The Empire of the Senses

The Empire of the Senses

Alexis Landau

Pantheon Books, New York

Copyright © 2014 by Alexis Landau

All rights reserved. Published in the United States by Pantheon Books, a division of Random House LLC, New York, and in Canada by Random House of Canada Limited, Toronto, Penguin Random House companies.

Pantheon Books and colophon are registered trademarks of Random House LLC.

Library of Congress Cataloging-in-Publication Data

Landau, Alexis.
The empire of the senses : a novel / Alexis Landau.
pages   cm
ISBN 978-1-101-87007-5 (hardcover). ISBN 978-1-101-87008-2 (eBook).
1. Jews—Germany—Fiction. 2. Interfaith marriage—Fiction.
3. World War, 1914–1918—Campaigns—Eastern Front. 4. Germany—
Social conditions—1918–1933—Fiction. 5. Life change events—Fiction.
6. Identity (Psychology)—Fiction. 7. Jewish fiction. I. Title.

PS3612.A547495E47 2015 813'.6—dc23 2014023895

www.pantheonbooks.com

Jacket images: (left) John Chillingworth / Picture Post / Getty Images;
(right) George Marks / Retrofile / Getty Images
Jacket design by Janet Hansen

Printed in the United States of America

First Edition

2 4 6 8 9 7 5 3 1

For Philip

Part One

1

The Eastern Front, August 1914

At first, the men were drunk off the euphoria of leaving Berlin, dreaming of virgin battlefields, singing and sharing flasks of whiskey when night fell. But Lev could not join in, blocked by a numb indifference that had settled over him as he observed the others with a clinical eye, picking apart their features, imagining how grotesque some of these men would appear if he sketched them asleep, their open mouths inviting flies. Yes, he'd volunteered when war was announced— but that day, only two days ago, already appeared fantastical, full of heated parades and brass bands, too much drink, his oxford shirt sticking to his chest in the humid air, and Josephine, waiting for him at home in the shaded courtyard, clutching her hat in her hands. She'd nearly ruined it, the one with the velvet flowers. He gently took it away from her and explained how he'd volunteered, to ensure he'd be called up first, to ensure no one would accuse him of shirking. He had said *no one* darkly because they both knew whom he meant—her mother and father, her brother, her whole Christian family, who despised him because he was a Jew. Even after seven years of marriage, seven biblical years, they hated him.

Josephine had blinked back tears, mumbling something about how perhaps a shortage of equipment would delay his leave.

No, no, he said. It wouldn't. "And where did you hear that, about lack of equipment?"

"Marthe."

He suppressed a laugh. "Still consulting your housemaid on such matters?"

She shrugged.

Lev nodded, trying to sympathize, but really, procuring information from Marthe? Large bumbling Marthe, who, although she expertly ironed the bedsheets and brought in afternoon tea at three o'clock sharp, never forgetting the lemon wedges, knew nothing of military matters.

Josephine brushed a hair out of her eyes. "But why must you go directly?" Here she was, acting like a girl of eighteen when at twenty-five she had already suffered the agonies of childbirth, twice, giving him Franz and then Vicki. The children were asleep, napping in the nursery. Soon Marthe would wake them. He pushed away the thought of their warm sleepy bodies, of how they clung to him when they woke, as if he might slip away, as if they had already dreamed this. Tonight, Lev would explain his departure to Franz, who, at six, would understand, and Vicki, only four, who might not. After he went, Josephine would weave a grand story they could all believe, a story repeated over dinner and again at bedtime. A story that would lessen the blow of his absence. Was she capable? Or would she become so wrapped in her own sorrow, the tale would not hold? He must tell her what to say, exactly how to phrase it, so the children would understand why he had evaporated, like the receding condensation on the bathroom mirror Franz traced his finger through after Lev's daily shave, drawing a gun with his pinky.

He looked at her face. Admiral-blue eyes, as if spun from colored glass. The delicate bridge of her nose framed by high cheekbones. Her arched eyebrows the color of wheat, which now drew together in worry. Please tell them a good story, he thought.

"But we still have some time?"

He inhaled sharply. "I'm leaving tomorrow. On the three o'clock transport train." Saying *tomorrow* made his heart pound, for her and for him. Too soon. So little time. He wondered if she would let him inside her tonight, their last night. On special occasions, she proved more compliant. Tonight, he thought, was a special occasion. The thought of her turning away, saying her head hurt, flashing that half-apologetic smile, infuriated him.

He stared down at his lace-up oxfords. Scuffed tips. Should take them in, he thought. No point—tomorrow he'd be gone. He pictured his empty shoes standing in his dark closet, perfectly in line with the other pairs.

Josephine touched his arm. "What are you thinking?"

The courtyard's uneven stones made their chairs lean slightly off kilter, and for a moment, it looked as if she might slide off.

"My shoes are scuffed."

"What?" she said.

How afraid should he feel of war? The question burned. But it didn't matter how much fear he felt or didn't feel—he was already in it, signed up and registered. And desertion promised death. They made sure everyone understood that.

"How can you think of shoes, of all things? You'll be gone by night-fall tomorrow and you don't even know how to hold a gun." He detected a hint of malice in her voice, as if he should know how to hold a gun properly, like her brother did, from shooting pheasant in Grunewald forest. But Lev had grown up in the city. Never touched a gun in his life. Never killed, not even a deer or a bird. *Jews don't hunt,* he remembered his mother saying. *Nor do they ride horses, sail, swim, fight in duels, or drink.* And he remembered thinking: What do Jews *do* then? All the valiant heroic activities were reserved for gentiles. For men like Jose-phine's brother, Karl von Stressing, who taunted Lev with his gray-and-white dappled steed as he trotted through the Tiergarten, with his saber and his hunting rifle and his tall black boots. But now they were both privates enlisted in the German army, both fighting for Germany, both shooting and killing and then afterward, drinking in the trenches. Lev already tasted the vodka, clear and pure and burning in his throat.

"How will you learn in time?" Josephine asked, more gently.

"Training's in the barracks close to the front, for four weeks, and then we'll be sent off into the jaws of Hell," he said, realizing how flat it sounded.

"Please don't say that."

"I'm sorry." He looked into her watery light eyes. "Back by Christ-mas. I promise." When his mouth closed in on that word, *promise,* Lev knew it was a lie.

.   .   .

As each night passed, the men grew listless and stared out the train windows. A pale student from the university sat beside Lev, frowning. He was studying to be an engineer. He flipped his brass lighter open and closed, methodically. The farther away they were from Berlin, the denser and darker the forests grew. The endless pines caught most of the light in their branches, creating a tunneling effect.

Lev placed his palm against the cool glass of the windowpane. It was almost dawn. A hot rain had fallen, flooding the earth on either side of the tracks. Passing through Prussia, they clung to traces of home in an otherwise alien landscape: romantic ruined castles of the Teutonic Order with names like *Creuzburg* and *Dünaburg. We are reclaiming what is truthfully ours*, the men murmured. Lev nodded along, handing out wilted cigarettes. He felt an unexpected burst of goodwill for these strangers, shop assistants and students and businessmen and doctors and cobblers—they were all mixed together in the sweaty boxcar, and Lev marveled at the oneness war produces, a body of men breathing communal breaths, eating and sleeping and shitting together, who, when severed from their petty lives, from the realm of money and women, felt as free as in the fabled days of their boyhood summers.

Now the Lord had prepared a great fish to swallow up Jonah. And Jonah was in the belly of the fish three days and three nights. The verse sprung to mind, as if the overwhelming foliage sprinting past him padded the insides of a monstrous whale that would spit them out at the end of the journey. But as far as he could see, there was no end. Only a cyclical green and brown interrupted by flashes of white birches. As he glanced upward, his eyes watered from the sharp blueness of the sky that had shed off the mistiness of dawn. Man is always trying to get away from nature, for nature is wind, rain, sleet, scorching sun, and she cares nothing if we suffer, Lev thought. We're traveling deeper into her inhospitable womb. He blinked, trying to decipher this shade of blue. He had not seen it before; it was harsher, lacking the softness and civility of a Berlin sky.

The arches of his feet itched inside the hot boots and his feet had swelled, along with his hands. His wedding band dug into his flesh. He realized he might easily die with it on and wondered if a Russian would cut it off for the gold. Melt it down into a lump. The train stalled. The man across from him, a portly bar owner, woke up alarmed. Thick heat pressed down on them, and the lack of movement roused the other men, intuitively fearing stillness. Gnats and flies buzzed, attracted to the sweat and salt of their ripe bodies. Another man greedily drank from his mud-colored canteen, draining the last bits of water. His Adam's apple worked up and down, the odd bump accentuated by his thin red neck.

The bar owner stood up unsteadily and barked, "Why are we stopped?" His eyes bulged. Someone grunted. The engineer sniffed and glanced away. Last night, Lev had shared a bottle of whiskey with this bar owner, who was now pacing the small length of the train car. Between sips they had reminisced of home. It had been a comfort to say the name of his street out loud—Charlottenstrasse—and to picture the front door of his house, recently painted midnight blue, with its brass handle, and to learn that this man lived on the other side of the park, a mere ten-minute stroll away. But watching him strut back and forth in his sweat-stained fatigues, his eyes jumping at the slightest snap in the woods, Lev realized he disliked him intensely, that he was a hysteric and a troublemaker. He decided to stay clear of him. He had to protect himself from this kind of man because this kind of man, Lev thought, often took the first bullet, as if a metal spitzer could sense calamity and direct its pointed tip toward it.

The train lurched forward and back, sending the man into a defensive crouch. His stubby fingers searched for something to grip.

Lev closed his eyes, moving his tongue over his teeth, the metallic coating a result of little water and too much tobacco. The blueness of the sky vibrated behind his closed lids. He had not slept well last night, occupied with rereading the letter that Josephine had slipped into his satchel, along with the blood sausages and an orange. Using the flame of his lighter to decipher her neat and tiny scrawl, he had thought the letter would contain a necessary revelation, an outpouring of emotion that had been concealed by the hum of their quiet domesticity. His hands had trembled as he opened the letter, the cream paper appearing so white in contrast to his ashen fingertips. He read greedily, without pause.

Dear Lev,

My only hope is that you will return by Christmas. The children will miss you terribly, even though as I am writing this you are still here, in the next room, packing your things. Especially Vicki; it will be very hard on her while you're away. Try to come home safely even though I know you want to prove yourself. But you mustn't think of impressing my mother or getting the Blue Max. To me, you are a true German, regardless. I have such faith in this. Write regularly and protect yourself.

With love,
Josephine

The letter was dull. He had hoped she would return to the language of her girlhood, eight years ago when they had strolled through Schiller Park, protected by the velvety shade of the oak trees, and she had rested her head on his shoulder, her white neck outstretched, a sheen of sweat upon it, and she had whispered urgently about the physical need for him, how she felt a resolute tightness that must be this need and gestured to her pelvis shielded by white lace and starched cotton, her mouth finding his; the pressure of her palm against the back of his neck could still be felt if Lev concentrated hard enough to retrieve the moment. The letters then had been such grand explosions of feeling, of unearthed confessions, and yes, shame too. But the shame was rich and dark and full of the possibility for redemption. He folded her letter away.

Lev stretched his legs and drank some tepid water. Yes, she had let him inside her on that last night. But granting permission was very different from wanting him. He'd encountered her unyielding body and remembered the way she turned her head to the side when he entered her, the way she breathed a sigh of relief when he'd finished, how much happier she appeared after it was done, rosy-cheeked and safely encased in her silk robe, pulling the sash tighter around her narrow waist while he lay there naked, legs spread apart, an affront to her.

Feeling the resentment swell in his breast, Lev felt guilty. He might not ever see her again, and here he was enumerating her flaws, forgetting her attributes. And she had many attributes. She managed the household with searing practicality: she purchased the finest linens and employed the most competent housemaid and cook; she knew which flowers would bloom in the garden depending on the season and arranged the bouquets, expertly cut, into long glass vases so that every room contained fresh flowers straining toward the light. She kept the children clean and well looked after, clipping their nails and starching their shirt collars bright white—his own mother had failed at this.

Most important, she gave shape to his life, providing Lev with a foothold in the mossy overgrowth of his work and social position, which otherwise would have felt slippery. Effortlessly, she put twenty overweight men from Stuttgart—potential buyers of the tricots and canvas Lev's firm Bremer Woll-Kammerei produced—at ease as they sat at her dining table and ate from her impeccable china. The men, their eyes trained on her, laughed heartily when she joked about the ineffectiveness of lace garters or how her father had known Peter Ulff, founder of the Berlin ribbon factory that supplied the royal regiments of the Austro-Hungarian empire. "When I saw those silky blue ribbons fluttering on the breast of every soldier during flag day or some such parade, all I could think of was little Herr Ulff asking me which shade of violet did I prefer at one of the many family gatherings he attended at our home." Her eyes shone in the candlelight as she spoke, and her forceful command of the table allowed Lev to sink into the wine-infused darkness and admire how she animated the room with a charged energy that enlivened even the dullest of men, bringing color to their cheeks. Lev too would grow entranced with her performance, marveling at her ability to keep up the light, happy mood, stirring the blood of these stolid men, who by the end of the night agreed to purchase meters and meters of canvas from Bremer Woll-Kammerei for the production of their signature rucksacks.

After these business dinners, her performance continued in the bedroom. The exaltation she felt at being useful to him, at being admired and gazed upon for so many hours by a tableful of men, fueled Josephine to reveal more of herself than she normally would. Cupping her breasts with both hands, she requested that Lev undress her, bit by bit, until only her plain naked body lay before him on the silk duvet cover. The silk of her skin against the silk of the fabric, the silkiness of their bodies twining together once they were both undressed felt natural and unimpeded. She did not wince or tense her legs when he slipped into her. Her body: angular, lean, taut tendons that quivered under his touch, sensitive to the slightest movement of his fingertips grazing her hip bone, the curve of her torso, the indented nape of her neck. It always seemed to Lev as if she barely had enough skin to cover her knees, her elbows, her cheekbones, creating an economy in her form, which became even more visible when she slid off her Oriental robe and slipped into bed beside him, her long cool body nestled against his stockier, rougher build.

In these moments, their marriage felt full of blood and heat, pulsing with possibilities even they couldn't name. The risk of having wed a gentile woman, a woman so outside the realm of his family, his neighborhood, his known world, was swallowed up by having Josephine. It was rare, and in some circles unthinkable, that Lev, an Eastern European Jew from Galicia, would come into contact with Josephine, let alone marry her. Her aristocratic German blood, the long line of military men in her family, the castles and estates her relatives had enjoyed for centuries, the horses and fox hunts—such things reflected nothing of Lev's life. No matter that Lev's parents had given him music and art lessons, an English governess from Bristol, a Latin tutor, admission into the best schools. This was not enough to skim the world of Josephine. So when he chanced upon her at the Ice Palace and she spoke to him freely, as if there wasn't any difference between them, as if he had not grown up in the Jewish section of Berlin, a yeshiva student with trousers that were sometimes too short, it seemed as if a pale white light seeped through the cracks of a stone wall he had always thought impenetrable. The light expanded, deepening into that rich golden afternoon when he took her hand, touched her wrist, and she said yes with her eyes, yes through her fingertips, a yes that meant more than coffee under the watchful gaze of her chaperone.

And why, Lev often wondered, had Josephine chosen him? At the start, he kept waiting for her to discover the error in her ways and apologetically, gently, end their relations. The opposite occurred. She grew more insistent, clinging to him with a fierce determination, as if Lev was her savior from the monotonous line of suitors who all reminded her of her brother, Karl, in their slim-fitting military uniforms, expert at making lighthearted quips while twisting the ends of their mustaches into fine points. "I don't want to sit under a parasol at a fox hunt and clap breathlessly for my husband," she would cry. "I've been doing that all my life."

"What do you want then?" Lev would ask, bewildered by her impassioned speech.

"You," she would murmur, lowering her eyes, suddenly aware of her need for him, which felt ungovernable, reckless. "I want to be where you are."

But potential, Lev realized, was a treacherous thing, because promises— her hope for a music career, his desire to paint, her plan to sever herself from her family—made in the semidarkness of their bedroom had turned into disappointment, regret, the sense of having overlooked some vital piece of information.

The phrase *a vital piece of information* echoed in Lev's head, the cadence of it taunting and sardonic. His boss, Herr Friedlaender, had employed that exact phrasing. The day war was announced, he had called Lev into his office and said all he needed to do was pass on that vital piece of information to the right government officials indicating how much he needed Lev in Berlin, at the textile plant, to ensure the production of woolen blankets for each soldier. When Lev replied that he was joining up to fight, Herr Friedlaender looked confused. He smoothed down his shiny silver hair, parted expertly to the side, and inhaled deeply.

"Why would you go to war, perhaps even to your death, when you have *everything* here?" Before Lev could answer, Herr Friedlaender exclaimed he would happily increase Lev's salary, and if the title of production manager was no longer satisfactory, he would even consider promoting Lev to vice president. He moved around the perimeter of his large walnut desk, picking up paperweights, putting them down, opening and closing his cigarette case, touching his silver hair. Lev had seen him perform these same fluid movements during client meetings, all the while talking and talking until, as if mesmerized by such a dance, the clients agreed to Herr Friedlaender's terms, which were always slightly tipped in his favor. But this hypnotic dance did not work on Lev, who remained seated, stoically staring out the large window, which looked out onto other buildings with similar large windows.

Herr Friedlaender readjusted his suspenders and smoothed down the front pockets of his trousers. "You're listening, yes? I'll pass along that vital piece of information regarding your usefulness to the firm, which will enable you to remain here. Josephine will be indebted to me—perhaps she'll even come to like me."

With the mention of Josephine's name, Lev started. "She wants me to join up. In fact, she said so herself. It's important to her that I fight for Germany, that I prove myself." Catching Herr Friedlaender's frown, Lev added, "Almost all the men in her family have fought, at one point or another." The part about Josephine saying it was important to fight was untrue, but Lev was certain she felt this way. It would allow her to feel proudly patriotic when her mother, the church ladies, the baker's wife, the seamstress at the tailor's shop, the teachers at Franz's school, or even the mail carrier asked after Lev. Josephine could then announce with the appropriate quiver in her voice, "He's fighting for Germany." But underneath this, what she really meant was: *Yes, I married a Jew, but look how loyal he is to Germany, how good,* erasing any question of his Jewishness surmounting his Germanness. German, only German. This was what Lev wanted and what he believed Josephine wanted: to escape the faint doubt, the shadowy presence of another past, another history, he kept trying to outrun.

Friedlaender stopped what he was doing, holding an unlit cigarette in midair. "If she thinks this, she's a shortsighted woman—the most important thing is survival, *personal* survival. If you haven't learned that yet, I don't know what else to say."

And then Friedlaender added, "I'll save your place here, for when you come home." He paused, observing Lev, his sharp dark eyes running over the contours of Lev's face as if he might be seeing him for the last time. Then the question of Lev's loyalties, how German he really was, would no longer matter to anyone.

Lying next to Lev on the transport train, the sleeping men looked peaceful. To escape the flies, many of them had placed pine branches over their faces. A forest of breathing wood. Outside, the trees exhibited the first signs of destruction. Bullet holes had pierced long delicate birches. Then there would be stretches of unmarked trees, white and gleaming. He wondered how recently the Russians had been here. The task of the Eighth Army, according to the officer who'd announced this when they'd boarded the train, was to regain areas that had been occupied by the Russians, as well as advancing over the border area in combat. It was impossible to tell if they'd crossed over the border or not. Lev also did not know if he would be stationed in Königsberg, northeast along the Baltic Sea near the Nemen River, or Mitau, which was more isolated, closer to the Russian border. The Russians had deserted both towns, leaving behind a wake of women and children, probably starving. When Lev had left his house, it smelled of bread. His children's skin shone from plentiful amounts of milk and butter. Berlin, of all places, would not suffer food shortages, he hoped.

Leaving Vicki behind had felt especially painful. On his last night at home, he tucked her into bed as he usually did. In the next room, he heard Josephine reading to Franz, stories about soldiers fighting in the snow, in the forests, and against all odds, winning. The window was open, letting in warm summer air. In a thin white nightgown, dark curls spilling over her shoulders, Vicki sat propped up on pillows asking him to sing song after song, delaying the moment when he would switch off the light and darkness would envelop the room.

"When you're gone, what if I can't sleep?" she asked.

He told her to think of her best memory, and she asked him how large or small the memory should be, and could the memory include other people, like her best friend, Greta, and could she change a memory so that, for instance, Franz would not have gone along to the candy store with them on the last day of school, and then he would not have picked out the best salted caramel piece, stuffing it into his mouth.

Amused, Lev had said, "It's your memory. You can do with it what you please."

"I wouldn't be lying?"

"No," he said, holding her small hand, hoping this moment would stick in his mind months from now, years from now: the warmth of her palm, the healthy pink under her fingernails, her brown almond-shaped eyes scanning his face, trying to decipher how serious it really was, his leaving.

"You're coming back by Christmas?" she asked for the fourth time that night.

He squeezed her hand. "Yes, Christmas."

She looked doubtful. Possibly she read the fear on his face, which he tried to mask with an overconfident tone.

"Are you sad?" Lev asked. But she only nestled into him, the side of her head pressed against his chest, her body curled into a ball. He stroked her back, her hair, and tears pricked his eyes. He didn't want her to see the anguish distorting his face, and so he swiftly switched off the lamp next to her bed. He held her for a long time, until, from the hallway, Josephine's voice cut through the stillness, asking if he'd finished packing his things.

The day he left, Lev watched Josephine through the train window. All in white, standing on the platform, she examined her fan. She didn't even bother to look up when the train started moving, until the last minute, as if she feared holding his gaze too long, as if such emotion would seem indulgent. She peered at the car behind his, and he could see that she searched for his face, but Lev did not call her name or wave a handkerchief to attract her attention. He had wanted her to feel remorse, to suffer his absence, to curse herself for missing the vital moment. But, Lev thought, nudging the knapsack with the edge of his soiled boot, perhaps she did not really suffer, at rest within her imperial bearing. Maybe she had walked home and felt more bothered by the afternoon heat than his departure. Maybe she stopped for a lemon ice and fanned her moist face, hoping the powder she had so carefully applied that morning had not streaked. She might pass another soldier and his wife walking to the train with stricken faces, and then she would nod to them in solidarity, reveling in the performance of mourning without really mourning him. And if she sought comfort in the church's lit candles, Lev knew she would pray for Germany and victory and large faceless things, because praying for a husband was ungenerous to the rest. A monarchist, with her fervent loyalty to the Son and the Holy Ghost, after crossing herself, would she linger a moment and pray for him?

His head rested on his rolled-up canvas pack, which was jammed against the train window. Before the others woke and started arguing about whether they were bound for Mitau or not, Lev slept. Already the coolness of early morning was gone and a thick heat bathed his face, softening the thoughts that kept him up at night: Josephine spending countless hours with her mother, or the fact that her brother, Karl, had been sent to the Western Front to build the first trenches, which somehow seemed more heroic than Lev's coming here.

It was a deep sleep, and Lev dreamed the unspeakable, as if the morning hours permitted obscenities. A woman with marble skin and dark-red hair, the color of October leaves, was naked save for a green velvet vest. She writhed beneath him, and his tongue explored her cunt, the smooth contours of it, although they were in the army medical office, in the white antiseptic room where Lev had been examined before joining up. The whole time Lev felt nervous a doctor might open the door and discover them beneath the bright medical lights. The urgency and uneasiness he felt melded into another dream, in which his mother would not let him wash his hands before dinner, forbidding him to use the same sink basin as she. When Lev asked why, she called him a Jew in disguise as a goy, and she grimaced when she said this, half smiling, half taunting. Lev froze, his hands outstretched before him.

He woke up with the sun bright on his face, his hands outstretched as if carrying something sacred, a tallith, or a Torah wrapped in embroidered velvet. A man leaned over him, trying to jam the window farther down, cursing the stubborn wooden frame. Lev peered up at his unshaven chin. It was an odd sight, made odder when the man vigorously shook his head in disapproval, the skin hanging from his chin swinging back and forth. Dazzled by the bright sun coming through the trees, Lev's eyes watered, blurring the sight of men milling about, spitting morning phlegm out the windows, scratching themselves, sharing cigarettes. The man above him cursed and stared down at Lev. His eyes were savage, bloodshot. "Does this damn window open any farther? It's sweltering."

Lev got up. He still felt the light warmth of the red-haired woman's body. They pushed down the window in a joint effort. The man grunted with satisfaction when gusts of hot wind blew into their faces. He poked his head out the window, grinning through his unruly mustache, and said, "Smells like horse shit and burning fields."

Lev grinned back, not wanting to betray his fear. He smelled fire. "Are we near the front?"

The man basked in the wind, his hair wild around his face.

Lev rested his forearms on the window ledge, almost touching the other man's elbow. He asked again, "Are we near the front?"

"Who knows?" the man said into the wind.

Gradually, the lushness and green protection of the forest grew sparse. Acres and acres of farmland on either side of the train had been scorched, burned out by the Russians before their retreat. Along the road, destroyed houses were bullet-ridden, and in the remaining potato fields, Lev saw oblong little mounds with wooden crosses stuck into them, helmets on top, cocked to the side. If the other man saw the helmets, he didn't let on. Lev could tell they were German helmets because of their pointed spikes catching the light. They passed through towns filled with deserted houses, no one on the streets, the gutters full of horse manure. A few starving cows blinked from a field. Lev breathed into his sleeve, the smell of manure and ash overpowering. Diaphanous farmhouses followed one after another as if ghostly bones hung languidly in midair. The man pointed to a broken-down doorway, and then a person appeared, gripping the wooden door frame, only to vomit on the doorstep before retreating back inside. The man grinned again, as if the burnt fields and the people left behind already proved a German victory. He held out a cigarette.

"Thank you," Lev said, surprised at how the man lit it, with the courtesy of a headwaiter. The train stalled. "Perhaps we're here."

The man shrugged, unconvinced.

Lev hoped this might be their stopping place, as the redness of the sun sadly vibrating through the fir trees struck him as beautiful. Beside the train tracks, two women wielded picks in the potato fields, backing away from the ground with alarming force before plunging into the soil again. One of the women looked up at him with eyes as black as prunes, and Lev detected both reproach and fear in her glance. The other woman paid them no notice, as if the bouts of bloody turmoil, whether it was the Russians or the Germans or the French or another invading group, were always occurring and would continue to occur. The way she wielded her pick said this much, radiating a passive acceptance of tragedy, an enduring knowledge that it was not that this one terrible thing had happened to her, but terrible things were always happening. Her passivity was galling, an affront to everything Lev put stock in. It reminded him of his parents. They had left Galicia for Berlin when Lev was two years old—their one act of will. But after this, they lived snugly in the Jewish quarter speaking only Yiddish and treating the rabbis as if they were gods. They refused to venture outside the limits of Scheunenviertel because they did not feel entitled. When Lev asked why, his mother would throw her hands into the air and exclaim, "We should be happy for this much." Her mouth would set into a tense line, and she would point to Lev's light eyes as if this caused his arrogance. "You always want so much. You always ask why, why. This," she yelled, waving a cloth around the dimly lit kitchen, "is more than enough."

Lev took the last drag of his cigarette, watching the women walk away, retreating into the thick woods, their scythes on their shoulders.

"I think," the man said after flicking his cigarette out the window, "we're here." His face glowed in the red sun. "But we're not at the front." He tapped his ear. "No artillery fire." His head tilted to the right, as alert as a bird listening for a mating call. "Faintly. I hear some fire faintly in that direction." He gestured in the opposite direction of where the women had gone.

Lev's stomach knotted with hunger. They had not eaten all day. He tasted nicotine mixed with the orange peel he occasionally bit into. The man told him at camp a hot meal would be served. "And maybe if we're lucky, we'll have a wash and some whiskey."

"Where are you from?" Lev now felt convinced this man was a Berlin waiter in one of the posh dining clubs where he liked to take Josephine dancing.

"Dachau." The man twisted one end of his mustache into a fine point. "I was a policeman there." He paused and then began twisting the other end. "Have you been?"

"I haven't been south of Frankfurt."

"It's a beautiful place."

The general hum of discussion, as they lined up in the aisles of the train, established they were at Königsberg. The man with the mustache forged ahead and then blended in with the other men as they waited to debark the train. Lev could still see the back of his clean neck, the close shave he must have enjoyed before leaving Dachau. A huddled silence fell, followed by one voice speaking above the rest, a confident and conspiratorial stream of words radiating from the front of the train, where one man stood, small in stature with sharp clear eyes that roved the crowd as he described what lay ahead. Lev heard snatches of conversation from others commenting on what the man was saying. Most of them couldn't hear him very well. Someone standing behind Lev breathed in quickly and asked, "Did he say we're leaving for the front today?" Lev felt a renewed shower of sweat break over his chest. The man spoke quickly and energetically and had a lean animated face. His eyes darted around the car as he explained that the front line was only a few kilometers away, that some of them would be sent there, and some would be held at camp until needed.

The engineer clamored toward the man, placing a thin hand on his shoulder. "Do you think I'll be sent to the front directly?"

The man rubbed his chin. "It's possible. You are young. But"—he paused—"they are always changing their minds. From what I hear, it's not as organized as it seems." Other men nodded. Lev watched him with fascination. His information was merely speculative, and yet he had fashioned himself into an authority on what the authorities were thinking. His name, Lev heard, was Hermann Streich. Physically, he was round-shouldered and slight, his oblong face wagging back and forth with various theories, but Lev felt drawn to him, as the other men did.

When they arrived at the camp, there was drinking and music. The air was celebratory over the recent taking of the Polish fortresses of Kowno and Wilna, which had driven the Russians farther east. Forty officers ate outside at a long wooden table, the red stripe of the general staff on their pants. They toasted and cheered the new crop of men. Another table was set up, where Lev and the rest were served mutton with small sickly beets. As he was cutting through his meat, he heard cannons sounding off, and then two columns of troops appeared, all in field gray.

Hermann leaned over his plate, whispering, "They're going to the front line. We're still fighting the Russians. They did not retreat as easily as our good officers would have us believe." He motioned toward the other table, where the officers ate. Lev tried to eat the beets sitting in a pool of oil. His stomach protested, but everyone had said, eat what is in front of you as fast as you can. As he ate, Lev overheard the officers talking about how even though the land was ruinous and barbaric, they would build it up again, cultivate and nurture it, as this was the German way. "We take what is backward and diseased, and with the strength of our will and hard work, we transform this"—an officer gestured with disgust at the surroundings—"into fertile, productive, and useful resources."

Lev glanced across the table at Hermann, who was also listening intently, storing away this information for later, when he would repeat it to others as if he had overheard a secret meeting behind closed doors.

He finished the beets. For a moment, he allowed himself to miss home. The starched white sheets on his bed, the quiet of the house after the children were asleep, and the lingering smell of bread and wine filtering through the hallways. How Marthe sang when she cleaned the kitchen late at night, preparing for the next day, and the sight of Josephine before her mirror in their bedroom, silently brushing her golden hair with a faraway look in her eyes, as if she was already dreaming, and how she would smile softly when Lev finally broke her reverie with the question, "What are you thinking?" A vague haze would overtake her, and to get closer to her, he would have to accept this dreamy state. Her abstraction would continue during the physicality of sex. She would sigh and arch her back and stare into his face without seeing him, with these bottomless liquid eyes, and he felt as if he was penetrating a shimmering mist. If he tried to break the spell and depart from this odd realm in which their skin felt translucent, his lips pressed into her shoulder blade somehow muted and unreal, she would recoil as if he had transformed into a vulgar and horrifying creature. She would fold into herself, clamoring for the lace pillows, burying her head in them, and muttering accusations Lev could never quite hear. She would fall asleep quickly, one hand frozen on her breast as if still experiencing an affront, and Lev would stare helplessly into the dark room, wondering how long it would be until she would give herself to him again. A month. Or two. He would have to wait. This he did not miss.

That night, they slept on the second floor of a deserted farmhouse. The first floor was filthy; the Russians had left piles of horse manure inside, and the process of removing it and cleaning the building was ongoing. The windows stood wide open, and he listened to the sound of a dogcart clattering down pavement and a salvo pushing through the night. He shared this room with twenty other men who breathed hoarsely, fitfully turning in their sleep. Hermann sat cross-legged in the corner, nearest the window, smoking. After dinner, Lev noticed he had become spent and sullen, worn out by his own personality, and when they unloaded their packs here, he had retreated to the farthest corner of the room. They were the only two people awake, but Hermann acted as if he did not notice Lev sitting up against the wall, smoking too. Every so often the black sky filled with fireworks from rising and falling signal flares, and Lev tried to distinguish the difference between machine-gun fire and rifle fire. Hermann also studied the sky, and Lev wondered if he was playing the same game.

The next morning, Lev found out that he would stay at camp and work in the field hospital until further notice. His job was to record any changes in the soldiers' wounds in the morning, make rounds, and clean the operating rooms in the afternoon. Relieved, he knew the possibility of death was at bay for a little while longer, and for an instant, Lev pictured that hated neighborhood dog of his youth, the mangy German shepherd who snarled and jumped up against the wooden fence that Lev passed on his way to school. The dog jumped so high, frantically clawing his paws on the slats, but never quite high enough. The stinging fear, the beating heart, the sweat under his arms never failed to surprise Lev even though he was safe, on the other side of the fence. This was how he felt now, on the other side of death, on the other side of the line. But in his relief, to stroll past the monstrosity but not into it, he felt shame too. Why had he been held back? Save for a few preliminary medical courses at university, he had no experience. Could they tell he lacked the conviction of his peers, who believed in war as if it was a necessary rite, a passage to manhood, whereas Lev slinked by, happy and ashamed all at once to remain on the sidelines and bide his time until he could return to his scented sheets, his scuffed wingtips, his wife's golden hair tangled around his fingers.

The other men had already gone ahead to breakfast. Lev lingered in the barracks, neatly folding his blanket, marveling at his fate, which felt like a beautifully wrapped gift he should save and hide away. Placing the blanket squarely at the foot of his cot, he smoothed down the rough wool fabric and wondered if Josephine still slept on her side of the bed, never crossing over to his side, or did she take up the whole bed now that he was gone, loose-limbed and languid among those lavender-scented sheets? Would she allow Vicki and Franz into bed with her when the nights grew dark and cold? Or if Vicki woke from a bad dream, would Josephine carry her down the hall, as Lev did, and take her into their bed until she fell back to sleep? When Lev did this, Josephine insisted he was spoiling Vicki. "She's not a baby anymore," she had protested, and Lev promised that next time he would not gather up Vicki in his arms, her long legs dangling on either side of him. But he never kept this promise. He always picked her up, carried her, held her close. His heart contracted, imagining Vicki alone and terrified of the darkness, of the invented demons lurking beneath her bed, of the red fox sinking its sharp white teeth into her ankle—a recurrent bad dream that caused her, upon waking, to race down the hallway crying, believing her ankle still pulsed from the phantom bite.

When Lev arrived at the mess hall for breakfast, men milled around the long tables, smoking and talking. The cooks ran in and out of the kitchen, ferrying bowls of porridge. His stomach, tight with hunger, grumbled even though the porridge looked gray and watery. Hermann grinned at Lev, coming over to him. "The damn Russians and Poles still live on Russian time. So every morning breakfast is either too early or too late. Even though we changed all the clocks to German time." He shook his head. "Incredible." Up close his eyes were slate gray, an indefinable color that changed with the light.

Lev glanced around the mess hall. "The natives aren't so cooperative after all." When he said this, his voice sounded stiff and detached. He sat down next to Hermann. Bowls, filled with the indistinguishable lukewarm grain, had been placed on the table. Hermann nudged Lev with his elbow. "But we're better than the czarist army—they terrorized their own people. Killed them if they didn't evacuate within twenty-four hours. Burned down their houses and slaughtered their livestock. Brutal, unpredictable rule—these people have lived under the worst kind of fear." Hermann's eyes flickered when he said *fear*.

"We're here to rebuild." Lev didn't know what else to say.

Hermann smiled sarcastically. "We'll make all the Poles, Lithuanians, White Russians, Latvians, and Estonians into Germans. They'll realize they always were German." He stopped short, pressing his thin hands together. "Even the Jews will become German here."

Lev stared at Hermann's slate-colored eyes and nodded, as if he had nothing to do with Jews.

Hermann continued, now eating his porridge vigorously. "The clocks and the fields and the slant-eyed women picking potatoes, even the animals will be German by the time we're done." His spoon dropped into his empty bowl, clattering against the tin.

2

For three weeks, Lev worked in the field hospital, recording how fast the wounds decayed and the agony of the men who housed them. He got used to the sharp smell of putrefaction hovering in the halls, even though fans were blowing and the rooms were well lit, giving off the impression of cleanliness and order. Sometimes, after he was done with his rounds, he lingered in the empty operating room, his hands sore from cleaning, and wrote in his diary, the snatched half hour a boon. He wrote about how yesterday a first lieutenant's chest wound appeared like a ruby. He had stated calmly to Lev, "The bullet entered here," pointing to the dark cavity lodged in his white chest. Then he added, "Not much longer, eh?" Lev recorded his death in the ledger two hours later. But the lieutenant did not shake. Brain contusions, abdominal wounds, and the effects of machine-gun fire made most of the men shake unapologetically. They suffered lockjaw, wheezing, their eyes searching the corners of the ceiling. What struck him were not so much their faces but the radiant colors; white gleaming skin contrasted with crimson blood, the wounds under bandages that would inevitably turn, after a few days, a dark muddy yellow. He wished he'd brought his oils, his canvases and brushes. But he hadn't packed any materials because it had seemed embarrassing, almost blasphemous, to suggest war provided leisure time to paint landscapes, and worse, that he expected this for himself. But here he was, bereft of his tools, save for a stubby piece of charcoal, which he tried on vellum, but the paper easily tore, only furthering his frustration at his ineptness for not having done any drawing or painting over the last few years. He cursed himself for even thinking he could take it up again, and under such circumstances.

But still, his desire to capture the odd, wondrous details that surrounded him persisted. Especially when hospital days were uneventful,
or when he was granted the afternoon off, feeling slovenly and empty,
the insides of his hands itched for his brushes.

Days passed into nights, and Lev, exhausted, would make his way to the
barracks in the predawn hours. Walking back, a cool voluptuous rain
fell. He would look up into the dripping tree branches and no longer
feel as if the land was hostile. He held his face up to the rain, licking
his chapped lips, his eyes opening and closing in response to the heavy
drops, the sky emptying out its distress. When he reached the barracks,
he would collapse onto his cot as the sky grew paler, his clothes sticking
to his skin. He didn't mind getting his woolen blanket damp beneath
him. It was too much trouble to remove it. He lay there, staring out the
window at the thick gray rain, thinking, You and the world have drifted
away.

A few days later, he wrote this at the end of a letter to Josephine.
She took it too literally and in response included reminders of home in
her next package, a lock of her hair, for instance. Sometimes, he flicked
the bottom of his chin with her silky lock, not thinking of her at all, but
merely enjoying the immediate pleasure of something soft and ticklish.

And sometimes he directed his thoughts back to that particular
moment when he first saw her at the Ice Palace, in Schöneberg. It was
late summer 1907. He had just turned twenty, and she eighteen.

That day, Lev had worn his best suit, a recently purchased three-piece
with a white cravat and bowler hat. He wore it stiffly and wondered if
anyone noticed how the starched collar pulled at his neck. He wanted to
look languorous and smooth in it, as if he had been born in such a suit,
as if he didn't save away two months' salary just to feel the delicate light
wool under his fingers while catching a brief glance in the mirror at how
perfectly the lapels rested on his chest, the fluidity of the double vent
in back, the fine length of the sleeves covering his gangly wrists. There
were mirrors everywhere, so it wasn't too obvious when he checked his

reflection. The mirrors were high and arched, causing the Ice Palace to appear grander than it actually was. Lev had heard all the pretty girls came here on Saturdays to escape the Berlin heat. He'd abandoned his university friends—they would play scat all day at the beach, happy to listen to the mingling of the seagulls and lake tides. So Lev ventured here alone, feeling strangely shy when he saw all the mirrors and the music. Dimly lit chandeliers hung over the ice rink. Sun streamed in through the long arcade of windows on the second floor. Lev positioned himself on the upper balustrade, peering up at the domed ceiling, wondering what this was before it became an ice-skating rink. He considered ordering a coffee and watched the skaters.

There were all sorts of combinations. Men with women, women with women, unruly gangs of children colliding into the paneled walls, a few older men dignified in their top hats, hands in pockets. A waltz played. His feet were starting to get cold. He thought about skating, but he wasn't very good. Well, the pretty girls were here, plenty of them. Lev lit a cigarette and smoked thoughtfully, as he often liked to do when surveying the opposite sex. On the ice, girls glided past painted frescoes on the walls. An alpine scene, full of snowy peaks. A cottage on a lake, the lake mirroring the reflection of the cottage and the surrounding firs. Supposed to make you think you're out in the country, Lev mused. As if we're all hearty peasants having a day off, our cheeks ruddy and full of blood. But the long silk dresses the women wore, with full skirts and shawls and elaborate hats, and some girls even skating with parasols, to block the rectangles of sun that fell across the ice from marring their untouched skin, gave them away as Berliners of a certain class. Old aunties sat at the café, stuffing their mouths with lemon cake while their younger versions, lithe and angular, pirouetted on the ice, the girls laughing and throwing their heads back as if they'd never seen the way the Wannsee freezes over every January, as if this was all new and sparkling. But it was summer outside, and the novelty of feeling a wintry chill while the rest of the city sweated was what made them all laugh so gleefully, as if they alone were exempt from the elements, inside the Ice Palace.

It happened quickly, as he was contemplating how hot the apartment would feel when he returned, and how much he must have already sweated through his white shirt because it had turned into a cold sweat, and how his collar really was too tight, and he might as well leave because his feet hurt, and he was hungry but sitting down didn't seem right, although the idea of a coffee tingled his tongue, the hot black liquid: she sliced across the ice, instantly, her long lean form frozen in an arabesque, one arm stretching over her head on the same level as her extended leg, making the most exquisite but impossible shape. Her dress was a golden brown, the color of fall leaves, a color I could paint, Lev thought as he leaned farther over the balustrade. In the last moment, when it seemed as if she might crash into the wall, she swiftly swung her leg down and performed a tight turn. Her neck looked extraordinarily long and white. The color of her hair, golden, flashed in the light. She was with two other girls, who stuck together, and occasionally she glided past them to make some remark, but by the time they could respond, she was off again. She weaved between couples and children, lost in her own world, impervious. Lev lifted his chin, as if to challenge her. He forgot the chilly air, warmed by her lunar beauty. A few times, he thought she might have glanced up at him, an averted haughty glance. Now she spun, her skirt billowing out, her arms crossed over her chest, like a Russian doll. Her friends watched, tugging on their hats. They were round-shouldered and awkward. She suddenly stopped, boring the pointed tip of her skate into the ice, as if to say voilà. Then she held his gaze. It was a piercing wintry gaze. Lev felt his chest cave and groped for a newspaper or another cigarette, though he knew he didn't have one. All he could do was stare back. She carefully placed a hand on her hair as if to smooth it down, but her plait was perfectly coiled around her head, and this little movement called attention to how she knew there was nothing out of place. Lev nodded, acknowledging this. She smiled. A small faint smile, but enough to make Lev move from his spot where he'd been gripping the balustrade and rush down the wooden stairs, almost slipping on the last stair, wet from a spill, until he came to the edge of the ice, the tips of his oxfords butting up against the frozen surface.

Fists in his pockets, he raised his eyebrows, an invitation. After taking a few moments to fix her laces, her gloved fingers working nimbly, she skated over.

"Hello," she said simply, her pale face tinged rose.

Her friends pretended not to watch, but Lev was fully aware of their darting glances.

"You're a very fine skater." He'd had these words ready on his tongue, so they came out crisply confident, exactly how he wanted to sound.

"Don't you skate?"

"I'm not at all good. I couldn't keep up with you."

"Well," she said, fingering her dress, "I've skated since I was a girl, at my family's winter cottage."

"Where's that?" Lev asked, noticing the perfect smallness of her ears nearly hidden under her golden hair. As small as seashells.

"Very far," she said in an exaggerated way. "In the Bavarian woods."

Lev grinned. "Just like that one—over there." He motioned to the fresco of the cottage on the lake.

She turned to look, and ice-blue veins along her neck appeared, a faint map of her body. "Almost exactly. Even with the same trees, the sky the same purple before the sun goes. You'd think they'd copied it, to remind us of my winter cottage," she went on, moving slightly back and forth on her skates, until she caught Lev's eye and saw that maybe he was mocking her, or mocking the idea of her winter cottage, implying how unremarkable it was to have such a place, because here it was, on the wall, reproduced. She stopped talking and put her hand to her face, the cream leather against her cream skin. "It's been sold since," she added somewhat wistfully.

Lev tried to rearrange his face. He had been smiling at her naïveté—it was charming. He hadn't been mocking her, not really.

The music changed from Strauss to Beethoven. The lights dimmed to amber, matching the late afternoon light outside. Josephine had taken out a fan, and the sharp quick movement of her wrist reminded Lev of a hummingbird.

"I always love this piece," she said airily, waiting to see if he could name it.

Men and women paired off, skating arm in arm, long sensuous strides.

Children waited on the edge of the rink, bored.

Lev smiled. "Doesn't everyone love Beethoven's piano sonatas?"

She paused, flustered. "But why the *adagio sostenuto*, in C sharp minor?"

The thought of kissing her crackled through him. Her mouth, berry-colored, delicately shaped. And her body already promised this kiss, the way she fluttered her hands to make a point, opening and closing with suggestiveness, her neck inclined toward him, as if their bodies were already intertwined.

She glanced down at the ice. "I mean," she said, "how does the music make you feel?"

"Would you like to sit down for a coffee?" Lev asked.

She shifted her gaze to the other side of the rink where an older woman waved a hat. "That's my auntie. Well, actually, chaperone. But I call her auntie. She's been with us forever. Ever since I was seven. She thinks I'll catch my death bareheaded like this." Josephine paused, giving Lev the chance to tip his hat to the heavy woman with steel-gray hair who appeared too tired to intervene. "But I refuse to wear a hat because what's the point of skating with a big hat?"

Lev reached out and clasped her wrist, his thumb pressing down between the edge of her glove and the beginning of her sleeve, a luxuriant swath of warm bare skin. He led her to one of the tables at the edge of the crowd, next to a tall window. In the sunlight, Josephine's hair shimmered. The dizzying threads of color—wheat, straw, copper, white-blond, honey—made Lev want to reach out and touch it. Instead, he ordered them two coffees and plum cake with cream. Teacups placed down on saucers, glasses clinking with glasses, spoons knocking against porcelain, and knives scraping the last bits of cake off plates filtered through the long drafty hall, creating a music of its own. For a moment, Lev and Josephine sat silently, listening to the drone of eating and drinking and the skaters on the ice, their steel blades skidding.

She placed the hand Lev had touched on the table and then quickly overlaid it with her other hand. Lev stared at her, wondering if she wanted him to touch her wrist again. Forcing a smile, she looked out the window and brightly said, "It's a beautiful day. Summer. And here we are, in the Ice Palace. All winter I waited for summer and now I can't bear the heat."

He couldn't think of what to say. The bravado he'd felt on the ice had evaporated and now he was back to his clumsy self, with stiff leather shoes that pressed down on his toes. The slanted caved rooftops of Mitte, where he lived, flashed through his mind, and he was sure such a place was far from her.

Carefully, she sipped her coffee and dabbed her mouth with a handkerchief, asking him various questions, all benign. Did he enjoy music? What was his favorite opera? What was he studying at university? She's good at this, Lev thought. He wondered how many suitors she had tolerated and entertained, asking them the same questions, smiling at the right moments.

She stared at him.

"I'm sorry?" Lev asked. "What did you say?"

"Oh. I only wondered what you study?" She leaned forward. A waiter poured more coffee into their cups, the black liquid streaming from the chrome pot. He finished off the pour with a flourish.

"I'm studying law and economics at Berlin University. I'm also working in the accounting department for a large matchstick company. The factories are in Galicia."

Josephine raised her eyebrows.

He went on, "It's training. I'm more interested in textiles."

"Textiles?" she said faintly.

Lev swallowed down the remains of his coffee. "I actually wanted to be an artist. I still paint on occasion. Oils mainly." The last time he'd painted was two months ago. A dark derelict courtyard where an old woman leaned against a lamppost. And lurking in the background, a man with a top hat was frequenting a place he wouldn't normally visit.

Framing the scene, brick walls were crumbling, revealing a masticated layer of gray, and the windows in the surrounding buildings were dark, save for a few pools of light here and there, to add depth. The court-yard had captured Lev's attention on his way home from work, and he reproduced it from memory when early the next morning he brought out his canvases.

After he mentioned painting, there was a pause, almost as if he could feel her body softening, her face opening into a new expres-sion, one that did not intend to delight or to show off the best angle of her face, which she knew could be accomplished by tilting her head to the right, revealing the long run of her neck. He savored this unadulterated version of herself—her eyes open and clear, her lips slightly parted, the sheen of her pearl earrings unself-consciously catching the late afternoon sun. If they were alone under trees, if he knew her better, he would kiss her on the mouth, his palm against her neck, the fine boning of her corset pushed up against him, their breath mingling in a shaded reprieve, away from all the brightness and chatter.

Lev noticed, from the other side of the rink, her chaperone lumber-ing toward them, moving at a slow but steady pace.

Propelling himself forward, Lev asked in a hurried whisper, "May I call on you?"

"We are in Wilhelmstadt, Spandau. Wasserstrasse ten. If you get lost, ask the grocer where the Von Stressings live. Our family is very old. It's easy to find us."

"Josephine." Out of breath, her chaperone clutched the back of her chair. "It's time for us to say good-bye to this young gentleman. He is a friend of Karl's?"

She shook her head. "He doesn't know Karl."

The woman reminded Lev of a ruffled dusty bed skirt. Her wrist wobbled on the cane in front of her, which upheld her momentous weight. She thrust an elaborate hat with flowers and a tiny fabricated bird in Josephine's direction. Josephine absently took it. After this, she said lightly how very enjoyable the coffee had been and how pleased she would be if he cared to call on her. The words grated, but such phrases were reserved for chaperones and introductions in public places—it seemed to Lev most of his daily interactions were composed of these airy words that, once uttered, took flight and meant nothing.

After she left, Lev sat in the café, fingering the prongs of the fork where she had put her mouth.

3

Already it was late September, and the Indian summer rolled on, bringing heat and rain followed by sun-drenched days. The temperate climate tricked Lev into thinking this war was barely a war, that he had somehow skirted it, or skipped it, or managed to delay it. He fell into a routine—the hospital by day, then five hours off, then night watch at the ward again, where he often dozed, only awakened by the occasional call for water or morphine. And yet even as he reveled in his luck, he knew it was precarious, this delight in his surroundings, in the friendship he shared with Hermann, in the joy he took in constructing the dollhouse for Polina.

She was a small girl from the village, nearly the same age as Vicki, with the same mischievous eyes. Her hair was blond, but her black eyes, almond-shaped, always made him feel as if he were seeing a version of his daughter. One day, he'd seen her traipsing along the road with her doll. Her small body against the large trees generated a surge of fatherly concern. She was crying and holding her doll to her chest. The doll had no arms or legs. He'd picked up a little Russian, but children didn't need much to communicate. When he asked her what happened, she mumbled something about a beast who'd chewed off the baby's limbs. Then she took his hand and said she wanted to show him the house where they played. She pointed to an abandoned estate, which rose up in the distance. Lev knew the place—it had once belonged to the Vichniakov family, Russian nobles who had fled, leaving trunks full of silk and silver the German army then confiscated.

She led him through the broken-down estate, filled with light and shadow and dust. Gangs of children had proclaimed ownership of different rooms. The blue room, with its torn and ripped satin paneling along the walls, belonged to Uri and his gang. The boys huddled together, protecting their loot of fallen Greek statues, heads broken off, wielding the torsos as if they'd found swords. They eyed Lev suspiciously.

Polina's tiny hand swept over the long grand hall. "This is where they had parties."

"Yes," Lev said, "it must have been spectacular." He looked up at the chandeliers, broken in so many places, and at the oil portraits of the Vichniakovs' ancestors in gilded frames, each one sliced through with a blade. A lanky boy, his fiery hair like a torch, sprinted down the hall wearing a brocaded drape slung over his body. "Come back here," he shrieked to no one in particular.

Polina shrugged and then she continued to lead Lev through the rooms, each with its own vibrant color, as if passing through a prism of semiprecious stones. The emerald room. The sapphire room. The crimson and the canary-yellow room. After a succession of rooms, a smaller one stood at the end of the hallway. A diamond window let in some dull light, but otherwise, it was shadowy and decrepit.

"My room," Polina said, gesturing to the canopy bed with silk pillows in the shape of logs positioned at the foot and the head. The canopy bed was missing its canopy. Lev immediately thought of the boy tearing through the hallway, and how he must have ripped off the blue silk canopy from the wooden carapace, which appeared barren and desolate. One salvaged portrait, of a little girl holding a gray poodle in an oval frame, hung next to the bed. Her rosy cheeks gleamed with health and her lips curled into a faint smile. The poodle's gray curls tickled her dimpled chin. Polina tucked her legless baby underneath the soiled bedcovers. She patted the baby's chest. "This is where we live."

Lev knelt down to her level. "What about your parents?"

"I don't know them."

No parents? Would Vicki say the same when asked about her father? What if she was forgetting him—his face, the sound of his voice? He felt his lungs shrink, his throat tighten. "But you mustn't sleep here—"

She rolled her eyes. "We don't *really* live here. Even though the cow lives *inside* with us, my aunt's house isn't terribly bad." She wrinkled her nose.

"Oh," Lev said, sighing.

In the meantime, Polina had busied herself with rearranging the baby's bed and feeding the baby an imaginary piece of apple and brushing the baby's imaginary hair. "Now, now," she whispered, "don't cry. I have to brush your hair; otherwise it will be a horrible mess in the morning."

Lev watched her, both saddened and cheered by her playing. He noticed the peeling wallpaper, a pattern of interlocking garlands, and how a few of the wooden floorboards had been pulled loose, and the general destruction of the room, and then he had an idea. He tore off a bit of wallpaper and held it between his fingers, reminded of Vicki's dollhouse, an opulent three-story one he bought her for Christmas last year, and how she loved it, peering inside the rooms, tinkering with the furniture, tracing her finger along the brocaded wallpaper, looking in on the nursery with motherly concern. Yes, that was it! He would build Polina a similar dollhouse. Of course it would not be as professional, but he had all the materials he needed right here, in this abandoned estate—the fabrics, the wood, the scraps for those little details he knew would bring her such delight.

He told Polina his plan, and she listened with rapt attention, her dark eyes alight. Tomorrow could she bring him some ribbon? Yes, yes, she said, I will get ribbon! But then she brooded over what color. Lev, to humor her, said red or blue would be best, but anything would do. Yes, yes, she said more to herself than to him, red or blue. I think I can snatch it from Anna. Perfect, Lev said, as he peeled off a swath of wallpaper and stuffed it into his pocket.

Over the next days and weeks, Lev amassed the materials, as if he was a rabid collector. He filched gauze from the hospital for the coverlets that would grace each miniature bed. When Hermann received a pack of letters wrapped in navy silk ribbon from an old sweetheart, Lev asked for the ribbon.

Hermann grinned, twining the ribbon around his finger. "For Polina's dollhouse?"

Lev smiled. "What else would I want your ribbon for?"

Hermann handed Lev the strip of ribbon and then tossed the stack of letters over to the side. "Keepsakes. Amulets. These things from home. They won't save us when the bullet goes through."

Lev gestured to the return address. "Tell me you won't think of Elena, sweet Elena Karpovich, who wrote you all those letters in such a fine hand."

Hermann's thin mouth formed a bitter smile, cold and sardonic. "She had small pitiful breasts and she would never let me touch them, as if they were such a prize, those wilted drooping pendulums of flesh."

"Aha! So you *do* remember her." Lev slipped the ribbon into his back pocket. Perhaps it would serve as a runner along the miniature grand piano he planned to carve and place in the sitting room.

"*Remember* is a strong word." Hermann flopped down on his cot. He put his hands behind his head and gazed up at the water-damaged ceiling. "More like a flash of thigh, the rub of her smooth pubic hair against my groin, the way she moaned and convulsed, as if I was stabbing her."

"Delightful," Lev said.

Hermann rolled over onto his side and stared at Lev. "Better than nothing."

The word *nothing* cut to the quick. Could Hermann tell Lev often got nothing? The nothing of Josephine's silent refusal, the nothing of her ghostly vertebrae when she turned away from him in bed, the nothing of her garnet lamp on the bedside table switching off, an act so much more definite than extinguishing a candle, which still left that burnt earthy smell in the air long after the flame was gone.

After a month, Lev was relieved from night watch in the hospital, and Hermann convinced him to go to the taverns. The taverns were strategically placed close to the front. On the way there, Hermann told him it was army supervised, meaning the women had been checked for VD. "They're clean. Just don't go sneaking into any villages. One night over there"—Hermann gestured toward a dense grouping of trees through

which a few lights glimmered—"you'll come back with your dick burning off."

"I'm married." Again, he felt like a schoolboy after the words
escaped him. Hermann had this effect.

"I would say that's irrelevant." Hermann's eyes glinted in the
moonlight. "At the edge of the earth, there are no judges."

Lev lit Hermann's cigarette. "And you?"

"Once."

"Not anymore?"

Hermann took a drag. "She left."

Lev did not ask why. He knew how easy it was to fall out of love,
like sand falling through a half-clenched fist. He had felt twinges of
this with Josephine before he left, when she would turn her back to
him in the kitchen and he did not know to whom that back belonged.
Or when she talked over dinner, the way her mouth moved would suddenly appear grotesque, the food churning around her tongue, followed by a forceful swallow. He would watch her throat working so
that she could resume her sentence. And it would end up being such
a meaningless sentence, not worth the effort or the patience. But these
flashes of un-love lasted only momentarily, and in a rush, Lev would
feel at home with her again, triggered by an equally small but valuable
gesture. She might stroke his forehead in bed. Or run her lips under
his ear when he came home at night, whispering, "Have you eaten?"
But Lev worried that over time the un-love moments would gradually
overtake the other moments, and that in a decade or less, they would
be left with nothing to bind them. It was pessimistic, yes, but he had
watched his parents' affections dissolve into a haze of tobacco smoke,
which thickened as the night wore on, the arguing climbing to a pitch
of hysteria in the crammed living room. The porcelain plates in the
glass armoire vibrated as the noise level increased, his mother's voice
high and tight, a rising crescendo of accusation. She had held a longstanding hatred for what his father did, for his talent of twisting numbers so people paid less taxes. A Communist, an admirer of Trotsky and
Rosa Luxemburg, she had even wanted to change her name from Mara

to Rosa, but his father forbid it. And then he stopped coming home for dinner.

It took Lev and Hermann thirty minutes, wading through the wide flooded roads, mud splashing on their boots and pants, to reach the tavern. The moon shone brightly, revealing the scurrying of large rats alongside the road. The rats burrowed into the ditches created by past explosions, searching for food and cover. Hermann aimed at one, but it got away. The bullet ricocheted off a birch tree. They silently walked on. Lev saw another one in plain view. He could easily shoot it. He placed his hand on his pistol, the cool gunmetal welcome to his sweaty palm. The dark fur under the white moon gleamed, raised up and wet. Hermann didn't notice, and Lev let the rat dissolve into the darkness. Silently slipping into the dense foliage, the rat reminded Lev of himself walking in the shadow of Hermann, who was by contrast much more forthright and direct. If he wanted to kill a rat, he did so, whereas Lev wavered and waited and developed an association with the vile animal, which prevented him from killing it. And Hermann advertised who he was, even if many men disliked him for such brashness. His voice was the last one they heard before they dropped off to sleep. His laughter trailed his own jokes. But Lev treaded carefully within his surroundings, first observing the various alliances and then calculating where he fit in, not revealing too much of himself lest someone dislike him. He was careful not to discuss his background, which he had buried long ago, just as these rats burrowed into the fetid soil, leaving behind only the thin line of their tails, until those too disappeared.

Inside the tavern, people carried on as if they did not hear the thundering guns echoing from the front. Lev recognized the policeman from Dachau sitting on a woman's lap, his arm slung over her flushed neck. In the corner, a man played the accordion accompanied by a boy, possibly his son, who sat with a violin positioned under his quivering chin. The policeman was drunk, his head lolling. He sat with three other soldiers, all of them with their shirts open, their pistols still in their holsters, their boots kicked up onto chairs in front of them. He saw Lev through the dense smoke and gestured for him to come over. Hermann whispered into his ear, "He's being sent to the front tomorrow." His breath was stale from hunger.

Three Rubenesque women approached, their skin glowing in the dim candlelight. They spoke with their eyes, velvety and dark. Lev felt the heat and pressure of their bodies, solicitous and warm. They spoke Russian, from what he could decipher, and pantomimed drinking, tilting their chins back, leading Hermann and Lev to an empty table near the blaring music. The women were burned from working outdoors, the strength of the sun evident on their high cheekbones, delicate creases fanning out at the sides of their eyes. Josephine's preserved white face remained smooth and untouched by the elements. Lev preferred her when she woke in the morning, a disheveled and messier version of herself, before the perfection of the day crowned her. The women leaned forward, laughing strangely at a joke Hermann made. One of the women, with reddish hair braided into a thick plait, came up behind Lev, massaging his neck, her breath in his ear. She smelled of beets and hay, and when he glanced down, he noticed how her nails carried a line of dirt beneath them, the same dirt that corrugated under his boots from the roads and that was now crusted on his pants. He caught the sour scent of dried sweat from her armpits. So different from pine and soap and lavender. The policeman and the other soldiers had peeled off their shirts, their bare chests shining with sweat, small crosses dangling. They clapped in time with the music. Flushed women danced around them, their hands on their hips. The men playfully slapped the women from behind, and the women threw back their heads. The musicians stomped their boots on the wooden floorboards. Lev wondered absently if one of the women belonged to the accordion player.

Hermann nudged him in the ribs. "Coming upstairs?"

The bare-chested men stumbled toward the dim stairwell with their women in tow. They sang in unison, an old drinking song. A song from home. The women struggled to sing along, their voices bending to the German.

Hermann added, "They have three rooms up there. Five marks for both." He looked at Lev savagely, his jaw slack from too much drink.

The women cooed and pressed their soft bodies against them. Lev felt his groin tighten, a building pressure. He tapped his boot methodically on the floor, frustrated by his hesitation. Again, the image of the sleuthing rat crouching alongside the road came to mind—why could he not emit a simple yes to pleasure? What did it matter if it was base? They were all, at bottom, base creatures. The thundering guns continued—so close, and yet such amorous activities continued as if it was a Saturday night in Berlin and all they cared for was plentiful schnapps and the feeling of a woman moving beneath them.

"Are they safe?" Lev whispered hoarsely, stalling.

"Hoffman was here last week. Inspecting the cleanliness of the"—a slyness enveloped Hermann's face—"merchandise."

"Are you certain?"

"The officers are terrified of disease spreading. They wouldn't take the chance."

Lev imagined himself walking back alone with the rats. He stood up from the table. "All right."

Hermann threw down a few damp bills. The women quickly stuffed the money into the front of their dresses, the bills disappearing between their milky white breasts.

If anything, it was a wonderful sensation, the taking of a woman. She did not stiffen or recoil. To plunge into the formidable darkness and not feel resistance but a lukewarm flow coursing between them. His thumbs pressed against the insides of her soft forearms, which were splayed above her head, her auburn hair radiating outward on the filthy pillow. At first, he heard Hermann grunting and a light muffled laughter in the next room, but then his own breathing overtook him like the rush of ocean inside a shell, and he forgot how close the war raged, and how the floorboards creaked, and how the heavy moon hung low and bloody in the black sky, illuminating her freckled, downy stomach. He forgot everything except his sex churning through her, and her surprising fluid receptiveness was a womanly quality he had not experienced for a long time, for it had been so long since sex was not a conversation where he was always trying to convince, dissolving pleasure and exhausting him.

Lev now held his palm over this woman's mouth, and her eyes glittered, apparently wanting to be silenced. He could not believe that she invited such shadows of brutality, that she preferred his improvised force.

After they finished, her face set hard and stony in the moonlight. She closed her eyes, closing out the image of him, as if the curtains in a theater swiftly met, and with it, shut down the openness of her body. The performance of pleasure was over.

At four a.m., Lev and Hermann walked back along the muddy road. Lev's limbs worked loosely and freely, his lungs expanding, opening to the cool dawn. They walked with their backs to the sound of thunder. Or guns? Thunder or guns: that was always the question. The rumble from the front layered with the chorus of birds vibrating through the trees created an odd score for their meditative silence.

Lev grinned, picking up his pace. "Was Hoffman really there last week?"

The edges of Hermann's mouth curled upward. "You had a good time, didn't you?"

"Yes." *You and the world have drifted away.* "Yes. I did."

The red sun was rising. Lev realized they had been here for a month, and he felt comfortable with Hermann, walking along this shared road. If he let his mind settle into the rhythm of his steps, let his face bathe in the red light creeping through the firs, and let himself wander back to that forceful plunging into her body, he felt satisfied, close to whole. He did not especially want to return home just now. He let out a sharp laugh.

4

The air was changing. No longer plagued by the torpid heat that had slowed Lev's days at the field hospital and made it hard to sleep at night with a sheet drenched in sweat, there were now signs of this being replaced by a much fiercer enemy. When he woke, his bed was no longer hot and damp but a cocoon of warmth where he hibernated until the last possible moment, and when they assembled outside at dawn, the crystalline air shimmered with an icy cold, turning noses yellow-white, all the blood retracting from the surface of the skin. They were ordered to watch over one another, to make sure extremities did not freeze. Headgear was introduced, and a demonstration of how to properly cover oneself was conducted on a gray morning in the middle of November. Frost ointment was distributed, as well as instructions for how to identify frostbite. Throughout the days, men constantly told one another in passing, *You have a white nose.* Lev remembered a man who'd lost his nose from artillery fire. A gaping hole marked the center of his face, and when the bandage came off, a hollowed-out crater dipped from under his eyes to the top of his lips.

In the mornings, Lev made Hermann rub frost ointment on his ears, which were slightly distended from Lev's head. Then Hermann bandaged them up, an extra precaution. And Lev rubbed the ointment on Hermann's cheekbones, sharp and pronounced, jutting out of his gaunt face. His cheekbones had been the reason why Lev had initially mistrusted Hermann. They lent him a womanly air of seduction, leading Lev to anticipate a betrayal of some sort, Hermann's obsidian eyes flitting from one face to another, procuring rumors about who would be sent to the front. Last night, when Hermann whispered to him that tomorrow Lev would be going to the front, it was a golden nugget of knowledge.

"For how long?" His chest tightened, the blood stiffening in his veins. *War tomorrow. War tomorrow.*

Hermann's cigarette burned a dulcet orange in the dark room. "I don't know."

"How do you know I'm going?"

A man moaned in his sleep. Someone smacked him with a rolled-up newspaper.

"Ludendorff's third in command knows things. I bring him the raspberry soda my sister sends me. He says it's the best raspberry soda he's ever tasted. Addicted to it." Hermann leaned back into his pillow. "The war's far from over."

Lev put his head in his hands. "I'm not finished. Polina will be devastated."

"The dollhouse?" Hermann asked sleepily.

Lev fought the urge to cry out, thinking about how he had constructed the frame and some of the furniture pieces, but all the details—those sumptuous details—had not been added. Right now it just looked skeletal, a bombed-out house, and she'd had enough of that, he thought. "Who will finish it for her?"

Hermann slapped him on the back. "She'll forget about the whole thing in a few weeks. That's how children are."

Sunday morning, before dawn, they started marching. They would march until reaching the transport station. No one knew how long the march would last. Some said a day. Others guessed a week. They were headed for Lodz, which was closer to Germany and farther south. The movement felt retrograde, as if they were retreating as opposed to pressing forward into the hinterlands of the Russian empire. But the officer of Lev's unit explained that by securing Lodz, the Russian advance toward Breslau in Germany would prove untenable. "We are defending Berlin." His voice grandly rolled over the words with an enticing richness. At the mention of Berlin, the officer's eyes misted over, as if he too kept a wife there who, at this very moment, was attending Mass, making the sign of the cross.

Lev had forgotten the heaviness of extra gear. Even his head felt heavier wearing the pointed metal helmet rather than the soft field cap. Across his chest, he'd strapped a rifle, as instructed to do when on the march. On top of his knapsack, a M1914 shelter quarter and mess tin. Connected to the lower half of his knapsack, he carried a bayonet, M1915 water bottle, and M1914 bread bag. His greatcoat, made of coarse gray cloth, sported dull brass buttons. He sweated under these layers of material and weaponry. Each man carried the exact same items in the exact same manner. No one spoke. They were too cold and the burden of equipment forced everyone to concentrate on maintaining a steady clipped pace. Lev couldn't tell one man from another, and he knew this was the point—to unite them into one moving body for more efficient killing.

Lev instinctually looked around for Hermann, Hermann who would always drop him a wink or a grin, a secret glance acknowledging that they were not strangers in a room full of strangers. But Hermann had stayed behind at base, joking how his job in the press office reassuring Germans back home that they were achieving stunning victory after stunning victory was quite important. He pantomimed an artist bent over his work. "Coloring in the facts—that's why they keep me here. Only yesterday did they announce our defeat at the Marne, which happened two months ago. But they call it"—Hermann had paused, lowering his voice—"the strategic release of information."

When they'd parted, Hermann's metallic eyes blinked as he explained strategies for survival. "Forget the Russians," he'd said with a dismissive wave of his hand. "The real terror is nature. The snow. We're not as used to it as they are. Frostbite's more likely than a bullet."

They marched for two days and then took a train to Lodz. Halfway there, the train derailed because the tracks had been blown up. The Russians had done it during their retreat. Lev and the other men crawled out of windows and smashed doors into the blinding whiteness of snow. Sharp hail drummed their helmets. The first two cars had crumpled up against the trees, leaving a pile of smoking machinery and men with entangled limbs cocked at unusual angles. There was no time to drag them out of the cars, to bury them with proper wooden crosses, to recite any kind of benediction, because the Austrians were losing to the Russians. The officer reminded them again of Berlin, of the mothers and wives they must save from the Tatar hordes. "Imagine what they could do, those eastern barbarians," he said, his breath white and full before him. He left Lev to imagine the possibilities as they marched the rest of the way to the front, passing through abandoned town after abandoned town, the houses and shops and churches and markets closed up and cleared out, the streets echoing with the sound of their synchronized lockstep. Lev wondered if Poles huddled inside the silent buildings, afraid of their own breath, afraid to shuffle an inch lest they be discovered by their executioners or their liberators: there wasn't much difference between the two.

They first entered through the reserve trenches, a mile behind the front line. At the edge of the forest, they passed a pile of wounded oxen baring their teeth in malicious grins, dusted with snow, frozen into uselessness. The distinct sound of cannons drummed from the front coupled with machine-gun fire. All around them, the snowy earth had been plowed by exploding shells. Broken wagons and dead horses had been moved to the side of the road. Dead soldiers had been arranged to the side as well; their eyes stared up at Lev. Sometimes, an arm or leg was missing. Beyond this, at the edge of a clearing, about fifty canvas packs were scattered on the ground, waiting to be searched for letters and the odd treasured item such as a wedding ring, a handed-down pipe, a piece of ribbon, an engraved lighter that would then be sent to the next of kin. The packs belonged to dead Germans. In his own pack, Lev carried Josephine's silky lock of hair, Franz's crayon drawing of the Red Baron shooting through the sky, and a diary. He wrote on the cover: *Do not send home.* What would she think of the woman in the green velvet vest who had writhed beneath him? And if she read his doubts: Were they suited for each other? Would her intermittent coldness in the bedroom eventually stretch into one long period of retreat? And how her family belittled him with their subtle insidious comments, comments that

when repeated afterward to Josephine made him sound paranoid and
cynical, as if he only saw the worst in people. But they treated him as
if he'd grown up entirely in Galicia, in small-town Brody, whereas his
family had moved to Berlin when Lev was two. They had servants when
money permitted. There were violin lessons on Saturdays and box seats
at the opera and occasional trips to the galleries to see the new paintings. Josephine would read all this and deny the truth in it. He imagined
how she might resent him, even in death.

After sleeping poorly that night on an uneven dirt floor inside
a pitched tent, Lev woke to the smell of burnt potatoes. He peeked
through the canvas opening. A few men fried potatoes and leeks, ignoring a man who lay a few meters away, clutching his stomach. He complained of an ulcer. Lev joined the men sitting around the bonfire. They
passed him some frozen chocolate someone had sent from home. All
supplies had to be melted first. Even the bread arrived in rock-hard
bundles, delivered by ski. A soldier repeatedly banged a loaf against the
ground, trying to break through the layer of ice. The men complained
bitterly of the cold and how the officers were lounging inside the mess
hall smoking and drinking hot coffee. Someone said that at the front,
the officer's trenches were like salons, with wallpaper and mirrors and
Oriental rugs. Another soldier, who didn't look older than nineteen,
read out a news item: "Everything has gone splendidly. Our troops have
successfully carried out their missions, all counterattacks have been
repulsed and large numbers of prisoners taken." He laughed hysterically afterward. Two other men smiled grimly. Lev felt the blood leaving his fingertips and made a fist, punching it into his other hand. He
remembered something a soldier said to him on the march. "We wait in
the dirt, tormented by lice and hunger, praying that the endless boredom won't kill us before the Russians do." The man had kept his eyes
trained forward and said nothing else. Lev thought about how more
black nights filled with hunger would follow. They would be fed enough
not to starve but little enough to feel as if they were starving, occasionally placated by a cigarette, a thimble of whiskey, a trifle that would
remind them of their former appetites, their former selves. How silly
I've been, Lev thought, remembering his first letters home, exclaiming

how he was experiencing life instead of being shut away in the rarified office of the textile plant, believing army life was real life. He'd rejoiced in the physicality of it, in the use of his hands that were now calloused. And he wondered why Josephine did not match his excitement in her replies, why her tone was measured and restrained, chilly even. Perhaps she'd foreseen how he could become addicted to this life or killed by it or, at the very least, utterly changed.

"Hey." Someone punched Lev in the shoulder. "Look."

A few meters away three soldiers posed behind a crude wooden cross, grinning at their bounty. Dead rats hung by their tails from the arms of the cross, strung up in a row. Another soldier took a photograph.

"They do this every morning, to show off the rats they killed in the trench overnight."

Lev kept noticing their paws outstretched, clawing air, and their ash-colored fur.

The man speaking to him smelled of whiskey. "The rats become hysterical. They run into our flimsy shelters seeking refuge from artillery fire, from the fantastic noise. And then they get killed anyway."

"Like us," Lev said.

The man smiled, some of his teeth black.

The next morning Lev was sent to the front as a medic. Of course, this was what he'd done before at the base—it was what they'd trained him for—but still he felt a mixture of relief and shame. The soldier pictured on the poster back home only fought with his bayonet and hand grenade, charging into no-man's-land, his eyes wide open to meet death. This soldier had inhaled the fumes of combat so that his face was blackened from dirt and grime and sweat. There was little room in the public imagination for the mail carriers and sorters, the military policeman, the press officers, the heavy combat vehicle detachment unit, for the reserve infantry and the doctors and medical orderlies who dressed the wounds and recorded how many had fallen.

Lev stood a few meters from the dressing station, behind a wall of sandbags. He could hear his own breath beating in his ears, the only real sound. His arms dangled at his sides, waiting. A few meters away, other men were shooting over the tops of the trenches. The taller men always got shot through the jaw, the shorter ones through the eyes. Along the ridge of the trench, a soldier sprinted a meter and a bullet blew out all his teeth, a spray of blood bursting from his mouth. Three men methodically negotiated an MG 08 machine gun—one looked through the sight, another held the lengthy row of bullets, and a third directed them, binoculars pressed into his face. The air sounded as if it was being torn apart by the firing of one of the big guns, by the whistling and howling of the rifle bullets, which squealed like butchered pigs. Yellow and green clouds wafted by from sulfur grenades. Lev breathed in and out. This was all he could do, and yet his limbs were jacked up with adrenaline, his heart pumping as if he were expecting to run a great distance.

The moments passed. He waited for wounded men. He had been instructed to run out, and if possible hoist them onto a stretcher, and if not, drag them to the advanced dressing station, a tented structure about three hundred meters from the front line. Shells burst overhead. He clung to the sandbags, frantic, but at the same time, overly aware of the most insignificant details: the shape of the shrapnel shell bursting in the sky resembled an old boot, and the gas sentry, ringing various warning bells and rattles, sounded like one of Vicki's broken toys, a sinister lullaby. Suddenly, the shooting subsided, for how long he didn't know, and a soldier limped toward him, a cigarette dangling from his mouth. He stumbled to the side, trying to say something. Lev pulled him behind the sandbags. The man pointed to where it hurt—his knee was blown out.

His eyes shut with refusal when Lev motioned toward the tent.

Lev yelled, "I have to get you in there. See the wound—" Another big gun went off followed by a rain of bullets. The man clung to Lev. Soldiers ran from all directions. Lev held the man, awkwardly rocking him, trying to remember how he used to hold his son. He coiled his arm around the man, attempting to transmit security and confidence when all he felt was plain raw fear. He was shaking and this shaking made the man also shake. They waited and trembled together, the three or four minutes interminable. Lev tried not to think about whether or not this man's leg would have to be amputated or if they could insert a

metal disk in place of the knee, and whether or not the soft wall of sandbags they leaned against would blow up, eradicating them in an instant.
How much heat could the skin take before singeing? Would he think
of anything else beyond the rapid destruction of his body, the charring
of his hands, the flames crawling up the sides of his legs, the way his
boots would appear like two balls of fire beneath him? The man moaned
softly, burying his face deeper in the folds of Lev's field-gray coat. Lev
wondered if he was being punished for forsaking God when he had
spent so many evenings inside Berlin's fashionable cafés disputing His
very existence over coffee and kaiser rolls, proclaiming that any rational
man would not sacrifice his son out of blind faith, that the world no
longer ran on superstition and myth, and those who needed the illusion of order, refusing the true chaos of living, lived in fear. Everyone
had raised their glasses, their glowing faces framed by starched white
collars, reveling in a feeling of shared intellectual superiority, nodding
when Lev called out, "We only know what God isn't, not what He is.
Despite all the decoration of churches and priests and marble statuar-
ies, we are merely devoted to the absence of an idea."

Shells exploded, filling the air with thick gray smoke, and involuntarily Lev's lips began moving, the rise and fall of his father's tongue
a salve, a talisman. *Yit'gadal v'yit'kadash sh'mei rab, b'al'ma di v'ra
khir'utei.*

Later, when the firing ceased, Lev smoked a cigarette inside the dressing station, watching the man sleep, his leg elevated on a wool blanket.
Rows and rows of half-dead men filled the tent. Lev walked toward the
opening, and pulled back the heavy canvas. The air smelled of blood and
ashes. The severe sky indicated the onset of evening as daylight drained
away. Makeshift graves, pitiful wooden crosses, had been erected since
this morning, and now the division pastor conducted a funeral service
only a few meters away from the dressing station. Lev watched from
the tent opening. He could no longer mock the pastor and those solemn
soldiers praying. The howling of the cannons rose again. The pastor
tried to appear calm, but never before had Our Father been recited so
quickly. The words went like water through Lev's ears. The men were

fidgety, restless, on alert for the crash of a grenade, the whiz of rifle fire. Many of them looked as if they were ready to bolt, their jaws tight, fists clenched. The pastor was sweating. The two dark crimson strips decorating the front of his white robe fluttered in the wind. He tossed a bit of dirt over the shallow graves, barely covering the naked faces, his thin voice rushing, "Being raised in the glory of the resurrection, he may be refreshed among the Saints and Elect. Through Christ our Lord . . ." A shrill sound, and everyone threw themselves to the ground. A shell exploded fifty meters away. The pastor burrowed his face in the dirt. Lev crouched at the entrance of the tent. He studied the intricate layers of mud splashed over his boot.

After some minutes, the soldiers started getting up, glancing around sheepishly because no one was hurt.

But Lev could still hear the sound of bullets buzzing through his ears, as if a chorus of bees encircled him.

5

Berlin, 1915

In the early morning, when the pale violet light filtered into his bed-room, Franz whispered his prayers. He pressed his forehead against the icy glass windowpane, his lips moving silently. He had requested that Marthe not lower the wooden blinds before bedtime because he wanted a view of the night sky. Possibly, a very small possibility he knew, he would see the Red Baron flying his bright plane across the blanket of night, saving them from the English, saving his father who'd been gone over a year now, and saving his mother, and his sister too. Even though they were safe at home, his mother cried yesterday when the old man who delivered the mail did not have the little brown postcard. She received one every week, and when the little brown postcard was delayed or lost in the mail, she yelled at Franz for dropping his soup spoon or for playing with the brass button on his sailor suit or for los-ing his mitten in the snow. When they went outside yesterday afternoon to look for the mitten, their eyes scanning the inner courtyard of the house where he'd played with Wolf, a sheen of dazzling white covered the gray stone as if a winter sandstorm had transformed their famil-iar surroundings into an unrecognizable landscape of blankness. It was clear the mitten was absent from the iron garden chairs arranged in a desolate circle, absent from the lonely oak in the center of the court-yard, a withered version of its former self, and absent from the benevo-lent statue of St. Peter now shrouded in powdery snow. Josephine drew her black shawl tighter and tighter around her shoulders, turning round and round, as if a full circular view of the courtyard would somehow reveal the missing mitten. Her smooth motion reminded Franz of the ballerina inside Vicki's jewel box, the dainty figurine rotating to a melodic nursery rhyme until the lid closed. By the time Josephine faced Franz, her eyes were swollen and streaming tears, and Franz wondered if the tears would freeze on her cheeks, like the long pointed icicles that they broke off and sucked. He wanted to take her inside before the tears could freeze. He had a terror that if she did not warm herself by the fire, the rivers on her face would become permanent icicles affixed there, as sharp and pointed as fangs.

It had begun to snow early this morning, the crystalline flakes sticking to his bedroom window. The snowflakes told a story about the Eastern Front, where his father was fighting, and about the Red Baron, who was flying his red plane to get there, to greet his father, to present him with an award for courage, to ask if he had a son. "Yes, I have a son," his father would say, and he would show him the photograph of Franz in front of the Christmas tree, wearing his Sunday clothes, the white shirt with the wide lace collar. The baron would hold the photograph up to the sky, and he would pronounce in a clear ringing voice, "He will become a great German soldier and fly planes."

Franz stood by the window in his flannel nightgown, his bare feet on the wooden floor, knowing Mother would fly into hysterics if she saw him without slippers. She would say he was trying to catch his death after only having just recovered from the grippe. But it was still early; she would not open the door yet. School remained distant until she opened the door and the process of washing and dressing and eating began, all in preparation for the brisk walk there. In class, Herr Bedderhoff might call on Franz to recite the "Cavalier's Song" from *Wallenstein*. Franz turned away from the window and concentrated on the oil painting of Mitzi, the family dog, a black schnauzer. His father had captured the dog's true essence: the prominent bushy eyebrows nearly covered his curious eager eyes, and his salt-and-pepper beard was perpetually coated in saliva, as pictured here. Franz always stared at this painting when he could not remember the words exactly. In a harsh whisper, he sang, "To horse then, comrades, to horse and away! And into the field where freedom awaits us, in the field of battle man still has his worth. And the heart is still weighed in the balance." The last line always troubled him. Franz paced his bedroom, treading lightly, not wanting to wake Vicki in the next room, who would surely ruin this sacred ritual by barging in and wanting to play. When he refused, she would cry, and then Mother would hurry in, and these magical morning hours would be lost.

Franz plopped down on the floor next to his bed and hugged his pillow into his chest. What of that line about the heart in the balance? Yesterday, after Herr Bedderhoff had made them recite the song three times, and then a fourth for good measure, Wolf's arm shot up defiantly. Herr Bedderhoff appeared surprised when Wolf asked what the last line meant. Bedderhoff's neck turned pink, which had only occurred one other time, when his front trouser buttons were undone. After Wolf asked the question in his piercing high voice, Herr Bedderhoff arranged his face into a contemplative gaze and answered that we all must keep up our spirits and dismiss horrid rumors only used to dismantle German pride.

"Is that how we must keep our heart in the balance?" Wolf had persisted.

Herr Bedderhoff said of course that's what it meant, and then ordered the boys to take out their colored pencils and a piece of paper.

But Franz believed Bedderhoff did not really know the meaning of that last line because his voice had cracked slightly, and his neck had remained red and white for a long time afterward. But his father would know, because his father read many old and important books. Through the glass doors of the bookcase, Franz would catch his reflection in their spines. After dinner, his father always read in the sitting room by the fire, but he did not like the children to disturb him unless they were willing to listen. Only then would he read aloud, reciting the story about Hamlet's dead father, who became a ghost, or how Viola loved a prince so much she dressed as a boy to win his heart. That particular story was Franz's favorite. Mother would sit nearby, embroidering, and occasionally his parents would comment on a piece of family gossip or a news item from the paper. Franz thought that it must be very dull to be an adult, and to be married. In the winter evenings, his mother and father grew tired and quiet and they sat as still as statues, listening to a radio program. They did not laugh unless they were entertaining company, and then they laughed too much, as he could always hear the hearty relentless laughter of his father and the breathless protestations of his mother; their intermingled gaiety funneled down the narrow hallway as he tipped into sleep.

But their voices had been replaced by a deafening quiet since his father left. There were no more lavish dinner parties, and Mother dismissed Marthe early. Mother said of course everything happened earlier because it grew dark at 4:30. In November the clocks were set back, and what did Franz expect? That they not change the clocks just so he could stay up as late as he fancied? "In that case," she had joked, "you'll have to write the Kaiser, expressing your complaints and what you propose as an alternative." But it was not falling back an hour that bothered Franz. The new ghostly silence permeating the halls was crisp and singular, as if they were waiting with held breath for the renewal of salt rations, for the news of English soldiers slain by the thousands, for the recovery of the red mitten, for the brown postcard to arrive in the mail. Franz much preferred the shared silence of his parents when his father was home. Knowing they sat together in the sitting room by the light of the oil lamp, which shed an amber glow, and knowing that in about an hour he would listen for the sound of his mother's heavy dress brushing the floor past his bedroom as she looked in on him and the cadence of his father's walk as he passed by Vicki's room and their conspiratorial whispers as they headed toward their sleeping quarters, arm in arm— well, now he only heard the isolated ticking of the grandfather clock and the skeletal rattling of the pipes attempting to push heat through the radiator grates and his mother's weightless step as she gravitated toward sleep, hoping it would take her earlier and earlier each evening.

Franz sat cross-legged on the floor, feeling sleepy. The scent of baked apples floated into his room underneath the door. Marthe had possibly opened the inner sanctum of the oven, to check on the shriveling golden skin, and if this was true, then there will be baked apples for breakfast, a rarity since the war. Under his bed, Franz had built a secret shrine to the Red Baron. Using an old shoebox as the foundational structure for his panorama, Franz placed the baron's model red plane in the foreground, along with a photograph of the baron's kind, brave face, a photograph he filched from his mother's armoire. On the back of the photograph, someone had written in cursive: *Victory is imminent.* Franz did not know what *imminent* meant, but he assumed it had something to do with the Red Baron, a code name the English wouldn't understand. When Franz slept on the floor, he turned the panorama to face him so that he could fall into sleep with the baron's handsome face staring back at him. And he dreamed of shiny apple-red fighter planes bombing French villages, and of the baron dodging bullets, his plane dipping and swerving with the wind.

The bedroom door opened. "Franz!" The thick hem of his mother's dress approached. "What are you doing on the floor like this?"

Franz gazed up, blinking. His mother's face, framed by her wheat-colored curls, looked drawn and pale. Shadows fell under her eyes.

She knelt down, touching his forehead.

Over her shoulder, he saw Vicki in the hallway, sucking her thumb. Her teddy had been abandoned at her feet, dropped on its ear.

"Why have you been sleeping on the cold floor?"

Franz heard his own voice well up inside his throat, a choking needling sound. He might not get baked apple for breakfast. "I wanted to share their suffering."

Josephine searched his face. "Whose suffering?"

"The soldiers defending the fatherland." Franz fingered the edge of her organza skirt. Luckily, the panorama was hidden under the bed. He heard Marthe opening the oven in the kitchen. The smell of baked apples grew stronger. His nostrils flared out to catch more of the buttery golden scent.

Franz could tell his mother was deciding whether or not to get cross with him. He continued, his palm gathering up more organza, "They all have to sleep on the hard cold ground in the middle of the forest. In tents. While I'm here, warm and cozy." He paused. "It's not fair."

"Mutti," Vicki called from the hallway, in her black wool tights, her belly distended.

Josephine turned around, her teardrop earrings spinning with her. "Vicki, wait a moment please."

She pulled Franz into her chest, stroking his fine golden hair. "No, it's not fair. It's not fair at all."

He soaked up her clean pine scent, which always reminded him of summer Sundays on the Wannsee, when Papa would take out a rowboat and they would eat mustard sandwiches in the tall high grass. They would find a quiet spot surrounded by firs, and Mutti would sing "Bei Mannern" from act one of *The Magic Flute*. The color bloomed in her cheeks when she sang.

At breakfast, Marthe served the plump golden apples on a plate, with stewed raisins on top. She spooned an extra dollop of raisins onto Franz's apple, saying that he needed to grow strong for when Father returned. "He'll expect to see you much taller by then."

Franz stabbed his apple with his fork and smirked. "We need more nails for the *nagelsaulen*. Today's collection day."

"Again?" Marthe asked.

Josephine stood up and rummaged through one of the kitchen drawers. Every school boasted its own *nagelsaulen*, a wooden cross, studded with nails in commemoration of the war effort. Everyone was expected to hammer a nail into the structure every Friday to praise the soldiers.

Josephine parceled out five nails for Franz and then five for Vicki.

Studying the nails in the palm of her hand, Vicki said, "Will this save Papa?" Half of her apple remained on her plate, sunken in at the core.

Josephine sipped her coffee. "Papa is safe and sound."

Vicki fingered the nails. "Someone said Papa and other soldiers could be locked up in England and never let go. That they would be slaves!" Vicki's dark eyes widened, startled by her own words.

Franz glared at her, stabbing the last piece of apple with his fork. "That's stupid."

"Greta said her mother sent clothing and cigarettes and pictures of Germany because they're captured." Vicki stared at Josephine, who continued to sip her coffee, savoring the last drops of milk and sugar. They'd nearly run out of their sugar ration, and yet ten days still remained until the first of December.

"I've told you both to avoid listening to rumors."

Marthe turned on the radio, rolling the dial to the opera station. Strauss. Josephine always preferred Strauss. His waltz "Roses from the South" floated above the children's heads, cascading over the milk-splashed glasses and the plump raisins Franz had not eaten, despite Josephine's efforts. She restrained herself from waltzing around the kitchen table as she sometimes did when no one was home.

Josephine put down her coffee cup. "In fact, today I'm going to the church. We're sending off love packages to the front. And I'm sure Papa would appreciate your drawings in the package, along with the bottle of strawberry soda, his wrist warmers, and the chocolate bars."

The children stared at her.

"Well, go get them."

Franz and Vicki returned with their drawings. All children had been instructed to draw a picture for the front. The schoolmasters encouraged the use of bright colors and cheering images, such as an idyllic farm, a tranquil lake, a family reunited.

Franz proudly unrolled his drawing of the Red Baron's plane shooting down English soldiers, whose heads lolled off their stick necks. Large teardrops of blood ruptured from their hanging limbs. He had included a ring of fire encircling the picture, and off to the side a large cannonball exploded inside an English family's farmhouse. Two cows were blown open by bombs, along with the desecration of three pigs, whose spotted pink bodies were blasted into the air, their hoofs nearly touching the wing of the red airplane. "You'll send it to Papa?"

Josephine sighed. She would have to burn the picture in the stove after dropping them at school. Lev would be sickened by such images. He had written in the last letter how stupid, senseless, and utterly barbaric it seemed, fighting against soldiers barely old enough to carry a gun, the fear in their eyes as palpable as his own, boys on the brink of adulthood who, at seventeen, had not experienced the pleasures of a woman, who would die virgins with the belief that they'd served God and country. Lev had finished his letter stating, *I hope to God, although I fear He has fled in horror—but I hope for us at least that Franz never takes up arms, that he never fights for such a useless murderous cause that has already taken so many lives, that will only take more.*

"Here, take it. Pack it for Papa." Franz held out his picture, having neatly rolled it up.

"And mine too?" Vicki asked, spreading her picture out on the now cleared dining table, her fingers sticky with apple. She'd drawn a cemetery, with rows and rows of soldiers' graves. Angels with crooked halos and sorrowful long faces hovered over the graves, waiting to transport the soldiers' souls to heaven. "The angels will save the soldiers," Vicki said.

Josephine felt her throat thicken, her mouth secreting a metallic taste. Yesterday, Sophie, the next-door neighbor, had received a letter. On the outer envelope, the blue stamp read: *Dead—Return to Sender.* She'd doubled over, gripping the handrail leading up to her house.

It was time to walk the children to school. She would come home afterward and lie down on the divan in the sitting room. She would take a long bath and listen to Strauss. She would leaf through fashion magazines and imagine a time when she could buy rich fabrics again, tulle and satin and organza, for her dresses and dine with Lev at the Duke of Pomerania's summer residence in the Bavarian woods, where they would raise their crystal glasses and toast the Kaiser, the salty taste of ruby-red caviar still on her tongue, washed down by sweet champagne. She even missed the sullen servants who cleared away each course (a total of nine plates, excluding aperitifs), and the howling of the greyhounds when a new carriage arrived, the wheels crackling along the blue-gray gravel encircling the estate, and how the duke always drank too much, his red cheeks swelling with effort as he shamelessly flirted with her, a fact that she and Lev found infinitely amusing. Afterward, they would drift into sleep under velveteen covers, giggling and whispering like schoolchildren over how foolish, how ridiculous the duke had acted. But under the covers in the dark Josephine's chest swelled, too embarrassed to admit she'd secretly enjoyed the duke's attentions because he had made it brutally clear how she'd awakened his want—it made her giddy, flush, nearly drunk.

After she dropped off the children, snow began to fall, and a heavy gray eclipsed the blue brightness of the morning. The linden trees lining the streets were skeletal, their thin wiry branches reaching out to nothing. When she studied the tree branches for too long, it reminded her of the few horrid photographs the newspapers released: boyish bodies caught in a forward outstretched motion among barbed wire, their torsos arched, arms and head hanging.

Josephine sucked in the wet air and started walking to the bread depository. They needed bread for dinner, and yet the thought of waiting in line for at least two hours seemed intolerable. She had forgotten her gloves, so she shoved her raw hands into her coat pockets. At least the fur collar, made of fox, offered comfort as the hairs felt silky and smooth against her chin, generating an animal kind of warmth. Two winters ago, Lev had bought her this coat with the fur collar, as well as a matching fox stole, which she found a bit excessive, distastefully grandiose. Her mother and *tante* Agatha had mocked the stole, with the little glass eyes staring out at the world. They joked, between sips of Russian tea and plum cake, that Lev didn't understand, no matter how many meters of the finest silk his textile mill produced, that he would never achieve a certain status because it was purely a matter of blood.

It was better before she married Lev. At least then, her whole family said what they thought instead of this subdued stifled hatred they now emitted, like a faint malodorous scent. Back then, her father had slammed doors and thrown his reading glasses across the room and yelled, the color high in his cheeks, about how calamitous it was for her to marry a Jew, especially one from an unknown family, devoid of social and financial status. Her father doubted if Lev would ever make more than three thousand marks a year. "You will have no dowry. See how much the Jew wants you then," he shrieked, slamming his veiny fist into his desk. A long glass vase rattled. The carnations, pure white, remained untroubled by his outburst. Staring at the perforated pet-

als, Josephine remembered feeling a piercing shame at the mention of
money, something her family never discussed, as if having money was
as natural as breathing. But now her father barked figures and numbers
as if he had been thinking of money all along. Her cheeks burned as
he explained the burden of supporting her—did she understand how
much those stoles cost him? The silk umbrellas with ivory handles? The
kid gloves and linen petticoats and trips to the dressmaker at the start of
each social season? "All that expense, to make you appear beautiful, and
this is what I get in return?" He had persisted, even after the wedding,
in calling Lev by his last name, always handling him with cool formality, the way you would handle a servant. Her mother worried that Lev
expected her to convert. No, no, she'd said irritably, he's hardly a Jew.
He despises the religion, she had said, which wasn't entirely true, but
it put her mother at ease. Of course there was the question of Lev's
converting to Catholicism, a question they bandied about as if playing
table tennis. A lot of other well-off Jews had done so, particularly Jewish
women who married German officers from aristocratic families.

"What difference does it make," Lev had said lightheartedly. "I'm
not religious, so whichever religion I take up won't mean much."

"It doesn't mean much," Josephine had echoed, and the general
frivolity in how he brushed away the question made her feel that she
too should brush it away. Cruel, yes, it was cruel, the way Father had
cut her off, agreeing to the marriage only on the condition that he not
provide a dowry, but Lev said it was better not to owe anyone anything,
and perhaps her father was short of money, a thought that had never
occurred to Josephine before.

For a few years, she did not see her family. Then her father died
of a blood clot in the brain. Franz was born shortly thereafter, and her
mother, alone and bewildered, called on her. And so the tentative give-
and-take began again, slowly, like a returning disease. Josephine would
come to Sunday tea with the children once a week. They stayed for two
hours. Agatha, her aunt, had moved in with her mother, and the two
women found comfort in having both lost their husbands to swift and
unexpected deaths. The unspoken rule was that Lev not attend these
afternoons, a rule he didn't appear to mind. *Thank God,* he said, *to be*

spared the agony of their company. And she half laughed. One Sunday her mother tried to explain, in her usual fumbling way, now that her father was gone, there were some funds she would like to bestow. Josephine held up a hand and said, "No," more sharply than she intended. And in that moment, she felt a warm surging pride pour over her because they didn't need the money. Lev was performing brilliantly at the textile firm, receiving yearly promotions. The number of men working under him multiplied monthly. They planned to replant the garden, with Oriental lilies lining the path so the fragrant sweet scent would bathe visitors as they approached the house—the new house in Charlottenburg with the midnight-blue front door and brass handle, exactly how she wanted it.

The line for bread on Friedrichstrasse stretched down the block. She saw its formation up ahead, filled with women and children bundled against the cold, their faces peeking out from under hats and shawls and scarves. The sky had grown darker, and she wanted to forgo the bread. She felt her body turning away from the line, and yet, as she stood there indecisively, two more people took her place. She imagined telling Marthe how silly she'd been to let it slip her mind, and were there still red potatoes left? Three more women shuffled into line, dressed in heavy black wool, their movements stiff from the blue cold. Franz flashed before her; how thin he'd looked undressed this morning, his sharp shoulder blades pointing out of his back like baby sparrow wings. So thin she'd hurriedly slipped his undershirt over his head, his sharp bones disappearing into the soft fabric.

She forced herself to stand behind a large grandmotherly woman who stared down at her swollen feet stuffed into boots that were coming apart at the soles. They waited in silence as the line grew behind them.

Suddenly the old woman looked up and said, "They cover the bread in chalk." Her eyes laughed as if the world had become a ridiculous place.

"It's imitation flour," Josephine countered. "It makes the bread prettier."

"In the middle of the night I got up to wait in line, so I could be first for butter. But when the doors opened, they told me all the butter had been sold the day before. Only turnips, they had."

Josephine lowered her head, thinking of how two days ago a group of women had marched in protest because a butcher shop ran out of meat. The women had stormed down Unter den Linden shouting *Peace! Peace!* Josephine had heard the distant racket from where she sat by the bay window in the living room, reading. She never cared for politics.

"You're not a widow, I hope," the woman added, exposing a black tooth toward the back of her mouth when she grinned.

"No, thank God."

The old woman regarded her carefully. "Bless your husband."

"Thank you," Josephine said, not wanting to know how many sons this woman had lost. She could not bear to look at some faded photograph the woman might pull out, another boy about to leave for the front, posed unnaturally in uniform.

The line shifted forward.

The woman sighed, picking up her basket, which held a few bruised apples. "How long has he been away?"

"Since the very start," Josephine replied, irritated by the question. The woman really wanted to know how eager her husband had been to join up. Not everyone volunteered immediately. But Lev had.

A light snow began to fall again, and Josephine felt her eyes sting from the cold wet wind. Winter evenings before the war, she used to step out for the shopping at four o'clock in the Old West district, alone among the buildings and monuments bathed in a china-blue gaslight. Even for small things—a new hem for her silk slip, a pair of brass buttons for Franz, a handful of white gardenias for the table—walking with the setting sun as her guide offered a few solitary hours, freeing her from the ordinary household sounds: a running stream of water, a teapot bleating, Marthe scolding Franz for dropping a dollop of marmalade on the floor, the tearful voice of Vicki asking for Lev. On her walks, Josephine stole glances into the lit rooms of apartments. Most of the time, the windows were obscured by heavy curtains or wooden blinds or by a bulbous paraffin lamp emitting a faint glow. But if someone lingered, taking in the last bits of daylight, she would see a woman, like herself, pausing pensively before the window, or a child reading, or a man embracing a woman, their bodies fusing into one opaque shape. A thousand stories spinning just as her own story spun, all occurring at precisely the same moment, comforted her, and she felt less alone when she looked into these brightly lit windows, as if the people inside kept a vigil for her, and she kept one for them. A hushed pact.

Holding the bread to her chest, she made her way home, thinking of those dreamy winter afternoons, when the light looked as it did now, the crystalline blue of the sky slipping into a faded purple, as faint as a bruise. And the tree branches cut stark outlines into the sky, reminding her that soon, the clear-cut outlines would fade into the general darkness of night. She covered the paper bag with her shawl, wishing the bread was warm for the children when she surprised them with it. But they would still gleefully tear clumps off the loaf, stuffing the pieces into their mouths, laughing.

When she came home, padding through the silent house, Josephine often paused, examining the objects around her; the glass bookcase and the Oriental rug and the low rounded table and the sloping walnut backs of the chairs and the hanging medieval tapestry of a hunt—the war left no mark here. She wondered if she remained in this room, as still as the walls, if Lev would arrive at six as he used to, readying himself for a cigar, for the day to peel off him. But no. She scolded herself for such frivolous thoughts.

She brought the bread into the kitchen. Marthe had left to fetch the children from school. A cold purple light stretched across the white walls. Preparations for dinner had begun; a stew simmered on the stove, a wooden ladle next to it, and on the table, a chopping board with thinly sliced radishes, which appeared like transparent moons, lined up next to the stainless steel knife blade. She sighed, catching a glimpse of her face distorted in the blade.

6

Almost a year had passed since Lev had arrived in Mitau, a town in the heart of Courland, south of Riga, on the bank of the Lielupe River. At high-water level, the plain and sometimes the town flooded. Each month, the front had shifted to the Germans' advantage as they gained more territory from the Russians, occupying abandoned town after abandoned town. This was where Lev had ended up—in one of these towns.

When he had first landed here with his regiment, all the people were gone. They had escaped into the forest. But slowly, as the weeks passed and his unit began to reconstruct what was burned and destroyed, the people returned—filthy, feral, lice-ridden, leaving behind family members frozen among the trees. Women and children and the old reappeared, timidly reentering their broken houses. A few lucky men who had circumvented the Russian army also returned. Most startling was how these people tried to kiss the top of Lev's hand when he walked the town's streets. At first Lev recoiled. It was old and feudal and he did not want to touch them because the notion that this land and its peoples were inherently diseased had been ingrained in him from the start. But it became tiring to fend them off, especially the begging women, who moaned and badgered him until he would finally outstretch his hand to receive a dry pitiful kiss, a kiss that felt like dust. As a matter of course, the soldiers began holding out their hands whenever they were in the village, but the exhibition of such insistent superiority embarrassed Lev, so he extended his hand as discreetly as possible.

The very condition of the streets proved how these people needed them: the footing was unsteady; one had to walk on narrow slick planks where cobblestones had been blown up. Once, Lev thought he saw a femur buried under loose cobblestones. Signs pointed to nowhere. Open gutters flowed with sewage. The officers gave big speeches every few weeks about their purpose here. *Unlike the productive Nordic and German races, these peoples in the east are inherently lazy and parasitic. To make the land over in our own image, we must instill cleanliness and order, and promote a culture of hard work, sweat, and labor.*

The phrases circulated in Lev's mind while he was performing the most mundane of tasks, such as recording how much firewood had been amassed in one day or knocking on the peasants' doors, demanding a detailed account of how many chickens they had and cows, and how much grain they'd produced. They could not understand him, their wide foreheads sweating with effort to convey something entirely different. Yesterday, an old woman tried to give him a black pot. It was chipped, the handle broken off, but she pressed it into his chest, nodding when Lev refused to take it, as if his refusal was just a performance and sooner or later he would give in. He finally took it, but a few hours later, he placed the pot in front of her door, an absurd game of give-and-take. Even more absurd was the general's confident smile when he had said, raising his wineglass, that if one could cultivate the natives to become orderly, clean, and honest, then the land itself would transform into an agricultural surplus of wheat, cattle, and wood of the very highest quality. "This East," he said conclusively, "is the real utopia." And the thunder of clapping that followed engulfed the crowded dining hall, which had once belonged to a local farmer who was dead or gone.

Today, Lev stood before a ditch filled with blue-black mares put down because they were maimed, injured in the shin or carrying shrapnel in their chests. His fellow soldier shot each horse at the edge of the ditch, and then Lev recorded it in a ledger. The soldier positioned the revolver on the horse's downy brow, and in an instant, the horse collapsed, tumbling awkwardly into the ditch. When they finished, the blue-black torsos shimmered in the sun. Lev counted twelve. He wrote it neatly in pencil. They paused, observing the odd beauty of it, before they began tossing shovels of dirt over the ditch. The eyes of the horses were still open, rolling back, gleaming in the darkness of the hole. Bit by bit, their muscular necks and arched backs were covered until it was only a pile of dirt.

"Nearly done," Lev said, leaning into his shovel. He blinked the sweat out of his eyes.

The other man shrugged. The silence between them remained ungenerous, as it had been all morning. Lev barely knew him, but the least this man could do was nod or make some gesture of solidarity. But Lev had heard this man's wife had left him because he hadn't sent enough money home. She was hungry and without coal. News of unreliable wives traveled fast. It made the other men nervous, unleashing images of their women straddling faceless men, men who were exempt due to bad eyesight or flat-footedness, who were either too old or too young to serve.

The man squinted into the sun, the sides of his eyes crinkling like wrinkled silk. His mouth looked miserable, as if he couldn't speak.

"Or maybe the horses are the lucky ones. To be put out of their misery," Lev added, transferring the shovel from one hand to the other.

"I'm not miserable," the man said, jutting out his chin. The pock-marked sides of his face glinted in the sun.

"You're better off without her." Lev did not actually know if this was true, but he stretched out his arm, as if to pat him on the back. His hand, suspended in the humid air, felt heavy and false.

He searched Lev's face, as if looking for a place to put his grief. "Her mother was the one who wrote to tell me."

"I can't imagine." Lev's voice trailed off.

The man dug the heel of his boot into the earth. "She's probably in bed with a Jew." Then he vehemently spat. The white wet spittle sizzled before dissolving into the dirt. "Shirkers. Bankrolling the war without fighting. Profiting from our dead." He motioned to the pit they'd just dug. "And who'll be left when the war's over?"

Lev's throat closed up, a tiny knot of nausea developing there.

The man threw up his arms, his face animated and filled with color.

"They're vultures, circling and circling, and when the time's right, swooping down to take their share." His eyes gleamed and then he asked, "Smoke?" and held out a pack of cigarettes.

Lev stepped back. His insides heaved upward. He did not want to be sick in front of this man. Dropping his shovel, he managed to say, "That's twelve for today."

As he gulped water from his canteen, most of it missed his mouth, sliding down his chin. He coughed into his palm. He would rest in the shade. It was Friday, the October heat oppressive and golden. Leaning against a tree, Lev sank down to the ground and rested his elbows on his knees. He watched the other man walk to camp, back to the smoke and the smell of production that claimed this place.

Behind him he heard a thud. A little yellow apple fell. It had dropped from one of the small thatched huts arranged haphazardly nearby. People were eating inside them. He had seen the locals building these little huts over the last few days in celebration of the Feast of the Tabernacles, or as the Jews here called it, Sukkot. They hung branches and palm leaves and bright acorn squash and apples from the roofs, and when Lev had seen children decorating the huts, he thought of Vicki and Franz hanging ornaments on a Christmas tree, the innate pleasure children took in these things.

Inside the hut nearest him, people argued. Then a woman emerged to restore the fallen apple to its place. She glanced over at him, her head covered in a cream shawl. She arched her dark eyebrows, as if expecting Lev to say something. But he said nothing, struck by her open clear face, how light and free her movements were, unburdened by her body, which he could tell through the clothing was sylphlike and beautifully shaped, like an expensive vase. Standing there, she slowly bent down to the ground, keeping her eyes on Lev.

He glanced away, scrutinizing the discoloration of the tree bark.

She moved cautiously toward him, cupping the yellow apple in her palm.

"Would you like it?" she asked in Yiddish.

"Isn't it for your little hut?" he answered back, in Yiddish.

She grinned, still holding out her palm, the apple resting perfectly still in it. "It's only for decoration. Someone should eat it."

Her whole body urged him to take it, the curve of her back, the slope of her white neck escaping the thin shawl, her wrist straining slightly as she balanced the apple in her palm.

"Thank you," Lev blurted out, quickly scooping it up. Without touching her skin, he felt her heat. But it would have been offensive to let his fingertips graze the creases in her palm, and she had trusted him, knowing he would not trespass this simple rule. Whose rule was it? They didn't know. But they both knew it existed for people like them, in these types of situations.

A boy escaped from the hut, probably twisting out of someone's embrace. Lev imagined old men with beards, young children, and tired mothers stored away in there, dipping pieces of bread in salt water, discussing the harvest, how it never yielded enough.

"Leah?" the boy called out, even though he could see her clearly, a short distance away.

Leah. The name vibrated on his tongue.

She spun around. "Geza, don't be so blind."

"I'm not blind." He stuck his hands on his hips. Lev guessed he was about fourteen, although his bony shoulders and slim hips made him appear younger.

"You are too. Blind as a bat," she teased.

"Your son?" Lev asked, hoping he was. Then he could tell her about his son, and they would have sons in common.

"My sister's son," she said, her eyes slipping away from him. And then she yelled, "Geza, come," and walked over to him, playfully pinching his elbow. "We gave the polite soldier an apple and now we must finish our meal."

Lev waited for that moment when she would turn to look at him once more before disappearing into the hut, but she did not. When she lowered her head to enter, her shawl slipped back revealing such dark hair it turned deep blue in the sun.

7

We plunder, Lev thought, as the rich dark forests were razed for firewood, for fortifications at the front, for the building of bridges. They also confiscated local horses, even the old useless ones, making it impossible for the villagers to transport goods, something the army then punished the villagers for. The punishments were frivolous and unregulated: robbing a family of their entire food supply for winter or beating a man in the town square for miscounting his chickens (he had been hiding a fat red hen) or raping someone's daughter even when she yelled *"Krank"*—sickly, diseased—her hands fluttering in the air like birds let loose. But her performance was not convincing enough. The officer had pulled down her lower lip, inspecting her shiny pink gums. Her teeth were strong, her eyes clear, her color high. "I know health when I see it," he had said afterward, boastful that he had out-witted her. The officer told Lev this as they oversaw the collection of raw materials. Local Jews had been recruited to collect, working as middlemen, knocking on their neighbors' doors, requesting candlesticks, meekly transporting organ pipes from the churches for scrap metal, carting Hanukkah menorahs out of their own homes.

Lev and the officer stood, arms crossed, in the middle of a drafty farmhouse. Most of the windows had been broken, glass shards lying on the ground. A blue bird flew in and out of the room until the officer raised his rifle and shot it.

"Who else would do this?" the officer joked, motioning to the crowd as they lugged tin and copper and brass onto the growing pile of metal. He shook his head in disgust.

Lev noticed a middle-aged woman reluctantly parting with a bronze samovar. When she put it down, her whole body went with it, her arms embracing the baroque curves.

Lev contemplated knocking the officer's pipe out of his mouth. "They don't have a choice."

"These Jews are doing what they're naturally good at. Stealing."

Lev clenched his jaw. The target of malevolence. For centuries, it has made us afraid, Lev thought.

The officer took another puff from his pipe. He smiled sardonically. His eyes flickered over Lev's face. "You speak Yiddish, yes?"

"Yes." Saliva flooded his mouth.

"Good."

How did everyone seem to know? Lev thought, his head pounding. Even the Jewish soldiers with talliths wrapped around their knapsacks glanced at him furtively in the mess hall when the sun lowered on Friday evenings and Lev acted as jocular and ordinary as the others. Was it his name, Perlmutter? Should he have changed it into something more German? Were his almond-shaped eyes huddled too close? Did his ears protrude too far from his skull? In Berlin, his difference had never been quite as striking. It had been ameliorated by well-cut clothing, elaborate dinner parties, a wife with golden hair.

"Sir, I don't follow. What is good about speaking Yiddish?"

Another question kept rising, like a piano key hit over and over: *Where is the man I was in Berlin?*

"Because you speak Yiddish," the officer said, "tomorrow you'll arrange the procedure for the identity cards: name, age, occupation, residence, number of children. Religion." He paused, putting away his pipe. "You see, you'll explain to the Jews what we need. And then the Jews will translate for the locals. Otherwise, it's the tower of babble all over again." He laughed, fingering his front pocket where he'd put his pipe.

The Tower of Babel, Lev thought the next day when in the cold blue morning he unlocked the barn where the natives had been waiting since daybreak. All the nationalities were mixed together, a big mess. They sat on the benches in their finest clothes and yet they smelled from being locked up in here with the horses. They had been given numbers by the soldiers earlier this morning, but when Lev walked into the damp, dimly lit barn, he saw that many of them had dropped their numbers on the floor, the pieces of paper scattered in the hay, smeared with refuse.

Lev clapped his hands. "Pick up your numbers. You must present your number to process your identity card." The sound of his harsh German vibrated in the stale air. He inhaled cow dung mixed with onions and body odor. A photographer stood behind him. Two local Jews stepped forward and said they were the translators. They were young, no older than twenty. Lev wondered how they had escaped the Russian army. He imagined them hiding in the trees, their hands blistered and frozen.

They asked him to please repeat what he had said, but in Yiddish.

Lev motioned for them to come closer, and he could tell by their tentative steps, their hands clasped behind their backs, that they feared him.

"I need everyone to retrieve their number. Look—all the numbers are strewn this way and that. Without the numbers, we can't get them into groups of five. No one will know who comes first."

"Groups of five," the translator repeated absently. His wire-rimmed glasses caught the light coming through the dirty windows.

Lev glared at him, feeling a rising distaste for such backwardness. Didn't they see the need for organization, for categorization? Otherwise, you have a mass, a herd, no better than a flock of senseless sheep.

"Go and explain to them." Lev thrust him in front of the crowded benches where the people waited.

When the translator spoke, the Russian sounded as indecipherable as a wall of stones. Lev could not detect where one word began and another ended. When the translator had finished explaining, the crowd drew a long suspended breath, and then a cacophony of sound exploded. Mothers scolded their children, wiping their faces with saliva-licked thumbs, and the children cried, wielding their balled-up fists. Men foraged the ground for missing numbers, holding up crumpled pieces of paper, which were then snatched away by someone else. Women used one another as mirrors, asking if their collars were straight, their hair parted down the center, their brows smooth. And in the midst of the tumult, the rebbes sat stoically on the benches, their eyes turned inward, conversing with invisible forces.

The people were herded into groups and led outside into the court-yard, where the photographer and his assistant waited. Each person was photographed individually. "Look at the black box," the photographer urged, his breath pirouetting in the air. Some glanced away when the flash popped, distracted by the fussing and whispering of the others, who waited impatiently. "Again," the photographer would yell, draw-ing up his pants, which were loose. Not having a belt made him less efficient, Lev thought, as he had to pause between each photograph to execute this simple movement. And each time, Lev noticed that his lower back was exposed, beet red from the frigid air.

The translators worked in another room off the courtyard. They recorded on a white card, for the index, the information on each sub-ject, which was gleaned by asking a number of mandatory questions supplied by the army. After this, each person's inked fingertip was pressed into the blue Ober Ost pass. Holding the finger, still moist with black ink, away from their bodies, they would wipe the rest on their hair or the inner hem of their skirts. If found without the pass, they would have to pay ten marks to replace it at their own expense, Lev explained each time, handing over the newly minted passes. A happy confusion permeated the writing room. Lev was struck by how the natives were like children, easily pleased and made to feel important by their images cemented into this little blue book.

Lev roamed from the writing room to the barn to the courtyard. Vaguely, as he walked from one area to the next, he thought of the woman with the blue-black hair. He wondered, leaves crunching under-foot, if he had missed her as he circulated, if when he was bending over a white card complaining of sloppy penmanship, she'd stood in front of the Brownie camera, adjusting her face to supply an appealing smile, her dark eyes awaiting the flash. She would not flinch or look away, Lev decided, because that day under the trees she'd acted willful, even dar-ing. She had taken a risk to talk to him, to offer him a fallen apple.

He heard voices rising in the middle of the courtyard. The photographer asked an old man, in Yiddish, to please remove his cap or else the picture would not be valid, and then the pass could not be processed. The rebbe stood in front of the camera, shaking his head. His family surrounded him, urging him to obey. Lev recognized the teenage boy, and then he saw her, speaking in a low voice to the rebbe, trying to convince him to remove his embroidered skullcap.

He caught her saying, "I had to remove my shawl and show my hair. It was only for an instant."

The rebbe protested, "He will be offended, I am sure of it. How will I explain this to Him?" He jerked his hand forward, motioning to the bewildered photographer poised behind the camera. "God does not care for your black boxes, for your binoculars, for your airplanes, for the variety of your human inventions. Nothing good can come . . ." His voice trailed off. He tucked his chin into his snow-white beard.

The photographer, uncomfortable, pulled up his pants.

"Father, please." Her voice shook. She glanced around, fearful that the delay would be noticed, that the old man might get beaten for his resistance. When she scanned the edge of the courtyard, she caught Lev's eye. For a split second, recognition coursed between them. Lev wished to feel this recognition in his hands, to clasp it between his fingers, to bring the vibrating moment to his mouth. He felt overly grateful to see her, almost embarrassed by how happy it made him. And now he could help her solve her predicament.

Lev walked over, congenial, his hands in his pockets. He smiled but no one would look at him. She appeared stricken, her face as pale as the moon. The old woman fiddled with a handkerchief, her arthritic fingers working the cloth this way and that. The boy, Geza, dug his heel into the dirt, creating a miniature hole. Geza's mother held him against her, her arms crossed over his narrow chest, her chin buried in his lank hair. And the woman, Leah, with her blue-black hair, stared at the horizon of trees, at the bare branches straining upward into the gray sky. Her hand rested on her father's shoulder.

Lev broke the uncomfortable silence. "Only have him push the cap back from his forehead. So we can see his face better."

She nodded, slowly pushing back the velvet cap.

The photographer took the picture.

The rebbe flinched at the sound of the sharp pop, at the brightness of the flash.

The rest of the family sighed.

Geza asked, "Now for my picture?"

Lev cupped his hand behind the boy's slender neck. It felt warm and clean. "Go ahead. It's your turn."

Geza straightened his back, squared his shoulders. He flashed a toothy grin. His front teeth were too far apart. Lev thought one could probably fit the width of two pencils between those teeth. Geza's mother and grandmother clucked their tongues in approval. The rebbe rocked from side to side. He could barely stand this picture taking, the fuss of it all.

"Ready?" the photographer barked.

Geza drew in a breath, puffing out his spindly chest.

In the suspended interval before the picture was taken, Lev felt as if a muslin sheet billowed over his head and hers and enclosed them under its rippling shadow. He rested his eyes on her face, on her neck, on the graceful folds of her shawl covering her hair and its midnight color. She stared back, her eyes wide and glassy and brimming with unknowable questions. Holding each other's gaze, they recognized the mystery of this instantaneous closeness, as well as the instinctual knowledge of when to look away and not know each other again, because the world on the periphery of their vision encroached, ripping off the safety of the caparisoned muslin sheet, marked by the camera's exclamatory pop.

Geza laughed. His mother clapped. His grandmother clucked her tongue.

The moment was broken, and she looked away from him, her face reddening.

He waited for her in the writing room and watched through the small window the rest of the family get their pictures taken. When it was her turn, she stared directly into the camera, her dark eyes revealing the slightest hint of laughter. Afterward, they moved single file across the courtyard. The rebbe walked as if in sleep, as if this was all a dream life and his real life occurred, with all its machinations and irritations, somewhere else.

When they came into the room, Lev arranged it with the two other translators so that he would be asking her the questions. They sat opposite each other across a scarred wooden table. She had since readjusted her shawl, but wisps of blue-black hair still escaped from under her white earlobes. Lev suddenly worried, pen in hand, that she did not remember him from the other day, that the sheltered moment between them had been the workings of his imagination. She might think of all soldiers as the same man in field gray. She might have given fruit to others, carelessly, without a thought. If she had already forgotten him, then—

"Are you going to ask me the questions?" Her voice sliced through the air, and he realized he had been staring at her earlobes.

Lev smoothed down the piece of paper. "Of course."

"Well?" She raised her eyebrows. Again, her expectant gaze, the way her small red mouth curled upward seemed as if she was laughing at him, that he was somehow ridiculous with his epaulets, heavy boots, the holster on his hip.

Lev cleared his throat. "Name?" Of course he remembered. Leah: a crescent moon, the whiteness startling and smooth when it appeared in the purple twilight. Those were the hours when we don't know ourselves as well as we think, Lev thought. When buried thoughts burn to the surface. Leah. A crescent moon.

"Leah," she said.

Lev carefully wrote out her name, pausing before the next column, realizing she had only given her first name.

Leah smiled, gesturing to the next column. "Mitau."

Lev began writing, but stopped. "Perhaps you misunderstood. Not the town—your name."

Leah drew her shawl closer around her shoulders. She stared at the piece of paper, her eyes scanning the columns and blank spaces. "We are called by our first name followed by the first name of our father. I am Leah ben Samuel. But the czar commanded everyone to take a last name. So we take Mitau."

Lev nodded, writing this down. For a moment, they both listened to the translator interviewing her father at the next desk. The translator asked the rebbe his occupation. The rebbe said he studied the Torah, the words of God, that he did not concern himself with the entanglements of pedestrian pursuits. "In the holy books, every word, every letter even, contains thousands of pages and every page reveals the greatness of God." He sighed heavily. "Which is never sufficiently understood, nor should it be."

She flashed Lev a smile.

Lev drummed the pen against the table. "Occupation?"

She played with her wedding ring, a dull gold band. Lev hoped she might be a widow who, out of reverence, still wore it.

"We have a stall in the marketplace. Maize in the summer and naphtha for fuel in the winter as well as pickled cucumbers and beans. Small trade."

"Married?"

She paused, her eyes sliding over his face. "Yes." She blinked slowly, a watery film replenishing her green eyes. Lev looked closer. Green with flecks of gold. "He's in the Russian army." Her voice turned flat, and she clasped her hands together, her eyes fixed on the tip of his shoulder, as if a bird perched there. "The soldiers here, they don't speak Yiddish. Except for a few."

Lev nodded, pursing his lips.

"The orders posted in the town square—sometimes the translation from German to Russian is terribly wrong." She hesitated.

"Go on."

"Well, the order posted about only baking cakes on Wednesdays and Saturdays." She swallowed, trying to suppress the corners of her mouth, which wanted to curl upward. "Well, instead of reading, *The German court judged*, it read—" She stopped short, shaking her head. "I'm sorry, but I do not wish to offend."

Lev felt the urge to pull her forearms toward him, to bring her near. "Tell me?"

She glanced at the translator sitting to Lev's left. Then she leaned over the table, lowering her voice to a half whisper. "Instead, the sign read, *The German excrement shitted that cakes will only be baked on Wednesdays and Saturdays.*"

Lev's chest filled with pressure; the feeling rushed up into his throat and was about to burst forth from his mouth, a release of inane laughter. He looked away, staring down at his fingernails, which he had recently pared with meticulous care.

She scrutinized the blunt edge of her wool tunic.

Lev coughed and said he would look into it.

"And do you think," Leah said, her voice held at a hush, "you could change the order to say cakes may only be baked on Wednesdays and Sundays?"

"Instead of Saturdays?"

"Because of the Sabbath."

"The Sabbath," Lev repeated dumbly.

She searched his face. "Surely you understand. About these matters."

And now she was asking too much of him, drawing him in with her eyes and her intimate whispering so that he could better help her bake her cakes on days that were not holy. He returned to the questionnaire.

"Number of children?" The freckles splashing her neck reminded him of a distant constellation.

Her face flushed.

He repeated, "Do you have any children?"

"No." Her gaze moved away from his shoulder, and for a brief instant her green-gold eyes turned opaque. She watched him write down zero.

Lev took a quick sip of water. He wondered if he had been too harsh. Maybe he had repelled her.

She stared at him strangely. In a rush of breath, she asked, "Are you from Odessa because Jews from Odessa tend to have light eyes."

The next question on the sheet asked for her age. He tapped the edge of the pencil on the blank column, drawing her attention to it.

Then he looked up at her and felt his eyes become severe, foreboding.

She leaned back into her chair, folding her arms over her chest. She was retreating into herself, drifting away. He cursed himself and the divide that could rise up between two people without warning.

He put down the pencil with an air of defeat. "My parents moved to Berlin when I was very young and they don't talk about the east." He pursed his lips. Enough of that. A draft blew into the room, the door perpetually open.

After a pause, she asked him why this was important, these cards.

"You don't exist without a pass."

"But I am sitting right here in front of you." Again, the suppression of a smile. She hugged herself to stay warm, retreating farther into the folds of brown wool.

"We need a record of how many inhabitants are under German control."

"But what will the passes do?"

"Any movement within the territory requires documentation. Passes will soon be required for walking at night after curfew, taking in guests, for the use of one's own cart, for moving outside of the district. This pass is the basis for all other documentation. Without it"—Lev sighed—"it's difficult."

Her tone turned sharp, incredulous. "I heard even dogs are issued passes."

Lev shifted in his chair. "We need the pass to certify a dog tax has been paid." It sounded absurd, saying it aloud.

"A dog tax?" she repeated, hard laughter pressing the edges of her voice.

"The important thing is your pass." Lev brought the tips of his fingers together, creating a rounded hollowness. "When you are stopped, you must show your pass. It costs ten marks to replace."

"Ten marks," she repeated. He noted the pronouncement of her collarbone, the shallow blue dip beneath her eyes. She probably didn't remember giving him the apple, that day under the trees with the golden afternoon bathing her hair, turning the black an opalescent blue.

He stared down at the sheet of paper. He had forgotten her age. When he asked, she traced her finger around the oblong ring in the wooden table, as if she had lived too many rings, too many lives. "Thirty," she said.

Same as I am, Lev thought.

And then, as if remembering something amusing, she asked, "Did you enjoy the apple?" She smiled, revealing a flash of white teeth. "Or was it already too soft?" She leaned forward, pressing herself into the table's edge.

"It was perfect. Thank you." His chest pounded—over an apple, a stupid apple. "It was very kind of you."

She bit her lower lip, chewing on it. He almost reached out and cupped her chin to stop her, to say don't chew your lip, as he did with Vicki. He always told Vicki it would ruin her lipstick, and she would throw back her head and scream with delight, *But I don't wear lipstick,* and Lev would pretend to forget she was still a little girl.

Leah did not wear lipstick. She had probably never seen lipstick in a tube and would think it a novel and amusing invention, if not wholly trustworthy. Her lips were the color of the red gooseberries the army instructed them against eating. Whether or not the berries were poisonous was debatable.

8

Vast areas of land lay in waste, the memory of trees evident in the stubble of black stumps spreading outward until Lev lost count. In the raw morning mist, the stumps resembled the tops of smooth rocks protruding from a shifting body of water. The trees were needed for their valuable sap, for firewood, for fortifications at the front, for the building of bridges. In the morning when Lev arrived, he sometimes had to catch his breath at the clear, clean landscape. He expected voluminous trees, and the naked land confronted him with its bleakness. The villagers stared blankly at the clear-cut land, and Lev wondered, before he sounded the bugle and signaled the start of the workday, if they mourned the dissolution of the primeval forests, where spirits and rocks were still worshipped despite the efforts of the church to steer the people away from such pagan ways.

A new crop of workers had arrived this morning, some of them barely twelve or thirteen years old. Their mothers could no longer hide them, and soon, Lev thought, they would contract typhus or cholera or an inflammation of the lung. The conditions were unsanitary as the boys struggled together, working under a wet sky with little food, and at night they slept in a barn under dirty blankets, a draft blowing in through the many cracks and holes. Lev wondered how Geza had avoided getting lumped into this unfortunate crew—he didn't have any visible disability, and as far as Lev could tell, he hadn't maimed or blinded himself in an attempt to circumvent service. Perhaps he'd just been lucky. Lev then entertained the wild fantasy of coming to Geza's aid by putting in a good word so that the German army would not swoop him up for such backbreaking work. He imagined Leah's gratefulness, her face breaking into a glowing smile, thanking him, her hand on his arm, for how he had saved Geza, his boyhood uninterrupted, as opposed to the sorry sight Lev saw before him now—these poor boys forced to perform the work of men. For a moment, Lev returned to the idea of Leah's gratitude, how she would revere him, speaking softly, her lips close to his face, the intoxicating scent of her hair escaping from under her scarf.

But it wasn't only about saving Geza and basking in Leah's gratitude. Lev also felt ashamed of how these Russian boys were treated. True, they weren't German, but nonetheless they were young and able-bodied, until the harsh working conditions took away their youth, hollowing out their eyes, collapsing their lungs, bloodying their palms, turning their healthy skin gray. Given this abuse, it was no surprise to Lev that some locals, along with a handful of Russian soldiers and even a few German deserters, had escaped into the forests, that they were forming resistance groups. They raided villages for bread and supplies. They committed random acts of violence against German soldiers who foolishly stumbled home late at night from the taverns and teahouses. But Lev saw how some of the Germans behaved, drinking naked on top of a horse in the snow, shooting into the dense trees bordering the barracks, aiming at small animals. One soldier had killed a woman in the forest last night. On her way home, a bullet caught her by surprise, ripping through her side. She had worked as a cook in the mess hall. The officers repeated *Stay German*, a slogan Lev found ironic as all traces of western decorum diminished. And at breakfast this morning, over steaming bowls of semolina, the man next to him boasted about how they had used some village men as draft animals, harnessing them in teams to plows. "And we photographed it," he said proudly before offering Lev more coffee. This man was barely a man. He looked about eighteen. His sharp blue eyes, set too far apart, reminded him of Franz's eyes, but then he interrupted Lev's thoughts with the complaint that there was no cream this morning. "Probably because all the cows have starved," Lev snapped, irritated that this boy had not noticed the cows standing sickly and skeletal in the fields, cows they'd confiscated from the local farmers and then left to starve and rot.

So Lev didn't write Josephine about these things. He wrote about clearing the land and making it more useful, about modernizing the agricultural systems, which were truly backward here. He wrote about the hard black bread that nearly broke his teeth, the beauty of the white birches, how it was getting colder and colder. Much colder than Berlin. *This will be my third Russian winter,* he wrote last time, worried that if he didn't write this, he would lose count of the weeks and the months that passed through him. When he'd folded the letter, pressing the creases down with his thumb, another stab of guilt attacked him. He'd spent nearly a paragraph describing the slender white birches, how their trunks tilted gently toward the light, the crimson and gold leaves whispering in the wind. How birch sap contained various healing properties and the locals believed that if birches surrounded your home, the devil stayed away. But he was really describing Leah, who reminded him of the white birches and of the white crescent moon peeking through the thin delicate branches. Leah: his tonic, his refreshment, the one spot of beauty he'd found. He'd not seen her since the day he processed her identity card. This he could keep count of; precisely two weeks had passed since then. He'd even loitered around the patch of forest where the Sukkot hut had stood, but it had been taken down. He went out of his way to go into town, hoping perhaps he would find her selling her wares at the stalls on market day. But last time, the square was so crowded he could barely move. Hawkers came up to him, pushing caps and apples and woven baskets into his face, barking out prices and then clasping Lev's hand as if he had agreed. Lev kept repeating, No, no, I don't want this, I don't want it, and then the men looked offended and shuffled off. In the midst of all the confusion, the Yiddish and broken German and the stream of Russian words he still didn't recognize, he couldn't find her. The raven hair, the woolen shawl, the way he imagined her smiling at him, half-impish, half-serious, when he caught her eye. He walked back to base empty-handed, without even a glimpse.

For weeks now, Lev had overseen the native workers and a small army of POWs, mainly Russians and Belarusians hacking away for kilometers on either side of the rivers and burnt fields. Lev watched them, his feet cold from lack of movement, smoking cigarette after cigarette as these men cleared wide swaths of land for the building of roads. The men sweated and swore and hated him as he contemplated the blue smoke of his cigarette poised between two gloved fingers.

And then Otto showed up. He had a compact body, a square jaw, and a glorious nose, a nose that inspired confidence in its blunt bold shape. He smoked fiendishly and never ceased to express his love of women. A few minutes after meeting Lev, bored and fidgety, he launched into one of his favorite monologues. "The force that drives life forward is Eros. It is a force that creates, destroys, and then re-creates." He lit a new cigarette directly after disposing of the previous one. "A man experiences Eros most powerfully from women; they are the conduits between us and the life force." He grinned, lighting a match. The blue flame flickered before catching on the tightly packed tobacco leaves. "That is why sex, as much as possible, with as many women as possible, is *imperative*."

Lev grinned. "And I take it you've had plenty here?"

Otto threw back his head, as if the memory of it was too much. "You have no idea." He spoke as if he could not keep up with the speed of his own thoughts when he described the barbarity of the whorehouse at the edge of town. "Local women carried us on their backs, whinnying like mares, and we clutched their hair, and pulled it sharply so that their necks snapped back. Afterward, they threw us out on the snow—drunk, we rolled around on the ground, no—we writhed on the ground." He shook his head, his smile echoing debauchery, inexplicable deviance. "The snow at night is wonderfully refreshing."

Lev imagined what it would feel like to twine Leah's midnight hair through his fingers, to feel her slim torso bucking under his groin.

"To be dominated like that," Otto continued, "thrown into the snow." His dark eyes watered, stinging from the sharp wind. They watched the leaves rise up from the icy ground, circling and swirling along the half-built road in a fitful temper.

"In Königsberg, there was also a good teahouse." Lev recalled how Hermann had convinced him to go that night. The whore with the reddish hair, the shabby room upstairs on top of the bar, the thumping tambourines down below as he plunged into her. "But VD. You have to watch out for that," Lev added.

"If you worry about something like this, pleasure flies away like a little bird." Otto fashioned his hands into two bird wings that flapped through the air.

"Yes, but," Lev said, not entirely ready to forfeit, "I'm married, you see. I simply can't bring home some vile disease and pass it on to her." But this wasn't the only reason why Lev did not go to the taverns. He couldn't fully explain, but such places struck him as decidedly vulgar. The proprietors masked such taverns as cozy little cottages in the woods, but the women looked meek and anxious. Despite their rouge and scented bodies, these women pretended at pleasure, until afterward, when the truth collapsed around their faces.

The men had taken a break, leaning on their pickaxes and shovels. They were exhausted, sweating in the cold. A few of them smoked. The sun was setting, illuminating the dirt so that it appeared a fiery red.

"Should we keep them working?" Otto asked. He stomped his feet to get the blood flowing, grinding his discarded cigarette butts into the snowy ground with his heels.

"Give them a few minutes."

The men watched Otto and Lev with intensity, their mouths hanging open, their eyes squinting at the setting sun. Up above, an eagle emitted a piercing cry.

Otto cocked his head. "A mating call."

Lev had never seen such a large bird. He wondered how it didn't fall from its own weight.

"I greatly admire birds." Otto followed the figure eights the eagle drew in the air, the elaborate looping and swerving and sudden downward dives. Then Otto turned and strode toward the men, his heavy gray cloak flying behind him.

"Get to work! Get to work!" he shouted in Russian, his arms thrown up as if urging the wind to blow harder, faster. He kicked one of the men in the shin. The man yelped. Otto's gray form flew down the line. As he approached, they picked up their tools again, throwing the force of their bodies behind each swing.

The way the tip of Otto's sharp boot had shot out so unexpectedly and kicked the man, as if he routinely dispensed such bright and sure violence, made Lev uneasy. When Otto walked back, his jaw tensed and released. He reminded Lev of a powerful dray horse, the way one could detect a ripple of movement twitching beneath its skin.

Otto impatiently pulled out a cigarette, his eyes trained on the men hacking at the soil.

Lev, feeling the urge to speak, to explain, to fill up the still air with words, started telling Otto about the problem with the workers, how they dug around the stones because the stones were precious, holding secrets of the land, whereas he had been instructed to crush them up. "The natives, they're backward. Still on the three-field system of cultivation. And they leave big round stones sitting in the middle of a cleared field, as if afraid to touch them, as if their ancestors dwelled in the porous gray matter." Lev laughed. "Strange, no?"

The rushing urgency of a distant train echoed through the trees, causing the workers to pause for a moment.

Otto snorted. "They're pagans, protecting stones, thinking there's life in them. But it's better than Christ, our savior." He sneered. "A perfect lie."

Lev pulled up the collar of his coat. The wind cut through it. "You're not a Christian?"

"Turn the other cheek—do you think I would believe in something invented for the sole purpose of keeping us enslaved? It goes against our very instincts as men."

"Our instincts as men," Lev repeated.

"To fight and fuck and reap the infinite pleasures of aliveness—religion condemns this—condemns what it means to be human, what it means to exist in the world, in the here and now." His cheeks glowed carmine pink from the pleasure he took in the boom of his voice. But it was not an unpleasant voice, Lev thought. It vibrated with the warmth and vigor of a man who did not live in fear.

"Who knows what exists beyond this?" Otto stretched out his arms to encompass the whole of the surrounding forests, trees, the distant steppes, the dirt, the working men, the two of them. He added, "The meek shall inherit nothing," and with it, he unwittingly emitted a light spray of spittle.

Lev took a few steps back. "We don't know anything beyond this."

Otto's eyes shone in the diminishing light. "Precisely!"

Two hours later, Lev and Otto reclined on cushions, drinking tea from small steaming glasses. Otto had convinced Lev to come to his lodgings, where he was boarding with a Russian family—a middle-aged woman named Antonina and her uncle, who spoke fanatically of the Japanese war, the only war the Russians ever lost. But Antonina kept interrupting and shouting at him to fetch fresh water for the samovar. The uncle flinched every time she shouted, but he didn't move. He sat stationed on a pillow next to Lev and Otto, asking softly, "But how long will the war last?"

Antonina fussed over Otto, refilling his tea glass.

Otto sighed. "What do you care—so long as England gives money and the earth gives men."

The uncle nodded wisely, as if in agreement. His creased face was brown and spotted from working in the fields. Lev thought one could hide coins in the deep ravines of his forehead. The uncle added, "In the Japanese war, we didn't have a fighting chance. Before the Battle of Mukden, I saw entire regiments lying in a drunken stupor on the ground." He sucked on his cheroot, rocking forward and back on his haunches, a soft swaying movement that made Lev sleepy. Perhaps, Lev thought, I should remove my coat.

Antonina bellowed, "We need more water, Uncle. Get more water for tea." She fanned herself with a loose kerchief, but the shifting hot air did nothing to alleviate her discomfort.

Lev felt warm inside the cramped living room. The thatched ceiling was low, just above their heads when they were standing. He had not removed his jacket because he did not know how long he was staying, and now he was sweating, whereas Otto had stripped off most of his clothing, save for a white cotton undershirt. Antonina had immediately picked up his discarded shirt, gloves, and cloak, folding each item on the chair near the fire.

"Uncle. Get more water!" she shouted again.

He slowly rose, his stiff body unfurling. Lev thought he could hear the creaking of the old man's bones. The peeling wallpaper, a ghastly yellow, seemed as if it had been applied to the rotting walls over a century ago. Antonina smoked continuously, nearly keeping up with Otto's pace, and a cloud of rosy smoke encircled them. Her low-cut linen blouse revealed an ample bust, and under her long skirt, knitted booties encased her tiny feet. She fanned herself, causing the smoke to move swiftly about her face. Wind blew against the house, and for a moment, this distracted her from shouting at the old man, who was now shuffling back with fresh water and new tea leaves.

But she resumed. "Ah! You forgot the *zakouska*! Go back, go back."

Uncle turned around, sighing laboriously. Through his thin shirt, the progression of his vertebrae was visible.

Antonina turned to Otto, muttering, "We have no servants. For once, he could help me. That is all I ask." She shook her head.

Lev smiled; the Russian language always sounded as if the speakers were in a perpetual state of anguished dissatisfaction.

Uncle brought back plates of sardines, shirred eggs, smoked herrings, and pickles, which he indicated sharpened the appetite. Such a feast, Lev thought, his mouth watering as he restrained himself from being the first to eat. But when Otto started shuffling sardines down his throat, Lev reached for a piece of black bread, gingerly spooning a dollop of herring on top of it. Antonina sprung up to retrieve some cognac as well as Bénédictine and kummel. She poured the amber liquid into stout glasses. Along the rim, small pieces of glass had chipped off. Lev worried that imperceptible pieces of glass might be floating in the drink, but then he noticed Otto also had a chipped glass and he didn't even flinch, swallowing down his cognac in one fell swoop. Lev took a sip, the fiery liquor gathering in the pockets of his mouth.

"If only we had vodka," Uncle said, sipping his cognac.

"Is it really forbidden?" Otto asked, his eyes half-closed in the dim lamplight. His large body looked relaxed, louche, pantherlike in its uncoiled sleekness, his shapely head cradled in his enormous hand.

Antonina funneled the last drops of a blush-colored wine down her throat. She swallowed hard, wiping her mouth with the back of her hand. "The rich can still get it."

Uncle nodded, eyeing his cognac suspiciously. "I heard Mazel sells it in the back room of the apothecary."

Antonina grimaced. "All Jews are traitors to Russia. I would not set foot in that Jewish shop."

"You were at the tailor's last week getting your winter coat mended," Uncle reminded her.

The fire crackled. Otto yawned.

"And the cobbler's before that." Uncle pointed to her gleaming leather boots, which stood upright next to the fire. They had just been polished and given new soles.

Lev fingered his glass. "In Austria and Germany, the Jews are entirely loyal. In fact, they subscribed the greater part of the last two Austrian war loans."

Otto roused himself, slipping another sardine into his mouth. "This is true." He licked his thumb appreciatively.

Lev added, "Many Jews are fighting for Germany. Risking their lives in this war."

"That is different," Antonina snapped. "In Germany and Austria, the Jews have civil rights; therefore naturally they are patriotic. In Russia, however, the Jews have no civil rights. So they betray us. So we kill them." She paused. "But some vodka would be nice." She examined her hands, frowning at their roughness. "Does one really have to go to that dirty little apothecary?"

It would only be a waste of breath, Lev told himself, to argue with this cow of a woman. She reminded him of a farm animal—asinine, bullheaded, at constant war with the surrounding stimuli so that she could barely focus. Right now, she picked at her teeth with the long tapered nail of her pinky finger. Before this, she had been examining the end of her plait, which looked like a miniature broom. Lev glanced away. Such a lack of decorum, such beastly manners revolted him. Of course, over the years he had grown accustomed to Josephine's habits—her stringent cleanliness, her starched white dresses, her impeccable table manners. Even when Lev stared at Josephine from across the dining table with nothing to say, which had occurred more and more frequently before the war, she sat erect in her chair, her long neck daintily bent over her soup, her elbows suspended above the tablecloth as if little flames threatened to burn her otherwise—that was how fastidious she was about such details. He would watch her and drink his wine and think what a beautiful picture he saw before him, and sometimes, this would console him. Other times, when they did speak, she would obsess over the minutiae of the house—the gardener had ruined her lilies again, Marthe couldn't find a good housemaid to assist her, the other one had quit unexpectedly, the windows needed cleaning, and could they perhaps replace the faded rug in the sitting room? Lev always nodded, his eyes glazing over as he watched her mouth move but failed to hear the words.

It was nearly ten o'clock. Uncle had since retreated to the far corner of the room, where he sat by the window, smoking his cheroot, staring out at the flat dark fields. Antonina had excused herself to prepare Otto's bed. He reminded her that she had promised him fresh linens. She waved her hand impatiently, too tired to quarrel.

Otto poured himself more cognac. He sat with his legs splayed out on the floor, like an overgrown child. "How long have you been out here, in this wasteland?"

"Three years come spring."

"You're from Berlin?"

Lev nodded. "I worked in a textile factory. Production manager." He clearly pictured the office where he had spent his days, the glass-paneled walls designed so he could look out onto the machinery and survey the workers. He had a nice velvet chaise in his office, of a faded cobalt color. Sometimes, he took afternoon naps there.

Lev felt as if he were discussing a stranger's life, a life still ongoing, running parallel to the one he led now. He often stopped in the middle of a field or mused at the dirty wall of the latrine (someone always wrote some obscenity there, at eye level, damning the officers' better pay or extolling the merits of a particular prostitute) and thought, while his stream of urine shot into the hole: What would I be doing now if the war hadn't happened?

He told Otto, "I have a wife and two children." He saw Josephine, all in white, and Franz clinging to her. Vicki hung back from the picture, but she was there, on the edges. She had been so young when he left, just four, sucking her thumb. Afterward, she would reach up with her thumb coated in saliva, expecting someone to dry it off. Lev always did, using the perfectly folded handkerchief in his front pocket. "There," he would say as if performing a magic trick, "all clean." Josephine would complain that he had ruined his handkerchief and now Marthe would have to wash and iron it all due to the stubbornness of a little girl who refused to stop sucking her thumb. She would murmur that he was spoiling Vicki, and he should discipline her by applying a smack to the top of her hand. But he could never bring himself to do it.

"Your wife, is she beautiful?" Otto asked greedily.

They heard Antonina humming as she prepared Otto's bed, the Russian soft and melodic. The fire had died down, leaving only embers.

"Yes," Lev said. "Yes, she is."

Otto grinned, wolfish. "If I had a wife, no matter how beautiful, all I'd do is cheat on her." Then he frowned, as if trying to solve a difficult equation. Lev marveled at how quickly Otto's expression changed; it reminded him of Greek theater, the masks of comedy and tragedy, two sides of a face. Otto continued, "Marriage, or rather monogamy, it isn't natural." He shook his head. "But we've been forced into thinking it so. Let us observe nature, and imitate it. Animals do not endlessly carp and pine after one mate."

Lev glanced at the smoldering embers. Leah, her moonlike face, the way her almond eyes laughed at him, the freckled constellations scattering her neck. How would he find her again?

Antonina had stopped humming, maybe to eavesdrop, or maybe she had run out of songs. She passed from room to room, her head bowed and her full skirt trailing behind, catching dust and dirt on its hem. As she went, she blew out each candle within its glass sconce.

Otto sleepily lit a cigarette, the last one of the night, he promised. "My supply is running low," he added. Lev had no doubt he could get more. It seemed as if Otto had always been here, belonging to the massive forests and to the violence of the seasons—to the ice and wind, the springtime floods, the drenching summer heat. Lev could not picture him out of uniform, in civilian clothes walking jauntily along Berlin streets. He would look awkward in a suit. He wondered who made clothes for men with such broad shoulders and thick necks and arms that dangled almost down to the knees.

"What did you do before the war?"

"I am an artist," Otto replied, as if it should have been obvious. He said his art drove him to join the war, to obtain the full taste and range of human experience, to see death and hear cannons and record it all in his sketchbook. It was late, but Otto became reanimated, his face bright and awake as he took Lev by the arm, leading him into his small room, where he kept his sketches rolled up and stored under his bed. Lev wondered if he was any good, or just one of the many artists flocking to Berlin. He hoped Otto was a bad artist. It would make him feel better about the fact that he hadn't picked up a paintbrush in nearly six years.

In the dim candlelight Otto unrolled his drawings, done in charcoal on paper, and laid them tenderly on the bed. He instructed Lev to hold the candle near, not directly above to avoid wax dripping, but close enough so he could see the drawings. Lev stared at two abstract bodies intertwined, taking comfort in the softness of freshly mounded graves. He felt the creep of envy envelop him. The sketches were good. Otto explained while the man and woman create a new life, underneath their passionate embrace, another body slowly decomposes. "It's called *Lovers in a Grave,*" Otto added proudly. "It's a sketch for what I'll do later—I work in oils, but for now this will have to suffice." He then spoke of how human matter is constantly transforming, how Goya and Callot showed this too, and how amazingly demonic it was, the way in which human matter shifts, right before our eyes. Lev remembered the men in the hospital ward, the change in tone and texture of a person's skin once he had died, how a pale and damply twitching face transformed into a waxen one, tinged with a blue-purple glaze, the lips stiff, how the broken blood vessels, like miniature spider veins circling the nostrils, became more pronounced.

Otto continued, "I insisted on going to the front line. I couldn't possibly miss it. To know something of men, I had to witness them in their unfettered state."

"Must be important for an artist," Lev managed.

Otto rolled up each sketch. "So very important! The most intense emotions must be sought out and experienced through lovemaking and dancing and drinking too much . . . and warfare—these feelings strike at the root of us, instinctually, I mean. Enough of the intellect, cooped up in our studios trying to replicate life"—Otto wiped his forehead with his discarded shirt—"instead of living it."

The Gay Science lay atop his nightstand. His ideas were so transparently Nietzsche's, nearly quoted from the book, Lev thought smugly.

"Well," Lev said, "you weren't wounded, at least."

"Why do you think I'm here, exiled to the hinterlands?" He pointed to his shoulder. "Shell fragments."

"The bits of iron deprive the wound of blood. Can cause gangrene and then infection, bleeding and then putrefaction." Lev paused, weighing his next words. "I was a medic. Behind the front line—in the reserve trenches for a short time and then mostly at base."

"Ah, well, it doesn't really matter." Otto waved his cigarette in the air.

Lev instantly heard the disappointment in Otto's voice because he was only a medic, barely a witness to combat. It was the same restrained disappointment Lev found in Josephine's letters, when she asked how he fared at the base. Was it any trouble dealing with the locals? Had the Russians encroached over the lines into the newly minted German territories? Did he ever, she wrote in her last letter, fear for his life? And then she followed this question up with a paragraph about the tragic fate of returning soldiers, fresh from Flanders, with no legs or arms. Oh yes, she went on and on about the poor soldiers, trying to goad him into feeling somehow unworthy that he had remained unscathed. He felt certain she wished for a more heroic post for him. Even if it meant death. Especially if it meant death, for there was little heroism in safety.

"We need medics of course. Indispensable," Otto rejoined, jolting Lev back to this small room, to the drawings on the bed, to his stomach full of herring and egg.

"There was a great shortage of medics—I often had to—" but Lev stopped, seeing Otto had lost interest. He turned his back to Lev, whistling while he rolled up his last sketch.

Through the thin walls, Uncle snored.

Otto complained, "All night long, he never stops."

Startled by the heavy deep rhythm of his own breath, Uncle woke up shouting, "Siberia! Don't send me back there, I beg of you."

Otto rapped on the wall. "No one's going to Siberia. But if you keep snoring like an old bear, I'll deliver you there myself." In response, they heard the rustling of sheets followed by a sigh. The snoring, first light, then heavier, resumed.

In darkness, Lev walked back to the barracks. He was drunk and filled up with the salty smoked fish and strong liquor Antonina had pressed on them. Inhaling the scent of burning leaves from nearby houses, he remembered autumnal nights in Berlin when the dense foliage would fall to the sidewalks and be gathered for burning. Marthe would do this at the end of the day, after sunset, when the children had been given their bedtime stories. Lev and Josephine would be leaving for a party, and through the windowpane of Franz's room, after reassuring him that they would return before midnight, Lev would spy Marthe building a bonfire of leaves in the courtyard, and he would think of the three witches of *Macbeth* spinning havoc on the hillside, and how Marthe was a benevolent witch gazing whimsically into the fire and the smoke, as if expecting a seraphic form to arise from the burning leaves.

Now, crunching through leaves, Lev walked toward candles blazing in the windows of homes signaling the beginning of Shabbat. And the Sabbaths of his childhood washed over him: his mother's rituals of cleanliness and purification, as if she managed to wash away the week's grime. Each Friday there were fresh sheets and fresh linens, and then she went to the Jewish markets for carp and kosher chicken and, lastly, to the bathhouse. In the evening, the scent of roast chicken, onions, freshly baked challah, and floor polish flooded the house. Even now, when Lev witnessed a woman lighting candles, even if there was no blessing, even if it was only Marthe holding the end of a lit match, waiting for the flame to catch hold of the wick while she hummed a Bavarian folk song, even then, he remembered Friday night, its safety, its purity.

Walking past houses with lit-up windows, Lev spied a table strewn with the remains of the holy meal, the white linen tablecloth and the braided bread peeking out from under an embroidered cloth. In the adjoining kitchen, an old woman sat next to a sealed oven. She had fallen asleep, her cheek in her hand. At her feet, two children played, dressed in their best stiff clothing. What kind of game are they playing? Lev wondered, thinking how the games of children do not differ despite class and upbringing. At the back of the kitchen, Lev strained to see a woman standing in an open doorway, bathed in a pool of yellow light as she gestured to another woman standing in an opposite doorway across a shared courtyard.

He made his way to the clearing where the little huts with the hanging fruit had been standing during Sukkot. Beyond the clearing stood more houses with candles in the windows. He felt like an animal that only shows itself at night, stalking the scents and smells of congregating humans. It was quieter here. There were no women conversing in doorways. An owl's hoot echoed through the fir trees, and beyond this, silence. Through a wooden shutter left slightly ajar, he heard the sound of water washing over skin. An orange chink of light streamed from an otherwise dark house. Lev moved with stealth through the leaves until his line of vision was just above the windowsill into the house, and he saw, as if viewing a small framed photograph, a woman slowly washing her hair in the middle of the kitchen. She sat on a low stool next to a deep copper bin filled with steaming water. Sliding her hair over her shoulder, she dipped her thick flowing mane into the water. Lev could not see her face, but he gathered from the color of the hair and the undulating bare shoulder blades, which were scattered with the same rust-colored freckles, that he was watching Leah bathe, making herself pure and whole for the Sabbath, so when she went to temple, accompanying the stream of black-clothed Jews migrating toward the prayer house, her hair and her neck would smell of the mint leaves she had dropped into the steaming water. Lev held his breath, afraid even the shallow sound of his breathing would alert her to his presence and then the moment would be broken, and the next thing, whatever it was, would ensue: her fear as she moved toward the window pressing a cloth to her chest, his fleeing into the silent forest, the incessant barking of a dog sensing some disturbance, the kitchen flooded by women—her sister, her mother— asking, *What has happened? What did you see?* But this did not happen. She did not hear him, or maybe, she chose not to hear him, complicit in the revelation of her body, as it was from the waist up, unclothed, her delicate shoulders soft in the yellow light of the kitchen. From the steam's heat, blood rose to the surface of her skin. Lev could see her forearms blushing, the rose color spreading. Her movements were fluid and smooth as she took her mane of hair and slowly twisted it to the left, then to the right. Water dripped from it as if she were wringing out a wet towel. She performed these actions with somnambulant deftness. He imagined her mouth slack, her eyes obscured as she thought of what? Her husband in the Russian cavalry? Why he had not written in months? He imagined her husband's death, a terrible thing to do— these thoughts would probably secure his own death, but he couldn't help himself willing her into widowhood. If he had the power of King David, Lev thought, he would have made the same mistake, overcome by the beauty of a woman bathing. The story was meant to remind him of covetousness and its consequences, but instead, it only made him feel strangely validated, grasping for a woman who did not belong to him. A common affliction, otherwise such a story would not have been written and studied and commented on through various layers of midrash. The image of Bathsheba bathing on the rooftops bled into the image of Leah, who now wound a dry towel around her hair, creating a makeshift turban, which balanced atop her head, crowning her. She turned to face him. He sunk lower, his nose pressed to the splintered damp wood of the windowsill. Her mouth upturned, almost smiling. Her collarbone, bare and gleaming with water drops, rose and fell in time with her breath. And her breasts were two luminous orbs. She lifted one and then the other, patting the skin underneath each breast dry. The careful way she handled herself reminded Lev of a mother nursing, suckling her young, positioning the nipple into the mouth. The sudden slam of the shutter made Lev fall backward, hurtling toward the ground. The wind was knocked out of his chest. A shrill voice cried, "What are you doing, trying to catch your death?"

He scrambled to his feet. Someone pulled the shutter tightly closed, and then a lock bore down on it. "There, better," the woman said.

He heard Leah reply, "I didn't realize it was open."

"Such a draft," the woman wailed. "How did you not feel the icy air blowing in here, probably filled with dybbuks."

Leah sighed. "It wasn't blowing. There's not a stir of wind tonight."

"Haven't you wondered why your womb keeps losing children?" the woman snapped. "The dybbuks, those little demons, have been spiriting away your unborn. One after another . . ."

Lev remembered writing down *zero* after asking how many children Leah had and the way she had stared at the hollow number.

"Enough!" Leah cried. "Last week, you said it was because I eat too many radishes, that the spicy root irritates the stomach."

Lev pressed his palms against the wood of the house as if this would help him hear more clearly.

The woman's voice softened. "I'll take the pot. Go upstairs. Get warm." After a few minutes, the light was extinguished. Then from the back of the house, Lev saw the old woman, Leah's mother, emptying the copper pot. She poured the dirty bathwater into the vegetable garden, muttering under her breath. Before turning back inside, she peered into the darkness as if to catch wandering dybbuks or souls transmigrating among the still houses, traveling through chimney tops, windows left ajar, unattended kitchens, loose floorboards, all due to the carelessness of women who were not as watchful and vigilant as she.

Lev left his post under the window, transfixed by the image of Leah's rising breasts, how they were shaped differently from Josephine's—the areolas dark brown and large, as opposed to the pink tips of Josephine's, which often reminded Lev of erasers on the ends of pencils. He imagined the swell of Leah's breasts as he cupped them. The setting was a natural one; among the trees, under the sheltering canopy of branches heavy with new foliage, the sun shedding disparate rays onto their nakedness, he would plunge into her. Blood rushed to his groin. He considered going behind a nearby tree to release the mounting pressure. Stopping in the middle of the road, he gripped his growing hardness under his coat. The strong scent of bark and the wet dark night surrounded him, but if he closed his eyes, he could place himself in that imaginary summer's day, Leah's naked back pressed against his chest, his hands massaging her hips. Her skin warm from the sun. She would roll her shoulders back, and he would bite the smooth rounded brownness. Enough. It almost hurt to walk. Hurrying toward the woods, he felt feral. The moon was unusually bright, illuminating the deserted road. Just when Lev grasped onto branches, about to pitch himself into the darkness, into relief, an approaching soldier shouted, "Stop!"

Lev, panting, sheepishly drew back from the inviting bushes.

The soldier, his gun drawn, advanced.

"I'm a German soldier," Lev yelled. He could see him clearly now in the bright moonlight: wire-rimmed spectacles, a receding hairline, thin, reedy, with worried eyes darting left and right.

He lowered his gun, shaking his head. "I thought you were a deserter. Rebel groups are forming in the woods, you know, raiding villages. Killing soldiers."

"It's gotten that bad?" Reaching under his heavy coat, Lev readjusted himself. "I've heard of a few mishaps here and there, but nothing we can't contain."

The soldier sighed. "I've been patrolling nights." He looked defeated. "And it's getting worse; more Germans are catching on, leaving to join the Russians. They don't want to get sent to the Western Front, where they know they'll die. Better to hide in the forest."

Lev noticed the tallith wrapped around the man's knapsack. He was one of the Jewish soldiers. There were about twenty who did this, flaunting their Jewishness with the tallith, hesitant to eat sausage, acting overly modest in the urinals, their hands encircling their penises to shield how the foreskin had been removed, as if they were extra naked without that silly little cap an uncircumcised penis donned. Lev was not ashamed of his circumcised penis because it was exceptionally large.

When other soldiers saw it, he wanted them to assume it was representative of the race.

"But I understand deserting." His spectacles glinted in the white light.

"Because we're losing the war and our children are starving at home?"

"Well, that. Of course that." He paused, studying Lev. "Haven't you heard?"

Lev shrugged.

"The Judenzählung. It's already started on the Western Front. They're counting us."

Lev's back stiffened. "All Jewish soldiers?"

The man swiveled on his heel in what looked like the beginning of a folk dance, a dance to taunt him. "Yes. All. Do you believe you are somehow exempt?" He laughed, sharp and bitter. "Von Hohenborn signed an order sent to all German military commands at the front, behind the front, in German-occupied territory, and in the homeland to determine, by means of a census taken on November first, how many Jews subject to military duty were serving on that date in every unit of the German armies."

"It's November ninth," Lev said, breathing heavily. "Maybe they've abandoned the idea."

"Oh, no. The Germans are just behind on their administrative duties out here," he said, drawing out a newspaper clipping. "You see, I have it here." And then, adjusting his spectacles he read the order lit by the light of the moon: *The War Ministry is continually receiving complaints from the population that large numbers of men of the Israelitic faith who are fit for military service are either exempt from military duties or are evading their obligation to serve under every conceivable pretext. According to these reports, large numbers of Jews in military service are also said to have obtained assignments in administrative or clerical posts far away from the front lines, either with the rear echelon or in the homeland.* "He stopped, panting, as if excited by the news. "You see, it's done. They are counting each and every Jew."

Lev face burned with embarrassment, the same burning he had felt as a boy when the schoolmaster pointed out in front of the class, "Your ears are as large as an elephant's. You would think with such large ears you would listen better." And all the schoolchildren would grip their sides with laughter at the Jew with the big ears. And Lev would run home, tripping and falling over his stumbling feet, run home with torn knees. And his mother would say, while stroking his hair, "They will always turn on you. Always."

The soldier interrupted Lev's thoughts, clucking his tongue like an old woman. "No matter where you fought, they'll count you."

Lev's heart beat quickly. "Where did you fight?"

"Flanders. But"—he turned his head to the side—"my ear got blown off." In the spectral light, the patch of swathed-over skin looked smooth and incandescent. "Thought I might get a *Heimatschuss* but no such luck. I was sent here instead for rehabilitation and when I got better, night patrol."

"It doesn't matter you lost an ear."

"Nothing matters anymore," the man echoed.

His throat tightened. "How will they count us, do you think?"

"How?" the man shook his head in disbelief. "Haven't you seen how good they are at counting? From the eggs to the chickens to the amount of paper and pencils and coffee each unit consumes—they will count us the way they count everything."

Lev stared down the road, and beyond that, at the cemetery in the distance, an apparition of gravestones, row after row, glowing white under the moon. "There are many more graves than when we first arrived," Lev said, pulling out a cigarette.

The man nodded, fingering his moustache, the hairs wiry and frosted. "In the middle of the night, I saw a dead Jew carried on a board into the cemetery, wrapped in a shroud. But when they'd gotten to the farthest corner, where the graves are twisted and broken, he lightly hopped off the *taharah bret*. Two peasants emerged from an underground tunnel, and they did a deal, what looked like the exchange of a bottle of vodka for a dead chicken. And then the Jew got back on the board, his friend wrapped him up again, with the dead chicken hiding underneath the shroud, and off they went. I watched the whole thing."

"Trading among the graves," Lev said.

"It's not a myth."

"Let's walk back together," Lev said, offering him a cigarette. "It's safer."

It was almost dawn. The red sun slowly rose in the east, lending hints of light to the dark sky. "Palestine," his companion whispered. "That's where I'm going after the war."

The birds were waking up, rustling in the trees, their calls sharp and scattered.

"Palestine," Lev repeated, the syllables rolling off his tongue. "They manufacture cigarette cases there."

The soldier shielded his eyes from the rising eastern sun. It was too bright. Piercing. It made his eyes water behind his spectacles. "It's the only place for us."

Lev wondered if this was true.

"Where we won't be rounded up and counted," he added sharply. The insistence in his voice urged Lev to agree, to shout, Yes, on to Palestine we go! But no. He couldn't picture Josephine in a desert among bronzed *halutizim*. The strong sun would burn her porcelain skin. She would shrivel up from a lack of moisture, from a lack of green. The olive trees, with their thin dry branches, would offer her no relief. But in Berlin, she often said how the heavy clouds rocked her into a gentle calm. On days when the sun did not show itself, she rejoiced in the sky's milky protection. Her eyes shone and her cheeks bloomed when she didn't have to contend with the sun, as if the two were in competition. But when it grew hot in summer, she became agitated, bored. She snapped at the children and refused to eat. She fanned herself impetuously and dismissed the glasses of lemonade Marthe ferried to her—no, she would not survive Palestine.

And Leah? Leah would survive. It was in her blood to cope, to make do. Unperturbed by her husband's long absence in the Russian army, by the German occupation, by all the new rules and strictures, by the harsh winter and lack of food, she had merely folded her heavy shawl over her shoulders and smiled at him, mischievous and goading, asking with her eyes, *What do you want from me?*

A funeral procession passed them on the road. A body wrapped in a white linen shroud was being carried, feetfirst, toward them. Two pieces of broken pottery, *sharves,* had been placed over the eyes. The two men leading the procession quickly looked up at Lev and then glanced away. Women trailed the tail end of the procession, wailing *"Zdakah tazil mi-mavet"* (alms for the dead). They rattled bulky charity boxes. There was no coffin because the use of wood for coffins had been forbidden. Bodies were buried only in cloth and lowered into the grave with nothing between the flesh and the earth. And recently, the Germans had outlawed the ritual washing of dead bodies in an attempt to maintain a certain level of sanitation.

The soldier smiled sarcastically at the wailing women. Then he whispered to Lev, "Bottles of vodka are under that linen cloth."

Looking back at the slow procession, Lev thought he saw a small movement from under the shroud; an arm readjusting itself, or possibly it was only a bit of wind lifting up the shroud for a split second before it settled down again.

When they got to town, hysteria tinged people's faces. Peasants rushed through the streets, yelling loudly in multiple dialects. A priest lumbered past, his oblong gray face turned inward. The Jewish women were quietly packing up their stalls in the marketplace. The church bells rang. The soldier told Lev, before disappearing down a narrow side street, that today the Germans were rounding up all natives for delousing, followed by inoculations at the military bathhouse.

Lev stared at him.

He threw up his hands. "They think the locals are filthy, that they're carrying disease. And we can't suffer another typhus endemic. It nearly wiped out the Serbian army."

All through the streets soldiers on horseback herded villagers in droves to the bathhouse at the edge of town. They marched them past the horse market and the abandoned church garden, and past the mill and the Belarusian cemetery, past the kerosene shop and the taverns and the iron goods store and the low brick building that housed the shul. The Jewish bars were deserted, empty of their elderly patrons, who enjoyed drinking kvass and playing cards out front for hours at a time. All the houses had been checked for shirkers. Front doors swung open, revealing empty dusty rooms with overturned chairs, a carpet pushed out of the way in case someone had attempted to hide beneath the floorboards, scattered newspapers, a samovar still steaming. A cat yawned, stretched out along a windowsill.

Lev started running toward Leah's house, down Tanner Strasse, retracing his steps from the night before. He passed soldiers coercing women into lines. The women begged and cried, offering small mis-shapen lumps of gold they had sewed into the hems of their skirts. They'd heard the inoculations would cause them to go barren. One woman threw back her head and opened her mouth, pointing to a gold filling. "You can take that, can't you?" The soldier shook his head disdainfully and used the butt of his rifle to herd her down the street with the rest. Lev kept running. He'd heard that at the bathhouse men and women had to strip off their clothing and stand naked in the cold brick room before going into the showers, where they would be assaulted by huge blocks of ersatz soap and canisters of disinfectant. Soldiers, outfitted in white short-sleeved gowns, administered the cleaning process, armed with scrubbers, hand brushes, loofahs, and rough towels, bombarding the natives with torrents of hot water, after which they brushed them with canvas sacking. And oftentimes, after seeing to it that a woman had been completely disinfected and scrubbed clean of all possible lice, they raped her.

At Leah's house, the door stood open. Beyond the house, Yatke bridge stretched over a rapid stream. Across the stream, fields upon fields of dry, flat yellow land. In the distance, the slaughterhouse and a scattering of red barns.

He spun around at the sound of leaves crunching; someone darted between the trees.

"Leah?"

He saw nothing now, only trees and dirt and a fallen bird's nest with tiny white eggs inside.

In Yiddish he said, "I'm not taking you to the bathhouse."

A few moments passed. Stillness surrounded him. Even the rushes in the trees stopped fluttering.

She stepped out from behind a birch, squinting.

"I'm alone," he said.

Leah nodded, one hand pressed against the birch, the other hand motionless at her side. Her eyes, animated with fear, appeared brighter and larger than Lev had remembered. He walked to her, and after a brief moment of hesitation, took hold of her hand and marveled at how perfectly it fit into his. "Let's find someplace to hide you," he said, leading her over the bridge, in the direction of the fields.

He hid her in the loft of an empty barn. With handfuls upon handfuls of hay, Lev covered her body. His fingertips lightly touched her heavy clothing, moving over the outline of her chest and her hips and her shoulders and her hair until only her face was visible. She reminded him of a living sarcophagus, immobile, inert, but one that blinked and breathed when the back of his hand accidentally brushed the side of her cheek or his calloused knuckle skimmed the bottom of her soft earlobe. And when this brief point of contact occurred, her liquid eyes would scan his face, searching for clues to who he was when not outfitted in field gray, and where he lived and with whom, for she had not failed to notice his wedding band, just as he had not failed to notice hers. As he covered her, Lev felt the heat radiating off her body, and this womanly heat shortened his breath, made it hard to think.

Weak afternoon sun shone through the diamond-cut window. Soon it would grow dark. And then she could return home, Lev told her. Leah nodded from under the hay. He dropped another handful over her forehead. She squinted and smiled.

"Now you look like a mummy," he whispered.

"What is a mummy?"

"At the Kaiser-Frederich-Museum," Lev began, "which is an enormous domed building, bigger than all the churches here put together. . . ." He paused, as if a spectral self had taken Franz to see the Münzkabinett, the "coin cabinet museum," and Franz, an avid collector, had stared at the large odd coins from Asia Minor, from the seventh century B.C. He had pressed his nose to the glass, leaving a smudge.

"Go on," Leah urged, raising her chin.

Lev balanced on his knees, listening to a shuffling from down below. But it was only a stray dog that had wandered into the barn, peering up at them, and then, after realizing there was no food, it wandered out.

"I can't quite explain," Lev whispered. "It's too foreign from this." He motioned to the darkened barn, to the low-hanging beams and the scattered hay and the cracked windowpane. Voices shouted outside. Through the window, Lev saw two German soldiers strolling lazily in the fields. One drew out a flask and drank from it in long lusty gulps. The other soldier threw his cap on the ground. His hair was as red as fire. They argued for a moment before the soldier with the flask handed it over to his comrade.

Lev turned away from the window. "You should stay here until dark. Completely dark."

"Stay with me until then," she said.

He made out her eyes and mouth more clearly than the rest of her face. She breathed quickly. Her neck gleamed. He wanted to take her neck in his hands and run his mouth along her collarbone, feel the pulse of her blood under his parted lips. She raised her hand up out of the hay and Lev clasped it, crushing his palm into her palm. Her cheeks flushed in the dimming light, she slowly told him about the wonder-rabbi, the cabalist. "He will bless you," she said. After a pause, their hands still locked together, she added, "He blessed me. He drove the dybbuks from my house. The dybbuks who were wreaking havoc on my womb." Her eyes were wet and shining. "I am a childless mother. Everyone knows this. Women will not touch me for fear of catching what I have caught. But the rabbi saw them, the dybbuks, dancing in my womb, rejoicing because they had spirited away my unborn children. And after he saw this, he blessed me. And now, he told me, like Sarah, I will have children. He said it's not too late."

Lev watched her mouth, her warm breath visible when she added,

"He blessed ten men when the war started, and they are all still alive."
She studied him. "Come next month, during the festival of lights. His
doors are open then."

He nodded, moving his thumb in circles along the inside of her
wrist, and wondered if this was the closest he would ever get to her skin,
her heat. Abruptly, she propped herself up on her elbows, her thick hair
falling around her shoulders. "Tell me, what does your wife look like?"

"I don't remember," he joked, brushing the last few strands of hay
off her shoulders. A snapshot of Josephine was safely tucked into his
shirt pocket, inches from his chest.

She didn't laugh. "It doesn't matter anyway, what you remember or
don't remember."

"No?"

"The way you look at me," she drew a breath, "tells me it doesn't."

That night, Lev leafed through Josephine's letters. He tried to shut out
the other men's voices, as well as the fleeting touch of Leah's hand upon
his face when they had parted in the trees behind her house. She had
smelled of hay and mint, and beneath that, her innate scent of heather
heated in the sun. "My cousin was killed at Maubeuge," someone said
gruffly while unbuttoning his uniform. Another man replied that he
thought he had crabs, moaning how he itched all over. "At least you're
not in the trenches," someone else said, spitting. "The rainwater is half
a meter deep there. Those boys in the trenches paddle in the water as
they fire, and the constant dampness causes bladder and kidney trouble," after which he punctuated his point by spitting out another wad of
tobacco onto the earth-packed floor.

Lev kept her letters in a stack tied with a string under his wire mattress. She had been writing less frequently because she was busy working for the DRK, the German Red Cross, as a nurse. She described how
the troop trains arrived every hour, packed with wounded, hungry men.
In between these trains, passenger trains also came, full of Prussian refugees with nowhere to go. She said they looked wild and rabid, wrapped
in dirty wool blankets. The women always had too many children, none
of whom they could feed. She wrote about how one woman had to be

detained because she suspected every person on the train wanted to shoot her. She was shrieking and sobbing, while her three boys looked on in silence. Some of the trains had been converted into stationary makeshift hospital wards. She emphasized how she was always busy, ferrying bread, coffee, and soup to the soldiers. But she did not seem to mind this. On the contrary—her letters were full of the energy and urgency war produces; she felt useful, and Lev imagined how the soldiers admired and complimented her. He thought she must enjoy her new role, playing Florence Nightingale, the lady with the lamp, gliding down the aisles of the infirm, a glowing apparition. It suited her. Lev reread part of a letter from two months ago: *I try to keep the children at home, but Franz insists on coming to see the wounded soldiers, and his will often proves stronger than mine. He desperately wishes he could fight and thinks being a child during the war is utterly useless. But I am secretly overjoyed that he is not old enough, for we would have surely lost him by now to one of the battlefields. Don't you think so?*

Lev drew up his knees, his back pressed into the iron grilling of the headboard. Below him, in the bottom bunk, a soldier was describing the pink and newly scrubbed bodies of the peasants after today's delousing. "They still seemed dirty. It's in their blood. You can't wash out that kind of filth."

Another man commented, "There's no such thing as dirty blood. Blood is blood."

Lev picked up her last letter, the one at the bottom of the stack. She wrote: *Yesterday, the children and I went to the cinema for a Henny Porten film—one of your favorites, I know. A Red Cross nurse was passing out candy and cigarettes to the wounded beforehand. One man's leg had not entirely healed; he was dripping a little blood on the velour seats. When Vicki and her friend Isabella saw his blood dripping, they burst into tears and ran out of the theater. I had to run after them for two whole blocks. When I caught up to them, they were still whimpering like puppies, and I slapped Vicki. Afterward, I felt badly, but she must learn the value of empathy. I think Isabella is too dreamy, and Vicki is always with her now. She claims her mother is an Italian countess. And when her father came home from the east (he was discharged—his left foot was blown to bits), she asked*

her mother, "Who is that strange man from Russia with the tall fur hat?"
Which makes me wonder, how do you look? Please let me know in advance if
you look terribly different, or if you are missing any parts. For the children's
sake, so I can prepare them. But it seems, thank God, that you have been
quite lucky thus far.

Lev put away this last letter. She had written it on October 1, 1917, more than a month ago. She wished he had been wounded just enough so she could tell others about it, but not so much that he'd be a pitiful case, like the man in the theater. He wondered if she resented his "luck," as she put it, and resented how relatively safe he was, stationed far from real battles, in the backwoods of the east, where soldiers fought typhus and lice instead of men, and staged *fronttheater*, such as Schiller's *Wallensteins Lager*, reenacting the Thirty Years' War, as if this war were not enough.

9

The first snowfall left the town glittering and white. In the early dawn, Lev walked outside with the other soldiers, their eyes blinking and watering from the new brightness. The air shimmered with cold. Lev thought his eyelashes might have frozen and stuck together in the short walk from the barracks to the mess hall. In the mess hall, everyone grumbled over another Christmas in Mitau. They drank weak coffee and smoked cigarettes and reminisced about marzipan and gifts wrapped in gold foil under the tree and the excitement of their children—children they wouldn't recognize by now. "They grow too quickly," a man grunted, sitting next to Lev. "My wife wrote how my boy is taller than I am." He took a violent bite out of his ham and butter roll.

Lev felt a cold despondency creep into his bones. How old was Franz again? Nine. Which would make Vicki seven. Maybe she had long hair in plaits and maybe she had outgrown her thumb-sucking. Maybe she slept better now, through the night without waking. But he could only guess at these things. The snatches of information he gleaned from Josephine's letters about the children often left him feeling bereft. They ate fairly well, they knew their multiplication tables, they missed him—this was about all she wrote. On occasion she tucked in a detail about Vicki's rebelliousness, which made Lev happy, or about how Franz had played one of the three wise men in the Christmas pageant, but otherwise she relied on stock phrases to fill the pages of her letters: *take care; write often; we're humming along just fine over here; it won't be long now; miss you.* Even her closing—*Love, Josephine*—at the bottom of the page felt rehearsed, mechanical, as if her hand automatically wrote the word *love* without the accompanying emotion. But perhaps he was only imagining this so he could think of Leah, freely and with abandon. He wanted to feel her skin again, kiss her—he almost had done it in the hayloft but had felt too afraid of spoiling the moment. He wanted to do all this and more without those pinpricks of guilt.

The man next to him finished off his sandwich and stood up abruptly. "It started again," he said, motioning to the heavy snow falling through the steamed-up windows. Then he walked off. Lev stared into his watery coffee and made a mental note to request that Josephine please include Franz and Vicki's birthdates in her next letter. She would think he was losing track of time, of home, of his footing in the world, and maybe he was.

Lev sighed, lingering a moment longer. There was nowhere to go anyway. It was impossible to work the roads and clear the fields because everything was frozen. Beneath the snow ran a layer of impenetrable ice. A sense of hiatus had overtaken the camp. The soldiers played cards indoors and started drinking before noon. The gramophone perpetually played folk songs. Lev sometimes watched with amusement as the men solemnly waltzed together. They dressed some of the youngest soldiers in wigs and aprons and pretended they were German farm girls from the high clear mountains. With their smooth beardless faces, the young men giggled and trounced from soldier to soldier, sitting on laps and blowing kisses. Lev found the whole scene drenched with despair, but he also laughed from time to time. What else was there to do? The officers, smoking their cigars, enjoyed the gaiety, believing everyone needed a reprieve, that the endless days of snow and fog and ice, with intermittent bursts of blinding sun, were damaging morale.

After breakfast, Lev went to Otto's lodgings. Exiting the mess hall, he already heard the garish vibrations of those folk songs echoing behind him. It seemed that each day they started earlier with the drinking and the meaningless frivolity. He sighed. His shoulders felt heavy, his legs lethargic. He missed home and he missed Leah, and the bleak gray sky promised nothing. Trudging through the empty snow-swept streets, he thought about the last time he'd seen Leah. A few days ago, but it felt like years. It had been unsatisfying because she was with her sister and they were headed to market. So bundled, he could barely see her face and she was in a hurry. For only a few moments, she stopped on the street and introduced him to Altke, her sister. Leah's breath was white in the freezing air. Her eyes laughed from under her wool hat. Then she gave him a quick nod, and they continued on their route, chattering away about the price of turnips. He had stood there for a long time, just watching her walk away, even though cold seeped into his boots and he swore his nose would freeze, turn blue, and fall off.

He hoped, in the middle of these silent streets, he would suddenly see her—highly unlikely, but still he glanced around. Every other house was marked with the red warning sign of infection, the windows boarded up for fear the virus would seep into the open air. Lev thought he saw, from behind a lace curtain, a furtive glance through the elaborate patterning. The only imperfections in the new snow were ashes, scraped from the ovens and scattered in front of each doorstep to keep people from slipping. He passed the cemetery and remembered how Aaron had told him about the secret business deals done here among the graves. He stopped a moment, musing at the graves, how the stones were run-down and crooked and jammed together, and in the process of lighting a match for his first cigarette of the day, the blue flame flickered and a dream resurfaced from the night before, a dream he would rather forget. He stood at the end of a long snaking line in the middle of a forest—ahead of him he recognized Aaron and some other Jewish soldiers from his division. An officer made his way down the line, counting off the Jews. He motioned for the first soldier to speak, who said he was a *Vaterlandsverteidiger,* defender of the Fatherland. The officer nodded in approval, moving on. The next soldier stepped forward and stated *Mosaischer Konfession,* of the Mosaic faith. A third soldier proclaimed Israelit, an Israelite, and then the fourth soldier in line proudly announced *Deutscher jüdischen Glaubens,* a German of the Jewish faith, as if he should win an honorary medal for this. When the German officer paused before the fifth soldier, a soldier who vaguely resembled Lev, the man could not speak. The officer swiftly shouted, *"Auf jeden Fall ein Jude."* Definitely a Jew.

. . .

Lev walked faster. The biting cold snaked through his open collar. The image of the German officer's laughing face when he shouted *Auf jeden Fall ein Jude* danced before him. Such triumph in identifying a Jew, as if the officer had a particular knack for catching difference—a glee akin to a banker's wife spotting that the diamonds hanging from her rival's neck were not real stones but cheap glittering imitations. Despite Lev's dream, the actual count had been orchestrated discreetly. He and the other Jewish soldiers filled out a form with their names, occupations, the date they joined the army, their duties, if they had fought on the front line, if they had been wounded, and if so, what type of wound. They handed back the papers to the officers with the obedience of schoolchildren.

When he reached Antonina's house, she was cursing and smoking and holding a bowl of steaming water. Uncle was nowhere to be seen. The house was overheated, as usual, and Antonina's flushed chest heaved as she recounted the morning's horrors. Otto's toe was inflamed and he couldn't walk. He had been hollering all through the night, demanding this and that, and she did not sleep a wink. Wisps of flaxen hair stuck to the sides of her temples. She begged Lev to see what the trouble was. "Maybe you can help with the pain. Maybe you can tell him to stop shouting," she breathed, a hot garlicky breath, into Lev's face. "I bring him a poultice, a balsam, but nothing, nothing works." Sighing, she followed Lev into Otto's room. Otto, with one sheet twisted around his leg, the pillows thrown to the ground, lay stretched out across the bed diagonally. He gripped the tarnished brass bars behind his head, emitting a low guttural moan, but when he saw Lev, he moaned more dramatically and gestured to his big toe, red and swollen, pulsating with pressure.

Antonina said, "Even a sheet over his toe and he screams."

Otto nodded weakly.

Lev studied the toe. "It's gout."

"Gout?" Antonina repeated.

"How can I get rid of gout?" Otto murmured, straining to lift his head.

"My brother-in-law, he had gout, and they chopped off his toe."
She sharply swung her arm through the air, illustrating the amputation.

"Shut up," Otto roared.

"Milk and cherries lessen the pain," Lev said.

"Milk and cherries?" Antonina waved a wet rag through air. Droplets of water sprinkled Lev's face. "Cherries in the dead of winter? Only the czarina eats cherries in winter."

"Cherries?" Otto asked. His eyes were glazed over, his ears crimson.

Lev pulled up a chair next to the bed. "Listen. I heard of a wonder-rabbi, a cabalist, who could possibly heal your toe. We could go. I could take you." He felt his spirits lighten at the thought of this adventure—better than playing cards with his tobacco-stained fingers, thinking about how his son was growing taller, mixed together with his yearning to see Leah again, alone. Then guilt always tried to chase away this desire, and Josephine's admonishing face appeared before him. What would she say if she knew about Leah?

Antonina kept waving the wet rag through the air in a circular motion. "Are you telling him lies about me? I've done everything I could, everything—"

"Get out," Otto shouted, wincing from a new shot of pain.

Protesting, she left the room.

They trudged through the snow, Otto hanging on Lev's arm, Lev shouldering most of Otto's weight, telling him about the wonder-rabbi's powers. "People seek him out, go to him with their problems." They stopped to rest a moment. They were near Leah's house, but he could not hear the stream because it had frozen. Over the last month, he had been ferrying her a handful of flour, a few potatoes, a dead chicken, a thimble of vodka—anything he could pilfer from the mess hall's kitchen, from the army's meager supplies. Anything that provided him a chance to see her, if even for a moment, when their fingertips touched during the exchange of these provisions. But even with the extra food, her sister had fallen ill from typhus. These days, due to the biting cold and lowered immunity, people were less resistant to diseases transmitted through lice. But somehow, even when there wasn't enough to eat, behind each frosted window six candles blazed, marking the fifth day of Hanukkah.

Lev gestured to the lit candles, recalling what Leah had told him. "During the holidays, that is when he sees people. He holds court in one of the prayer houses. Jews, gentiles, all types, seek him out to be blessed, to be cured, if someone is sick, if their wife is barren, if they cannot ejaculate, if they are lusting after another man's wife"—he paused—"they line up and wait for days to see him."

Otto lifted up his bad foot, which was swaddled in wool. His toe was too sensitive and swollen to fit into his boot. "I'm not waiting for days."

"Look," Lev said. Down the snow-packed street, the doors of the prayer house stood open. Men filtered in and out, in black caftans, smoking cigars and strong pipe tobacco. As Lev and Otto approached, they heard grumbling and arguing, voices rising to a pitch of irritation while others conferred in murmured tones. Otto gripped on to fences along the way, but most houses had no fences. He was covered in sweat, his neck red and pulsating. He tore open his coat, sending a few brass buttons flying. He eyed the plain wooden doors and broken stone steps and hesitated to enter. Exiting, an old man in a tall fur hat threw his cigar butt into the bushes and stormed off.

Inside, it was dark and crowded, and all the men converged around a staunch red-haired man in a velvet cap who guarded the entrance to the next room, where, from what Lev and Otto gathered, the wonder-rabbi held court. The door was closed, and the man in the velvet cap smiled grimly with his arms crossed over his chest. He avoided eye contact even though various men came up to him and pleaded, saying they'd been waiting since dawn; their daughters had diphtheria, their cows no longer yielded milk, or soldiers had taken away their sons. The litany of need rose and fell like a chorus. Otto held on to Lev's shoulder, breathing heavily. The smoke burned their eyes and made it hard to see. The small windows embedded in the stone walls were dirty and let in dull gray light. Some men didn't bother with the doorkeeper. They griped and lamented, carrying on dramatic monologues for an invisible listener. One man whined and wrangled with God, accusing Him of providing a bad harvest, and on top of that, his wife had taken to her bed. Her hair was falling out. She was coughing up blood. Her chest had sunken into a cavity. "Like a hollow bowl!" he cried and threw down his fur-trimmed hat. "This winter is an empty desert in which You have stranded me—You, merciless and unforgiving, are preparing that I should soon become a widower."

Otto leaned into Lev. "No one cares."

Lev shrugged. "At least he has the comfort of saying such things out loud."

Otto nudged Lev again. "Let me tell you, this is what will happen. His wife will die and he'll take up with another woman, a prettier one who is a better cook. He'll be much happier and will barely remember his first wife. In a year's time, he'll be back here, praising God. Simple as that."

Lev said, "It's human nature, to forget so we can survive."

The smell of wet wool and sweat filled the small prayer room. There was barely any space to move forward. Lev elbowed a few men aside, trying to reach the doorkeeper. He felt as if he was part of a larger human body, this crowd clothed in black.

Finally, they got to the front of the crowd. Behind him, Lev felt nudges and shoves from the other men. He could smell their smoke-infused beards and the saltiness of their last meal. The red-bearded man stared ahead. He was unusually short, but his muscular arms and protruding chest made him appear less so.

Lev said in Yiddish, "We need to see the rabbi."

The man did nothing, his mouth a tight line.

Otto tried in German, "We are German officers and we have an appointment with the rabbi."

The man picked a piece of lint off his sleeve and examined it. Lev palmed him ten marks. He glanced at Lev with faint curiosity. His red beard glinted copper and gold, and he now played with the very tip of it. Lev palmed him another ten. Otto swore but Lev elbowed him silent.

The small man shifted his weight from one hip to the other, his legs straddled before the door. "The rabbi is very busy, as you can see. What makes you think I will just let you inside? Others have been waiting for days." He continued to finger his beard.

The back of Lev's neck started to itch. He wanted to shake this little man. Instead, he folded an additional ten-mark note into the man's palm.

The man smiled, and the money disappeared into his coat pocket. For a prolonged moment, he patted the outside of his pocket. Then he opened the door.

They entered into a plain room with one window looking out onto a courtyard. The air was cold and blue. It seemed as if no one was here, but behind a wooden desk sat the wonder-rabbi. He had black hair, a black beard sprinkled with white, and gray uncertain eyes. His long bony face reminded Lev of an El Greco painting, along with his delicate hands and tapered fingers and papery white skin. A slight flush animated his cheeks, which only made the rest of his face appear paler. He acknowledged Lev and Otto, while at the same time he looked distracted, as if he saw many men before him.

Lev wondered if they should sit down on the faded brown rug, a dusty square of wool in front of the desk. "Samuel ben Abraham, thank you for seeing us." His Yiddish was coming back.

The rabbi massaged his temples with his index fingers. He looked down at his desk, a clean wooden surface. "I deal between God and man. Between man and man is more difficult." He squinted at Lev and Otto, and his blue lips curled back. "Christian and Jew?"

Otto said, "I can't walk because of my swollen toe."

The rabbi closed his eyes. A slight wind shook the windowpane. It was fiercely cold inside the room, but he had no need for heat or food or light, as if he sprang from ether. He mumbled, "A Christian is better than a Zionist. If they build a Jewish nation, such a place will no longer have any Jews in it."

Otto nodded in agreement.

The rabbi opened his eyes. "You are not a Zionist, are you?"

Lev shook his head. "I'm German." He hesitated. "A German Jew." It sounded like a lie.

The rabbi snorted. "God is all-knowing. We must thank Him for His wisdom."

For a moment, they held their breath, unsure if the rabbi would continue in this vein, but he did not. He tugged on his beard and told Otto to soak his foot in a tub of cold water filled with mint leaves and to elevate it during sleep. He added that he should not walk or run or wear boots or drink alcohol or speak often because this would agitate the blood and he could see that Otto had agitated blood. "Your face is always flushed. Your hands are never still." His tone was accusatory but understanding, like a scolding father, and Otto, suddenly the wayward son, became obedient. "Yes, of course. Whatever you suggest."

The rabbi nodded, satisfied. Then he reminded them, "God gave us this insight. It is not of human invention but all made and created by Him." He paused and focused his wintry gaze on Lev. "The fear of God is more trustworthy than your so-called modern humanism."

Lev felt his cheeks burn, and out of the shadows of his mind, he heard his mother yell that, to his university friends, he would always be an eastern Jew from Galicia, despite his silk cravat and newly acquired monocle—a silly thing he wore for a semester, which his mother nearly tore off his face in one of her fits. Staring at the rabbi's bluish-white face, the way he passively sat in his chair not expecting anything from this world, infuriated Lev. He remembered such holy men shuffling down Hirtenstrasse, a street all shades of gray, unpaved and maze-like, peppered with little shacks housing whole families in one room, trapped yellow light emanating from cracked windows, rubbish in door-ways composed of old newspapers, torn stockings, shoelaces, and apron strings. And he was sure the rabbi would think such remnants were worth preserving instead of the glittering facades of new buildings, the white lights in the trees lining Unter den Linden, the cinema palaces of Alexanderplatz, overlaid in gilt.

Lev averted his eyes and examined the dusty rug with its frayed edges and threadbare middle.

Otto stepped forward, leading with his bad foot. "Thank you, Rabbi. Thank you for your help. Already, it's less swollen."

The rabbi glared at Lev and threw up his hands, his eyes rolling back. "Why? Why must I set sight on your clean-shaven face? It nearly contaminates my eyes to see a Jew shave off his beard, to grow so distant from God."

Otto, his head bent forward in supplication, a pose Lev had never seen him occupy, started explaining army regulations, but Lev gripped his shoulder. He only wanted to escape, to flee, lest he be cursed, but then he cursed himself for entertaining such thoughts, for being drawn into this cloistered realm where rabbis cursed and blessed whole families for generations, crippling men into believing the reason their son died or a fire destroyed their house was because a wonder-rabbi once glanced at him in the wrong way ten years ago. He was about to lunge for the handle when the oak door sprung open as if the red-bearded man knew exactly when their meeting had ended.

10

While they had been inside with the rabbi, the solid gray sky broke apart into brilliant blue patches, the afternoon sun illuminating the remaining clouds as if a flame burned within each one. People spilled out of their homes, relieved the grim day had lightened. Children chased one another, throwing snowballs, yelling and running, their cheeks blotchy from the icy air.

Otto and Lev walked back to the barracks along the blindingly white streets, and Otto talked the whole time about how wonderful the rabbi was, how his toe had healed, how he barely felt even a trace of pain. Occasionally, he held Lev's arm to steady himself before striding ahead with the newfound fervor of a patient miraculously healed.

"Yes, the rabbi," Lev said, pausing at the sight of a boy with bright blond hair, the same color as Franz's, who ran ahead of the pack, clearly the leader. Victoriously, he did not wear a hat, and it seemed that this freedom lightened his step, made him enviable in the eyes of the others.

Otto said over his shoulder, "He offended you. I saw it on your face, as if you were battling an angry ghost."

Lev kicked at the snow, his boot dirtying the pristine whiteness. "The way people treat these rabbis, with such reverence and esteem. As if they can solve the world's problems with one wave of their hand, as if they alone know the infinite secrets of the universe. I don't like it."

"That's not to say some men don't have a gift—" Otto doubled over, groaning.

"A gift?" Lev teased.

Otto leaned against a snowbank, his bad foot dangling in the air. "Help me again?"

Lev suppressed a smile and offered Otto his arm.

Otto murmured, "I suppose sometimes the pain returns in flashes."

"Slowly, Otto, go slowly," Lev said, scanning the streets. He had led them in the direction of Leah's house without really meaning to, his feet mysteriously carrying them toward the river, the flat yellow fields and the white birches, toward the abandoned farmhouse where he had last touched her.

Otto glanced around. "The base is the other way."

Lev kept walking, ignoring him. "No cure is immediate. You have to follow what the rabbi said—no alcohol, no excitement. Rest, Otto. Plenty of rest."

Otto nodded morosely, still holding on to Lev for support, allowing Lev to lead him even if they were walking in the wrong direction. "Antonina won't let me rest. She chatters day and night about the most inane subjects—her sister's husband, who is a brute, how she doesn't have enough flour to bake bread and could I get her some, the best way to clean out a chamber pot, how the consumption of pumpkin seeds would benefit my constitution. I fight the impulse to strangle her, to cease her incessant chatter. My palms itch; it takes all my will not to clutch that fat neck of hers and wring it."

"Yes, yes," Lev replied, his senses heightened, wondering if Leah might be walking this way, if he could at least catch a glimpse of her. He observed all the people on the street, searching for her face in the crowd. The physical need to be in her presence tricked him into thinking he had seen her when it was another woman with black hair, not as lustrous, bending over a small child who had lost her boot in the snow. When she glanced up, with her narrow eyes and thin downturned mouth, the woman's unfamiliar face jarred him. But the unexpected fine weather, the sharp sun hitting the back of his neck coupled with the general air of frivolity that overtook the people on the streets, infused Lev with the hope that perhaps he would find Leah today. He imagined how they would marvel over seeing each other unplanned.

"Aren't you listening?" Otto cried.

"You were telling me about Antonina," Lev said, suddenly overcome with gloom: *I'm lost in the fog of a daydream that will amount to nothing.*

"She refuses to let me rest! Purposefully, she's wearing me down, sapping my strength as Delilah did Samson."

"I would hardly compare her to Delilah," Lev muttered, spying the rooftop of Leah's house peeking through the fir trees. Perhaps she was at home. Perhaps she would step outside to collect firewood or tend to the chickens and she would see him there, walking by. Perhaps, perhaps.

Otto tugged on Lev's coat sleeve. "You've taken us back the long way making it only harder for me to walk. Do you realize if we'd turned right at the mill—"

The same hatless blond boy ran past, a snowball hidden in the folds of his jacket. He accidentally bumped into Otto, knocking him off balance. Otto cursed the boy, who glanced back with a malicious smile.

Geza ran after the boy and hurled a snowball at his head. He missed and the snowball broke apart, revealing a stone packed away inside of it.

The boy kept running, disappearing into the trees.

"Geza!" Lev shouted.

He turned around, hands stuffed into his pockets.

"Are you throwing stones now?"

Geza jerked his hands out of his pockets. "He stole my pencils and tore apart my school notebook."

Otto shook his fist, half joking. "Assert your dominance—catch the blond beast!"

"Don't encourage him," Lev said, worried Leah would hear the commotion and frown upon what had happened, thinking Lev had instructed Geza to throw the stone.

"Officer, if I have violated some code of conduct I apologize," Geza replied with a touch of sarcasm. How bold and unruly the boy was, his hair loose around his eyes, without a scarf, not even in this frigid cold, as if he thought himself immortal.

"My name is Lev." He paused. "Did your mother receive the medicinal teas I gave to Leah for her? Such concoctions work quite well to cure the disease."

Geza nodded, lowering his gaze. "Yes, thank you, Officer. I mean Lev."

He sighed. "All right. Go home. Don't cause any more trouble with that boy. I'll get you more pencils, another notebook."

Otto snorted. "I'd go after him if I were you."

"Thank you," Geza repeated, his voice softening.

Lev patted his arm. "Think nothing of it." He resisted the urge to ask after Leah and paused, hoping she might appear, but the moment dissolved and nothing happened. Geza said good-bye and walked back to his house.

The sky tipped into violet and the cold chill of evening rustled through the trees. "Let's go," Lev said, and Otto grumbled about his foot, how it was acting up again because Lev had taken them the round-about way and now it was getting dark and he was tired. Lev pretended to listen while trying to quell the pinpricking heartsickness, as if her absence pierced his vital organs, leaving holes and tears.

A few days later, Lev returned to Leah's house bearing new colored pencils and a notebook for Geza, both individually wrapped in brown paper, tied with string. He had placed a sprig of holly under the string, an added touch of delicacy he hoped Leah would notice and like. The house was quiet and still, encircled by the green hush of the forest. The other houses nearby appeared equally deserted when normally the neighborhood bustled with activity, with children playing and women gossiping and men, in huddled groups, discussing portions of the Torah. After leaving the packages on the front step, Lev lingered, glancing through the dusty windows, remembering the night when he had seen her bathing, her skin gleaming in the candlelight. He gazed longingly at the dark window, catching his own forlorn reflection in the glass, when he saw a figure move through the room. He froze, overcome with nervousness. It would look strange if someone saw him lurking here without any discernible purpose. He lightly stepped off the porch, but the old wood creaked under his boots. The front door swung open.

"Lev!"

Leah stood before him, her hair swept up into a bun with little dark wisps escaping around her temples. She looked lovely like this, her elegant white neck bare and inviting.

He tried to smile but his face felt tight and ungainly. Their time in the hayloft, the fluid conversation, her relaxed body breathing beneath the hay felt strangely separate from this moment, the clear daylight illuminating every detail. The broken capillaries around her nose, the blue shadowy skin under her eyes, her bitten-down fingernails. And yet seeing her so clearly, he wanted her even more.

"Hello, Leah," he managed. "I didn't expect to find you at home."

"Oh," she replied, biting her lower lip. They stared at each other, and then she bent down to pick up the packages, and at the same time, he bent down to help her. Their foreheads collided. He touched her shoulder, apologizing profusely while she also apologized. Words and sentences flew between them, none of which Lev actually heard, transfixed as he was by her presence.

She hugged the packages to her chest. "Thank you for these. Geza told me about the other day. He must not provoke those boys."

"He's young."

There was an uncomfortable pause. She looked down at the packages and smiled. "The holly is pretty."

His heart thundered in his chest, and he said a little too excitedly, "It's for you—I thought you might like it."

She brushed away a stray hair from her mouth. "Thank you."

Lev shifted on his feet, the porch creaking beneath him. "It's quiet today."

"Everyone's at services."

"Oh, of course. It's Saturday." Lev gulped, feeling embarrassed he hadn't realized this simple fact. "The quiet dark houses. Not even a candle is lit."

"Not even a candle," she repeated, smiling ruefully.

"You're not at services with your family?"

She touched her forehead. "Headache."

Lev stepped back. "I apologize—I didn't mean to disturb you. Rest, rest—you must rest."

Her hand slid down her neck, lingering there as if she was taking her pulse. Behind her, the hearth blazed, the room's warmth filtering onto the porch. She gripped the door frame, holding out her hand. "Don't go."

Lev grabbed it; her warmth funneled into his fingertips, up his arm, spreading through his chest.

She pulled him inside.

In a rush, in a stream, she explained how he infiltrated her thoughts, her dreams, as if a demon possessed her. "You are not alone with these feelings," Lev said, kneading her defined jaw line with his thumbs. Then he touched her hair, her neck, where her collarbone rose and fell with her quickening breath. His hands running over the coarse fabric of her clothes, he felt her torso, her hips, the backs of her thighs—he wanted to undress her but not here with the windows facing the street for all to witness. Leah gestured to the hallway, and they stumbled into the narrow dark space, gripping each other, as if letting go would sever the moment.

Her room was simple, spare, with a few loose floorboards. A neatly made bed in the corner, a rickety table with a small vase, empty of flowers. A diamond window looked out onto the garden, and Leah immediately drew the curtains. Then she turned around, her mouth open, peering at him anxiously as if she was about to explain, but Lev didn't want her to explain. He swooped her up, slung her over his shoulder, feeling the crush of her breasts, her stomach, her pelvic bone against him. She breathlessly uttered a few words of protest, but her hands slid down his lower back, and she playfully tried to pull off his belt, tugging on the tough leather. He threw her down on the bed and removed each layer of clothing, as if unpacking a precious gift. When he came to her undergarments, she nodded for him to remove these too, and he did. Her body vibrated before him on the little bed, her black hair against the white sheets, her legs parted, her breathing labored. He started to touch the dark softness between her legs when she whispered, "Let me see you too."

Lev slipped out of his uniform, tearing off his undershirt and long underwear until he stood naked before her. The image of Adam and Eve swam into his head—their mutual shame upon the realization of their nakedness contrasted with his joy. He wanted to laugh out loud, to shout with delight. He wanted to gather her up into his arms and swirl her around the room as if they were the first humans to revel in the pleasure of their bodies, skin on skin, her hair in his mouth when he kissed her neck, her hot palms pressing down on his shoulder blades, urging him into her without the slightest resistance, as if gravity had released them as they swam in and out of each other, free of the world's heavy materiality.

Afterward, they languished in the messy bed, watching the sky darken through the drawn curtains. The cat slept in a gray ball next to Lev's foot. His head on her chest, listening to the rise and fall of her breath, Lev wondered when her family would come home, and as if reading his thoughts, Leah said they were still at services and would be for another hour.

She stroked his hair. "We have a little more time."

He inhaled her sweaty milky scent. "I don't want to leave you."

"Then stay," she joked, tickling his ear.

Lev stroked her stomach, his fingers running over a raised brown mole above her hipbone. He marveled at the surprise of her body, how different it felt from Josephine's. Leah's skin was thicker, rougher, with moles splashed in unexpected places. She had smaller breasts, broader hips. Her taste in his mouth was sharper, more pungent. Recalling their reflection in the smudged oblong mirror made his blood rise to the surface, and he wanted her again. In the mirror, he had held her hips, his chest pressed into her back, her face turned to the side. Her half-closed eyes and open mouth, which occasionally twitched with pleasure. At one point, she opened her eyes wide and watched their reflection. He watched her watching, which caused him to finish too soon, exploding into her. Afterward, he buried his face into her smooth back, apologizing, but she laughed lightly and reassured him that this was only the beginning. There was time to practice.

"Lev," Leah said, interrupting his reverie.

He pulled her close, their skin sticky and warm.

She freed herself, sitting up and wrapping the sheet around her. "I wouldn't want you to think—"

He smiled. "I don't."

She shook her head, frustrated. "I am serious. I would never do such a thing as this." She blushed. "Normally."

The cat continued to purr, nestling up against Lev's bare leg. The soft fur lulled him, made him sleepy even though he could see Leah wanted to discuss important matters. She told him, twining the sheet more tightly around her, how two weeks ago she had received a letter about her husband. Zalman had died on a Carpathian mountain pass. Of course she felt sad he had suffered such a tragic end, but they had never been happy, not before the war, not even on their wedding day. Zalman. Such a name sounded like the salted pumpkin seeds that always got stuck between his teeth. Leah explained how she hadn't engaged in sexual relations since her husband left over two years ago, and even then, she barely felt it was intercourse between a man and wife. "He would service himself with his hand, sometimes using mine, but I never moved it fast enough for him—doing this felt like pulling off an old stubborn boot that is too small." She said this bitterly, with little acknowledgment of the humor such an image evoked.

He waited for her to ask about his wife, but she didn't. Perhaps she feared any mention of Josephine would immediately darken his mood, make him grow distant and uncertain, and maybe it would.

He reached for her hand. "I also didn't expect such a thing to happen between us. Of course I dreamed it, wanted it, but I never thought it would. But it has happened."

"It has," she said, her eyes shining.

"Do you want it to keep happening?" he asked, already knowing the answer.

She threw herself onto him, crushing her mouth against his neck and chanted into the warm darkness of his body, *Yes, yes, yes.*

11

Otto had lost his voice from yelling because the workers were not clearing the forests quickly enough. The road should have been built before the first frost, and already the ground had nearly frozen into a slick grayish surface, making it that much harder to dig. In the late afternoon, Otto sat down on the frosted ground, unable to speak. His toe was better, although he still wore a felt boot. He took out a cigarette, debating whether or not to light it. Lev watched the men. Their hands bled through their mittens. Dark shadows played under their eyes. They coughed into their armpits while working, hoarse sounds full of fluid. Fewer and fewer men reported to work, their numbers dwindling because of the typhus outbreak, while others just disappeared.

Lev turned away, scanning the massive forest. He couldn't look at the men. Sometimes, they pitched forward onto the icy ground. The others carried on working, as if this were a natural occurrence. A few times, men died this way, and Lev had to arrange for a burial.

He glanced down at Otto, who still sat motionless on the icy ground.

"I'm leaving. It's too cold." Perhaps he could get to the hayloft in time to see Leah. It had become their agreed-upon meeting place. But he never knew when exactly he might meet her, as they had to orchestrate the timing of their rendezvous strategically. If they grew reckless, greedy, her family asked too many questions concerning Leah's whereabouts, and Leah was a poor liar. Every day, Lev looked for the piece of red string. If Leah tied it to the branch of the birch tree closest to her house, it meant she would be waiting for him in the hayloft. If the red string was not on the branch, Lev turned away, sullen and disappointed, and waited anxiously for tomorrow.

Otto stared moodily at the men, some of whom had paused, sensing a break.

"It's nearly dark," Lev said, motioning to the gray sky.

Otto shrugged. He was in one of his black moods when he refused all entreaties. Lev knew to leave him alone, that the more he cajoled him or tried to persuade him, the more disagreeable Otto would become. Hesitating for a few seconds, Lev walked away, knowing that later this evening Otto would come bearing libations, a bottle of schnapps tucked under one arm, bandying about cigarettes among the barracks, full of goodwill, the whole episode of this afternoon forgotten.

Walking back along the river, Lev thought that the only way men knew how to reconcile was over a good deal of alcohol and a shared appreciation for women. The more specific the conversation—which whore did he prefer and what position—combined with the refilling of their vodka glasses, lubricated any resentment that had gathered between them, until it dissolved completely into one of Otto's tirades on the beauty of war, the bestiality of men, or the inherent duplicity of women. He circulated among these three topics depending on his audience and which topic he had opined on last. Continuing along the river, Lev imagined what Otto would speak of tonight, and already he heard the sonorous tremor of his voice, booming through the smoke-infused barracks, and the lackluster laughs of the men, too lazy and insipid to rouse themselves from their cots.

The river was frozen over, and a group of peasants stood along the bank, pouring beet juice over the white surface. Lev strained to look, realizing the juice was being poured over the outline of a cross in the ice. After they finished, they crossed themselves and then burst into chatter. The girls' wheat-colored braids, adorned with bows and glass beads, stuck out of their coats. They exchanged parcels wrapped in newspaper. The young men, in wide-cut pants tucked into high boots, waved their hats over the girls' heads, teasing them. Lev glimpsed a flash of green ribbon on a girl's blouse, and the lightness of her hair—it lit up the whole scene—reminded him of Josephine's hair, how even in the dullness of winter it shone in a darkening room. He would come over to where she sat and kiss her head, his lips running along the white part in her hair. Oftentimes, she would remain still, engrossed in her reading or sewing until the weight of his hands on her shoulders would make her turn around, asking, "What is it?"

He walked on toward the village, Josephine's hair still pressed against his nostrils. But the smell of something burning interrupted such thoughts. Up ahead, above the marketplace, plumes of black smoke billowed. On the streets, people sprinted between doorways. Windows had been smashed. Doors swung open. Inside houses, pots rolled on the floors. Lev ran past a man lying in a doorway clinging to his shoes, moaning something indecipherable. The infernal murmur of pigeons perched on the rooftops foretold some catastrophe. Lev ran faster, his chest tight and pounding. He had to find Leah.

When he reached her house, the door was unlocked, probably to save the trouble of having it broken down, since the neighboring doors had been yanked off their hinges. He had already checked the birch tree—no red string. The main sitting room was in complete disarray. The hat stand was broken in two. The long wooden table had disappeared. The drawing of Baal Shem Tov had been dashed to the floor, the glass frame in shards. He stepped forward. "Leah?" The sound of his voice vibrated in a futile echo. "What has happened here?" He strained to hear an answer. Slowly, footsteps creaked down the stairs from the attic. He heard whispering. The room was almost dark, as no candles had been lit. Leah appeared at the foot of the stairs. She absently touched her face and then brushed her hair back from her eyes. "Lev?" she whispered.

Lev stepped forward, careful to avoid the shards. His hand rested on his holster. He felt his body tense, but he was useless now. "Cossacks?" The word was as old as childhood stories of men in black, each with a saber in its curved scabbard hanging from his sash, leather boots, and a tall fur hat. Such men had killed his mother's father and burned down their fields.

She yawned and shook her head. "Peasants. Simple goyim from the town." She smiled halfheartedly. "It usually comes this time of year. At

Christmas." She knelt down to retrieve the crushed picture frame, her hair loose around her shoulders.

Lev bent down. He touched her hair. Her eyes were unfocused. "They weren't shy. They took all the kitchen utensils. Even the bread shovel and the fire poker. And the underwear. Muslin underwear we were saving for spring, to give at Passover." She rubbed her eyes, taking in the bareness of the room. "They thought the tefillin contained valuables, but when they found just old yellow pieces of paper inside, they flung it on the floor." Pausing, she bit her lower lip. "Not even a Jewish woman is pure enough to touch the tefillin." Lev encircled his hand around her wrist. She shuddered.

Upstairs, her family started arguing about whether or not it was safe to get water from the river and to eat a little bread. Geza raised his voice in the dark: "The least we can do is get out of this corner. We're huddled here, as frightened as children."

"You are still a child," his mother retorted.

"Ouch!" Geza yelled.

The women whispered harshly, "Quiet. Do you want them to return?"

"Haven't they already done enough to you?" Geza's mother lamented, her voice trembling.

Lev said, "They won't come back. Everyone should come down now."

Leah picked up a piece of broken glass, dropping it into her apron. "We thought the Germans would intervene. But it started very early this morning, and no one did anything." She picked up another shard, her white fingers navigating the pieces.

"Let me do this. You'll hurt yourself." Again, he took her wrist. This time, she did not shudder. Instead, she just looked at him, embittered.

"When the peasants came crashing through our door, some German soldiers strolled by our house, smoking cigarettes." She violently scooped up a handful of glass, dumping the remains into her lap. Little red cuts emerged between her fingers. Lev wanted to hold her hands and kiss them. "The soldiers saw how our coats and chairs and tables were carried out, as if it was the natural order of things."

Leah started to rise from her squatting position, but Lev cupped her shoulders. He whispered, "I was out in the forest, clearing roads. You know . . ."

"And that's how it's always been—the natural order of things!" Geza bellowed from the attic, and then he stormed down the stairs, breathless. He kicked aside the broken picture frame. "Can you believe it?" he said, tearing off the dangling arm of the hat stand.

In the moonlight, Lev saw the gash across Geza's lower jaw. "I can fix that."

Geza automatically touched it.

The others trailed down the stairs. Leah's mother emerged first, fisting her woolen skirts up around her knees. She said at least the goyim had not taken the good linens, which she hid behind the oven. Leah's sister followed, her hair patchy and uneven from typhus. And then Leah's father, the rabbi, descended without a hint of effort, a frail figure in the darkening room.

Leah stood up, dropping the glass pieces into a pile on a remaining chair. Leah's mother went up to Lev, clutching his sleeve. "Do you think you could get our things back? They even took his *kapote*, the long black frock coat he always wears to *Shabbos*." She was tiny, enfolded in dark wool, her little pale face sticking out of the cloth.

Leah sighed. "Mother, he knows what a *kapote* is. You don't have to explain everything to him."

"How do I know what he knows?" She eyed Lev, his clean-shaven face, his German uniform, his head uncovered, provoking God. At least this is what Lev thought she saw: an anesthetized Jew, scrubbed of any hint that he shared their history.

"It's better not to know what these meaningless things mean," Geza muttered, touching his cut again, this time out of curiosity. His mother pulled his hand away from his face. He shrugged her off and strode over to the broken window. After contemplating the silent streets, he stuffed a rag through the jagged hole. "And there's nowhere to sit now."

Leah's father pointed to the wooden benches jammed up against the walls. He spoke softly but with deliberation. "God has provided us with a place to sit and to sleep."

Still gazing at the windswept streets, Geza said in a low voice, "But we built those benches into the walls for this precise purpose, when inevitably, every year and sometimes twice, we are robbed of all our belongings and have to sleep and eat on benches until we can afford to buy back our things, for double." He fingered his wound, which made Lev wince, thinking how it was only getting dirtier and should be cleaned immediately, with soap and water, then dressed. He would return later tonight, after pilfering gauze and soap from the medical ward.

The rabbi closed his eyes and murmured something indecipherable, holding one arm out while he lowered himself onto a wooden bench.

"Geza, please," Leah sighed, motioning to her father. "At least we are still here, together."

Geza reluctantly left his post by the window, pulling the rag out of the broken pane as he stepped away. Lev could tell how he thought blocking the wind with a rag was futile given this barren room with no candles or forks, the floors stripped bare of rugs, the trunks overturned and emptied of shawls and shirts.

Geza slapped the rag against his thigh. "I'm going to fetch water from the river. Then we'll have tea."

His mother protested; the streets were still empty. She told him to wait until more people came out, until it was safe.

"Safe?" His breath stood in the still air. He charged through the front door, grabbing the bucket as he left.

They held their breath, watching him stride across the street, kicking at the bluish snow, until his form receded, blending into the black trees. Lev stood behind Leah, inhaling her hair, the scent of a river after it has rained. The rabbi had fallen asleep, and his snoring, akin to the sound of a failing engine, filled the room. Lev quickly squeezed Leah's hand, and then he turned around, addressing Geza's mother and grandmother, who hunched despairingly on the one rug the villagers had left behind.

"I'm going to fetch some supplies to treat that wound of his. Don't worry—it only needs cleaning, a few stitches."

. . .

A few hours later, Lev sat with Leah and her family on cushions borrowed from a neighbor, drinking hot elderflower tea, their faces illuminated by candlelight as they dipped pieces of bread into a pot of honey Leah's mother had managed to hide. On the wall, the glass paraffin lamp that usually gave light was shattered. Leah pinched a bit of salt onto Lev's bread, as if she were serving him at a proper table. Leah's mother had filled empty glass bottles with hot water from the samovar, corked them, and then wrapped them in rags to use as hand and foot warmers. "At least," her mother said after a long silence in which the only sounds were the ones of eating and drinking, "we are warm and we are eating."

Geza chewed his bread awkwardly because of his cut. Lev had cleaned and dressed the wound, but it would scar. When he mentioned this, Geza burst out, "It will look as if I've fought in a duel."

"Jews don't fight duels," Leah retorted, lightly leaning her arm into Lev's, as if she didn't notice this small intimacy, an intimacy that brought to mind her naked limbs and bare torso melting into his own nakedness. He chewed on the bread.

"Jews didn't fight in duels because they were not thought honorable enough to participate," Lev said.

Geza sipped his tea pensively, leaning toward the flickering candle. His eyes fixed on Lev. "In Berlin, I bet Jews fight duels all the time. Did you ever fight in one?"

Leah cut in to say it was impolite to ask such questions, and her mother muttered, "Who would want to tempt God in that way? There are already too many ways to die." Leah's sister, with her brown liquid eyes, sat there silently, watching her son.

Lev rocked to and fro, as if to reposition himself, but he only wanted to brush against Leah's arm again. As he did this, he said, "I fought in a duel, at one of the fraternities."

Geza ravenously chewed on his bread. "And what happened? Did you win? Do you have a scar somewhere?"

The rabbi interjected, his voice thin and wary, "Goyim *naches*. The games goys play. And I am unimpressed with your new muscle-Jew. Is it he who is supposed to rebuild the holy land, in Palestine?"

Geza kept looking at Lev, as if they were coconspirators. "Scholars hunched over the Talmud, what have they done?"

"You can't build a road to the Sabbath." The old man closed his eyes and nodded to himself. The candle was burning down. Soon they would all be sitting in the dark.

"After the war, I'm going to Palestine." Geza took in the surroundings, as if impressing upon his memory the mud-packed floor and the broken lamp, the smashed windowpane and the hard benches, because one day, when picking tomatoes in the dusty heat, he would remember this small, dilapidated place.

The old man opened his eyes, and within his dark pupils, Lev saw a flare of anger. "I'd sooner see you go to Spain, the land of the curse. But the *cherem,* the curse, will end. At least in Spain there are God-fearing Christians, and wherever there are religious people, Jews can live too."

They went back and forth like this, debating, and the women listened, and Lev took the opportunity to offer Leah his bottle warmer, their fingertips touching.

"Won't you be cold?" she asked, nestling his bottle warmer into her armpit, drawing it up against her breast. He stared at where she had put the bottle, wishing it was his own hand pressed there. He didn't notice Geza asking about Berlin again.

Leah looked away, suppressing a faint smile.

Geza persisted, "And what about the streetlamps? Are there no more lamplighters?"

Lev said the streets were so bright you could read a newspaper while walking to dinner. "Electric lights," he added, pulling out a cigarette, offering one to Geza. Geza took it and then asked about the motorcar, the subway, the gramophone. Did he own one? What music did it play? In between Geza's questions, Leah's mother took the opportunity to ask Lev if he was blessed with any children. When he said their ages, seven and nine, his throat thickened. He answered these questions about his life carefully, feeling Leah's eyes on him, wondering if he hurt her by talking like this, wondering if the names of his children and the name of his wife uttered in this dark room sounded unnecessarily cruel after how he had touched her wrist, offered her his bottle warmer, been inside her repeatedly.

While Leah's mother gleaned information about him, Geza argued with his grandfather. "But in the west, there's even legal protection against pogroms. Jews can become government ministers. Viceroys!"

Samuel stroked his beard. "I fail to see the appeal in the house-trained animality of the western Jew—his feigned civility, his adopted customs, his so-called gentility and rich furnishings. A mere mimic of his persecutors."

Geza grinned. "You used to have a picture of Moses Montefiore hanging on the wall, before it was stolen."

Leah's mother poured more tea into their glasses, stirring the elder-flower petals first.

Geza continued, his large hands spread over each knee. "Monte-fiore dined with the king of England. What of that?"

Samuel mumbled into his tea, "Montefiore is an exceptional case. And he never forgot his people."

Leah began, "When Adi came back . . ."

Leah's mother added, "My brother."

Leah fixed her eyes on Geza. "Adi was taken away by the Russian army at fourteen, and twenty years later, when he returned here as a lieutenant general, there wasn't a trace of his Jewishness left." She paused, pressing a small piece of bread between her thumb and index finger. "Even though he cried on his mother's grave and wished he had never been taken from his home, everyone disowned him."

Leah's mother stared into the flickering light and said it was a terrible thing, taking young boys away from their homes and converting them in the army. After this, they fell silent. Geza glared moodily at Leah and his grandmother, as if it were their fault Adi could not come home.

That night, falling asleep in his cot, Lev thought about the songs Leah and her family sang before the light died out entirely and how his cheeks had burned because he did not know any of the words and he had tried to appear as if he knew some of the songs, but it was all foreign. Leah had started the singing as a way to ease Geza's dark mood, and

soon they were all singing their hearts out. Lev winced at such
ness, but he also wanted to sing freely, without feeling fraudulei
time he had opened his mouth and hummed along, he felt ashar
he also felt ashamed remaining silent. It was no use. He wondered if
Leah had noticed how stonily he'd sat beside her rolling voice, which
sounded as open as the sky. And then he revisited Josephine's most
recent letter, opened this afternoon, and how she had mentioned, in
between a story about Vicki's stubbornness and the decorations needed
for the soldiers' Christmas pageant, how the members of Granny's sis-
terhood had decided to boycott Jewish businesses. But Frau Schiller
had just sent quite a generous basket of fruit, bread, and cheese for the
soldiers at the station. *You know Frau Schiller, she lives on Alte Bahnhof-
strasse. We do a lot of shopping at Schillers and we will continue to do so.* It
was a strange way to end the letter; did she want him to feel reassured
that at least she was not boycotting Jewish shops? Or was she trying to
say how Schillers would be the exception to the rule, because there were
good Jews and bad Jews, just as some cuts of meat were better than others? And then he drifted back to his last conservation with Leah, after
all the songs had been sung. She had walked him to the door while the
rest of the family still sat on cushions, talking about which goyim might
be wearing their coats and hats by now.

Leah's mother raised her voice. "Tomorrow that dirty peasant Tola
will be wearing my woolen shawl. She'll be smugly selling apples, and
when I pass by, she won't even feel a prick of shame."

On the doorstep, Leah took Lev's hand in hers—he felt the softness
in the middle of her palm, the slight roughness of her fingers—and she
started talking about how, when spring came, she would take him to see
the going of the ice. She drew closer, her voice low, describing how the
river would first break in one place and then the cracks would spread
over the surface. Huge blocks of blue-green ice then floated down the
river, taking along small trees, even once a dog. "And before you know
it, it's summer," she whispered, pressing his hand into hers, "and the
acacia trees bloom sweet flowers, eight blossoms on each leaf. And the
chestnut trees, with their creamy white flowers, so soft and fragrant
you'll want to run your cheek against them. And in the heat, the dust

from the roads sticks to your skin, making it look brownish gray. But then we'll swim and wash it all away." A sharp wind blew through them, and Lev wetly kissed her chapped knuckles and said yes with his eyes, yes, summer would come, and they would swim and sit together under trees, and he would feel her milky white body under his.

The electric streetlamps, the color of Josephine's hair, the sound of his children's voices, and even the war, faded away. She was the only real thing to him.

12

By the end of July 1918, Lev and the rest of the men heard the German advance on the Marne River had failed. They cursed Ferdinand Foch, the victorious Allied commander, they cursed the Americans, and they cursed Ludendorff, who had spoken so highly of the spring and summer offensives, promising they would push through the Hindenburg Line and win the war. By March, men under thirty-five were sent west to replace the wounded and the killed there. When collected for the transports to the Western Front, they chalked on the wagons: *Cattle for Slaughter in Flanders* and *Criminals from the East.*

Late into the night, with his usual audience in attendance at the barracks, Otto opined on the power of the February Revolution worming its way into the hearts of German soldiers. He'd heard that along the quieter stretches of the Eastern Front, Russians and Germans fraternized, and German units began to imitate Russian revolutionaries by organizing a soviet, forming councils to criticize the officers, thinking they had the upper hand, or should have it. Otto cleared his throat. "Mother Russia will overtake us."

Someone snickered.

Lev said, his legs dangling from the cot, "But we don't notice, too busy leaning over our maps, calculating the distance from here to Germany."

A few men sipped their beer.

Otto kicked a chair out of the way, his hands gesticulating.

Lev drew in a breath, preparing himself for one of Otto's monologues, which never failed to entertain and embolden.

Otto's voice thundered, "Here we sit, susceptible to various dangers, both known and unknown, as this eastern wilderness encroaches, gaining strength and power over us, many of whom are rear-guard troops, too old, weak, or injured to put up a real fight. The best we can offer is watch duty, or office work. And the moment we're shipped west, we'll die at the hands of the French or the English, I promise you." The men nodded, heavy with liquor, their breath sour.

"Remember Melsbach," someone called out. A general chorus of agreement rose up. Melsbach had proclaimed himself a Lithuanian. He fell in love with Domizella, a village girl, and he said returning to Germany meant spiritual death. Two days earlier, he had packed his bags and shot himself in the woods. And then there was the translator, Seidel, the only one able to write in White Ruthenian, who'd slowly, over time, fashioned himself into a White Ruthenian, conversing with local pastors, delving into their native history and songs, which he published in Ober Ost's bulletin. "His Germanness disintegrated," Otto said, his tone both severe and mocking, "and he's been singled out as a traitor with double loyalties. His activity has become"—Otto paused for dramatic effect—"difficult to manage."

Lev sighed, thinking how poor Seidel had lost his grip on the world. As if I have any sense, Lev thought, a twinge of cold irony washing over him. He was actually worse off than Seidel—at least Seidel knew what he wanted, whereas Lev suffered as if living under a death sentence, the days dwindling down, one by one, to when he would abandon this place. He dreaded it, passively waiting yet tormented by the thought of leaving Leah. To return to what? An unknown wife and unknown children. His wife would pretend to love him again, and he would go along with the pretending because what else could he do? But he felt sure they would be strangers. And as he grew more and more entangled with Leah and her family, he traced and retraced Josephine's negative qualities, as if this justified his desire for Leah and their fantasies of marrying and moving away . . . to Palestine, or some other eternally warm place. Leah often joked about how he could sell textiles there just as he'd done in Berlin. Sometimes, he went along with the fantasy, adding that he would grow a beard. She would run her hand along his clean-shaven cheek and say, "A beard would suit you."

But then he held Leah's hands, squeezing them. "My children."

And Leah would suddenly stop talking, her whole face flushed with embarrassment. "Of course not. I was only dreaming." Then she would touch her abdomen because she knew how it felt, to lose children.

But when Lev sat with Leah and her family at their dinner table, they discussed the preparations for Altke's wedding, whether the rabbi would lose his voice again—his vocal chords were quite fragile, due to mysterious lesions; and remember, Leah's mother said worriedly, the raspy way he read the Torah portion last Saturday? Amid all this, Lev revisited Josephine's frigidity, her superficial letters that told nothing of her feelings for him, her obsessive cleanliness and banal dinner chatter, and her family, who had always hated him.

Yes, Josephine really was a cold unfeeling wife, or rather, Lev chose only to remember the times when she had acted as such. Fashioning Josephine into this kind of woman made it easier to meet Leah in the deserted hayloft, his heart singing when he saw the red string on the birch branch, readying himself to touch her soft unfolding body. Because Josephine was a supercilious gentile who refused his advances with countless excuses: migraines, stomach cramps, seasonal allergies. "Which is grounds for divorce," Leah often reminded him.

"Well, yes," Lev said, "in Jewish law, this is true."

"Is there any other law?" she asked, a slight smile on her lips because she knew Lev came from a place where Jewish laws appeared antiquated, arbitrary. Perhaps even meaningless.

But then Lev, feeling a sudden onslaught of guilt, would rejoin, "We were not such a good match. I shouldn't blame her for everything."

And Leah, sensing it more beneficial to appear generous to this phantom of a wife, replied, "Poor matches are poor matches. We shouldn't blame anyone for it."

"No, we shouldn't," Lev would repeat, and then, as if they had washed off his guilt together, he would touch her body slowly, starting at the nape of her neck, uncoiling her beautiful black braid, his palms cupping her gently rounded shoulders, her full smooth breasts, and the swell of her abdomen and the curve of her hips all fell under his command, as if he was molding her from clay.

He marveled at the wet darkness of her sex, how liquid and open she felt, even when he only brushed her there with his fingers. Even when his hand just rested there, dark heat radiated from her coarse hair. When he straddled her, she gazed up at him with an open guileless expression and guided his fingers into her mouth, the same fingers that had only seconds before been inside her, and she sucked on his dirty fingers with an air of contentment he did not think possible. With this small gesture, she made her desire so explicitly understood that he dove into her with such force she emitted a yelp of surprise. To reassure him it was pleasure and not pain she felt, she folded her legs around his waist, her thighs open and yielding. Lev watched in disbelief when her eyelids fluttered closed, her body tense and attuned to his smallest movements as she frantically clutched his chest, his shoulders, sighing and heaving and twisting as if he was tormenting her, but when he asked in a whisper if he should stop, she shook her head violently and pleaded, "Don't. Stop."

Worried and mystified, he obeyed. Suddenly, at what seemed a crucial moment, her back arched and her limbs trembled, as if she hovered over a dark precipice, and some untrammeled force swallowed her whole. After a few suspended moments—Lev watched her intently; her face contorted, her breathing grew shallow, and she made sounds that reminded him of a small wounded animal—she collapsed, turned her head to the side, and smiled. Then she whispered, somewhat ruefully, "Thank you."

When Lev asked Leah about this, she shrugged and said the act of orgasm was as necessary for women as it was for men. She added it was healthy and good for the complexion, as if it was just one more feat the body could perform. Then she planted a perfunctory kiss on his amazed forehead and began braiding her lustrous hair back into its tame plait.

Though it had happened many times since, her body's extreme reaction still took Lev by surprise because he had never seen a woman behave this way. Before Josephine, he knew a few girls, Jewish girls from his old neighborhood who let him kiss and fondle them, but when he forayed under their stockings and petticoat layers, they merely laughed, throwing back their long necks, because the idea of sexual relations before a marriage promise was unthinkable. "Oh Lev," he remembered Eva Bauer saying halfheartedly, her young face flushed with excitement, "you don't really care about painting my portrait after all!" When he called on her again, she gave no reply. So at sixteen, he surrendered to what many other young men did and went to a prostitute. She was old, nearly thirty, with dark hair and startling white skin. Coarse black hairs encircled her nipples, and it disgusted him, but in the end, he managed, despite the way she stared at him blankly, her lips curved into a half smile. He had believed the female orgasm was some mythological state, some exaggerated tale men attributed to certain women who were anatomically gifted or oversexed, but now that he experienced it on a regular basis with Leah, who was just a country woman, who sold maize at the market and lovingly ran her fingers through his hair, who told stories of village gossip, Josephine grew into even more of an oddity. In his mind's eye, Josephine's face turned paler, anemic, and withered down to brittle bone whereas Leah's body grew more and more luxuriant, hot to the touch.

With summer ending, Lev noticed how the other soldiers grew restless. They sang songs about unmarked graves awaiting them in the Russian forests, about the Bolsheviks cutting their throats in retaliation for the harsh terms of the Brest-Litovsk Treaty, about being sent off to the Western Front in their already broken state, too weak or too old to fight the French. Lev listened to these songs at night in his cot, contemplating the blue smoke of his cigarette as it traveled up into the air. He did not sing along because the sound of his voice embarrassed him. He was content to listen in the darkness. In this way, he could be in agreement with their despair, while at the same time he inwardly criticized their flair for the dramatic, how they shouted and moaned over imminent death, when this had always been the case. Sometimes at night, when everyone was singing and drinking, Otto would come up to Lev's bunk and rest his chin on the mattress. He'd whisper that their only option was desertion. "During the train ride through Germany, we jump off"—his two fingers galloped along the edge of Lev's cot—"and home we'll be."

"We'll die doing it."

Otto grinned. "We'll die if we don't do it." He propped his lit cigarette on Lev's boot. "Two thousand men due for transport mutinied in
Kharkov."

Lev rested on his elbows. "The other option is we stay here." He
resisted adding how he had thought of it many times, beginning a new
life with Leah. But the impossibility of this had recently been cemented
by a piece of recent news: Leah's husband was not dead. She had long
believed he'd died in the Carpathian Mountains, in the winter of 1915,
near the Polish town of Tarnów. That had been the story told by Altke's
fiancé, Slotnik, whose brother Misha had served in the infantry division with Leah's husband against the Austro-Hungarian army. According to Misha, Leah's husband had slipped and fallen to his death while
they advanced across the rocky peaks. But Misha famously exaggerated
facts, and the veracity of his letter had been brought into question by a
recent sighting. The pharmacist's wife had a cousin in Novgorod who
saw Leah's husband drinking in a tavern with some officers of the Red
Army. Apparently he had defected from the czarist army and was now
with the Reds, as most of the peasants were. He looked alive and well,
his eyes flashing as they always had, his reddish hair rakish and long,
flowing from under his army cap. The cousin wrote that he was drunk
and cursing, toasting to the new Russia with his comrades. The cousin
believed he would return home soon, to Mitau, because the war was
ending and Russia was now a free state.

After the pharmacist's wife had read this letter, she ran with unprec-
edented speed to Leah's house, the letter clenched in her sweaty hand.
No matter it was early evening, and Leah and her family were just settling down for dinner. When she burst through the door, her shrill voice,
in a mixture of triumph and panic, announced that Leah's husband was
coming home. This had occurred five days ago, and since then, Leah
existed in a state of high agitation. She asked Lev the same questions
over and over again: How did the cousin know it was Zalman for sure?
Many Russians had red hair—he couldn't possibly base his evidence on
this. And Zalman did not enjoy drinking, another reason why the cousin
might be wrong. And what about Misha's letter? Although Misha did

not actually see Zalman die with his own eyes, the timing of Misha's letter was precisely when Zalman's letters stopped arriving, indicating Zalman's death. How could such timing be mere coincidence? But the last question, which continuously haunted her, was this: How could she have felt so sure of his death and now be wrong? She repeated, as if in a trance, "In dreams, I saw the Angel of Death myself, and he told me Zalman died along the mountain range, that snowy November."

When Leah consulted her father on this, as he was a Talmudic scholar, he recalled such a passage in the Gemara about the Angel of Death making a mistake. The rebbe drew a labored sigh and explained that in the story heard by Rabbi Bibi bar Abaye, who was often visited by the Angel of Death, a nurse by the name of Miriam had mistakenly been taken instead of a hairdresser by the same name. So the nurse was brought back and exchanged for the hairdresser. Then the rebbe brought the tips of his slender bluish fingers together and shrugged, indicating this must be the case with Zalman.

Amid her fretting and worrying, Leah revealed a few details about her husband, details Lev greedily collected regarding her former life. Zalman had fiendishly red hair and green eyes as narrow as those of a fox. He was bowlegged and he suffered from indigestion. His feet sported painful bunions, and she often had to massage almond oil into the big red lumps. Days passed, sometimes weeks, when he refused to get out of bed. When Lev asked why, Leah said that melancholia, a black bile, would seize him. She had tried everything to help him, even laying tefillin on his weaker arm as a reminder of God's holy words, which was said to relieve those in his condition, but the only remedy was time passing. After ten days, he would sunnily jump out of bed as if nothing had happened and resume his work at the tannery. But Leah knew it was only a matter of time until it would happen again. Just before the war, the periods between his bouts of melancholy grew shorter and shorter. She feared that soon the darkness would eclipse him. "It's because I couldn't give him a child. At least that's what he always said. He said he was stuck with a barren woman for a wife, the worst kind of luck. Then he would laugh bitterly about never having a son to call his own." When she explained this, her eyes welled up, and she appeared weaker, more breakable, as if her bones had instantaneously thinned. "He accused me of withholding this precious thing from him—a child—as if I meant to do so. As if I did not suffer as much as he suffered. As if it was a contest of suffering and he always the victor." And then she broke into long inconsolable sobs. Lev held her in his arms, felt her quaking body, and so badly wanted to rescue her from this Zalman, this fiendish red-haired demon who was surely riding back to Mitau within the fortnight, licking his lips, anticipating a triumphant return full of carnage and bloody revenge in which he would kill, with the help of his comrades, White Russians, Germans, Austrians, shifty landowners, disloyal peasants, anarchists from the Black Army, and anyone else who stood in his way. Lev couldn't help imagining Zalman's face: the green slanted eyes, the unshaven beard, the pointy chin and greasy hairline, the flecks of blood that peppered his cheekbones from some recent pillaging.

Otto shook the metal bedpost, which momentarily dissipated the image of Zalman's bloodthirsty smile. "Lev—are you listening? If we stay here, we'll only get slaughtered by the Reds." Then he added, "The Bolsheviks have begun their advance, attacking our positions at Narva, northeast of here."

"Yes, I heard that," Lev said, rubbing his eyes.

"Where did you hear this? I thought it was only a rumor."

Lev tensed at the uncharacteristic alarm in Otto's voice. "Yesterday, in the officers' mess hall." He waited for Otto to ask what he'd been doing there—and he would probably tell him the truth. He'd been stealing provisions for Leah and her family because they were slowly starving. All the locals were, whereas the officers let food rot and crops go bad while they drank their coffee and cognac, the surplus evident on their well-fed faces and in their wide girths.

Otto stubbed out his cigarette against the bottom of Lev's boot. He came closer to Lev, and Lev noticed the sweat on his brow, the ingrown hairs of his beard, how his eyes narrowed. Again, Lev was reminded of Zalman. He shook his head, as if to shake off the menacing apparition of this imaginary face that he himself had created.

Otto whispered, "Officers are deserting their troops in the north, fleeing for Germany. And men are burning their uniforms, selling off military horses, selling anything they can get their hands on."

Lev inhaled the strong scent of schnapps from Otto's breath, debating whether or not he should tell him about Reval, the German base on the Gulf of Finland. The soldiers there had sold off nearly all the seaplanes and gasoline they had been guarding.

Otto palmed Lev a few damp cigarettes, and before departing, he again galloped two fingers along the edge of Lev's cot.

Lev tried to sleep to the sound of other men's breathing and tried to concern himself with what they would do if the treaty was annulled and the Reds returned or if they were transported west, but he only thought of Leah. He wanted to know what she was thinking at every moment, what she was doing now. He imagined she might be washing her feet in the kitchen, in the bucket filled with hot water and mint leaves, or she might be helping her sister with the wedding preparations, taking preserves out of the cellar and choosing the best ones for the feast. Or she might be braiding her wet hair into a thick plait, as she often did after a bath, so it didn't get in the way, only to wait for Lev to unravel it. The dampness of her hair through his fingers, the smell of bark in the strands, the feel of her cool neck under his palm—it had been five days since they'd met at the barn. Five eternal days! Yesterday he waited for her behind the abandoned farmhouse, but she never came, too upset, he assumed, by the recent news. But because of the red ribbon fluttering in the warm wind, he waited in the dusty heat, smoking, unable to tear himself away from the post lest she arrive at the last minute, out of breath, full of apologies. The agony of the wait would make their reunion even sweeter as he anticipated the run of his tongue through her mouth, the way she clung to him and whispered affectionate nicknames into his neck. He turned onto his side, his face to the wall, moving his hand under his drawers. Another man, a few cots over, sighed and grunted an ejaculatory grunt. Someone else swore in his sleep, banging his leg against the iron cot rail. Lev closed his eyes, seeing the shape and swell of her breasts, tasting the taste of her—a mix of sweat and wheat.

That night Lev suffered from dark swirling dreams. Zalman returned to Mitau in the form of a satyr; his red beard flowed down to his groin, and he pranced the cobblestoned streets on hooved feet, the sound of which echoed through each and every house. When Zalman found Leah, he dragged her by the hair through the apple orchards. He dragged her and she screamed and screamed, crying for Lev. When Lev heard her screams, he followed the distant sounds, but he could not find her. Every street abruptly ended in a stone wall littered with garbage. Every forest empty of Leah. He could only hear her cries and follow them, as if Zalman demonically led him into some dark trap. When Lev woke, sweat soaked the front of his shirt. He rubbed his eyes and touched the thin sheet and felt his arms. The reassurance that he was physically here, in his army cot among sleeping comrades, did nothing to smooth out the sharp terror spreading through him, as if someone had injected the remnants of that poisonous dream into his veins.

The following Thursday, Leah's sister, Altke, got married—the marriage had to take place on a Thursday because widows always remarried on Thursdays. Her husband had been dead more than seven years, and everyone agreed she was still a young woman, despite her limp. Zlotnik, short, with a patchy beard, and lacking in Talmudic scholarship, had courted her not only because she came from a respected family, but because she had already borne a son, Geza, her fertility proven. Lev's presence at the wedding went unquestioned. He had become part son, part brother, and in terms of Leah, part husband to the family, and they accepted him without ever saying so. They invited him to Sabbath meals, asked after his health, mended his clothes, and overlooked the fact that Leah had fallen in love with him. Lev had often taken Geza shooting for birds, and on these long walks, Geza told him about leaving Mitau, about the girls he liked, about how he couldn't care less for his studies because none of it would matter soon, despite what his grandfather thought. When Lev asked him about Leah's husband, Geza would shrug and politely say he did not remember much. Leah's mother would even go so far as to criticize Zalman. She complained that he had picked his teeth after meals, having the manners of a farm animal, and that he did not bathe properly, until Leah would interrupt and say, "Do not speak ill of the dead." To Lev, these were wonderful words, the way she had assumed his death so easily, as if he had been dead many years when now he might return any day.

Lev walked behind the groom's party as they made their way to the bride's home, trailed by musicians playing a mournful waltz. The sun sat low and heavy in the trees. People had locked up early. A few stragglers hurried out of the public bathhouse, their cheeks rosy from the steam. Candles blazed in the windows overlooking the alleys, lanes, and streets leading to the *schulhof,* where the wedding canopy stood, draped in white muslin that rose and fell with the breeze. Water carriers and the poor stationed themselves along the road for the wedding procession. Zlotnik, nervous and dazed, sported a smudge of black ash on his forehead, a reminder of the Temple's destruction. Lev blended into the families that poured out of houses, dressed in their finest clothing, and yet he imagined he was the one getting married, anticipating the sight of Leah veiled in white. The pressing throng irritated him; a man stepped on his heel and a small child clung to his pant leg, peering up at him with a runny nose before realizing Lev was not his father. An old woman said something to him he didn't understand. She smiled, toothless.

Last night Otto had told him they would be transported west in two days, but no one knew for sure. Lev tried to imagine telling Leah this, but all the possible combinations of words and sentences sounded callous.

The melody of the *klezmorim* swelled to a frenzied pitch as the procession neared Leah's house, and in front of the house, Altke awkwardly sat on an elaborately decorated chair positioned on top of an upside-down trough covered with a brightly woven rug. Lev heard a woman whisper, "She looks like a horse." Another woman agreed, and added that her jaw was too big for her face, her hair had the same coarseness as a horse's tail. Altke gazed out at the crowd, her liquid eyes listless and uncomprehending. "She has a limp," someone added, his hot breath sweeping over Lev's neck. "I saw her walking fine," a man countered.

Lev strained to see Leah, who stood with a group of women behind the trough. He only saw her dark hair catching the sun and the green silk scarf fluttering around her face. The man added, "Her sister's the real beauty."

The rabbi's voice rose above the din. He placed his hands on Altke's head. "May God make thee as Sarah, Rachel, Leah, and Rebecca who built the House of Israel." Then Zlotnik stumbled forward, pushed from the crowd, and lowered the veil over Altke's face. A few people snickered. Leah's eyes laughed, chastising the clumsy Zlotnik, and her gaze drifted over to Lev. He still caught the laughter on her face, but when their eyes met, her smile faded into a more serious and meaningful look. He knew what she was thinking: that he should be the one lowering the veil over her face, and then they would walk at the head of the procession toward the shul with men carrying burning torches and women holding lit candles trailing them across the sprawling market square, past the beggars and the water carriers with their buckets ready to receive the good luck coins people tossed into the water. As he held Leah's hand, they would feel the gentle pelting of wheat kernels women threw at bridal couples for fertility and health. And the old and the sick, too weak to walk, would stand on stoops as they passed, holding a pair of doves, ready for release.

Someone handed Lev a torch. He held it away from his chest, and the flickering heat made his eyes sting. Following the procession to the shul, he saw Leah's head bobbing up and down. She spoke with a woman he did not recognize, a woman who seemed coarse and matronly. These minutes she spent with someone superfluous, when here he was, only a few paces away. But this is her life, he thought, rooted in many things that did not depend upon his presence. And didn't he want her to still have these things after he left? Yes, of course. And no, not at all. He wanted her to pine for him and cling to his memory so furiously that no man would come near her—not even Zalman. Especially not Zalman.

"Fools, they still believe in this kind of nonsense!"

Lev looked up, jolted by the crowing of an ancient woman perched on a stoop. She glanced at him, her eyes sharp and bright as if she'd overheard his selfish thoughts. After the wedding couple passed by, and she'd guffawed about the price of lace and silk, all that finery for foolish love, she muttered, "May God bless them."

Leah, suddenly at his side, touched his sleeve. Her hair was dangerously close to the flame of his torch. "Watch out," he said, more forcefully than he'd intended.

She laughed, infected by the general mood of the procession. People were talking all around them about Zlotnik, who now stood under the canopy waiting for the bride. He was a forlorn figure in his heavy gray suit, his eyes trained on his shiny shoes. Leah pointed to the fluttering of Altke's veil. Her parents led her to the canopy.

"She's almost married."

"Almost," Lev said, squeezing Leah's hand.

The rabbi intoned blessings. The red sun dipped behind the apple trees, the same apple trees where Lev had first seen Leah, among the same little huts constructed for Sukkot. It was September again, and the huts were up, just as he remembered them, fruit dangling from the thatched roofs, makeshift rugs over dirt floors, the feeling of coolness and reprieve inside. Leah's breath tunneled into his ear: *Ich liebe dich.* The glass smashed under Zlotnik's shoe. Everyone cheered and the music started, a demonic swirl. He touched his ear, unsure. It could have been the wind or her breath playing tricks, but his chest contracted. He looked at her. She was smiling and laughing again, the music humming through her body as she led him toward the stable attached to the shul where the main celebration took place. He marveled at her show of happiness, transforming her face into a mask of gaiety, erasing, for this one night, the circular discussions they'd had over the last few weeks about the return of Zalman and Lev's departure, the future foreboding and miserable to them both. She had cried so often she had trouble opening her eyes in the morning from the swelling. While Leah fixated on whether Zalman would really return and if he was really alive, Lev fixated on when Zalman would return and take her back as his wife. They quarreled over this. Lev wanted her to realize that most likely the letter from the pharmacist's cousin was true so she would be prepared for Zalman, whereas Leah still clung to the belief that somehow there had been a mistake, some misunderstanding, and in fact Zalman had died in the Carpathians.

Oddly, Leah reminded him of Josephine tonight, deceptive in her sparkle, adept at making others feel comfortable when she herself felt the most uncomfortable. But with Josephine, such a display of careless ease had irritated him because after the party ended and the guests left, she would continue the facade with such precise determination, such unbending resolution, he wanted to shake her.

Leah, even as she laughed and cajoled, gave Lev quick glances full of clouded doubt, and he would nod, because they were in this together. Even in her distressed state, Lev found her sadly luminous. Dark shadows hung around her eyes and her lips were dry and cracked, but it was a side of her, this fragility, he had rarely seen, and he felt a protective desire to fold away her troubles, to fold away the past and the future so they only knew the present. But he could only hold her smooth white hand and impress upon her, through their shared touch, that he loved her.

The stable had been cleaned for the wedding with yellow sand strewn on the floor. Strings of paper lanterns hung from the rafters, long tables were covered in coarse muslin, and on the tables waiting to be served: jellied calves feet, carrots with prunes, sauerkraut with red berries and pickles, cooked apples, tea and beer. Against the far wall, wooden planks on top of barrels served as a stage. Leah turned her head this way and that to talk to relatives who passed by while she held Lev's hand. She was his and also not his. He studied her face, the way her eyes lit up when her aunt said she looked beautiful. Leah frowned and said she had no use for beauty, but her aunt disagreed, saying beauty is never useless.

Lev thought about telling her what Otto had said, about leaving in two days, but why ruin this blessed night? He wanted her to have the chance to feel beautiful, even with her protestations, to dance and sing and laugh without the encroaching dread of their separation. He stood next to her warm light body and she almost made him forget, with her fluttering movements, how time was passing. How he would soon see Josephine, if he made it home. How he would resume his old life.

Leah guided him from one gathering of relatives to the next, always clutching his hand, their palms sweaty and intertwined. Old women appraised him knowingly. He avoided their glances, feeling ashamed, already imagining the gossip that would ensue after his departure. He knew these women well now, having overheard them talk of errant men in the marketplace, at the dinner table, on the street. *He left without a note, without a word. She's alone with the children, another's on the way, and winter's coming.* Yes, he heard them.

Lev closed his eyes, his jaw tensing. He had to tell Leah, but how? He looked at her searchingly. She smiled back, mistaking his look for the question of when they could safely slip away from the wedding party unnoticed.

"No one will miss us once the *badkhn* starts," Leah whispered. She tightened her grasp around his arm. A squirrelly man in baggy trousers, his linen shirt breathing open at the neck, clamored onto the stage accompanied by the yelling and cheering of guests. He bowed deeply to the crowd, an imperious smile on his lips. He began rummaging through the gifts stacked neatly in piles at the edge of the stage. He scratched his head and frowned. More laughter erupted. Lev looked at Leah, wondering what this was all about. She clapped her hands with the rest of them but when she felt Lev's eyes on her, she said, "He's the master of ceremonies. He announces each gift, commenting on the giver of the gift, and then shows it off to the audience." Lev wanted to say such a ritual seemed uncouth, embarrassing those who had not been able to afford enough, and vaunting those who had given richly. But the way she enjoyed the spectacle, her face flushed, stopped him. Yet he felt repelled by this little man who bellowed out that the fine silver kiddush cup was from the Mazurskies, "An illustrious and notable family I might add." The *badkhn* grinned, his teeth crowding his mouth. Next he frowned a clown's frown, holding up a tattered prayer book, letting the cover flap open to reveal yellowed pages. "Is this all that Boris Lachmann could afford? But how well he eats!"

Leah covered her face in her hands, her shoulders shaking with tremulous laughter. "It's true," she said between parted fingers. "He's so stingy."

Lev sipped his beer, wondering who Boris was and why everyone cared so much. A cool wave of condescension passed through him as he took in the revelers, how the men drank on one side of the room, shrouded in a cloud of smoke, the women on the other, their heads covered since their wedding day, the din of voices rising and falling, and the excited face of the *badkhn* as he held up an embroidered pillowcase, a candelabra, his scrawny arms gesticulating. He waved the next gift in the air, a gilded mirror that reflected the blurry faces of the guests, and asked in a falsetto voice, "What is love?"

Leah tugged on Lev's sleeve. "The light is dying."

Through the windows, the fiery sun backlit the branches of the apple trees. She motioned with her head toward the door.

They slipped out of the stable, beer-filled laughter trailing them. The air still held the day's heat, a heavy moist heat Lev could clench in his fist.

They heard the *badkhn*'s hearty voice as they walked farther into the trees toward the little huts. He asked again, raising his voice, "What is love?" and not waiting for a reply, he answered, "It is a small candle flickering on the mantel. Briefly, it leaves its mark. Then once again fades into the dark."

Lev motioned to a hut at the edge of the orchard. "Here is where I first saw you."

She blinked at the fading twilight. "Was it really here?"

"You don't remember?"

She buried her face in his sleeve. "I remember everything."

He breathed in her hair, pulling off her scarf. It fluttered in the warm wind.

She tried to reach for it but he held it up high.

She cupped his cheek. "Someone will see us."

"Who can see in the dark?"

"There are always eyes."

.   .   .

He led her into their hut, as he called it, but another family's rugs and plates had been left on the ground. A little salt dish stood in the corner along with some stale bread. Through the roof of pine branches, slices of night could be seen. Leah flicked her finger against a hanging lemon. Lev tried to take a bite out of an *etrog* but it hit his chin.

She sat down on the rug, staring up at him. "People will wonder where I am."

"With me, naturally." Lev twirled her green scarf above her head. She didn't say anything, and he noticed her eyes were wet. He bent down to his knees and straddled her. The heat of her body moved through her clothing, seeping into his. He thrust his pelvis into hers and fumbled with her difficult undergarments. She did not assist or protest. Her legs felt like lead in his hands. "After you leave," she began.

His heart bloomed into his throat. "After I leave, what?" he repeated roughly, instantly regretting it.

"Everyone will know I've been with you." She stared at the ground, her thick hair covering half her face. With the back of his hand, he brushed it aside like a curtain.

He ran his hands along her legs, and she softened, hugging his hips with her thighs. "How will they know?" But he already knew—the old women with their glances, the way people observed them. It was clear they were in love.

The night wind wafted through the thin wooden walls. She leaned back on her elbows, staring into his eyes. "And then—" She breathed in sharply. "What will happen to us?"

He felt his throat tighten. "In two days—" He stopped, trying to collect himself. "The Russians are coming back—Zalman is coming back. If I stay here, they'll kill me. If I go, I might make it."

She regarded him thoughtfully. "I know. I heard some of the other soldiers talking."

He touched her face. "Nonetheless, we have tonight. This moment. That's still something."

"Is it?" she murmured, staring down at the packed earth.

He moved his hand up her inner thigh, and rested his palm between her legs, feeling the softness there. She lay down, pulling him with her, and he undid his pants, raising up his hips for a brief moment. Partly it was a lie, what he had said about the immediacy of this moment and the uncertainty of their future, and partly true. True in the abstract sense, but they did not live in abstracts. Guiltily, he gripped the back of her neck and covered her mouth with his so she couldn't talk more of the future, unknowable as it was.

13

Two days after the wedding, Lev and Otto found themselves on a transport train heading west. All the young able men had been roused at five in the morning and told they were needed where the fighting counted. "Belgium, Brussels, France, we'll be slaughtered within hours," Otto said to no one in particular. The men around them dozed off, drank, played cards. They had been traveling for half a day, barely out of the dense forests. Otto had packed a spare change of civilian clothes, and Lev had done the same. They were prepared to burn their uniforms and rip up their identity cards, but they would wait until they reached Prussian soil to hurl themselves from the train onto some unknown stretch of land. This was their plan. Otto smoked fiendishly, his bloodshot eyes flashing at the slightest change in the train's movement. Lev asked about Antonina, trying to fend off the urge to talk about Leah. He knew if he did, he would sound sentimental, and Otto would say all women were the same, that what Lev felt was only an illusion. His eyes burned from the smoke and from the autumnal wind, which blew dirt and dust through the open windows. It stuck to his face, to the surface of his teeth.

Otto shrugged, studying his dirty fingernails. "Antonina wailed, begging me to take her. She didn't want to be left for dead, for the Reds to pick apart. Uncle watched from the corner and offered me a bottle of vodka. I have it here, if you want."

"Maybe later," Lev said, waving away a mosquito.

"Women," Otto mused, "they turn quickly. She played the czarina in the beginning, and now, my last image of her is with her hair strewn around her face, her eyes puffy from crying, her chest heaving. Well"—Otto unscrewed the vodka bottle—"what about your precious Leah?"

Lev motioned for the bottle. "She wanted me to stay and become a rebbe. Well, not quite that. But a tradesman, as if I hadn't left behind an entire family and profession in Berlin." He took a long sip, the astringent liquid burning. Talking about her in this way momentarily lifted the heaviness that filled his throat like a pile of stones so that every time he spoke it didn't sound like his voice.

Otto rubbed his eyes. "She was a simple woman."

Lev felt the urge to argue this point. Yes, she was in some ways simple. She wanted a child and she wanted his love. She worried about how long the food supply would last through winter, if the cows were sick, if her sister's typhus had healed, if the season would be harsh or gentle and when the ice would melt. She looked forward to summer, and when summer came, she walked barefoot, little particles of dirt collecting between her toes. She swam in the same river where she washed her clothing, the same river from which they drew water. She loved gossip and often whispered secrets to Lev about a cousin or an aunt, secrets that meant nothing to him, but it was a delight to hear the incredulity in her voice, the pleasure she took in the telling. But she was not simple when Lev tried to tell her about his life in Berlin. She would play with her hair and grow distracted, and after a few minutes, she would tell him to stop. She would say Berlin, a city she would never see, only made her less real to him. "And what is this? What am I?" she raised her voice, gripping the sleeves of her dress. He would comfort her, his embraces easily lapsing into lust, and then they forgot about Berlin, which is what she wanted in the first place.

Lev took another sip from the bottle. "She wasn't so simple."

Otto punched him in the arm. "When you see your Josephine, Leah will melt away." He made an obscene gesture with his hands, and Lev felt nauseated by Otto's thick fingers. But he didn't have the will to argue, knowing Otto would turn their private discussion into a public forum, enlisting the other sleepy men to debate the merits of monogamy, the futility of fidelity, if a man could live as happily with one lover as with another.

The lowering red sun shone on Otto's face, making him appear beastly. "You look like a devil," Lev said, flicking his cigarette butt out the window.

"And you look like a half-drowned water rat, with that patchy beard and the weight you've lost."

Lev touched his face, feeling the hollows under his eyes. He hadn't shaved because Leah preferred a beard, and all decorum had fallen away at the base. In the heat, the men strutted bare-chested, suspenders hanging down around their waists, their fatigue pants shredded and dirty.

Otto gripped his crotch. "Josephine won't recognize you."

Lev bit into a stale piece of bread.

Based on their calculations, tomorrow they would cross into Prussia, and then they would jump, positioning themselves as close to the German border as possible. But after this, a blank. Where would they burn their uniforms? Their papers? How would they avoid other units? If caught, they would be killed for desertion. Would they find shelter, food? They'd packed some tobacco, bread, rotten fruit, enough for a few days. After that? Otto's face, as he dozed off, his large head angled against the window, appeared unbothered, as if jumping off this train was merely a strategic detail. He had said, before closing his eyes, that the next days would be difficult, so better to sleep now. But Lev couldn't stop agonizing over each step of the plan: How does one jump from a speeding train? And seeing Josephine for the first time, his children, his house—would it all be there as he left it? Worst of all, Leah's expression when he'd told her he was definitely leaving hung before his eyes. The day after the wedding, they sat on cushions in the far corner of the room, while her mother yelled from the kitchen over the smell of burning bread, and Geza had just brought fresh water through the door, and the samovar emitted a shrill whine.

After he told her, she said flatly, "You're leaving because Germany has lost the war."

Lev shrugged, said he wasn't sure, but they needed men in the west, and Geza burst out, "I'm leaving too, once this is all over!"

Leah's mother walked into the room, holding Sezja the cat in her arms, massaging his gray fur. "What's this about you leaving us?"

"Yes," Lev said, resisting the urge to prevaricate, something he often did when a situation turned uncomfortable.

Leah asked hoarsely, "When exactly?"

He took her outside, behind the house, even though the back door was open and he knew her mother was listening, and probably Geza too. "Tomorrow morning, very early." He felt guilty, like she should punish him, but she only hugged him close, and little sobs escaped her mouth, little pockets of air filled with sorrow.

When Lev woke, the dawn carried an uncharacteristic coolness. The other men on the train slept soundly. If today was the day he would die, each surrounding detail assumed an enhanced meaning. A flock of crows lifted off the ground, circling fir trees. Black birds are a bad omen, Lev thought. A bluebird or a dove would have reassured him. Someone whistled a low melancholy tune, and it seemed the tune was his death knell. He started to sweat in his undershirt, and at the same time, he felt a chill sweeping through him. When they jumped, would he fall and break his bones? Or get shot in the back while running away? He rummaged in his front pocket for cigarettes. If he had an odd number of cigarettes left, a bad sign. Touching the tips of the cigarettes, he counted five. He shoved the pack deep into his pocket again.

They were the only ones awake at this hour, but Lev wondered if others were planning the same thing, feigning sleep, their muscles as tense and ready as his had been all night. Lev nudged Otto with his foot, tapping the face of his watch. Otto held up two fingers—two more hours. With a blanket folded around his shoulders, Otto unpacked the contents of his knapsack: a knife, two pairs of socks, tobacco, a pipe, the bottle of vodka, a comb, his civilian clothes, his identity papers, his rolled-up drawings, a pair of underwear. Otto instructed Lev to make sure his civilian clothes lay on top so he could easily change. At the bottom of his pack, a stack of Josephine's letters. On top of the letters, a loaf of bread Leah had baked before he left. The bread was wrapped in a white muslin cloth, embroidered with birds. "Something from home," she had said, because she couldn't read or write, only knowing how to account for a barrel of apples, a pint of pickles, or the price of coral beads by making a few marks in a ledger.

He touched the birds' wings, thinking how her nimble fingers had sewn together the strands of color.

Lev and Otto sat facing each other, their knees pulled up into their chests, their arms crossed over their legs. The sun rose steadily, heating the compartment. Otto assumed a stoic expression. Whenever they locked eyes, Otto would slowly nod but then look away, as if it were bad luck to hold Lev's gaze for too long.

Lev smoked a cigarette, ate a soft apple, examined his boots. He tapped his watch again. In response, Otto mouthed, *Soon.* With the sun beating down on the windows, and the other men stretching and standing up, they were close. Otto watched the passing landscape, his mind working, trying to estimate if they had gone far enough, or too far already.

He suddenly lunged forward, grasping Lev's arm. "I don't feel so well," Otto moaned, holding his stomach. No one paid much attention, despite Otto's performance. Together, they stumbled toward the exit door, which one had to slide forcibly open.

Lev clutched Otto's shoulder and in the other hand his knapsack.

Otto yelled, "Open the door—I have to vomit."

Lev pulled open the door. Otto threw his pack out the window, into the blur of fields and brown earth. And then he stepped off the train as casually as stepping out of a cab, feetfirst, his arms loose around his sides. Lev caught sight of two soldiers a few meters away, near the window. The one lighting a cigarette frowned and started to say something.

Lev jumped and yelled. The roar of the train swallowed up his voice. On either side of him, other deserters also dove into the blurry landscape, and it reminded Lev, for a split second, of relay races in the gymnasium pool, how he would sense in his peripheral vision the long lean white bodies of his schoolmates jumping into the water headfirst, arms outstretched and tense, all of them acutely aware of one another and yet intensely focused on their own success.

His knees hit earth. His elbows smarted. He scrambled upright, feeling the grains of dirt infiltrate the open cuts in his palms. Somehow, he still held his knapsack in one hand. The other hand fisted the air. Ahead of him, Otto zigzagged across the field. Lev's eyes watered, his ears filled with the sound of whizzing bullets. He ran toward Otto, bracing for the feeling of a bullet lodging itself into his flesh. Only once did Otto turn around, and when he saw Lev, he jerked his head toward a gathering of trees up ahead and cut across the field as quickly and smoothly as an animal in his natural habitat. Lev followed, running parallel. He didn't notice that the train had passed. He heard bullets even though there were none. He saw fir trees and Otto's thick neck. He couldn't even say for sure if he had been shot, his chest tight and burning, but he kept running for the coolness of the trees and the lone figure of Otto up ahead, hurling insults into the still morning air.

Over the course of a month, they made it back to Berlin. They burned their uniforms and identity papers in the forest. For a while, Otto and Lev crossed through the countryside with two other deserters. Boys, barely twenty, who were careless, smoking at night and shooting into the sky at inopportune times, although they occasionally caught fowl to roast over an open fire.

Otto was against them. "The greater our number, the greater our risk," he whispered to Lev after the boys had fallen asleep. Yes, the boys were senseless and scared. But if left alone, they would be captured and killed. Lev also knew Otto was right.

When they reached the banks of the Vistula River, Otto feigned a chest pain and told the boys to go ahead, promising they would catch up with them. "See you in a few days," Otto had said, waving his hand in the air, assuming his most paternalistic tone. The boys strode away into the blue-gray morning.

Lev and Otto waited half a day and took an alternate route. They slept in barns, taverns, fields, brothels. No one asked where they came from or where they were going. They only wanted to know if the war was over. "Germany is victorious," Otto would roar. This statement always yielded a free beer and a small plate of food. As Otto and Lev drank, each person recounted their own brand of suffering: burnt crops, dead sons, hungry children, a lover who had stopped writing months ago. When they spoke, they stared at Lev as if he held some secret knowledge. Where is my husband? When will the windowpanes stop vibrating from artillery fire? Is my son really dead? He tried to project a kindly expression even though his stomach growled and his fingernails hurt from the dirt packed underneath each nail, and a perpetual sheen of sweat bathed him despite the frigid mornings and nights. As he listened to these people recount their wartime grievances, their ugly mouths moving, the words senselessly pouring from their lips, Lev contemplated his own situation. He'd heard so many stories: Berlin had fallen to the Spartacists; armed workers had taken over the newspaper district as in Russia; Bavaria was now a free state; the Kaiser had fled to Holland; Germany had become a Socialist republic; the monarchy had been restored. And where was Josephine? His children? Had she managed to keep the house? He stroked his beard, which reminded him of how mangy he looked, like a stray dog. He feared Josephine would not recognize him or that she would not want to recognize him.

Otto and Lev made a pact—once they got to Berlin, they would part at Pariser Platz near the Brandenburg Gate. They had been prisoners of the Russians and they had escaped. "Feel free to elaborate," Otto joked. "Details make a lie more believable."

Otto repeated this when they approached Pariser Platz one morning in late November. After four years, Lev had imagined it would look changed, but the Adlon Hotel still stood grandly on the corner, and the pillars of the Brandenburg Gate rose up out of the wet morning, as formidable and massive as Lev remembered. Instead of the crisp blue sky and sharp sun and open faces of Berliners stringing garlands around his neck, as he had often imagined of his homecoming, the women wore black, their faces withered. Even the young ones appeared old and thin, staring down at the wet slick stones. When they did look up at him, disappointment filled their eyes, and he glanced away, ashamed somehow of returning to this cold and hungry place, as if he had singlehandedly lost the war. There were hardly any men around, but the few he did see hobbled across the square on makeshift crutches or begged on the busier street corners, shaking a worn hat. In the middle of the square, a contortionist balanced on his hands, his legs bent over his head, feet dangling around his ears. The chipped porcelain bowl in front of his mat stood empty of coins. Another young woman passed by who appeared far older than her years. She limped and stared at Lev contemptuously. Lev swallowed, terror spreading through him—what if she could tell he had deserted? What if she reported him? Was it evident by his civilian clothes?

He turned to Otto, who was finishing a cigarette. "Otto," he whispered. "Did you notice that woman?"

Otto flicked away his cigarette butt. "I don't like cripples. I know men who prefer them, a fetish of sorts, but I find it disgusting."

"No," Lev hissed. "I don't mean that. She looked at us strangely, as if she could tell we're deserters." He envisioned a firing squad and felt the softness of the black cloth they would use to blindfold him. He imagined shitting his pants right before the shot went off; he would die filthy and alone, and then his executioners would toss him into a communal grave.

Otto slung a bear arm around him. "Confidence, Lev. Confidence. Otherwise, every wayward glance, every slur or slip of the tongue will plague you and you'll lose your mind. Don't let it come to that."

The raw wind cut through his threadbare shirt, and Lev stuffed his hands into his pockets, clenching his fists. It started to rain. He shivered under Otto's weighty arm. "You're right. You're right."

Otto surveyed the now empty square. "Go home to that lovely wife of yours. And the child, Vicki."

"Yes, Vicki," Lev said, feeling his eyes well up. "And Franz," he added. What did they look like now? Would they recoil from him? His reflection appeared frightful in the store windows. A throbbing desire to see his children overtook him. He had survived and here he was, in Berlin, alive! Those faceless executioners would never catch him— there was no proof of desertion. His story would hold. Lev ran a hand through his dirty hair, sighing.

"Well," Lev began, thinking he should say something meaningful, something monumental. "Here we part."

They embraced.

"Thank you, brother," Otto murmured into Lev's ear.

"If I smell anything like you," Lev said with a laugh, "she'll never take me back."

Otto grinned. "Urine, sweat, beer—absolutely irresistible, I assure you."

Lev gripped Otto's shoulder; it felt massive under his hand. "Take care, my friend." He paused. "What are you going to do now?"

Otto stared pensively into the fog. "Maybe I'll go south. My brother lives there."

"Your brother?"

"Yes." Otto paused. "Do you have any brothers?"

"No."

Otto shrugged. "Strange."

Out of the corner of his eye, Lev thought he saw a bear. A man in a dark hat led the beast by a chain around its neck, a leather muzzle fixed to its mouth. A ragtag group of children, all shoeless, followed the brown bear. He walked on his hind legs with his paws flopping in front of him. The man, a gypsy, smiled sweetly. He held a tambourine but had no intention of using it.

Otto let out a labored sigh and nodded to Lev, casting him a glance that was both sentimental and savage, a look that summed up the whole of his personality.

Lev wanted to say something more, but he only saluted him and watched Otto cross the square. He wanted to see if he would go into the bar on the corner or if he would buy cigarettes first, but he couldn't stand here all day.

He made himself start walking in the direction of Charlottenburg. He might see her on the street, before even reaching the house. Many times he had constructed the scenario of their reunification: at home in the garden, a mild spring day, her hair loose and swimming over her shoulders. A moment alone, their lips brushing, his hand on her cool skin before the children rushed toward them. But already, it felt so different: the sky dark with clouds, the rain, she would be sitting inside by the window, the rose garden soaked and indifferent to his fantasy. He wasn't even in uniform. Straightaway, he would have to lie. Lie about how he left Mitau, lie about Leah and his life there. Another thing that hadn't entered into his homecoming until now: he was in love with Leah. He had tried to push away her image as they made their way back to Berlin. When he thought of her, he lost focus, stumbled over his words, made sloppy mistakes that Otto said would cost them their lives if repeated. "Stay focused and alert!" Otto had barked. "Don't think about the past," he had added, as if he knew what hummed inside of Lev. But now that he had survived—he was here, in Berlin!—his mind freely retrieved her image, and the sensations and details of their love affair bled into this old life, this old city, as if he had opened a familiar book, one he had read many times, and yet underneath the pages another story, the real one, sang beneath it, an intractable melody.

Down the main avenue, a streetcar approached, and he jumped onto the back of it, the way he used to when he was a boy. For an instant, he worried what the other passengers thought of him in his ragged state. *Confidence.* He mouthed the word, Otto's deep voice echoing in his head. A little girl stared at him from under her bonnet, but when he smiled, she pretended not to see him. She looked about nine—the same age as Vicki would be now! She held her white rabbit muff close to her chest, and faintly, Lev recalled giving Vicki a similar one attached to a silk cord that hung from her neck. The streetcar trundled down the main road running along the Tiergarten. Up ahead he could see the Zoological Garden, and his heart leapt at the sight of two disgruntled pandas munching leaves. Franz and Vicki loved the pandas. At least the pandas were still here. Hardly anyone strolled the park save for a few darkly clad figures, and Lev tried to remember what day it was, perhaps a Monday or a Tuesday when fewer people visited. The air, the trees, the stones all carried a bluish-gray tint, which would have depressed Lev if he didn't feel elated and nervous, revisiting each street corner, each signpost and archway that reminded him of another life. The stall where he often got flowers was shuttered, but that didn't prevent him from remembering how he purchased white gardenias for Josephine on Fridays from an elderly man who wore one thick-soled shoe to compensate for his shorter leg. Did Josephine still insist on Oriental lilies for the garden? Did she still prefer freshly cut tulips in the foyer? Were these luxuries still necessities or had the war changed her into a more sensible, frugal woman? He gripped the streetcar railing, gulping in the wet cold air, his mind racing—would she still be beautiful? Could he still love her? Had the Russians returned to Mitau? Had Leah's husband returned? Would Leah embrace Zalman, kiss his face, as if she still loved him? A stab of jealousy attacked him, unfair as it was. As he rode home to his wife, why did he begrudge Leah the same fate? Human nature. That's what Otto would say. After a man possesses a woman, he must ensure biological certainty; he needs to know that if there's a child, it's his. Hence his repugnance at the thought of Leah coupling with another man. All other emotions—jealousy, pain, obsession—were only symptomatic of the desire to secure paternity. Perhaps this simple biological explanation would make sense if Otto still stood next to him, hollering on about it, but alone with his thoughts, it broke down into a rubble heap. He returned to the image of Zalman reuniting with Leah. The roughness of his ginger beard against her perfect cheek. The plundering of her dark hair through his thick fingers. Her thighs spreading . . . he would have trouble breathing if he lingered too long here. His chest ached—he touched his heart. It seemed to contract, to recoil under his skin. He squeezed his eyes shut at the sound of Leah's shallow breath, warm on his neck when they made love, but now it would be Zalman's neck. Without warning, Lev doubled over the brass railing and retched into the moving street. Luckily, the piercing trolley bell signaling the next stop covered his guttural sounds, but the little girl in the bonnet saw.

At the next stop, Lev stumbled off. Leaning against a low brick wall, he gripped his knees, his knuckles white. *Not like this—I can't return like this.* Again, it was true; he would need focus and control for this next step as well. He stood up and breathed deeply, acknowledging the chestnut trees, their bare branches impervious to the wind.

Only a short distance more to the house.

Angrily, he pushed away the images of Leah. She's with her Zalman now, he thought, starting down the familiar route to his house. Enjoying him. Taking him into her arms. Into her bed. He inhaled the sharp air, his chest expanding, his stride more decisive.

Even though he knew his anger was false, and these images were counterfeit, he clung to his jealousy. It was the only way he could come home, without collapsing with rage, with grief, over what he had lost.

He started to run but then stopped and tried to maintain a steady pace. He didn't want to draw attention to himself. He broke into a run again. Two officers conferred in a doorway, and Lev suddenly called out, "I'm going home—I was in a Russian POW camp."

"Good for you," one of them said kindly. The other one nodded with approval. Lev grinned back stupidly, self-conscious of this blatant lie.

He slowed his pace again and hoped they were not still looking at him.

Two blocks away, he broke into a sweat. He leaned against a lamppost and touched his face. Would she still find him handsome? He had been unable to dislodge the dirt from under his fingernails. His hands looked ugly. A familiar woman strode past. The baker's wife? She wore a wide lace collar, a jovial smile. He smoothed down his hair, kept walking, his legs unsteady. The apartments and buildings appeared the same, the same brick and stone, the same ivy flowering on fences, the same corner where he used to turn left, the house in sight. Dirty snow covered the low gate enclosing the courtyard. The two windows facing the street on the upper floor were dark, the curtains drawn. He unlatched the gate and treaded into the courtyard. The blue door gleamed with its brass handle. Resting his hand on the door handle, he drew in a breath. Should he open it? Then he pushed down. Locked. Would he have to ring the bell to his own house? Just then he heard the back door to the kitchen open and saw Marthe shaking out a rug. She gazed into the gray morning, her face expressionless.

"Marthe," he whispered, breaking into a smile. Inside the house, he thought he heard the shrill vibration of a piano key landing on a high note. He imagined the admonishments of Josephine, who did not like the children to play with the piano. "A musical instrument is not a toy," she used to say, running her hand over the music stand where she kept sheet music.

Marthe inspected the rug, frowning. Lev wanted to speak to her before entering the house. This felt hugely important.

She saw him. "Herr Perlmutter," she gasped, dropping the rug.

"Hello, Marthe."

She bent down to retrieve the rug, but Lev stopped her, holding her shoulder for a moment. She took his hand. "When did you arrive?"

"Just now."

She nodded. "You look . . ." Her voice trailed off.

"Filthy. I know."

"We hadn't heard anything from you for the past two months." He tried to figure if her tone sounded accusatory or just worried. Or was she trying to tell him bad news?

He peered over her shoulder, through the half-open door to the kitchen. The walls were still that gray blue, because the color blue, he remembered Josephine saying, warded off flies. Nonsense, he had said. Flies are color-blind.

"Where is she?"

"Upstairs. Dressing."

"And the children?"

"In the nursery." Thank God they were safe in the nursery with the white miniature furniture, the floor of flower-patterned linoleum, the frieze on the walls depicting summer, fall, winter, spring. The stuffed bear with wheels for feet. The life-size ballerina doll Vicki loved.

Lev touched his face. "What if I frighten the children? Do you think they'll recognize me? What if I frighten her?" He shivered in the damp air. His head pounded.

Marthe took him by the arm and led him into the kitchen, where the stove radiated heat. "Don't think of it."

He sat down at the table, his head in his hands.

"It will be all right," she whispered. She pressed a warm wet cloth to his face. He took it and breathed in the soapy scent, running it along his forehead and neck. For a while, he just sat there with his face covered by the cloth, his mind blank and dark. He couldn't believe he was here in this kitchen, with the same red cast-iron pots on the stove, logs of wood piled in the wicker basket, the same blue-and-white china from which he had eaten many meals. It all appeared still and serene, as if he had stumbled into a doll's house, a place too small, too neat for his clumsy body. When he opened his eyes, Marthe placed a cup of coffee in front of him. "Drink this. You'll feel better." Her hand trembled holding the delicate saucer.

Lev took a long greedy sip, and Marthe started to ask him how he got home, but Franz ran through the doorway, at first not seeing Lev, only demanding a warm roll. "Can I please—" He stopped short, his mouth hanging open.

His ash-blond hair hung in his eyes, which were large and blue and darted around the kitchen, settling on Lev's face.

Lev smiled wryly. "Don't you recognize me?" His voice caught in his throat.

The boy barreled into Lev, clung to him. Lev felt his fine soft hair, so bright and blond, like his mother's.

"Papa, you smell!" He laughed, throwing back his head. A sharp pointed laughter.

Lev looked at Marthe and shrugged. "I suppose I do."

She suppressed a laugh, her eyes wet and shining.

Franz touched his rough beard. "Do you have any medals?"

"I lost them all."

He tugged at his father's shirt. "Did the French take them? Where's your uniform? Your saber?"

Lev hoisted him onto his knee. "How did you grow so tall?" The boy felt much heavier and his long legs dangled down, his feet touching the floor. A lean face had replaced the one Lev remembered—the round childish chin, the faint dimples.

Franz narrowed his eyes. "Did you kill loads of Englishmen? I bet you did. I bet you blew them to smithereens!"

"Loads of men killed and were killed."

"Germans too?"

"Loads," Lev said, absently stroking Franz's hair.

"When we meet the trains, soldiers come out without legs and arms and faces. It's quite terrible." For such a young boy, his voice sounded affected, theatrical.

Marthe gently touched Franz's arm. "Why don't we—"

Vicki shouted down the hallway, "It's not fair if Franz gets a roll and I don't."

Josephine's voice, clear and crisp with that innate melody to it, called after her. "Vicki, don't run. Don't run. You'll fall and hurt yourself. Vicki, don't run." She paused in the hallway, probably stopping in front of the half-moon table upon which lay a few unopened letters. He imagined her fingertips grazing the edges of the envelopes.

Lev bolted upright in the chair. He gripped the table, feeling a new wave of sweat break over his body.

Marthe whispered something into Franz's ear.

"But I can't," he said loudly.

"You can't what?" Vicki stormed into the kitchen. She wore wool tights paired with a ballerina tutu. Her hair parted down the middle in two braids.

Lev stretched out his arms.

She paused, studying his face. Thin and angular, she'd lost her round little body, the body of a four-year-old. She doesn't remember me, Lev thought, running a hand through his hair. And why should she, with my dirty beard, gaunt face? He leaned forward, whispering, "Vicki, it's me."

Her lower lip trembled.

Franz stomped his foot. "It's Papa, stupid!"

Vicki ran to Marthe. Safely in her arms, she turned her face toward Lev. When he smiled, she swiftly looked away, squeezing her eyes shut. Then she slowly turned to look at him again, her cheek pressed against Marthe's apron.

Sentences floated through him from the soldier's manual: *What to expect upon your return home? Shock and excitement. Try to prevent frightening your children; attempt a gentle, slow reintroduction into domestic life. Send word first of your return to prepare family members for your arrival. It is especially important to alert your wife in order to avoid finding her in any unexpected circumstances.* They had laughed over that one and rephrased it among themselves: *to avoid finding your wife fucking the neighbor, to avoid finding your wife in flagrante delicto, to avoid finding your wife receiving vigorous cunnilingus from your best mate,* and so on. Whenever they needed a laugh, which was often, they just murmured: *to avoid finding your wife* . . .

He watched Josephine moving down the hall with envelopes in her hand. He couldn't see her clearly at first because she was backlit with the light coming through the rectangular windows flanking the front door. "Franz?" She sounded tired, put out. She walked into the kitchen studying the return addresses on the envelopes.

Not bothering to look up, she asked, "Franz?"

"I'm here. With Papa."

Lev stood up.

She clenched the envelopes, staring at him. The way the morning light hit her hair instantly brought him back to the Ice Palace, where he had first seen her so many years ago, how unreachable she appeared, how anxious and inadequate he had felt peering down at her from the upper balcony. How uncouth he must have looked in his new suit and tight shoes, and now, he was equally uncouth in his tattered civilian clothes, with his dirty fingernails, gaunt face. When he looked into her eyes, the initial excitement of this first encounter pulsed through him, shortening his breath, making it hard to breathe, and then so many other memories crashed down. Infinitesimally small ones mixed together with grand ones: Franz's birth, his tiny body swaddled in white muslin, Josephine holding him to her milky breast, her long elegant fingers playing the piano on Sunday afternoons, her dulcet voice calling to him in the forest, the sweet sound ringing through the coniferous trees, her hair long and wet down her back when she ascended from the bath, how he spied her clean dripping body reaching for a towel, and when he hugged her, the scent of pine and lavender tingling his nostrils, a scent belonging only to her.

His eyes watered and he choked back a sob—so many images, so many days and years.

Franz grabbed his hand, shaking it. "Papa."

"Franz," Lev said, shielding his eyes with his hand.

Josephine held his other hand—her cool touch, her smooth palm. He inhaled sharply, gulping down air.

"Lev."

He opened his eyes, taking the measure of her. Gone was that certain lustrous quality to her skin. Her hair was still golden and thick, but her face appeared tighter and more fragile, her skin paler and more translucent than Lev remembered. Once, he thought her delicate, but now she seemed breakable, on the verge of snapping, a brittle reed. So many tiny blue veins ran down her neck. *To avoid finding your wife . . .* Of course, the severe food shortages, the British blockade. She never mentioned hunger, but he could see it on her face.

"We thought . . . after you stopped writing—" She looked away and started to cry. He took her into his arms. Her cheek pressing to his chest, she murmured, "You're here."

Then she pulled back, her eyes flickering over his civilian clothes. Before she could ask about this, Lev said, "When the Russians came, we caught the first transport train heading west. We only got so far. Then we had to walk the rest of the way from Poland. Our uniforms—"

She shushed him, putting a finger to his lips.

Marthe started banging around the stove, making more coffee. He wished Marthe would talk, to lessen the cool detachment leaking into his chest.

He hugged Josephine again and felt her body stiffen. "I know. I'm filthy," he apologized, thinking it absurd, this apology.

She touched his face. "A bath will do you good." Her lower lip was dry, oddly whitish. He ran his thumb along it.

She flinched, pursing her lips. "Franz, Vicki—give Papa a hug. Tell him how happy you are that he's returned to us in one piece."

He winked at Vicki and she gave him a half smile. Franz clasped Lev's hand with both of his hands, as if greeting a dinner guest. "So glad you're back, Papa. We read the casualty lists every day, you know."

The kettle let out a shrill whistle, but Marthe had left the room, knowing when to make herself invisible.

The four of them stood in the center of the kitchen, their arms interlocked. Cold air blew in from the back door, which had been left open.

Josephine blinked and rubbed her eyes. "I'm so happy." Her voice, pinched and clipped, held back all the things she couldn't say in front of the children.

"I'm happy too." The words sounded false. Again, he noticed Josephine staring at his tattered clothes. He touched his chest, the worn sleeve of his shirt, and told her how they burned their uniforms when the Russians invaded, and to avoid getting killed, they jumped onto transport trains at the very last moment while it was still possible. "Many of us didn't make it out." The words, once uttered, sounded believable and real. He even felt a pang of guilt for the men he imagined still stranded in Mitau.

"Oh, I don't care about the particulars." She squeezed his hand.

The children watched them, transfixed.

"It's so cold in here," Josephine said, breaking the momentary silence. "Let's move into the sitting room." She looped her arm around him. "You're much thinner."

He tugged at her waist. "So are you."

"Not too, I hope?"

"Still lovely," he reassured her, thinking of how easily Otto could convince a woman of her beauty even when she had none. "Just as lovely," Lev added.

Josephine blushed. "Every woman worries, after such a long absence."

Lev stroked her back. The warm bodies of his children pressed against them. They moved down the hallway toward the sitting room.

Vicki grabbed his free hand and kissed it.

"Sweetheart," Lev said.

She gazed up at him as if he was a stone monument suddenly come to life.

Franz talked continuously about what they had done at school to help the soldiers, what kinds of weapons different regiments used, the types of uniforms and medals. "You'll tell me all your stories?" he asked.

"Yes," Lev said, catching Josephine's eye.

"All of them? Even the bloodiest and scariest ones?"

"Even those," Lev said, feeling the weight of his body in his bones, in the small of his back, in his shoulders.

"We'll see," Josephine said, ushering them into the sitting room.

The coffee Marthe had given him helped, but his stomach felt raw and tight—the last meal had been two days ago, blood sausage on a kaiser roll. He also had to urinate. He could not think of much else, though here he was, sitting on the velvet couch, his children at his feet, and Josephine fussing with a pillow, saying something about how it needed mending. The body always wins, he thought, trying to lean back into the soft cushions, but it felt unnatural. Outside he heard the whimpering of a small dog and the owner commanding him to keep walking. Through the half-drawn curtains, he could see the sun breaking through the clouds, casting the room in a yellow glow.

Franz reverently touched the tip of his boot.

Vicky nestled herself against his calf, hugging his leg.

His children, yes: that's why he came back. He rested his hand on Vicki's small shapely head. Her soft brown hair, the clean white part. She looked up at him in adoration. He smiled down at her and felt tears prick his eyes. Mitau—Leah—that old life was receding, as if new skin was already growing over a wound.

Lev let his head fall back onto the velvet couch. Was it this easy to surrender the past? Vicki squeezed his leg and murmured, "Papa. Papa," in the same insistent way she used to chant when she could only utter a few words, when she was a year old.

Josephine settled into the couch, assuming her most fetching pose. It reminded him of when he used to court her, when she was barely nineteen, and she would sit in the most unnatural way with her back slightly arched and head tilted to the side, her shoulders pressed down to accentuate her long neck. She would carry on long conversations with him seated in that pose.

She smiled brightly. "Don't you think—"

He interrupted her. "I'm sorry." He got up and rushed to the bathroom, enclosing himself in the small white marble chamber. He jerked the brass faucet handle to the left. Icy water rushed out, and he splashed his face before he let down his pants and urinated into the pristine toilet bowl. His head fell back, and he observed the mosaic on the ceiling of a faun peeking out from behind a tree, watching a woman with a lyre. His eyes swam, and he blinked hard, revisiting the apple orchards and Leah's body under the branches, his hands touching the earth as he balanced himself above her. The lean white birches swaying in the wind, the calm sound of leaves as he fell asleep, his cheek on her chest.

"Darling?" Josephine called from outside the door.

He jerked on the chain next to the toilet. The swish of water drowned out her voice.

She lightly tapped on the door.

He leaned over the sink, both hands pressing down on the marble countertop. Water still gushed from the faucet. If he could prolong the moment and not open the door—a moment more before the morning unfurled and rolled into more days and mornings.

Josephine sighed. "Lev?"

"Yes, darling—I'm coming," he said, cupping his hand under the running water and swallowing it down. He ran his mouth along his sleeve. Then he rushed out, closing the door behind him.

Part Two

14

Vicki leaned into the gilded vanity mirror, purring words into the glass. She liked the way her mouth looked when she said: *sex, flirt, five'o clock, cocktail, kiss, cigarette.* Her breath left little circles of condensation on the mirror, magical words remaining there until evaporating away. She repeated: *flirt, cocktail, sex,* attempting to catch the American cadence, mimicking what she heard on the radio, the endless stream of exotic sounds flowing out of the wireless on late golden afternoons when no one else was around. On those afternoons, she knelt on the plush carpet, her head against the velvet couch cushions, and closed her eyes, willing the American jazz, with the intermittent bursts of lively conversation, to transform the cloistered and heavily draped living room into New York City's roaring streets. If she waited long enough, and kept her eyes closed, she would suddenly be floating down Madison Avenue in a light cotton shift, the gleaming store windows reflecting her figure, appearing more boyish and lithe than she really was.

She sighed, standing back from the mirror, rubbing the rouged lipstick off her lips with the inside of her wrist. She wasn't allowed to wear makeup during the day. Only streetwalkers did that. But tonight, Elsa would take her to a special club, where she could wear lipstick and her best dress, the one with the golden spangles. Vicki smiled at her reflection again, shaking her head left and right, relishing her new bob. Her auburn hair skimmed just under her earlobes, accentuating the slender flutes of her oblong lapis lazuli earrings. For the first time, the image she carried in her head, of what she wanted to look like, coincided with the image before her.

Two days ago, she had gone up to the roof of Elsa's apartment building, where yellowing grass sprouted up in haphazard patches. The two girls often met here on Thursdays to listen to records and study *Elite*, a fashion magazine, imagining themselves in a zeppelin-printed dress or shimmering evening gown. Vicky had met Elsa in a drawing class where Elsa was the model. Vicki had sketched her long, bracingly white back for more than an hour, impressed by Elsa's stillness. She'd only moved once, to brush away a lock of hair from her faintly open mouth. By day, Elsa worked as a typist in a large office with other typists. She claimed she could still hear the staccato sound of the keys ringing in her ears, and sometimes, at night in bed, her fingers moved of their own accord, striking at the keys. Which was how she became an insomniac. She went out to clubs and cafés, smoke-filled music halls and cabarets, bars and opium dens, cellars and rented rooms where clandestine entertainment was offered to those who wanted something a little different. She'd been to the Resi and the Josty, which made the best Turkish coffee to treat hangovers, the Femina, the Aleifa, the Eldorado, the Oh La La, and the Mikado Bar, best for transvestites. But bisexuals had the most fun, according to Elsa. She'd said this to shock Vicki, who wasn't all that shocked, knowing Elsa had an ex-boyfriend who worked at Siemens, building generators for power plants, and that she was still hung up on him. She knew Elsa only ate rice pudding sprinkled with a little sugar and cinnamon for dinner because she worried about her figure, and that she read *Die Rote Fahne* religiously. Even knowing this, Vicki felt pangs of jealousy whenever Elsa described the little lanterns flickering in the Tiergarten, the cigarette lighters illuminating beautiful young faces for a quick instant before velvety night enveloped them again, the warm air throbbing with a sense of expectancy as they discussed Rilke, Picasso, whether or not marriage was compatible with modern life, whether it was wise or foolish to commit suicide, whether sunbathing produced a greater clarity of mind.

. . .

Vicki waited for Elsa on the roof, wondering if she would be late again, as Elsa was often late and disheveled, but in a sumptuous, alluring way. Rolling her silk stockings down her legs, Vicki looked out at the brick chimneys sprouting from the tops of the buildings, a staggering line of them as far as she could see, and she noticed how on the next rooftop, stray newspapers and gum wrappers littered the dying grass. Down below in the darkened courtyard, a boy yelled. Vicki glanced over the ledge; a group of children hovered behind an ice wagon, and a boy held up a block of ice while the others tried to touch it. "Get back, get back," he shouted. "It's mine." It was awful, Vicki thought, the need in his voice, as if it could all be taken away from him in an instant. The sun warmed her bare legs. She sighed, wondering about the time, and wondering if the Reds were indeed gaining ground as Papa said, and wondering which record Elsa would bring today. Leaning back on her elbows, Vicki absently studied the fluttering red flag hanging from the next apartment window; on it was the hammer and sickle. She didn't see this flag much in her neighborhood because, as Papa joked, they were the rich capitalists, and it would be quite unwise to advertise their own destruction.

When Elsa finally arrived, twenty minutes late, she brought a phonograph and planted it between them. Elsa also brought Vicki a handful of blue grapes wrapped in brown paper. "Apologies for my lateness." She grinned, popping one into her mouth.

The two girls sprawled on the grass, the blades tickling the backs of their knees. The grapes nested between them, and when Vicki reached for a grape, her hand skimmed Elsa's slim cool fingers, sending a slight rush through her wrist, up her arm.

"Something new today." Elsa balanced a record between her flat palms.

Vicki turned her head, shielding her eyes from the sun. "What's that?"

Elsa raised an eyebrow and then put the record on the phonograph. A deep husky voice began to sing in French, about lovely things.

"Her voice is as rich as Sarotti chocolate," Vicki said, admiring the lines of Elsa's swanlike neck, which was sporadically splashed with a spray of rust-colored freckles. She knew Elsa hated her freckles and often used powder to cover them up, but Vicki thought they were pretty little additions.

"Josephine Baker," Elsa replied. "She's really got it."

"It?"

"Sex appeal." Elsa said this with a fatal air, as if it were the most essential thing in the world.

Stories below them, a policeman blew his high-pitched whistle and a woman shouted. Vicki didn't dare look over the ledge this time. In the working-class district where Elsa lived, there was always commotion and fighting on the streets. And Vicki didn't want to appear too curious or naive about such a place. Elsa often teased her about her posh upbringing, saying that she was out of touch with the proletariat, that soon there would be a revolution, and didn't she want to be on the right side of history?

Vicki tugged on the dry yellow grass. She'd been inside Elsa's flat a few times. She lived in Mietskaserne, a six-story housing block built around a maze of internal courtyards. Out-of-work men leaned against walls, smoking. The toilet was on the second level, and Vicki didn't like to use it because it was shared. She didn't want Elsa to know, so last time she waited until she got home, her bladder almost exploding.

"Hey V," Elsa said, interrupting her thoughts, "I've got an idea." She called her V because, as she explained when they first met, it sounded more modern, more androgynous.

Vicki pulled her knees into her chest. Elsa often had ideas that were not wholly acceptable, ideas that, if her mother knew about them, would cause her to consider Vicki a stranger. Last week, Elsa had convinced her to skinny dip in the murky green waters of the Wannsee, and when they were both underwater, Elsa had twined her legs round Vicki's waist and the brush of her pubic hair had rubbed up against Vicki's abdomen. Vicki blushed, thinking about it.

"I think," Elsa said, on all fours, crawling toward Vicki, "you need to create a change."

With Elsa's smiling face inches away from hers, Vicki noticed how the blue grapes had slightly stained Elsa's lips and how she smelled of cotton and sweat and cigarettes.

"You don't like my clothes?" Vicki glanced down at her sundress, muslin yellow with a scalloped hem.

Elsa suppressed a laugh, suddenly brandishing a pair of sewing scissors. "*Bubikopf*—you must."

Vicki gasped. "You know I can't."

Elsa steadied her eyes on Vicki. "Frau von Stressing Perlmutter will understand."

Her mother, with an equally long weighty braid, would not understand. The way her mother used to dress, like a historical object! Laced in corsets, covered to the neck in pleated cloth, layered in skirts and petticoats that made her every movement and motion artificial, her mother now seemed baffled without the security of all that clothing. She was sheepishly exposed, surprised by how the new silk shifts merely floated over her figure. Sometimes, Vicki would find her mother before the looking glass in a new dress cut to the knee, the fabric diaphanous and light, with an expression similar to the one Mitzi the dog wore after getting a summer shave: bewildered, mystified, self-conscious.

Elsa touched the back of her neck, and Vicki instantly felt deliciously calm and pliant.

She uncoiled Vicki's braid. As her fingers worked her hair loose, she scolded Vicki. "You've been wearing it back like this, pretending it's short, when all you have to do is cut it."

"I know," Vicki said, breathless, the sun suddenly too hot, sweat trickling down the sides of her torso, under her slip. She inhaled sharply. The cool metal scissor blade pressed against her neck as Elsa cut off a chunk of hair.

"See?" Elsa said, shaking a fist full of chestnut strands.

Vicki stared, recalling her mother's advice about how a woman's hair was a prized possession.

"Almost done," Elsa announced, clipping off the last chunk.

Vicki's hair fell around them, scattered on the grass, gleaming in the sunlight.

She bent back her head, turning her face up to the sun, suppressing the fear of going home. She shook her head left and right. Weightless.

Elsa whispered, "Don't you like it?"

She faced Elsa, fingering the thick edge of her hair, where it ended now. "I think so."

"You didn't do this for me, did you?" Elsa's eyes narrowed, as if such obedience was worse than refusal.

"Oh, no," Vicki said, her breath catching in her throat. Although in part, she had.

Elsa smoothed down Vicki's hair, running her palms along her temples. "Well, you have *it* now." When she said *it* her chin jutted forward, challenging Vicki to accept this new gift.

Vicki grinned. *"Sex appeal."* On a nearby roof, two pigeons cooed.

Elsa laughed, throwing back her head, a movement Vicki had tried to emulate countless times alone in front of the mirror.

She languished on the grass, puffing on her cigarette. "It looks good." Then she added, "Don't worry about your mother."

"I'm not worried," Vicki said.

Walking home, Vicki pulled down her straw hat, as if any one of the nameless pedestrians would instinctively know she'd just cut it all off and scold her. But no one noticed. Maybe if she took off her hat? She pulled on the brim, her heart accelerating. What would it feel like to walk these streets with her new hair, her neck bare in the wind, an open invitation to be touched and kissed there? She passed street merchants selling their wares and noticed a woman with so much hair on her head, piled high in twisted coils, it must have survived since the last century. She passed a number of streets under construction. They were digging up the roads again, the steam of hot asphalt offensive. The facade of buildings had been reduced to wooden scaffolding, and she failed to recall what was here before. She walked at a clipped pace, humming with an internal nervousness every time she felt the breeze sweep over her neck. Off the main street, she caught sight of a sign: RUNS REPAIRED. She'd pricked her stockings on the roof with Elsa, the silk catching on her ring. She looked down at her thigh, her white skin gleaming through the run, almost insolently. Why should she fix it? What was the point of this constant fixing and washing and straightening that occupied her mother to no end? No, Vicki thought, she wasn't going to be like that. Not ever. She pulled off her hat, glancing around, ready to challenge anyone. But no one cared.

Vicki arrived home earlier than she'd intended, too early to avoid her mother, who was in the sitting room, probably working on her needle-point or reading over sheet music. Every time she came through the front door, she felt as if she was entering an antiquated domain: the frieze of grapes above the kitchen door, the sculpture of two naked Greek youths in the alcove along the hallway, the stained-glass window above the staircase throwing patterns of red, purple, and green light over the dark wood paneling. Vicki used to delight in the odd objects her mother preserved in the glass cabinet: an English doll dressed in taffeta, a bridal wreath from the eighteenth century spun from the finest silk, a tobacco box carved out of rose quartz, family portraits of women with curled powdered hair and delicate rose-colored lips, those carved and lacquered figurines, mostly little dogs, from Josephine's mother, Marie. Entering the living room, she caught sight of herself in the glass cabinet, her hair brazenly short, especially when her startled expression overlapped the English doll's placid face.

Her mother didn't bother to look up from her needlepoint. Vicki still had a few suspended seconds to dash out of the room, but something kept her feet planted on the plush carpet.

"Vicki," her mother paused, making a tiny loophole and stringing the needle and thread through it. "Are you going out again before dinner?"

Vicki held her breath.

Josephine slowly looked up.

Vicki heard the distinct tick of the grandfather clock. Mitzi stirred at Josephine's feet, realizing something was amiss.

Blood rushed to Josephine's face.

"I wanted to. I've wanted to for a long time, and today Elsa finally helped me cut it." Her voice sounded more confident, more even and smooth than she'd anticipated, and she felt, instead of fear, a rising triumph.

"Elsa," her mother said darkly.

"Yes, Elsa."

"Oh my God," her mother said, touching her forehead.

With the blinds drawn in the semidarkness, the room felt oppressive, the heat thick.

"She's the stenographer. Do you want to look like a stenographer?"

"And what do stenographers look like?" Vicki said, crossing the room. She leaned against the window, yanking the curtain aside.

"Don't," Josephine warned. "Letting in the light only heats the room more."

Vicki shook the curtain. Dust particles rose up. She thought about how her mother still slept in an old four-poster bed *a la duchesse*. How she probably still wore a nightcap and night gloves. How she'd found a copy of *An Ideal Marriage* under a pillow in the sitting room—a sex and marriage manual claiming to cure "sexual misery," a state her mother had surely brought upon herself. You couldn't solve sexual problems with a book! Just uttering the word *sex* would drive her mother screaming from the house.

Josephine snapped shut her needle case. "You're only fashioning yourself into a *Ypsi*." *Ypsi* was shorthand for the type of girl whose greatest fear was to appear unmodern even if the new styles didn't suit her. Especially to Josephine, such a woman, in addition to the bobbed hair, had that ridiculous fringe hanging just above the eyebrows, constantly tempting someone to part it, as if it was a curtain that, once swept aside, would only reveal a pale sweaty forehead. *Ypsi* meant fastidious dieting in an attempt to appear as slim as Louise Brooks when sadly, she never would be, while smoking too many cigarettes and saying she never wanted children when she'd really love to have them. Vicki often heard her mother bemoan the new fashions to Marthe, complaining how the other day she saw a stocky girl parading around in the shortest shift with such bulging calves that it was tragic.

Josephine edged off the sofa, lowering her voice. "You are a pretty girl, Vicki. But since the war—"

"I know," Vicki interrupted. "Since the war, women look artificially thin. And romance is nowhere to be found, with men propositioning women on the streets, and such short dresses interrupt the line of the leg, and so many girls with pitiful stocky legs tramp around in their short dresses and short haircuts—it's a real shame!"

"It is a shame," Josephine said, observing her coldly.

"What's a shame?" Lev called out in his jovial tone, the front door slamming behind him. His whistle echoed in the foyer. He took a moment to hang his hat, and in this interval, Josephine flashed Vicki a stern look. Lev walked into the living room, his hands in his pockets, curious about the latest domestic drama. His eyes, light and joyful, rested on Vicki's face. He'd caught some sun, his cheeks rosy against his olive complexion. They exchanged a secret smile, and then Lev turned to Josephine. "Well? What's the problem?"

Josephine smoothed down her dress. "Just look at your daughter's hair."

Lev turned around, studied Vicki for a moment, his hand on his chin, trying to suppress another smile, and then he turned back to Josephine. "Yes, I see what you mean. It does appear a bit shorter than it was this morning."

Josephine kneaded her palm into her forehead. "You don't understand the implications."

"Let's have some lemonade. Vicki, open a window!"

Vicki yanked back the curtains and unlatched the window latch. Sticking her head all the way out, she enjoyed a brief reprieve. At least her father understood.

Her parents started to argue. Vicki observed the linden trees, thinking it was always a shame after they'd just been pruned. They looked so Spartan. But pruning helped them grow. She heard her mother's voice, rising and tightening: "It's not at all womanly. She looks like a prepubescent boy. And they've started slicking back their hair, cutting it shorter, without even a curl or a wave to it."

Her father, soothing her mother, probably with his hand on her shoulder, said, "On Leipziger Strasse, I saw some very elegant women with short haircuts."

sler, had commented in his high-pitched nervous voice about the new vitality of youth. A few nights ago at a dinner party, he'd explained how people now want to bask in the light, the sun, the health of their bodies. The longer he spoke, the higher his voice climbed: "It's no longer restricted to an exclusive circle, as you might think—it's a mass movement spreading all over Germany. The new architecture, which creates a much more modern domestic setting, is how the young people wish to live these days." And he charged ahead with this argument through coffee and dessert, the specifics of his examples ballooned into generalities as he consumed more and more port wine from a crystal glass, his pinky finger raised in the air. From here, Lev could only see the sharp motion of the women's white legs slicing through blue sky. Even though the count loved the sound of his own voice, he had a point about this new passion for physical training, irrepressible for certain teenagers, such as his son, Franz, who had to fill every waking moment with cycling, hiking, javelin throwing, gymnastics, fencing, and so on.

A chorus of horns sounded at a stalled truck. A balloon seller stood on the corner, and the bobbing red, orange, and blue helium orbs entranced a child who ignored her mother's command to keep walking. A horse harnessed to a cab glanced around, lowering its head into its nose bag. White-jacketed waiters wove in and out of the small tables on café terraces. In front of the expensive hotels, porters dressed in navy blue waited. On the corner, a huge advertisement for Manoli cigarettes loomed above the intersection—*Enjoy it while it lasts!* A young woman stepped out of a cab, slender and light, her silk stockings shimmering in the afternoon sun. She glanced around to see if anyone noticed her, and catching Lev's eye, she smiled coyly. Lev grinned at the confidence of youth, at how clearly no catastrophe had touched her yet by the way she strode into the café terrace, not bothering to give any notice to the young men exiting at the same time. Of course she could feel them looking at her, but she only smiled inwardly, imperviously scanning the terrace for her friends. The way she cut through the crowd reminded him of Vicki—they all moved so quickly now, as if a pause would cause instantaneous death.

Vicki had cut off her hair yesterday, and it had upset Josephine greatly—they were yelling at each other in the living room when he'd come home, Vicki nearly in tears and Josephine emitting that cool fury with which he was all too familiar. He had tried to mediate but failed. Why shouldn't she look like other girls? It was the fashion. Surely Josephine should understand. Vicki had flung her arms around his neck, her breath short and quick. "Thank you, Papa. You understand. You really do." He'd guiltily held her in his arms while Josephine surveyed them with a steely glare. In that moment, Lev saw the age on her face: the shadows under her eyes, the slightly dull pallor of her once radiant skin, the thinness of her upper lip. "Forgive me for trying to maintain some semblance of order in this household," she'd said, before retreating upstairs to their bedroom, where she'd stayed for the rest of the night, not speaking to Lev until this morning. Even then, she answered in a monosyllable when he asked what was for dinner tonight. "Fish." And then she'd turned away, avoiding the perfunctory kiss he always placed on her forehead before leaving.

The way she'd averted her eyes and recoiled when Lev touched her cheek—all because of what Vicki had done to her hair? No, not all. Josephine's anger contained various layers, layers that could be excavated, akin to the findings of a massive archaeological dig. On the outer layer, she was angry over a specific, quite recent event, such as Vicki's hair. Underneath this, her anger percolated over a series of other infractions committed in the past weeks: he'd misplaced her ivory hairbrush; Vicki hadn't yet sewn the ribbons on her pointe shoes; Marthe burnt the roast again; the dog Mitzi had forgotten herself and urinated on the pillow with a needlepoint of the Kaiser's imperial palace, a keepsake from her aunt Agatha. And beneath this second layer existed a third layer, filled with the defeat and regret of having surrendered to life's manifold disappointments. When they had nasty fights, this third layer revealed itself in sharp bright flashes. Her face turned from hardened dissatisfaction to a hollow vibrating sadness, and Lev had to look away, leave the room. He didn't want to know more of this third layer, but he could guess its contents: a failed music career, the death of her mother, the trouble with Franz—something about the boy wasn't entirely right—and the end of a certain way of life, from before the war, before he'd left and returned with pieces of himself missing, pieces neither he nor she could recover.

He touched his hair, felt how the strands fell through his fingers. Time for a cut and a shave. The strong sun hit his face and its warmth felt good even though he sweated under his white shirt. Lev watched the panoply of people on the streets. They rushed past, their briefcases bumping up against his arm. He scratched his chin, feeling the emergent stubble. He considered buying the afternoon edition; the newsboy waved it around on the corner. He would leaf though it at the barbershop.

Inside, the moist air mingled with the smell of lather and scented after-shave. Sunlight streamed into the room through the dusty wooden blinds. Scissors snapped open and closed, slicing off unwanted hair and a heavy black fly hovered over one of the sinks. Lev listened to snippets of conversation: someone's wife had left him and now wanted to come back after realizing how depressing Frankfurt was—her lover lived in Frankfurt, but she hated it there. Someone else discussed an investment gone bad—apparently manufacturing umbrella handles had not turned out well. Lev sat down in one of the empty chairs.

"Shall we leave the mustache?" the barber asked.

Lev ran his finger along the rough fringe. "No, take it off. I look younger without it." *Younger without it . . .* The phrase gave him pause. Always unexpected, how a word, an image, the combination of certain colors would pierce through the present moment and leave a perforation in his heart. Instantaneously, he felt Leah's soft hands on his face, her teasing tone as she tried to convince him to keep his beard, she liked him better that way. *But I look younger without it,* he had protested. She smiled and nestled her face into his neck. *You look like a real scholar with a beard,* she murmured, her breath soft and light on his skin. *A rebbe,* he had joked, *you really want me to become a rebbe like your father and remain here.* Then she would turn serious and ask, "Would that be so terrible?"

No, not terrible. Not terrible at all. It would be too beautiful to imagine, Lev thought, leaning back into the creaking leather seat. He touched his mustache. "Yes, take it all off."

The barber nodded and started preparing his tools. The ceiling fan emitted a faint whooshing sound, reminding Lev again of the one they'd just bought for the bedroom, how it only made the room hotter, becoming yet another irritant to Josephine's already delicate state. He sank farther down into the chair, inhaling the musty smell of the leather. The glee he'd felt when he'd left the office early this afternoon, the June air, full of summer, faded. His head hurt a little. It suddenly felt too warm in the barbershop. And the barber was taking his time, lingering over every little detail as he arranged his tools on the chrome tray.

Lev observed himself in the cloudy mirror. *What would Leah think if she saw me now?* Had these nine years taken much of a toll? He turned his head to the side. He had no jowls. He still had nice hair, full and wavy on top. But thirty-nine sounded old, older than the version of himself he carried around, older than the age he believed he truly was: thirty. He had been thirty when he'd fallen in love with Leah.

If she saw me now, for the first time, would she fall for me? He frowned. *Maybe.* Wiping his brow, he tried to imagine what she must look like now, but his memory clung to her youthful body, her open laughing face, her freckles, rust colored, her black hair, so black it turned midnight blue in the sun. Why try to imagine her differently? What was the use? Better to revel in what he remembered and not trouble with where she was now. Probably still in Mitau, with Zalman. Perhaps they'd moved to a more prosperous town, but this was as far as Lev's imagination would stretch. Because he couldn't find out—contact only endangered her. He had told her they should not exchange letters after his departure. She couldn't read anyway, so she would have to get someone else to read, and then gossip would spread, and Zalman would use the letters to prove she'd been unfaithful in his absence. He remembered Leah asking if perhaps Geza could read the letters to her. She had asked this weakly, because they both knew Geza was too young and volatile to act as an intermediary. Then she got angry and flung a wooden spoon at his head. "I'll never see you again. It's what you really want! To return to that shiksa!" They stood in the garden, in the back of her mother's house, but the kitchen door was ajar, and Lev knew everyone was listening inside. Listening for what he would say next. He told her it was for her protection—she would be a penniless divorcée if Zalman found out and left her. She could even be killed for sympathizing with the enemy. A traitor.

"I don't want to ruin your life," he said.

"You've already ruined it," she countered before bursting into sobs and kissing his face through her tears. The salt he could still taste.

The door to the barbershop flew open, ripping Lev away from his reverie. The barber paused, holding the sharp blade away from his neck. A man with oiled curls close to his head strode into the shop, accidentally causing the front door to bang against the wall, interrupting the dreamy inertia Lev had been so enjoying. The man was talking about how ridiculous it was, the ban on public speech, as if continuing a conversation he'd been having on the street. "Or course, he has others to speak for him, to advance the cause, Strasser and Goebbels and such, but it's shameful the way he's already suffered so much at the hands of the government and still they persist with that damn ban."

Lev didn't look at the man directly but watched him in the mirror. His cheeks, a flushed crimson, appeared perpetually inflamed regardless of the heat. The man rambled on about how he would be ready when Germany was ready. "Not long now, I'll tell you," he added as the barber tied the smock around his thick neck.

The blade glided down Lev's cheek, sluicing off a thick layer of lather. Then the man jumped to another story—how the other day, on an errand for his wife, he popped into a shop on Leipziger Strasse only to be confronted by a tangle of women buying up all the summer gloves on display. "They descended on the merchandise as hungry as a flock of dirty pigeons. Bickering, arguing, chattering away—before I entered the shop, through the glass, I thought they were German, but then of course once inside, it became clear to me they were only imposters, believing their overly expensive clothing could hide the fact."

"Hide the fact?" Lev repeated.

"They're just a bunch of uninhibited Russian refugees! And how they mix our language with their own, producing such a guttural stream, I nearly had to cover my ears!"

Lev said, "You did, huh?"

"By God, I did!"

The man finally stopped talking. The green quiet of the room settled over them. Lev listened to the faint buzzing of the fly, the fan whooshing overhead, the scissor blades sluicing through hair, the scratchy sound of the razor gliding down lathered chins, and the razor then dunking into soapy water, tapping melodiously against the porcelain bowl. When the barber placed the wet hot towel over his face, Lev closed his eyes and tried to think of nothing.

Leaving the shop, his face tingling from the citrus aftershave, Lev smiled at how the curly-haired man had fallen asleep, snoring as the barber clip, clip, clipped around his large head. Like an infant who tires himself out after a bout of crankiness and then sleeps deeply. Yes, he was an infant—belligerent, loud, unable to distinguish where he began and the rest of the world ended.

As he walked with no real direction in mind, something pelted his hat. It was the drop of chestnuts from the trees lining the streets, splattering the concrete, leaving behind those unmistakable dark brownish spots. He walked past a bearded man, his side locks visible from under his hat. He smiled mischievously at Lev through his glinting spectacles. He carried an umbrella even though the sky, a piercing blue, showed no trace of rain. That black hat, the heavy overcoat—the old Jew had chosen to move about life with a dark cloud hanging over his head. Lev watched him amble past the redbrick institutional buildings, all stone and mass in comparison to his slight body swathed in that thick overcoat.

In the distance, the domes and spires of the New Synagogue rose up. His mother still lived there, in Scheunenviertel. She didn't like it there but said she was too old to move to Palestine. And you can start the revolution anywhere, no matter where you live, she'd said. His mother would have liked Leah. He had often wanted to tell her about Leah, but he always stopped himself, and now, nine years later, what was the point? It would only give his mother more ammunition against Josephine. He could already hear her chiding: *See? See how much better off you would have been with a Jewish woman? One of our own?* She would then endlessly carp on about how he had lost his one chance at happiness when he left Leah behind, forgetting the essential details: Leah was married. Lev would have gotten killed if he stayed there. And did she expect him to abandon Josephine and the children? Her precious Vicki?

Without wanting to, Lev boarded the S-Bahn. He would make it a short visit. Remembering it was Friday, he pictured his mother preparing food, laying down a fresh tablecloth, lighting candles—his most sympathetic memories. The train rattled past Rummelsburg, where the old-age home was, and past the windows of people's homes. Someone listened to a phonograph from an open apartment window. Billboards invaded the summer sky, advertising Sarotti chocolate, shoeshine polish, cigars, bootlaces. Kaloderma soup used an Asian motif, evoking Madame Butterfly. *After the revolution, Montblanc remains the king of fountain pens,* another advert read.

A tired-looking woman sitting across from him stroked her little dog, which she had stuffed into her purse. His shaggy ears perked up at the sound of someone unwrapping a sandwich two seats down. On either side of the tracks, workmen dug up the street, the sound of construction melding with the staccato vibration of the streetcar as it raced along. Lev paged through his paper, skimming an article on the cycling races, but the thought of seeing his mother unfocused him, made him uneasy. Every time he saw her, she complained it had been too long and the visit too short. When he arrived, she was unsatisfied, and even more so when he left. He could skip it altogether, but something about the Friday afternoon light, golden and burnt orange, drew him back to her.

He walked on the sidewalk, a rarity here as the Jews had a predisposition for walking in the middle of the street or, rather than walking, roaming, Lev thought. There were hardly any automobiles, just carts, so the streets invited foot traffic, fruit stands, stalls selling eggs, cheese, butter. Lev insisted on walking correctly, on the sidewalk. No one noticed him. They were accustomed to the stray Berliner stumbling into this section of the city unofficially designated for recent refugees from Poland,

Romania, Hungary, and Russia, as well as home to religious Jews, well-off Jews, pickpockets, counterfeiters, and people like his mother who couldn't be bothered to leave. A slow-moving group of men with long beards waded through the street as if confronting a rough surf. Lev heard snatches of Yiddish mixed with German and Polish. Prayer houses dotted the sidewalk. By day, they served as storefronts where you could buy pencils, notebooks, soap, sheets of paper. Lev passed the Jewish boys' school with its commemorative bust of Moses Mendelssohn planted next to the arched entryway. Children trudged along with their tallith under their arms; they appeared thin, almost transparent. As if it were still wartime. As if these children had just arrived from the east, underfed, hair full of lice, combatting typhus, diphtheria, and God knows what else. Lev shivered, remembering how children died in Mitau from disease, the miniature coffins lowered into graves, their mothers throwing themselves over heaps of unearthed soil. He shook his head, guiltily relieved that his own children had survived the war and were now vibrant and healthy, consumed with their studies, with their clubs, with their haircuts. He smiled again, thinking of Vicki's short hair, how it really suited her.

A group of young men stood on the corner, arguing in Yiddish. Yeshiva students, Lev thought. Their pale skin appeared even paler against their somber clothing. They didn't notice anyone else, not even the pretty girl who passed wearing a silk summer dress. "He is everywhere and nowhere," one of them proclaimed. "Why this absence? Always this maddening absence!" another in a skullcap interjected, only to be cut off by a tall wiry youth who commanded the group, "We cannot keep defining ourselves by what we are not. Then we are nothing. The fate of modern Judaism lies in our hands. We must speak in positive terms." They were talking about God. Lev lingered on the corner, amused by their naive passion for the unknowable. The students crossed the street, their voices rising to a crescendo of incredulity. They didn't see the truck rounding the corner, bounding toward them. The driver hit the brakes and then he leapt out, waving his arms and cursing in Russian. Two men wearing similar velvet caps turned to look, pausing for a moment from the business deal they were discussing. But the students kept arguing and gesticulating, having crossed the street without realizing they'd brushed up against death.

Bracing for the visit with his mother, Lev eyed the bar across the street. It would be impossible to withstand her recriminations otherwise. The door was open—no one ever closed it. The place, as he'd expected, was run-down, shoddy, with a backroom where people ate and a front room with a public bar, the kitchen separating the two sections. They served good brown bread, smoked fish in various sauces, blood sausage from Warsaw. Russian émigrés who had escaped the revolution just in time enjoyed schnapps at the bar, commenting on how the particular sharp taste of the liquor, akin to black licorice, reminded them of home. Two old women with crinkled white skin considered Lev with suspicion before returning to their conversation about how unhappy Rabbi Reznick was over the low attendance for shul on Saturday mornings. "But he doesn't make it very enticing," one of the women complained. The other one took a quick sip of tea and replied, "I suppose everything these days must have something *enticing* about it."

Lev sat down and ordered a glass of vodka, remembering the refreshing crisp taste he used to enjoy during the war. When he took a sip, the sharp clear liquid felt strangely comforting. From across the bar, Lev spied Benesh and immediately glanced away, not wanting to attract him. He had seen Benesh here many times, always closing deals, weaving between the tables, greeting customers as if he'd known them all his life, hoping they would prove lucrative in some way. He had tried to involve Lev in a moneymaking scheme a few years back—was it buying up tenement buildings in Hallesches Tor or investing in that revue near Potsdamer Platz? Lev couldn't recall—he only remembered the distaste he'd felt when Benesh had pressed his fleshy moist palm into his own hand, swearing that Lev would regret missing out on such an opportunity.

Lev drained his glass and thought about getting another. But he sensed Benesh's eyes on him, sizing him up, as he moved from table to table, inching toward Lev. As usual, he wore that same cream-colored suit, the same monocle. His shoes—lace-up oxfords, extremely shiny ones, a deep mahogany brown—always appeared too small for his feet. The top of his balding head sported a sheen of sweat. "Hello, my friend," Benesh said in Yiddish, pulling up a chair. "May I offer you a cigar?"

Lev stood up and signaled for the bill. The woman behind the bar stared at him blankly.

Benesh waved his hand in the air. "No one pays here. They just write it down on a ledger." He gestured for Lev to sit. Lev said he was late to see his mother.

"Never keep your mother waiting!" Benesh called after Lev, who moved through the heavy blue smoke toward the open door. "The wrath of a mother is unparalleled," he added and then laughed hoarsely.

His mother still looked like a refugee from Galicia. Even though she wore modern clothes, a knee-length burgundy skirt, stockings, stacked heels, a white blouse, her eyes continually peeked out from under her dark hair, suspicious, unsatisfied, restless. She smoked incessantly, despite her hacking cough. The small house was falling apart. Termites had eaten through the windowsills, leaving behind miniature mountains of fecal matter that looked like sand. The brass doorknobs were loose on the doors. The wallpaper was peeling in the bathroom. But she didn't care and refused to leave, unmoved by Lev's persuading or by the checks he regularly sent her. He suspected she donated the money to the KPD, the German Communist Party. Her three cats, Trotsky, Lenin, and Mayakovsky, white with splashes of brown, were old and didn't move much, preferring the sun-drenched windowsills or the hot cobblestone pathway. As he approached the house, he thought he'd at least have a few last moments of reprieve before knocking on the door, but she was out front, shaking crumbs from a tablecloth. The heat of the day had subsided, promising a cooler evening. When she saw him, her eyes lit up, but then she barked, "I haven't seen you in months. How is that shiksa of yours?"

"Josephine?"

"Who else would I mean? Or are you faithfully following in your father's footsteps, keeping someone on the side?"

He kissed her on both cheeks, her skin still soft and smooth, dusted with a little rouge.

"And you arrive like this, on my doorstep, unannounced, so I don't have time to prepare anything. You do this on purpose."

"I can only stay an hour."

"There's herring, potato dumplings. A few marinated beets."

Lev's mouth watered even though she was a terrible cook. Still, he hadn't eaten all day. One of the cats, possibly Mayakovsky, sidled up against his leg.

"How are you?"

She shook her head, coughing. "I'm not well. I'm not well at all. But you wouldn't know the difference. The Angel of Death could have taken me two months ago, and who would know?"

"It seems as if you're still here."

"Barely," she said, encircling his arm with a firm grip and leading him inside.

He sat down on the couch, which was partially covered in cat hair. Lev tried to sit on the cleaner end of it but then gave up. The late-afternoon sun filtered in through the windows, illuminating the golden dust particles. His mother sat in the reading chair opposite him, the chair where his father used to sit. She sat there triumphantly, nestled into the deep-seated cushions. His father had died of a heart attack before the war, or as his mother put it, Lev's marriage to the gentile Josephine killed his father. Not that she missed him. He'd been an argumentative drunk as well as innately mercantile—there wasn't a thing he couldn't sell and he'd sold everything from prayer shawls to life insurance, and this, of course, disgusted her. Lev had always taken his mother's side, witnessing her despair when his father left for days on end, only to return drunk. When he mysteriously came into money, he spent it recklessly, buying his mother a fur coat and Lev a sailor outfit, both of which they did not especially want. When his deals went badly, he would lie in bed and swear at the ceiling. He buried his head under a pillow and moaned over his mistakes. Lev brought him tea and cigarettes and pickled herring, but nothing cheered him. Once recovered, he tried to talk to Lev about his studies, to engage him, but the attempts

were paltry and halfhearted, and Lev came to view his father as a volatile unsettling presence.

And so when he suddenly died, Lev felt relief. Relief that he no longer had to listen to his mother's tirades against his father or witness his
father's crippling depression, the world turning dark not just for him
but for everyone. And Lev felt relief that money was no longer appearing and disappearing at a moment's notice. He'd often had to advance
his mother money for food and cigarettes only to come to dinner the
next week, the table flush with vodka and meat, his father jubilantly
playing the generous host. Yes, it was better now, even if the house felt
overly quiet, hushed.

His mother stood up abruptly. "The tea. I nearly forgot." She left
the room.

Lev eyed the altar in the corner, alight with candles dedicated
to Rosa Luxemburg. The fact that they shared the same birth date,
March 5, and that his mother had been born precisely ten years before
Rosa, in 1861, was only the starting point for her feelings of intense
kinship with the Polish Jewish revolutionary. Apparently, Rosa also suffered from a volatile husband, Gustav, who drank too much, and both
women endured physical ailments from an early age. Rosa had been
born with a congenital hip dislocation, which caused her to limp, and
Lev's mother had a similar fate: her left leg was slightly shorter than her
right. She believed the only way Jews would ever become equal citizens
of the world was through revolution, which would do away with petty
illusions of religion, nationality, gender, and class. Her favorite quote
of Rosa's had been recited so often Lev knew it by heart: "Why do you
come to me with your special Jewish sorrows? I feel just as sorry for
the wretched Indian victims in Putamayo, the Negroes in Africa . . . I
cannot find a special corner in my heart for the ghetto. I feel at home in
the entire world wherever there are clouds and birds and human tears."

She returned from the kitchen carrying a tray with two tall glasses
for black tea. In small bowls, she'd placed the dumplings and the beets.
She lowered the tray of food onto the coffee table in front of them.

"No herring?" Lev asked.

She sat down and immediately started smoking a cigarette. "Gave the little bit left to Lenin this morning. Plus, I didn't know you were coming. And now you criticize me for being empty-handed."

Lev leaned forward to pour the tea. "I'm not criticizing you, Mutti. I only wanted to see how you are doing."

"How am I doing?" She threw up her hands, waving a cigarette through the air. "I'm perfectly fine. Except for the fact that I never see my grandchildren. How's Vicki? She looks like me, that girl, but of course I wouldn't know. I haven't seen her since May."

Lev started to speak, but she held up her hand. "I already know what you're going to say—the ride is too far on the tram. An hour, at most. But to see me, an hour always lasts too long."

"It's not that," Lev explained, feeling guilty. "Franz is consumed by his studies. Every weekend he hikes with these nature groups. And Vicki has dance rehearsals for the fall performance."

She dusted off some hairs from her skirt. "They prefer Josephine's mother, who, by the way, still hasn't realized the nineteenth century is over." She puffed on her cigarette. "Oh, I forgot. She's dead."

Lev nodded. "It's had quite an effect on Josephine."

His mother sniffed. "Everything has quite an effect on her. Too fragile. Too delicate. I told you this before you married her. How can a woman like that endure even a fig of hardship? She can't."

"Well," Lev hedged, taking a sip of the too-hot tea. "Since her mother died . . ." but he didn't bother to finish the sentence. He didn't have the energy to defend Josephine, especially since he agreed with his mother.

Lev sunk back into the couch, not minding the feeling of all those little cat hairs peppering his shirt. Now Leah—his mother would have loved Leah. He often asked himself what his life would look like if he'd brought her back from Mitau. Or if he'd met her before Josephine. Leah, who smelled like the fresh river, whose name reminded him of the full moon. He still had dreams about her, certain images spinning through his mind long after he woke; the apple orchard and her body under the trees, the shadow of leaves scattering across her bare torso. In the last dream, he found her in Berlin at the fruit seller. She was buying fresh figs. He embraced her. She smiled sadly and said, "Imagine the children we could have made." And Lev had replied, "We would have three children by now, at least!"

He woke up exuberant, until he felt the cool emptiness next to him in bed, the vacant space indented by Josephine's long angular body.

When the sun started to set, his mother got up from the chair and lit the candles standing in their silver candlesticks.

"Are you keeping Sabbath?"

She smiled weakly. "A sentimental habit."

The image of her standing there, match in hand, candles flickering in the setting sun, made his heart contract. How often had he admired Leah performing the same task on a Friday evening? In his own home, such rituals were not done. They ate fish on Fridays, and the smell always lingered well after dark.

"Do you want me to stay?" Lev asked.

For a moment she hesitated, and then she blew out the match. "Herr Schonemann and his cousin Gilda, who helped with the pamphlets last week, are coming for dinner."

Lev held his hat to his chest. "So you won't be alone?"

She clasped his face, her hands icy cold. "Solitude is a blessing, my son. With your father . . ." She blinked hard, then forced a smile. "You know how it was."

He kissed her on both cheeks, and she followed him to the door, muttering the same stream of complaints that began and ended every visit: her back hurt, her right leg was acting up again, would Vicki ever visit her, and when was the next time she could expect him? Would he return before another six months passed?

"I'm sorry Lenin ate the last of the herring," she added.

"It's okay, Mutti," Lev said, putting on his hat.

"You'll come back before the High Holidays?"

"I'll try," Lev said, thinking she looked smaller than he remembered, standing there in the doorway, her shoulders hunched, her white face framed by her graying dark hair.

He rushed home, anticipating Josephine's anger at his lateness. She would assume he'd been with a woman, disbelieving he had actually used the free summer afternoon to visit his mother. But then she would reluctantly ask after Mara, feigning concern for her health and her leg when really Josephine wanted to wish that part of Lev away.

He walked briskly down the street filled with families making their way to synagogue. The stores had all closed early, candles lit in the windows. The door to the bar was finally shut after standing open all day. Lev saw Benesh lingering outside the bar, stretching himself, his plump body comic in the cream suit. Lev hurried on, not wanting to engage with him. The U-Bahn was just around the corner. The crowd thinned as he neared the end of the street. Not recognizing him at first, Lev saw Rabbi Landauer moving toward him in long mournful strides. The rabbi stared through Lev, his large eyes blinking as if continually startled.

"Rabbi Landauer," Lev said, touching his tattered coat sleeve. The rabbi was an emaciated version of himself. He had once been well fed, heavily bearded, the learned Torah teacher of Berlin, a fixture of the community.

"Oh," the rabbi replied, running a hand through his thinning hair. "I didn't see you."

"Rabbi Landauer—what happened to you?"

He motioned to his head. "As you can see, I'm uncovered before God. A walking disgrace."

Lev only then noticed he was not wearing his signature black velvet skullcap. The rabbi shook his head, hooking his arm through Lev's.

They walked some blocks while the rabbi told Lev his story. In a flurry of long tumbling sentences, he explained how he'd lost his faith after suffering from a series of depressive episodes. He was now in the midst of an existential crisis—a complete sea change. He'd turned to Buddhism. As he talked, he was clearly distracted, stopping mid-sentence to glance suspiciously over his shoulder. He looked half-starved, his hollow gray face having turned inward, his glassy brown eyes peering at Lev with an odd terror. On top of everything else, he'd recently become a vegetarian.

Lev almost smiled, but the intensity of the rabbi's expression stopped him. "Keeping kosher is enough to kill a man's appetite—wasn't that enough for you?"

Landauer muttered that he felt healthier than ever, that his mind was as clear as crystal and he no longer wanted to be a rabbi. "I've felt like a fraud my whole life. I've never really been certain about the nature of God, even though I've taught countless boys, such as yourself, to believe in His existence while at the same time declaring how any attempt to even understand God is a pompous, arrogant act." They'd walked for what seemed to Lev countless blocks. He felt empathy for the rabbi, but at the same time, he spotted a U-Bahn station out of the corner of his eye. And like all depressives, the rabbi remained unaware of time and the distance they'd covered. He continued the monologue of his spiritual breakdown, elaborating on details he'd already described, decrying his fallen place in life. The streetlights lit up, giving the rabbi's long sunken face a ghostly pallor, something akin to an El Greco painting. As the rabbi reiterated the healing effects of consuming tea derived from tree bark, Lev took his arm, nearly forcing him to stand still.

"How did this happen so suddenly?"

The rabbi shook his head, his gray beard thin and brittle. "I know now that I cannot return to the old ways. The old ways are dead."

At dinner, Lev turned this phrase over in his head—*the old ways are dead.* Were they? What were the old ways, as opposed to the new ones? Looking at his family around the table, he had his doubts about the future. His son, Franz, was a stranger to him. He clung to past heroes but knew nothing of battle. He was, in a word, not grown up. Under the influence of his friends in these reactionary groups, Franz, Lev noticed, was turning anti-intellectual, repudiating thinking as impotent. They clung to the rigidity of drill practice, ready for anyone who would command them, and yet when Lev tried to engage Franz on a subject he studied, Franz only stared at him blankly, answering, *Yes, No,* or *I don't know,* in an attempt to end the conversation as quickly as possible, as if talking with his father was a repellent exercise.

And his daughter, Vicki, who was in the middle of an argument about jazz—an argument she would never win with her mother—had such stubbornness, cutting off her hair without permission. When she shrugged, Lev admired her athletic shoulders, the way her face shimmered with just a touch of makeup under the chandelier, how when she leapt up to demonstrate the futility of the waltz, her body appeared weightless, nimble, free. Today, Vicki wore a striped dress hitting below the knee and she had a red pocketbook matching her openwork pumps, which were her two most recent purchases from Wertheim's, purchases Josephine had deemed indulgent. He thought he'd caught a whiff of cigarette smoke on her clothing when they waltzed around the dining table, possibly the unfiltered Turkish ones. Short hair, short dresses, cigarette smoking, gum chewing—this was how women acted today, their reckless determination admirable and confusing to Lev. On the train home, he watched young women like his daughter cut through the crowds on the sidewalk, their backs straight, eyes focused ahead, no chaperone in sight. The men his age offered up their seats to women on the train, which was now an apparently antiquated and boorish thing to do, but Lev did it. *As long as a man can still fall in love, he'll offer up his seat to a woman on the streetcar,* Lev told Vicki when she teased him about it. When he did so, younger women smiled as if he was in dire need of instruction. But women over forty almost always accepted his seat, whispering Thank you with such solemnity it was as if they were thanking him for upholding one of the last pillars of civilization. And maybe he was.

Franz mechanically stood up from the dinner table, averting his eyes. The boy is strange, Lev mused when Franz left the dining room, barely speaking. We have nothing in common—not music, not women, certainly not business. He said the other day he wanted to be a farmer, return to the soil. He worships that hermit Heidegger living in the Black Forest among the peasants, willfully provincial. But that is youth, confusing manual labor and living on the land for a certain purity of thought, an ideal that doesn't exist. Absolutes exist only for children . . . that's the problem—Franz is still a child.

Lost in thought, Lev hadn't realized that the table had been cleared, the lights dimmed, and he sat here alone. In the next room, he heard the radio on low, playing Vicki's beloved jazz. She'd probably knelt down next to it, her head resting on a cushion, dreaming of an alternate existence. He had hoped she would linger with him at the table, and the night would grow late, late enough for him to enter his bedroom and find Josephine already asleep.

When he went upstairs, Josephine was positioned at her vanity mirror, unhooking the coral necklace he'd given her some years back. He asked if she needed help, and she shook her head, the necklace sliding off her neck in one fell swoop. The clink of the coral beads against the crystal bowl, where she kept her less valuable jewelry, sounded like the start of an argument. Lev flopped down on his side of the bed, still wearing his shirt and tie and his lace-up oxfords. Josephine glanced with distaste at his shoes on the bedspread. Then she returned to examining her face in the mirror, tracing the faint lines around her eyes. The sound of a trumpet floated up the stairs. Mitzi growled from Franz's room.

Josephine sighed. "Franz seems out of sorts."

Lev pulled a cigarette from his case. "I wouldn't pay attention to it. Only makes it worse."

She started brushing her long fine hair. "I'm not."

"That's debatable."

She glared at him through the mirror. "Must we always have a debate?"

Lev smiled sarcastically. "Yes."

"I'm tired, Lev."

He stared at her long fine hair, the only part of her that had retained her girlishness, but hair was, ironically, dead matter.

She put down her brush and then picked it up again, scrutinizing the bristles. "When I called this afternoon—"

"I was out."

"Frau Blutcher didn't know where you'd gone. Is that how you instruct her to answer my calls?"

Lev peeled off his shirt. The room was stuffy and the ceiling fan sputtered. "I went to see my mother."

Josephine stopped brushing her hair and swiveled around on the miniature velvet stool. The front of her dressing gown flashed a slice of white skin. Instinctively, she tightened her robe. "Is she well?"

"No," Lev said. "She wants to see her grandchildren. Specifically Vicki."

Josephine strode across the room to retrieve her ivory comb. Twirling her hair into what looked like a long twisted ribbon, she tucked it up into a bun and speared the comb into it. Her fingertips lightly touching the sides of her head, she said, "I don't want Vicki exposed to the wrong elements."

Lev kicked off his shoes. His feet swelled in the heat. "She's old and lonely. Think of your own mother."

Josephine flinched. "My mother wasn't a Bolshevik."

"Your mother still sent the Kaiser a birthday card every year."

She suppressed a smile. For a moment, Lev thought they might not fight tonight. He stroked the hairs on his chest. It felt good to be touched, even by his own hand. Changing the subject, Lev said he'd heard that at Alfred Flechtheim's last private party during Fasching, Anita Berber wasn't allowed inside. She'd stood on the street yelling—everyone heard her all through the Tiergarten, but apparently she was fatally ill, having since gone south, to Baghdad of all places, to die of consumption.

Josephine perched on the foot of the bed. "Such a shame." She looked down at the satin bedspread, spreading her white hands over the smooth fabric. "I don't like Alfred Flechtheim much. I don't see why you still frequent his flat."

Lev sat up, no longer relaxed. "You don't like Flechtheim because he's a Jew."

She continued to concentrate on the bedspread. "I never said that."

"It's why you don't want Vicki to visit my mother, to know the Jewish side of the family."

She flashed him a nasty look. "You were with a woman this afternoon."

Lev crossed his arms over his chest. "Yes, it's true. My mother is a woman."

"Not your mother."

"Have you forgotten I'm a Jew too?"

She winced, as if she couldn't stand the sound of the word. "Why such insistence on this topic?" She paused. "What I mean is, you aren't exactly one of them, wearing those fur hats, speaking Yiddish, and praying in the corner." Then she slumped onto her side, resting her head in the crook of her arm. "I'm tired, Lev. Worn out. Exhausted."

"Are the meetings for the German Association for the Protection of Mothers so strenuous?"

Her lower lip trembled. For a moment, Lev felt sorry for her. The radio had been turned off, and the house was suddenly silent. He only heard the dog climbing the stairs, padding down the hall. He pulled at her robe, and she let it slip open. Shivering slightly, she glanced down at her bare shoulders. Lev's hands slipped under her breasts, as if weighing their merit. "So I'm a respectable Jew."

"Well," Josephine murmured, "yes."

They both laughed. A trace of hope dangled—Josephine's bare torso, her petulant smile, the way her hair caught the dim light. She stretched out on the bed, her naked body within reach. Lev slid on top of her, enjoying the mutual heat of her breasts pressing into him. She tugged on his earlobe. He nipped her shoulder and then buried his face into her neck, inhaling the soft darkness.

When he grew more decisive, wiggling out of his pants, pulling down her underwear, he felt her legs tense. He went ahead anyway. On top of her now, both of them naked, her thighs clamped around his waist. He could barely move forward or back. Her head turned to the side, her eyes shut. He didn't know how to proceed. Touching her face, he whispered, "Josephine? I can't move . . ."

"Herr K," she began weakly.

He dropped his head onto her chest. Ever since she'd started analysis, at Lev's prompting, this Herr K figure had emerged from the shadows of her girlhood with such force it seemed as if she still saw him at family dinners leering across the table, while her father looked on with the passive acknowledgment that his business partner fancied his fourteen-year-old daughter. She kept revisiting one episode in particular, which had occurred on a balcony overlooking a parade. Herr K had appeared out of the darkened living room and, closing the French double doors behind him, had tried to force himself on her. She'd described it to Lev in great detail: she felt the air empty from her chest, her nose rapidly filling with the strong tobacco he smoked. She'd tried to breathe through her mouth, but her throat closed like a fist clenching tighter and tighter. When she jerked her head to the side, she remembered seeing the slow-moving crowd below, the horse-drawn carriages, the brass band with their pageantry, the ladies twirling their parasols, children running. Her head grew light. A chilled sweat broke, soaking her underclothes. The parade dissolved into a blurry whiteness. The last thing she remembered was gripping Herr K's lapels, afraid she would pitch over the balustrade, headfirst into the throng. Afterward, no one understood what was so terrible about igniting the interest of a good-looking thirty-year-old bachelor with a promising career. She should feel flattered, her mother had said, and they apologized to Herr K, explaining away Josephine's rude behavior.

Josephine stroked Lev's hair, apologizing through her fingertips. Any chance was lost for tonight, as it had been for countless nights. Even before the emergence of Herr K, this cool reluctance, this inability of his wife's to fully capitulate had persisted; only now she attributed it to Herr K.

Lev drifted into sleep, vaguely aware of someone clipping the hedge outside. He curled onto his side, yanking the bedspread over his ear, and prepared himself for dreams of Leah, dreams he always had after seeing his mother.

16

North of Alexanderplatz, early evening, deafening traffic. Franz walked briskly, turning it over and over—why Wolf had looked at him with such disdain. They'd been eating luncheon in the cafeteria, and Wolf was telling Franz about a youth group, the Wandervogel (Wandering Bird), that met in the countryside on weekends. "Swimming and hiking and fresh air. Only men. Physical training and that sort of thing."

Franz had squeezed Wolf's arm and exclaimed, "Let's go, Wolffchen!" Wolf recoiled, as if Franz carried some infectious disease. Wolf's eyes—light blue with shards of a darker sea color—flickered for an instant before he wiped his mouth and threw down his napkin in a gesture that could only imply distaste. But everyone had nicknames in the fraternity—Oswald was Ossie, and Fritz, Fritzi—where did he misstep? The closeness they'd shared had unfolded so naturally over the spring term: fencing in the Tiergarten, swimming in the woods, the clear water submerging their light naked bodies. They shot water out of their mouths, propelling the limpid streams into each other's faces. But such a friendship proved an intricate dance, and he had stumbled.

He studied the second hand of his watch ticking. He ran his thumb along the smooth glass surface, chastising himself again for calling Wolf that silly name. He shouldn't have! A cigarette seller bumped into his shoulder. "Cigarettes?" His sour breath bloomed into Franz's face. Franz turned away muttering no thank you. Two women dressed as men strode by, bowler hats pulled down to their eyes. They walked arm in

arm, cutting through the throngs of people. He trailed them, noticing the way they laughed and smiled at each other, as if they alone felt
happy.

A boy grabbed at his jacket.

"Hey—what do you want? I don't have any money."

The boy smiled sheepishly. He had a beautiful mouth, lips the color
of raspberries. Long elegant limbs. Not so young in fact . . . close to
fifteen.

"Come on—I've got something to show you."

"Sure, but why make a point of it on the street?" Franz fingered the
banknotes in his jacket pocket—all there.

The boy shifted from one foot to the other, digging his hands deep
into his front pockets. "Come on, don't make this hard."

On an impulse, Franz ruffled the boy's hair, an auburn brown, soft
through his fingers. The boy looked up and a quiet smile passed between
them. "Let's go, then," he said, gesturing for Franz to follow him.

Last week, Wolf wrote a poem about his favorite whore. He described her legs, her ass, her breasts—Baudelaire's my inspiration, he'd
said. Franz didn't know Baudelaire—probably some damn French poet.
Then Wolf stopped his raving and asked Franz where he went for sex.
Right in front of everyone. "You never have a girl, so?" He'd raised
his golden eyebrows, his question so precise and mocking it cut right
through Franz.

The boy stopped in front of a looming apartment block on Breslauer
Strasse. The well-lit building led into a pitch-dark courtyard. Franz followed the boy up three flights of creaking stairs until they reached a
door illuminated by a paraffin lamp. The whole time Franz stared at the
boy's back, his legs, the way his light agile body easily climbed the stairs
made his chest tingle with anticipation. As the boy unlocked the door,
Franz stood close behind him and imagined grabbing him, sucking on
his soft downy earlobe.

The door opened into a dingy yellow kitchen that smelled of fried
fish and chopped onions. Franz took in the surroundings; the open
shelves for plates, the oilcloth covering the table, the cheap glass vase

engraved with flowers, the magazine *Die Dame* flung onto the seat of the chair. A sharp disappointment overwhelmed him when a woman emerged from behind the curtain separating the kitchen from the bedroom. She wore a slip dress and a silk robe over it. A string of fake pearls. A look of acknowledgment passed between the woman and the boy before he disappeared behind the curtain.

She sat down at the kitchen table and offered Franz a cigarette.

He stood behind the chair, gripping its frame. "I don't smoke."

She shrugged. "Suit yourself." She was clearly the boy's mother—the same auburn hair, freckles on the bridge of her nose, thin lips. Although he would have preferred the boy and was still recovering from feeling somewhat tricked, she wasn't bad looking—a little heavy in the hips, but her hair had a pleasing copper sheen to it, her hands white and delicate, fingernails clean.

She sighed and pulled the magazine from the chair. "Take a seat."

Franz sat down and folded his hands on the table. He heard a door open and close, and wondered if the boy had left.

She offered him sugar cookies arranged neatly on a chipped plate. He took one, bit into it.

She threw up her hands, her bracelets clanging together. "It's been hard since my husband died. I used to hang around Frankfurter Allee, near the railroad station, but it's easier with my son"—she hesitated—"lending a helping hand." She took a long drag and laughed bitterly. "We look after each other, in a way."

"How did your husband die, if I may ask?"

She pursed her lips. "Curiosity—that's what hooks men. We barely get by these days." She tapped the long column of gray ash into the ashtray. "So. What would you like?"

Franz rubbed his forehead, considering the question. He didn't know. He was still thinking about the boy, his long limbs, the way he'd smiled at him on the street with his open laughing face, hair in his eyes, that youthful dart around the corner as Franz followed closely behind, blood racing.

She continued, "I did hairdressing before he died. Respectable work." She sighed again, her freckled chest heaving. "You want to know how he died? He came back from the war in one piece. Two years later, crossing the street, a truck ran over him."

Behind her, the curtain rippled. Franz wondered if the boy stood on the other side, listening.

Her bed had already been turned down in anticipation. She'd put garnet-colored lampshades on the lamps to give off the impression of warmth. She bent over to roll down her silk stockings. Her backside, large, white, and gleaming, sickened him. A great deal of slack skin. When she sat up, her cheeks were flushed. Is this, Franz thought, what Wolf rushes off to on Thursday afternoons? What he boasts of? A waste of human energy. A shame. How he desecrates himself.

Franz told her to turn around. She nodded, and he gripped her fragile copper hair, some of the strands breaking off between his fingers. The back of her neck was thick and smelled of cigarettes. She grasped the brass bed frame, cried out a little, but she knew how to endure a certain amount of brutality. And yet, she probably didn't expect this from him—he seemed like a polite boy from a good family, wanting to know what regiment her husband had served in during the war. Franz dug his fingernails into her back and gripped her arm tightly. She would bruise from this.

Afterward, Franz threw a few crumpled bills onto the bedspread, which had been kicked down to the bottom of the bed. The woman lay on her side, her hand on her stomach. She watched him dress with dull gray eyes. He had exerted himself and it showed. He smoothed back his hair, wiped off his face with a towel he found lying by the freestanding sink. When he left the room, she tucked her chin into her chest and closed her eyes.

The boy was waiting for Franz in the kitchen. He started to cajole him into handing over more money, but Franz shoved him off, banging the front door behind him. As he descended the stairs, he heard a teakettle boiling, emitting a high-pitched whine.

. . .

"You're late," Marthe whispered, removing his linen blazer in the marble entry hall. His arms effortlessly slid out of the silk-lined sleeves. She
folded it over, smoothing down the jacket with affection.

Franz pinched her cheek. "Have they started?"

"Your mother insisted on waiting."

"What's for dinner? Anything good?"

"Oysters to start. Pea soup. Pike."

Franz wrinkled his nose. "Dessert?"

Marthe smiled. "Raspberry tart with marzipan icing."

"Delicious," Franz said, pinching her cheek again.

"Franz, don't," she said, suppressing a laugh. He'd done that since
he was little. But Josephine disapproved of such familiarity.

"Is that you finally?" Josephine called from the dining room.

He hesitated to answer.

She appeared at the end of the hallway, a slim apparition in navy
silk, the hemline hitting below her knee. She walked toward him,
already inspecting. Between her forefinger and thumb, she held the corner of her linen napkin, as if she hadn't the time to leave it on the table.
"Where have you been?"

"I'll just wash up first, Mother."

"Leave him be," Lev called from the dining room, followed by a
cough.

He started for the bathroom off the hallway.

"Wait." She touched his shoulder. "You're winded."

"It was crowded getting home."

She gazed at him, her eyes wide and gleaming. "Why are you late?"
She cupped his chin. "You smell of cabbage."

Franz gently removed her hand from his face. "The tram was full
of stenographers. Rush hour." He smiled. "Everyone coming home."

The dining room blazed with light; the crystal chandelier hanging over
the table and the lit candles flickering over the china and the glittery
hairpin fixed in Vicki's dark hair made Franz squint. She'd cut off her

hair yesterday—he thought it looked ugly. Vicki was talking about dancing; she was always talking about dancing. She wanted the radio on during dinner because that's when Radio Berlin broadcast her favorite jazz bands, but Josephine refused, saying music shouldn't be consumed as if standing at some lunch counter wolfing down a gherkin. It required patience, concentration. "That atonal noise you love—I wouldn't even call it music."

"It's called jazz, thank you very much." Vicki dissected her fish quickly, separating out the tiny white bones from the flesh. She did everything quickly, hardly ever still, unless Franz found her splayed on the couch after one of her dances in the early evening, her shoes kicked off, her feet up on the armrest, her toes curling and uncurling, encased in silk stockings. Then she would speak low and soft, staring dreamily into the brocaded wallpaper as if a pattern existed there that only she could see.

"It's Negro music," Franz said, taking a sip of water. "Primitive and frenetic." His hands felt dirty even though he had cleaned them thoroughly in the bathroom. That woman stuck on his skin—he wouldn't feel clean until standing under the shower for at least ten minutes, the water scalding hot. Afterward, he would use a nailbrush, dislodging any debris from her that might have gotten stuck. Her thick neck, the cigarette smell—he revisited this as he reached for the butter encased in a rectangle of porcelain.

Josephine anticipated this and handed him the butter dish. "Here." Her fingertips felt cool and soft.

"Thank you, Mutti." *The mind is a terrible master but a wonderful servant*—was that it? Franz wondered. Or had Wolf said, *The mind is a terrible servant but a wonderful master?*

Franz had taken the tram three extra stops just to recover from the nausea washing over him. He dragged himself home, inhaling the cool air, holding it in his lungs, releasing his breath slowly, trying to exorcize himself of the grimy apartment, the boy's sly smile, the way she'd tapped the long column of ash into the ashtray.

"You can't possibly reduce Erno Rapee down to that. He's a brilliant jazz symphonist. If you'd turn on the radio right now, you'd hear for yourself." Vicki banged her glass on the table. A little water spilled, discoloring the linen tablecloth.

"Vicki, please," Josephine said without looking up from her plate.

"Well, it's not primitive! Jazz is not created by merely playing a syncopated two/two bar. It is full of complex rhythm, harmonic precision, auditory and modulatory richness."

"You're only repeating what Herr Laban says."

Vicki rolled her eyes at Franz.

He stared at her and then said the barrette in her hair looked cheap.

Vicki touched it. "It's not."

Marthe cleared the soup bowls. She hesitated, glancing over Franz's shoulder. "You're not hungry?"

He held up his bowl. "Too much lunch." His stomach clenched and unclenched. All he could get down was water, possibly some clear broth, but the pea soup, heavy with cream, stuck in his throat.

"He should come home for lunch, like a civilized person. Otherwise, the digestion suffers," Josephine said, shaking her head.

Vicki threw down her napkin. "Can we please turn on the radio?"

Lev smiled at his daughter. "I agree with your mother. Jazz and its accompanying dances have lost that nostalgic sweeping grace from before the war. These new dances are hollow, mechanical, too fast and feverish . . ." He paused, searching for the right words. "And yet there's something liberating and free there too." He sat back in his chair, glancing at Josephine. "We used to waltz."

"It was a beautiful time," she said, fingering the long string of coral beads draped around her neck.

Lev stared into the flickering candlelight.

Vicki pushed back her chair. "There's no life in a waltz!"

Franz grumbled, "The Charleston, the shimmy. You all look like dancing monkeys high on caffeine."

Vicki laughed. "Excuse me, he who doesn't take alcohol or coffee or cigarettes. You should—just once—come out, listen to the bands. But instead, you insist on spending all your time in your room, doing whatever you do. Or hanging around Wolf."

"So?" Franz snapped.

She shrugged. "He's a bit . . ."

Lev stood up. "Vicki, I'll show you how to waltz. It's tranquil—you have time to gaze into your partner's eyes."

Josephine threw up her hands. "We haven't even finished with the second course."

Lev motioned to Marthe. She turned on the radio, the dial skimming through news programs, the daily weather, horse races, until a Strauss waltz filtered into the dining room.

Josephine sighed, pushing away her plate.

Lev walked over to Vicki, taking her hand. "Put your arm here," he instructed. "Tilt your head to the side, your gaze skimming just above my shoulder, as if you're looking out into a grand vista."

"A grand vista," Vicki repeated sarcastically. "I see yellow walls. Butter yellow. Not very inspiring."

They started waltzing around the table, Vicki trying to lead and Lev steering the small of her back. "Settle into the music."

Vicki shook her head, erupting into laughter. "I can't. It's just too boring."

"If you aren't cycling, jumping rope, and having a love affair all at once it's boring, isn't it?"

Vicki shrugged.

Marthe popped her head into the dining room. "Shall I bring out coffee with the cake?"

"You barely ate," Josephine whispered across the table.

"I'm really fine," Franz said.

"Are we dancing or not dancing?" Lev asked.

"Dancing, dancing!" Vicki protested, and then she settled down, laying her cheek on Lev's shoulder. He counted the time under his breath.

Josephine stood up in one long fluid motion.

Franz smiled weakly at his mother. She was coming over to inspect him again. "Darling," she said, stroking his hair. "What's troubling you?"

"Nothing," he muttered, staring down at the navy trim scalloping the edge of the white plate.

Lev and Vicki finally stopped swirling around the table and sat down again.

She caressed his neck. "Are you upset over a girl?"

A girl. He'd been with two girls and each time he'd felt nothing of the hot rush other men described. Nothing but the mechanical motion of two bodies mashing up against each other, followed by the revolting closeness women thought you owed them afterward, the way they twirled their hair and stared at their nails and flung a stray leg over his. Both times, he'd left in a hurry, wishing he'd never done it, furious at his own inability to feel what others boasted of in graphic detail.

"A girl?" Vicki echoed. "Franz doesn't even notice girls."

He frowned, still staring down at his plate.

Lev grinned. "He's very serious, wrapped up in his studies, and all the clubs. Cycling club. Fencing club. Reading club. Walking club. There's a club for everything, as if it isn't allowed to just go to the cinema or have a drink on one's own anymore."

"I heard there's a club for people who're third children," Vicki said, stabbing a limp green bean with her fork.

His head pounded, the yellow walls claustrophobic whenever he looked up from his plate. The smell of the offensive pea soup still lingered, even though Marthe had cleared it. He stood up and said he had to excuse himself. When he left the room, he felt his mother's eyes trailing his back with that pleading questioning look she reserved for him. It was intolerable, how she doted on him, but at the same time, when his head fell into her soft lap, and he let the sound of her voice wash over him as she told him bits and pieces of irreverent gossip, his body loosened, his jaw went slack, and the weight of his thoughts floated upward, toward the rise and fall of her breath.

He climbed the stairs, overhearing Lev tease Vicki about her figure. "So thin and athletic. You don't have enough meat on you to waltz!"

They were always speaking so loudly, he thought. Almost yelling. While his mother was soft and quiet, the way a woman should be. His father only encouraged Vicki's tendency to carry on with artists, smoking and drinking and dancing all night. And now she'd gone and cut off all her hair.

"So you have to be fat as well as boring to waltz?" Her voice rang out, followed by a peal of laughter.

Franz paused on the second to last stair, trying not to make a sound. If he waited here for a few more minutes, would they say something about him, about why he never had a girl? He clenched the banister, listening to the swish of the kitchen door, which carried the scent of marzipan and berries. His mouth salivated for the cake Marthe placed on the table. The dog Mitzi roamed down the hall and, spotting Franz, picked up her pace.

Franz knelt on the stairs, motioning for Mitzi to come to him.

"The fashion will inevitably change to a more Rubenesque figure. I heard in America they already have pills you can take, to fatten you up overnight," Lev said.

"I'm never taking those pills!" Again, such a loud voice, so piercing. He squeezed his eyes shut in aggravation. "No, no—just a little piece please," Vicki said. Now they're eating cake, he thought, running his fingers through Mitzi's coarse black fur.

Then his mother's voice, muffled and low in comparison. "I want to check on him. He might be ill."

"If I were dying, literally dying on my deathbed, you wouldn't even notice," Vicki retorted. Franz imagined her spearing her fork into a piece of cake to give her comment the full effect.

Sitting at the top of the stairs, Franz heard the start of that incessant clipping coming from next door, right below his bedroom window. The wind through the trees softened the sound, but he heard it whenever the wind died down. Feeling the heat rise in his chest, he stormed into his room and pushed the curtains back, and yes, as he expected, he saw Herr Lenevski, in the dying light, trimming the hedge that separated their two houses. A White Russian who wore a monocle and butchered the German language. Franz glared down at the bald spot blooming in the center of his head. He balanced on a ladder, his spectacles sitting low on the ridge of his nose as he snipped away, obsessed with the height of the hedge, that it was too high and blocked the necessary sunlight for his roses. He thought about opening the window and yelling at him to stop. But then Herr Lenevski would swear back at him in Russian and

Mitzi would start barking and then his mother and sister would run up into his room. He flopped down on his bed. *Clip, clip.* He resisted the magazines stashed underneath the bed in a shoebox because his mother might appear any moment now. If she saw these magazines, and what he did while he read them, she would be appalled. He let his hand slide down to the floor. He fingered the bed skirt, knowing the magazines lay on the other side of it. His two favorites: *Eros: Magazine for Friendship* and *Freedom, Love and Life-Art*, with lifelike illustrations of soldiers marching in time and then fornicating on the other side of the page. And *Ernst*, the more love-oriented magazine, with poetry in the style of Rilke and short stories accompanied by romantic drawings of men during the period of ancient Greece. They fed one another fruit, stroked one another's shoulder-length hair, and embraced next to fountains, water spouting forth. He tried not looking at the magazines too often, but when he was alone in his room, especially in the afternoons, when he came home from class and the house was quiet, he surrendered to the images, gorging on them. Afterward, he guiltily cleaned up the mess, not wanting Marthe or anyone else to find traces of his illicit activities. He always promised himself he would not look at the magazines again, but of course, within a few days, he always succumbed.

Clip, clip, clip. How much was he lopping off? Franz leapt over to the window, again pushing back the curtains. Mitzi picked up her head but didn't move from the foot of the bed. The Russian had vanished, his ladder abandoned against the brick wall.

Defeated, he slumped into his desk chair, and switched on the lamp. He fingered the open pages of the novel he'd started, Hans Grimm's *Volk ohne Raum* (A People Without Space), a long rant about the lack of living space in Germany. He sighed, closed the thick book, and stared at the snapshot of himself and Wolf taken last summer in one of the new photo booths where pictures develop within minutes. They'd waited in the photo booth, pressed together, their breath intermingling, wondering when the images would spit out of the little slot. Wolf sat on his lap because of the one stool, and Franz inhaled the particular scent of shaving lotion Wolf used, a lemony balsam. Wolf didn't notice the swell in Franz's pants, and if he did notice, he didn't recoil. He acted as if it wasn't happening, which Franz took as a hopeful sign. Wolf grinned while Franz assumed a dignified expression, as if posing for a family portrait. Wolf teased him about it afterward, how serious he'd been about the snapshots, how he'd wanted them to look a certain way. Walking away from the photo booth, Franz quickly draped his blazer over his arm and held it stiffly out in front of him, as a kind of curtain. Wolf shot him a sidelong glace and then tossed his copy of the photograph into a nearby trash bin.

Franz spent the rest of the afternoon despairing over whether Wolf had noticed or not, and if he did notice, was he utterly repelled? Which would justify how casually, almost cruelly, Wolf had thrown away their photograph. As punishment. And to explain, without having to explain, that he didn't care for Franz, at least not in that way. Afterward, when he'd sat next to Wolf at the bar, their knees knocking from time to time, Wolf appeared wholly unbothered, playing cards and describing a recent fox hunt at his grandfather's estate—how his horse had suffered a stress fracture in the splint bone and they almost had to call off the hunt. Franz tried to listen, arranging his face into an amused smile, but at one point he had to excuse himself for the lavatory, where he sat down in the stall, his face in his hands, breathing deeply, trying to ignore the stench of urine, the sticky floors, the sound of doors banging open and shut, trying to hold back his tears, the pressure building behind his eyes.

Franz sauntered over to the framed photograph of Wolf from that day, his own face nearly obscured. He had placed it on a low table next to his bed, which displayed other important items: a Hakenkreuz pin that he fixed to the knot of his tie, the black, white, and red banner of Imperial Germany draped over the table, serving as a makeshift tablecloth, and his DNVP membership card. He was now a young member of the German National People's Party. His father didn't know. At meetings, they spoke of restoring Germany to her former glory, that a moral and national rebirth was necessary to reestablish Germany's long-lost connection to the ancient Greeks—that the true German *volk* would only emerge when the foreigners, the Jews and the Slavs, had been expunged. And above this altar, as he called it, he'd hung two oil portraits to be enjoyed simultaneously: Frederick the Great on horseback and Bismarck, his domineering profile illuminated by a bloodred background.

He heard his mother's light footsteps ascend the staircase and down below the radio turned up, jazz blasting.

"Vicki—please! Lower the dial," Josephine called from the stairs.

Franz ran his finger along the edge of the gilt frame, as if he could touch Wolf von Trotta's perfect cheekbones.

17

In March, Geza arrived in Berlin. The changeable sky confounded him, compared to the constancy of his Russian sky. Here, clouds shifted unpredictably. Rain started and stopped, and the sun emerged, blindingly bright, without warning. Never knowing if the day would grow cold or hot, he often perspired too much or shivered in a thin shirt, ill prepared. In his view, the unreliable weather explained the irritable and frenetic nature of Berliners. They pushed and shoved on the tram. A simple exchange, for instance the buying of a sausage roll, was rushed, the vendor clearly impatient with how slowly Geza conducted himself. So he trained himself to speed up, moving his hands swiftly even for simple tasks—unlocking the door, buying bread, spooning his soup, taking off his hat. He carried out these mundane actions with alacrity, with an uncharacteristic crispness. And he started walking at a clipped pace down the street to keep up with the mass of moving bodies walking even faster alongside him. Avoiding eye contact was another behavior he copied, observing how people looked down at the pavement or just past his shoulder, as if acknowledging a fellow pedestrian indicated a softness, a weakness, or that you wanted something.

If Geza had stayed in Mitau, he would have joined the Red Army, as his friends had done. His mother and his stepfather, Zlotnik, also urged him to join, because if he enlisted, the family would receive food rations and assistance with farm work. He refused. He did not believe in the workers' movement, suspicious when they proclaimed that Jews were equal to Russians, using Trotsky, head of the Red Army, as a prime example of this new Russian Jew. Despite his mother's protestations, he had left Mitau two years ago and worked in Warsaw as an apprentice bricklayer, saving up enough money to come to Berlin. Eventually, he hoped to move to Palestine. When he got to Berlin, he first found work as a nightclub errand boy, but he should have known such a job would expose him to illegal activities, and after a near run-in with the law, he quit.

Now Geza worked as a bricklayer again, through the recommendation of his boss in Warsaw. It was fine work. He always had Fridays off, which he liked to spend in the Prussian State Library, in the cool confines of those rooms, leafing through newspapers or just staring into space. His life felt simple: he started work at seven and he finished at eight. The boardinghouse provided him with a cot, a blanket, and every Friday clean sheets that smelled of starch. Sure, he had to share a room with a family of four, and sometimes the joints in his hands hurt after work, but he didn't mind. He wore the same white apron and black pants, his uniform for bricklaying. He grew to like his fellow workers, a rowdy crew from Odessa who spent all their wages on vodka and then complained that they never earned enough to keep a girl. Geza smiled at them, bemused by their theatrics, while he quietly saved and saved.

Only one thing was not simple: the envelope sewn into his threadbare jacket. Inside the envelope was a letter from his aunt Leah for Lev Perlmutter. She had asked, just before he left Mitau two years ago, that if he made it to Berlin, he must find Lev Perlmutter and give him the letter. She had not really asked him. She had thrust the letter into his hands and demanded it. She had learned to read and write for this very purpose. It had taken her a year. "If you find him, give it to him," she had said, her face clouded with urgency. "Promise me," she insisted. Geza promised.

He carried this promise around his neck like a stone, even though he knew where Lev lived. He knew Lev's house in Charlottenburg with the blue door and the brass handle and the white lilies lining the pathway. He had seen the stately brick mailbox, a little house unto itself inside the low garden wall, into which he could easily slip the letter. But he had not done it.

That day in March, when he went to deliver the letter, he hovered outside the garden wall, watching for the right moment to dispense with it. He wanted to complete the task, as he found romantic entanglements such as these distasteful. Just then, the front door opened. Geza shivered in his white shirt and watched Lev skip down his steps, whistling a popular tune. He looked healthy and rich, smoking a cigarette, wearing an expensive fedora. About to turn away, Geza saw a young woman laughing and calling after Lev. The sound of her voice, as melodious as a little bell, entranced him. She wore a knit cap molded to the shape of her perfect head. Sunlight bounced off the crisp white fabric of her dress. Her long dark hair streamed down her back, and there was something intelligent and daring about her, despite how she still wore her hair long. Perhaps it was the way she teased her father or the way her agile movements gave the impression of lightness, fluttering before him like a skylark.

He couldn't stop looking at her.

She teased Lev, motioning to his bowtie, and they laughed. Then Lev took her arm and they made their way down the stone path.

Geza darted out of view, hiding behind one of the massive oak trees lining the street. After a few moments, a woman and a young man also emerged from the house. He concluded the woman, also in white, must be Lev's wife. She held her head high and wore an elaborate hat with feathers and pearls in it. The hat reminded him of an ostrich. The boy sulked and she tried to comfort him. Geza thought it was strange, how this boy, who was nearly a man, acted as if someone had taken away his toys. City life must make men soft, he thought. The mother and son walked behind Lev and his daughter. Clutching the letter, Geza trailed the family down the street for a few blocks. He tried to catch what the girl was saying, to know more about her, but he couldn't hear the exact words. Only the golden sound of her voice washed over him.

Leah's letter was still sewn into his coat pocket, even now, as he walked to the Prussian State Library with a few sheets of loose paper under his arm. He might write to his mother and reassure her all was well. Or he might let his mind wander in the vast octagonal reading room. So quiet and still, the reading room provided relief from the tumult of the boardinghouse, with cigar smoke lingering on the furniture, the running children and their mothers shouting after them.

Out of the corner of his eye, Geza noticed a woman leap over a puddle, and the lightness in her step reminded him of the girl he had seen that day, when he almost dropped off Leah's letter. Almost. But when he had his chance, after Lev and his family rounded the corner, he chose not to. Lev had looked comfortable in his life—and his beautiful daughter adored him. Despite his promise to Leah, Geza also thought such a letter, whatever its contents, might ruin this family. And then what? What did Leah want from Lev after all this time? The simple act of dropping her letter in Lev's mailbox would involve Geza in more tumult, more tears, more separation when the world with its Great War had already had enough of this. No, Geza had decided, I won't do it. I'll wait at least and see. He didn't know what he was waiting for, but it felt like enough to walk away with the letter still in his possession, convinced he had somehow helped the young girl with the ringing voice in her white dress, a sight of beauty he would otherwise never have seen.

18

When Vicki woke up the next morning, the house felt strangely quiet. Her father must have left for work already, her mother sequestered in one of the numerous rooms of the house where less heat could reach her, and Franz had jaunted off to one of those nature hikes in the woods. She couldn't think of anything less appealing than sleeping in a pitched tent and praising the merits of vegetarianism over an open fire. She dressed, grinning at herself in the mirror. Yes, it was still short. Nothing had changed overnight. Grabbing her watch, she paused, contemplating the time. Late: already nine. She should have been at the library by now, studying for her foreign language exams. Evil exams, forcing her to sit still in a silent room with other silent students, their spines curled into question marks, squinting at dusty fine print, when outside she could hear the activity of summer humming. The humming seeped into her blood, made her heart beat faster, made her arms swing along when she walked, appreciative of her youth at this particular moment in time. At least she would have the walk there before shutting herself away in the somber, gray stone Prussian State Library, sitting for hours in the octagonal reading room, the tables and chairs arranged around a weak circle of sunlight filtering through the dome.

She ran down the stairs, her hand gliding along the wooden banister. Marthe heard her from the kitchen and called out to ask if she wanted coffee.

"Can't. I'm late."

"At least take a roll!"

Fixing her hat at the bottom of the stairs, Vicki hollered, "No time!"

. . .

On Friedrichstrasse, little white flyers fell from the sky. Vicki caught one descending, and glancing over it—some right-wing group pushing their candidate for the elections—she let it fall from her fingers. There were always elections, parties forming and dissolving and forming again. It didn't matter to her. What mattered was the larger than life Marta Eggerth painted on the side of a building, smiling down on all those little flyers, her ruby lips, her pencil-thin eyebrows, her shorter than short hair. Vicki cut through the crowds of men in their suits and hats, some of them standing still, reading the flyer. Two girls chatted while riding their bicycles, and Vicki recognized them from French class. She admired the crocheted white beret one of the girls wore. Wondering where she'd bought it, maybe at Tietz's, Vicki leapt over a small puddle and, feeling more sprightly than usual, cleared it by a good meter.

She approached the library, staring up at the hulking stone structure, the imposing columns, the front blanketed with flowering ivy that would turn reddish brown in a few months. When she entered, the hushed quiet and the sight of other people working away at desks, the lit-up lamps giving off an air of studiousness and concentration, settled her mind. She knew her way around the interlocking rooms without giving it a thought, arriving at her spot, the great reading room with its odd octagonal shape. Sitting down in the third row from the center point of the room, there were two more rows of people in front of her, a necessary distraction, while at the same time, many more rows extended behind her. Shuffling papers, books opening and closing, someone furtively unwrapping a sandwich, an errant whisper—the din of work and study made Vicki feel less alone, as if she wasn't the only one stuck inside on a Friday, when she knew others were swimming and lounging on blankets and laughing their heads off.

Don't think about it, she commanded, reaching into her leather satchel for *A Student's Guide to French Language and Literature.* Was it essential she read Flaubert in the original? Did Madame Bovary care one way or another? Her father always said he regretted not learning French, wasting his time on Latin and Greek. Before opening the book, she glanced around at her reading companions. At the next desk, a girl leafed through *BIZ (Berliner Illustrirte Zeitung)*, scrutinizing a German film star smiling in the California sun; the next page showed the Egyptian pyramids from the air. Two middle-aged men in front of her bent over a medieval calendar of days. Many had staked their claim to a particular desk by leaving a briefcase or a stack of books on top of it while they smoked outside in one of the inner courtyards. Maybe, she thought, a cigarette first would help?

She reached down again into her satchel, groping for her metal cigarette case, when she felt someone watching her. Out of the corner of her eye, she saw a young man sitting a few rows back. He wore dark clothes, a dark hat next to him on the desk, his face long and lean. While he studied her, he fiddled with a toothpick. She detested men who used toothpicks in public. Pretending not to notice him, she glided out of the reading room, walking toward the arched doorways leading to the courtyard. As she pushed open the heavy door, she realized she'd forgotten her cigarette case on the table, but returning to fetch it would reveal more of herself than she wanted, giving him the idea that he'd flustered her. Instead, she waited lamely in the courtyard.

Enough time had elapsed to return to the reading room without seeming as if it was all a ploy or device to garner his attention. And maybe he wouldn't even be there. As she pushed the door open again into the hushed gray quiet, one of Elsa's phrases flashed through her mind: *Love grossly exaggerates the microscopic, nearly invisible differences between one bumbling human and another.* So typical of Elsa to say while she mooned over Heinz Lienek, who'd dumped her for Klara Manning, head of the KPD chapter in Wedding. Elsa could be annoying, Vicki thought, feeling her heart accelerate as she neared the reading room and saw that lone figure sitting in the same place, his dark hat in front of him. On impulse, she tossed back her hair, only to realize her long braid was gone, and so she must have looked odd, her neck jerking back like that. He watched her return to her seat, his eyes fixed on her neck, her back, her shoulders. Her short hair swung in front of her face, and she mechanically pushed it behind her ear. Before sitting down, she shot him a haughty look, but then without meaning to, she smiled a little and his eyes lit up.

She sat down. It was impossible to work now. He remained behind her, fidgeting with his hat. He didn't have any books. Only a few sheets of blank paper. Vicki felt pleased that she'd worn her openwork pumps with the matching red pocketbook, but then she chastised herself for caring. Why should she care what he thought of her? He looked shabby, wearing thick dark clothes in summer, his face wolfish with those slanted eyes and high cheekbones, and the way he just stared without a hint of embarrassment. He hadn't offered her a cigarette or a coffee. He hadn't asked where she studied, or if she liked jazz, or if she preferred the Charleston to the fox-trot, or if she followed the horse races, or if she'd seen the latest Hertha Schroeter film at the Capitol Filmpalast. And he wouldn't because it didn't seem as if he knew about these things.

In the distance, she heard the church bells mark the hour. Already one o'clock and she'd barely made progress. Ignoring hunger pains, she pressed on. Once, when he stood up to go, Vicki felt a stab of disappointment. But then she saw he'd left his hat and papers behind, and an unwarranted sense of relief washed over her. Alert to every minute that passed while he was gone, when he returned with a newspaper under his arm, she pretended to be engrossed in adverbial pronouns. Furrowing her brow, she read: *The French adverbial pronoun* y *is so tiny that one might think its role in a sentence is not very important, but in fact quite the opposite is true. It is extremely important in French.* She glanced at the pages of his newspaper and saw it was in Russian. His eyes darted from one article to the next until he noticed her looking at him. Vicki immediately glanced down, reading: *You cannot replace the noun with an object pronoun. For example: I'm going to think about your proposal. I'm going to think about it. Right: Je vais réfléchir à votre proposition. Je vais y réfléchir. Wrong: Je vais réfléchir, Je vais la réfléchir, Je vais lui réfléchir.*

She slowly lifted her eyes from the page, grateful to find his face obscured by an article about Diaghilev.

Late afternoon settled in, lending the room a melancholic, trembling light. People began to leave, packing up their belongings, the sounds of which echoed throughout the vast room. With the light dying and people drifting away from their desks, the reading room reminded her of a massive mausoleum, and she shivered at the thought of getting locked in, sleeping among the ghostly stacks, the words of forgotten authors breathing through the spines of dusty books. With that, she snapped her book closed and hastily slid the rest of her things into her leather satchel. The young man remained, leafing through the sports section, fixated by a large photograph of the boxer Max Schmeling shaking hands with the American vice president.

He didn't look up when she left. Stepping into the late-afternoon sun, which normally brought great relief, Vicki felt agitated. For all his staring, he didn't even bother to glance up from his newspaper when she walked by, swinging her satchel, clearly leaving for good this time. Maybe she had daydreamed the whole exchange, creating an imaginary dialogue between them out of nothing. Maybe he hadn't even noticed her. Maybe he stared that way at every woman. She started to walk down the steps, trying to forget the incident, when she felt a light tap on her shoulder. "Miss? Excuse me?"

She caught her breath, unprepared to find him standing right in front of her. The first thing she noticed was the long white scar running down his cheek, as if someone had slashed him there. At least he was freshly shaven, but he'd nicked his jaw, the cut covered over with a bit of gray paper.

"I'm sorry. I didn't mean to frighten you." He had a thick Russian accent.

Vicki forced a smile.

Pausing, he formulated the next sentence in his head before speaking—it was the same look of intent concentration Vicki often saw on the faces of her fellow students in French class, working out the subjunctive and the conditional, the formal or the informal, in hopes of not fumbling up the whole sentence.

"I believe you forgot this in the reading room?"

Her red pocketbook. "That was very kind of you," she said, taking it from him.

He shrugged, shoving his hands deep into his pockets. "You are welcome."

For a prolonged moment, they stood on the library steps. He studied his worn-down boots, which had been recently polished. Vicki fiddled with her bracelet, a thin gold chain with a pendant of a ballet slipper hanging from it, before saying, "Thank you again. I should be getting home." The sky had clouded over into a warm blanket of gray, trapping the heat.

He took his hands out of his pockets, gesturing to the busy street. "Would you prefer me to accompany you to your home?"

"Oh, no, that's all right."

"All right," he said, gently taking her by the elbow.

When she hesitated, he asked, "Shall we go now?"

"Oh, well, actually—" Vicki faltered.

His dark eyes scanned her face. His hair, so black it shone with a bluish tint, momentarily fell into his eyes before he brushed it back.

"Yes, all right," she said.

He strode beside her now, a slight smile curling on his lips. Whenever she paused, at a corner or a stop sign or a light, he joked that she knew the way to her own house; he did not. She said she was only figuring out the best way. What is the best way? he asked.

"The best way is the fastest way." Talking to him, she noticed how she used simple words and phrases, how she spoke more slowly because she couldn't tell how much he understood. He asked her what she was reading in the library.

"French," she said.

"Voltaire?"

She looked at him, surprised. "We did read him. Now we're reading Flaubert."

He grinned. "The materialistic impulse killed her."

"Who?"

"Madame Bovary," he said somewhat defensively.

She meant to turn right, toward the Tiergarten, but they kept walking down Kanonier Strasse. She wanted to walk with him through the heavy foliage of the park, where she would feel less distracted by the constant barrage of traffic and the oncoming waves of pedestrians, which sporadically separated them. She wanted to ask him why he went to the reading room and how long he'd been in Berlin, and what his name was, but then she'd spoil the mystery of the encounter.

They exchanged shy glances every now and then, as if they were still sitting a few rows apart in the library. Intermittently, he would make a comment about something they'd both witnessed, such as how the woman carrying her Pomeranian around in her purse, its little black nose sniffing the air, clearly had an unhealthy obsession with the animal, or could Vicki see in the second-story window that man getting ready for a party, putting on his waistcoat and tying his white tie?

Despite these comments, long stretches passed when he didn't talk much, and she couldn't tell if he was just shy or if his German was still too elementary. She didn't know his name or where he came from, and yet here they were, walking in silence as if they'd grown so comfortable with each other that they didn't feel compelled to converse. Luckily, the sounds of the city filled these fallow silences with passing sirens, news vendors repeating the latest headlines, the gust of a double-decker bus turning the corner, a policeman emitting a sharp whistle. A few times, his hand brushed against her gloved one, but he made no indication that he had intended to touch her hand or if it pleased him. As they walked, he occasionally asked her questions about things they passed, and to her surprise, she didn't always know the answer. He wanted to know what the *white weeks* meant when they walked by the KaDeWe department store windows advertising *White Weeks*. Everything in the display was white—white handkerchiefs, white linens, white lace collars, white gloves, white undergarments. Vicki replied that everything white must be on sale. But he wanted to know what was so special about white. "Is it highly demanded, here in Berlin?"

"I guess," she said, stealing a glance at him.

He frowned. "It's much more difficult to wash white. I would think people are less likely to buy such a color. The moment you step outside, dirt jumps on it."

She smiled. "That's probably why people like it. You would only wear it if you could afford to wash it often, as if all you did was lounge in drawing rooms, eating tea sandwiches."

He nodded, turning this over in his head. "I think it's arrogant, to wear white."

Vicki shrugged.

Passing a gourmet butcher, a hulking ham hung in the window. He wrinkled his nose, as if he could smell the pork through the plated glass.

"I would personally choose never to wear white," he added.

"Never?"

Next to the butcher, hydrangeas, carnations, tulips, and baby roses crowded a florist's window. Vicki stopped in front of the elaborate display, pressing her palm against the cool glass. "What if you were getting married?"

He looked down at his shoes. "I would wear a dark suit."

"But if you were a woman getting married, would you still refuse white on principle?" she teased.

"I am not a woman," he said curtly.

They stood in front of the florist's window, staring at the flowers, all of which looked artificially perfect. Vicki imagined that the dewdrops peppering the hydrangea leaves had been carefully dispensed with a syringe to suggest freshness.

He turned away from the window. "Those flowers look strange, wrapped up in red foil. I prefer wildflowers, just growing in the fields."

"Are the ones in Russia much prettier?"

"Of course."

Vicki thought he maintained quite strong opinions for an immigrant, disliking most of what he saw. And yet everyone else she knew always raved about everything, describing, for instance, the iced coffee at Hiller's as divine, fabulous, utterly supreme.

Their pace slowed to a more leisurely stroll. When she asked him where he was from, he flashed her a mysterious handsome smile. "You already know this, so why do you ask?"

"But where in Russia?"

He gazed at the church steeple rising up above the congested city.

"Mitau. Just a little village, about fifty kilometers from Riga. It used to be part of Courland, then Poland, then Russia, and now Poland again. I'm sure it will change twenty times over."

"Mitau," Vicki repeated, her face lighting up. "I know it."

He laughed. It was the first time she saw him laugh, the skin around his eyes crinkling up like the folds in a paper fan.

"I really do," she said, putting her hand on his arm. He stiffened and she felt the smooth shape of his musculature tensing under his thin coat. A warm flutter moved through her body, like a moth trapped inside her chest. "My father was stationed there during the war."

He glanced away uneasily. "Your father, is he from Berlin?"

"I grew up just across the park. My name's Vicki, by the way, short for Viktoria, but everyone calls me Vicki, or V."

"Vicki," he repeated, staring at her. "I like your hair short, even though it was beautiful long."

She frowned. "How did you know my hair used to be long?"

Heat traveled up his neck, blooming into his face. "I apologize—I only meant to say it must have been beautiful long. My German is still not as good as I would like." He rubbed his forehead and glanced down at the pavement.

She took his arm, and this time, he didn't tense under his jacket. "Your German is quite good."

"Let's keep walking. It's so nice to walk," he said.

As if in silent competition, the store windows lit up one by one, anticipating the moment when the sun would set and their bright facades would illuminate the streets, causing people to stop and desire what they saw. The lit windows reminded Vicki she didn't have all night to wander the streets. But she didn't want to rush off, especially after her blunder—she hadn't meant to make him feel self-conscious of his German, so she walked on a little longer, overly aware of the minutes ticking by on her watch. She tried not to glance down at her wrist, but a general sense of anxiety settled over her as she thought about her mother, who hated it when she ran late. And then she'd have to explain her lateness, and she couldn't possibly mention walking with a strange man down Potsdamer Strasse, which was already out of the way from her usual route. To get home, she'd have to cut back up to Kurfürstenstrasse. An omnibus heading in the direction of Charlottenburg stopped at the corner. Vicki dove her hand into the side pocket of her purse, confirming she had the fare of ten pfennigs, plus another five to tip the conductor.

She explained that she was already late, but it had been so enjoyable to walk with him, and maybe she would see him again at the reading room, but it was the weekend now, so she might not go until Monday, especially with the fine weather—but, oh, the bus was leaving any second, so unfortunately she'd have to say good-bye. The words tumbled from her mouth while he maintained a stony silence, which only caused her to grow more verbose. Finally, she stopped, out of breath, and said before hopping on the bus, "And after all that, I nearly forgot to ask your name!"

He looked stunned, as if she had asked him something extremely disagreeable.

As the bus pulled away from the curb, he shouted back, "Geza."

Her white-gloved hand fluttered in the early evening air. "Good-bye, Geza."

At dinner, his name lingered on her lips as she pushed bits of fish around her plate. She fought the urge to say his name, to mention how she'd met him at the library, even in a casual way, because then her father would surely ask too many questions and her mother would say she shouldn't walk with strange men on public streets without a proper introduction. Her mother sat very straight, her shoulders pushed back, her long neck tilted forward as she carefully inserted little bites of white fish into her mouth. She wondered if her mother had ever felt this anticipatory excitement, wondering when she would meet him again, if he would come to the reading room on Monday morning or if he would wait a few days, purposefully building a sense of expectancy around their next encounter. Her mother, so cool and controlled, only cared about Franz, who now slumped in his chair, staring at his soup, which he hadn't touched. Vicki smoothed down her hair, reminding herself of its shortness. Franz had barely noticed it yesterday, but when he did, he'd wrinkled up his nose in disgust and said now she looked even more unattractive than before.

Now her mother was talking about the radio again, how insufficient it was in conveying the true timbre of a musical composition. She put down her fork, always the signal that she was preparing to say something important, or at least something she thought important. "Radio trains the ear to such unrefined tones, produced in such a slapdash manner, that the delicate gradations are entirely lost over the airwaves. The beautiful tones"—she paused, clearing her throat—"the beautiful tones have been abandoned, resulting in that continuous, irritating stream of undifferentiated sound. For example, how can anyone distinguish a viola from a double bass?"

Lev listened with amusement—Vicki knew he'd trained his face to assume this expression whenever he disagreed with Josephine, which was often. Just the other day he'd exclaimed how amazing it was to hear the ringing of the church bells in Trier, the live reporting of a boxing match, including every bloody punch, or the deafening crush of horses galloping at full speed around the track, all within the comfort of his living room. He'd been talking to Marthe, trying to convince her that a plug-in phonograph was much handier than a hand-cranked gramophone.

Franz stared at his water glass as if it held other worlds in it, as if he wasn't even at the dinner table. Vicki tried to get his attention by making a face at him, but he ignored her. Lev leaned over his plate and said in a conspiratorial tone, "Remember the way Marie acted when we first explained the radio to her?"

Josephine smiled with affection.

"We told her that if someone played music in France or even America, you could hear it in Berlin." Lev grinned. "And then Marie said?"

Vicki rolled her eyes—how many times must they recount the same old stories?

Josephine gestured for Lev to keep going.

He took a sip of wine. "Marie said, 'But how can the music possibly be so loud?'" Lev clapped his hands together, trying to illicit a laugh from Vicki and Franz. Vicki smiled at her father; she couldn't help herself. His eyes danced mischievously. He poured himself more wine.

Josephine added, "But then I told her, 'No, Mother, the music is transformed into tiny mechanical waves and then travels through the air, sometimes over millions of kilometers, to where we are.' And then Mother said how barbaric it sounded—well, I think she's right in the end!" Josephine stroked her coral necklace, and Vicki wondered if she'd ever let her borrow it. Maybe. When Vicki came home that evening, out of breath and full of apologies for her lateness, Josephine had said, "The short hair—I think it might suit you after all." And then miraculously, she'd smiled.

Her mother continued to play with the coral beads, and Vicki, without even meaning to, pictured herself wearing the necklace the next time she met Geza. The bright pink stones would draw attention to her neck, his eyes resting on her clavicle and then moving down to her décolleté.

Josephine focused on the crystal chandelier hanging, in teardrop tiers, from the ceiling. "Do you think Mother senses it when we talk about her?"

Lev squeezed Josephine's hand. Lately, she made these vague spiritualistic statements, and despite her questioning tone, her eyes would take on a hard gleam as if she truly believed her mother hovered over their dining room table, listening.

Vicki asked if she could turn on the radio—she wanted to listen to Erno Rapee. Otherwise, it was tedious sitting here with Franz's long face and her mother's wistful sighing. She needed a place to put her pent-up energy. She wanted to dance wildly, to sweat, to feel her body move and twist and quake to the rhythm of jazz. Just then her father started reminiscing about the waltz, that bygone era before the war, and then he swooped her up in his arms, showing Vicki how to glide around the table in one smooth, controlled motion. Even though she disagreed with him, hearing herself shout, "No, it's too boring!," she loved it when he danced with her. He could always tell what she was thinking just by studying her face. She wondered, as he gazed into her eyes, if he could tell she'd met someone. "Relax your hands," Lev instructed. "Let me lead."

Vicki sighed.

"See? We're floating."

Vicki laid her cheek on his shoulder, closing her eyes. Lev counted the time under his breath: *One, two, three, one, two, three,* with the emphasis on the first beat. He'd smoked a cigar before dinner. She could smell it on his shirt, and even though she detested cigar smoke, she didn't mind the scent on him. It reminded her of all the times she would wander into her father's study to find him steeped in a fog of bluish smoke as he leaned back into his desk chair, turning something over in his mind. When she asked him what he was thinking, he would press his fingertips together, as if holding an invisible orb, and say, "Business." When she asked again, he would grin and say it didn't concern her; it was just a problem he was trying to solve. If he thought about it long enough, he would solve it. "It will come to me. It will come," he'd say, picking up his half-smoked cigar and puffing on it from time to time.

As she slowly opened her eyes, Lev started cajoling her about growing too thin.

"It's the fashion!"

He squeezed her arm. "The fashion? I think I feel your bone protruding, right here!"

Josephine leaned over Franz, massaging his hunched shoulders, asking if he felt ill. Vicki knew he found it tiresome, this fussing, yet Franz handled his mother like an antique vase, couching his frustration in gentle phrases, keeping his voice level and low as if she might break from the slightest hint of annoyance on his part. It was probably why she loved him more, because he never yelled at her, always taking the time to explain even the most mundane details of his day, whereas Vicki had no patience for her mother's questions. The minute Josephine asked her something, Vicki felt a red-hot irritation flash through her. Last week, Josephine innocently inquired if Vicki had any intention of mending the run in her stockings. Immediately, Vicki answered, "No, I don't. And I don't care." "But it will get worse," her mother had said, and this caused Vicki to ask her why everything must always get worse from her perspective. "If you leave them at the top of the stairs, I will mend them," her mother replied, her voice trembling, as if Vicki had wounded her greatly.

They stopped waltzing, and Vicki fell back into her chair. She sipped a spoonful of pea soup, but it had grown cold. Franz stood up abruptly, excusing himself. Josephine sprung up to follow, but Lev motioned for her to stay seated.

Her face reddened. "What if he's ill?"

Lev massaged her hand. "He's fine."

Marthe set down a marzipan cake, shaped like a dome and covered in pale green icing.

Vicki rolled her eyes. "If I were dying, literally dying on my deathbed, you wouldn't even notice."

Lev lowered his voice, pouring Josephine more wine even though she hadn't touched her glass. "Darling, I don't think that, in the future, you should ask about his girlfriends. He's a private type, and I think it embarrasses him to talk about those matters in front of everyone."

"Do you think now I could listen to my radio program? Erno Rapee and his band are performing live and—"

Lev nodded, but then he said, "Wait. Just wait one minute and have a coffee with your old father." He grinned, and this performance of self-pity always amused Vicki. She took a large bite of marzipan cake, letting the icing melt on her tongue. He launched into one of his stories, which often ended in a question that purposefully invited debate. But she didn't feel like debating tonight, and with Franz upstairs and her mother sitting here anxiously, the atmosphere felt strained. Lev soldiered on, recounting how he'd read that the last great Persian storyteller wandered through the Middle East, but no one cared to listen because everyone was inside, glued to the wireless for the latest news. "The old myths are dying out." Lev's eyes twinkled. "Capitalism has made everything into an object of mass consumption. We're all driven by what we can buy next."

Vicki crossed her arms over her chest, vaguely wondering how he started off with an Arab storyteller and then arrived at economics. "*You* produce objects of consumption."

"Yes," Lev said, folding his cloth napkin in half and then into thirds. "And the alternative?"

Vicki felt a wave of indignation sweep over her. "There are alternatives, Papa."

"Would you like to live in a *mietskaserne* with your friend Elsa, sharing a communal bathroom?"

"If everyone cooperated . . ."

"I can tell you, it would be much worse."

Her ears burned and her head hurt a little. But her father would keep sparring in this light playful tone until he won the argument. Utterly exhausting. She slumped farther down in her chair.

"Why do you think so many Russians are flooding Berlin every day? Why do you think Herr Levenski has moved in next door, when in Saint Petersburg he had a palatial estate ten times the size of this house? The Reds are killing their own people by the thousands. When I was in Mitau"—he paused for effect—"I saw the work of the Reds. Brutal. They killed without sense. At least you could reason with the czar's army."

With the mention of Mitau, she thought of him again. *Geza.* His name tingled through her, a tight buzzing nervousness she'd felt all through dinner. Struck with the sudden urge to ask her father if he'd known Geza from Mitau by any off chance, she scolded herself for such a naive thought. Of course not. Why would her father know him? He barely spoke of the war as it was . . . and if she did ask, he would tease and cajole, relentlessly questioning her about this Geza, how she knew him, if she fancied him, and Vicki wanted to keep Geza a secret. His lank blue-black hair that kept falling into his eyes, how closely he'd stood next to her, so close she could feel his breath, or the way he'd lightly taken her elbow at various points during their stroll—she didn't want anyone to know how often she'd retraced these little moments, and each time, a renewed excitement washed over her at the mere thought of him.

Her father continued, "It's easy for you to support *the cause*, as you say, sitting here in a comfortable dining room with plenty of food on your plate, your belly full, knowing tomorrow you will wake up in a warm bed, and buy new earrings at Wertheim's. Not a bad life, eh?"

He waved a finger in the air, his lips curling into a smile. "You and your grandmother prefer to see the world through red-tinted glasses."

Vicki fiddled with her coffee spoon.

"She asked after you today." Lev reached over, stroked her cheek. "You look more and more like her."

After dinner, in the sitting room, she switched on the radio. Upstairs, she heard the muffled voices of her parents arguing. Running water echoed from the kitchen as Marthe rinsed out the last coffee cups. She heard Franz jerk open his window, followed by the creaking of his heavy boots walking across the floor planks. As long as she kept the dial low, she could listen in peace. She pulled a velvet pillow off the couch, and spreading out a blanket on the carpet, she sank down. Pulling her knees into her chest, she closed her eyes to the sound of a lonely saxophone reaching into the darkened room, followed by a low throaty voice full of sorrow and longing, full of all the things she felt.

19

O n Friday mornings, Josephine went to Dr. Dührkoop, a psycho-
analyst with a private practice on the top floor of an imposing
stone town house on the southern border of the Tiergarten. She had
been seeing him for the last four months at Lev's insistence. At first,
she resisted, arguing there wasn't anything wrong with her, until Lev
started chronicling her migraines, which had grown more severe after
the death of her mother last fall, and her night terrors, which had also
increased. Now, she looked forward to the sessions, where, for a full fifty
minutes, once a week, she lay down on a soft chaise lounge and talked
about herself—behavior that, in any other setting, she would deem
utterly indulgent.

Today, having arrived early, she stood in the waiting room, staring at the framed photographs arranged in a line along the far wall.
She had glanced at them in the past, but never before had she actually
taken the time to study them, and as she did this, she felt somewhat
disturbed. The first photograph, in faded sepia, featured two little boys
dressed as court jesters in wide ruffled collars, black ballet slippers,
and knit bodysuits patterned with interlocking diamonds in a diagonal
arrangement. One boy faced the camera, his hands on his hips, while
the other boy hid behind him, one naughty eye peering out, the rest
of his face obscured. The boy facing the camera wore a leather belt
with a small knife attached to it, covered by a leather sheath. The other
boy held a knife, without its sheath, behind his back, as if to stab his
more confident brother. Underneath the photograph, a caption in cur-

sive script read: *The Children of the Suppancics Family*. The next photo-graph pictured the back of a woman's head, her bare neck, her wide back clothed in some kind of woolen jacket. She glanced slightly to the side, the beginnings of a double chin detectable. The bare blatant neck instantly reminded Josephine of Vicki's short hair and how upset she'd felt when Vicki had strode into the sitting room yesterday, ready to chal-lenge her when all Josephine felt was sadness, remembering Vicki's fine dark curls, the way she used to run her fingers unencumbered through Vicki's hair when she was a child. Dark curls with hints of copper and gold, a mercurial color that changed with the light. In the morning sun, a reddish brown, and by nightfall, a blackberry hue. Lev had tried to console her, saying it was only hair and it would grow back, while at the same time he took Vicki's side, playing the diplomat, tap dancing between them, or at least this was the image Josephine evoked when she thought about it.

The next photograph: a close-up of an eye—the pupil, the cornea, the white eyelashes, the delicate eyebrow arched over the upper eye-lid. Underneath, the same cursive script stated: *The Right Eye of My Daughter Sigrid*. She wondered if Sigrid was Dr. Dührkoop's niece, or the photographer's daughter, whoever he was. She could hear the muted murmur from behind the office door, where Dr. Dührkoop was in deep discussion with another patient. The walls, padded with green damask, had been purposefully designed to soften distinct sounds. Even as Jose-phine strained to listen, she could only pick out a few discernible words: cat, Arthur, Vienna. Mainly, a woman spoke, and Dr. Dührkoop prob-ably nodded and jotted down notes in his notebook. Josephine moved on to the next photograph, strangely comforted by the sound of the woman's voice droning on in the next room, as if she too had irresolv-able troubles. In another photograph, titled *Riki Raab,* a tall woman twined a long flowing piece of tapestry around her body, suggesting nakedness underneath. She wore a strange pointed hat, almost papal in character, and through half-closed lids, she glanced at the viewer with a mixture of arrogance and embarrassment.

The doorknob turned. A boy, about sixteen, walked out of the office.

His face reddened when he saw her, and he brushed past. As the doctor ushered Josephine into his office, she could hear the boy's hurried steps echoing down the long hallway that led to the stairs.

On the chaise lounge, she made herself comfortable. The doctor sat in the opposite chair, his legs crossed, his leather-bound notebook resting on his lap, a pen stuck between the pages. A low coffee table positioned in the middle of the room featured an array of African figurines carved from onyx. On the windowsill, orchids, a deep magenta, sprouted new buds. Through the window, Josephine stared at the tops of the linden trees swaying in the wind. Dr. Dührkoop always began each session in the same way, with a bout of silence that felt uncomfortably palpable. He studied her from behind his wire-rim glasses, his hands laced over his kneecap. His square garnet ring, set in gold, always caught her attention, the deep red color alluring. Josephine thought he kept his fingernails a tad too long, accentuating his slender tapered fingers. She swallowed, and it seemed as if he heard. "Would you like some tea before we start?"

"No, thank you, Doctor. It's much too hot out for tea."

"Hmm, yes, it is rather warm."

He adjusted the pillow behind his back and then refocused his gaze on her. Josephine had a fleeting image of the doctor licking her neck, the texture of his tongue rough like a cat's, the licks quick and precise as if he were lapping up milk. She tried to redirect her thoughts, but the image perversely stuck.

He opened his notebook, smoothing down a blank page. "How are you feeling this week?"

"I'm fine, thank you, Doctor." In the beginning of each session, she felt awkward lying on the couch, her feet dangling off the edge. He preferred her to lie on her back so she wouldn't have to face him, especially during the moments when she described more intimate details, but it seemed rude, staring up at the ceiling. And most of the time, she liked to look at his face. He reminded her of Mahler, a less handsome version, but with the same imposing forehead and Roman nose, the same style of spectacles and swept-back hair. But not facing him, he had explained, would allow her to speak more freely. Over the weeks, she had grown accustomed to the sound of his voice, low and calm, and the movement of his pen scratching against the paper whenever she said something noteworthy. But today, she felt the urge to see his reaction to her words, to gaze into his gray quiet eyes.

"You seem"—he leaned forward in his chair—"to be carrying tension. Especially in your upper spine."

She breathed, feeling her ribs rise and fall beneath her folded hands.

"Try to relax your shoulders, your jaw, your mouth, your eyes, your hands." When he said these things, she felt as if he were touching her in all of those places. Her head grew heavy, despite the morning sun filtering into the room. Her eyelids involuntarily started to close. She sighed. "My daughter."

"Vicki." His chair creaked as he shifted positions.

"Yes, Vicki." She paused, opening her eyes. "Yesterday, she cut off all her hair."

"And this has greatly upset you."

"Yes, it did."

"Why do you think it was so upsetting?"

She touched her forehead. "Well, I suppose if I really think about it . . ."

The doctor laughed lightly. "Yes, that is what we do here."

She turned her head to look at him. He smiled encouragingly.

"I suppose Vicki reminded me of that American ambassador's daughter who's always in the press, running around with foreign correspondents. She's only twenty, but they say she's had five lovers plus a broken-off engagement to some financier from Chicago. I don't want Vicki to become like that, but when she cut off her hair, I thought, Now this is the first step toward provocative behavior."

"Hmmm." He scribbled something down in his notebook.

"Young women these days are"—she searched for the right words—"sexually vivacious."

"'Sexually vivacious,'" he repeated, smiling again.

"Yes," Josephine replied, shifting onto her side so that she faced him squarely. Again, without meaning to, she thought of Titian's painting *Venus and the Lute Player*. Venus, positioned on her side, squarely faces the viewer, her white body exposed save for a light handkerchief draped across her lap. The lute player stops with his music to gaze at her lovely figure. Should seeing or hearing be the primary means of perceiving beauty? This was apparently the painting's question, and she had debated it with Lev when they first met. Because he used to paint, of course he vowed that sight was the primary function for perceiving beauty, whereas she remained convinced that sound conveyed beauty in its purest, most objective form. For a moment, she imagined herself as Venus and the doctor as the lute player, stopping to admire her. She blushed at this vain fantasy.

"What were you thinking just now?"

"That when I look at you, I feel as if you're listening to me more intently, as opposed to when I am staring up at the ceiling. Then I can't see your expression and I wonder what you're thinking."

"But that's not important."

"What isn't?"

"What I think."

"But it is."

He shook his head, taking off his glasses. "Josephine." When he said her name, her heart beat faster. He slid the stainless steel ashtray closer to him and then lit a cigarette. "Do you think the reason why you were so bothered by Vicki's haircut and by the amorous activities of the American ambassador's daughter is that you yourself had once been sexually vivacious, only to be punished for it by Herr K's sexual advances? This quality attracted him, and you don't want Vicki to suffer the same fate, or to carry on the tradition, so to speak?"

"I did feel it was my fault, with Herr K."

"Because you were young and very pretty. You told me your mother had said if you weren't so precocious, none of that business would have happened."

Josephine felt her cheeks burn. "Yes, she did say that."

"And you felt guilty about your attractiveness, and you thought, perhaps, if you were less appealing, he would have left you alone."

Herr K's pomaded moustache, the peppery scent of it, suddenly flooded her senses. Her throat tightened. "He probably would have."

Dr. Dührkoop leaned forward, his face growing more animated.

"Your sexuality was a liability, robbing you of your girlhood—and now you feel threatened by Vicki's burgeoning womanhood because it brings back the trauma."

Josephine clutched a pillow to her chest. "Yes, the trauma." The way he kept using the past tense—when she *was* pretty, *was* sexual, *was* appealing—made her wonder if he would still describe her in this way. Had she aged that much? Under her eyes, slight hollows had appeared, making her face, at certain times of day, more shadowy. The creases around her mouth were more pronounced. But beyond these minor signs of age, she still felt young and sprightly. Her carriage had remained erect, her neck long, her skin soft and pale, and her hair, heavy with golden strands, crowned the top of her head. She touched the end of her thick braid.

He leaned back into his chair, smoking thoughtfully. The desk clock indicated a few minutes still remained. But not enough time, Josephine thought, for the word association game, which had unsettled her last time. He'd barked a series of unrelated words, and after each one, she had to respond with a word she found similar in meaning, as a pathway into her subconscious mind.

He languorously folded one leg over the other. "Your anger toward Vicki is misguided. That helpless girl on the balcony, blamed for merely defending herself, is angry."

Josephine nodded, doubting if this was true. She had been angry with Vicki but not necessarily because of any girlhood trauma. She had been angry simply because the haircut was an act of defiance, and it seemed as if Vicki no longer wanted a mother, as if she could dispense with her as easily as discarding a pair of torn stockings. Old stockings thrown out in the trash.

She heard the waiting room door open and close. The doctor wrote down a few perfunctory notes in his notebook. Josephine watched him, wondering what he wrote. She suppressed a smile, imagining him jotting down a grocery list instead of an assessment of her psychological condition. With studied seriousness, he could be scribbling: *wine, cheese, black tea, endive, olives.* At least that's what she thought he ate, living the bachelor's life without anyone to cook for him properly, although she had heard his mother visited quite often.

She sat up, rubbing her forehead.

"We have a few more minutes. Is there anything else you would like to discuss today?"

The clock read five minutes to one. The sounds of lunchtime traffic filtered through the half-open window, jostling her out of this dim cocoon. A tram rattled past. A line of horses trotted down the street, headed for the park. Rearranging the pillows, even though Dührkoop told her not to bother, Josephine thought of something she could say to fill the last five minutes.

"I still think of my mother all the time. Sometimes, I feel as if she's lingering here, observing me, trying to make contact."

"I see."

"Do you think that's a strange thing to say?"

He scratched his clean-shaven face. "Not necessarily." He then produced a cream-colored card embossed with the name BALTHAZAR WEHDANNER, THE EVANGELICAL CHURCH OF ST. JOHN. He handed the card to Josephine. "His awakening meetings have a tendency toward fanaticism, but I do think he's a gifted spiritualist. A number of my patients have found him quite extraordinary."

She slipped the card into her purse, snapping the clasp shut. "Thank you, Doctor."

"Please," he said, walking her to the door. She enjoyed, for a brief moment, the feeling of his hand on her back. The lightness of his fingertips made her pliable, loose-limbed, off balance.

He opened the door. "Do feel free to call on me any time, outside of our regular sessions." He always said this at the end, but today, the timbre of his voice was different, as if he really wanted her to call.

"Of course, Doctor. Thank you." She still felt his hand on her back as she walked through the waiting room, past an elderly woman clutching a parasol. Down the hall, down the staircase, through the marble atrium, outside under the glass-plated portico, the bright sunlight hitting her face, she felt his hand there still, burning through her chiffon blouse.

. . .

That night, Franz came late to dinner. Josephine hovered over the pea soup on the stove, thinking how again Marthe had added too much cream. "Marthe," she sighed, "add more broth to the soup, please."

Marthe arranged red mullet fillets over pats of butter in a skillet. "I apologize, Frau Perlmutter—should I prepare the fish now?" She glanced at the clock on the wall. "Or would you prefer to wait until Franz arrives?"

"We'll wait."

"Also to serve the soup?"

Josephine sighed again. "Yes. I don't like to start without him."

At the dinner table, Lev complained he was hungry. Vicki sat next to him, playing with her silverware in a distracted manner. Her hair, Josephine mused, wasn't entirely bad. It accentuated her long neck. And she'd fastened a pretty clip to her hair, one with rhinestones.

Josephine dabbed her forehead with a lavender-scented handkerchief, relieved it had finally cooled after such a ferociously warm day. "What did you do today, Vicki?"

She looked up from the table. "Oh, nothing really."

Josephine raised her eyebrows. "Nothing?"

She shrugged. "Nothing of any note. I went to the library."

"That gloomy building," Lev said.

"Yes," Vicki replied, suppressing a smile. "It is gloomy. I felt like a prisoner locked away in there with it so beautiful and warm out."

Josephine stared out the window. Still no sign of Franz.

Lev poured himself a glass of red wine from the decanter. "I'm sure there were other prisoners, as you say, at the library."

Vicki studied her nails. "Do we have to wait all night for Franz? I'm famished."

Josephine's chest tightened at Vicki's demanding tone. Always so sharp, so quick to turn on her at a moment's notice.

Vicki continued, "If I were the one late, you'd all be on the third course by now."

"And if I were late," Lev chimed in, "you'd be drinking coffee in the library by now." Josephine flashed Lev a look. He was always

encouraging Vicki to be cheekier, more insolent than she already was.
About to disagree, she thought of Dr. Dührkoop's calm peaceful face,
the way her name rolled off his tongue, as if he'd known her all his life.
He had worn an ice-blue tie today offset by a starched white shirt. She
wondered if a woman had bought him the tie. A lover.

She heard the front door open and immediately she got up. Passing the kitchen, she motioned for Marthe to start serving the soup, but
Marthe wasn't there.

"Franz," she called, moving swiftly down the hallway. The mounting anxiety she'd felt—fantasies of a crushed bicycle, a car running him
over, a tram accident, one moment of distraction turning fatal—slowly
melted away when she saw his face. A bit winded, he waved. Marthe
took his coat. They were whispering, and this annoyed Josephine.
"Franz," she repeated, balling up a linen napkin in her palm, a napkin
she didn't realize until now she'd taken along from the dining table.
"Where were you?"

He appeared oddly disheveled. His shirt wrinkled and hair tousled
as if a woman had just run her fingers through it. She took his arm. He
said he needed to wash up first, but she had so many questions: *What did
you eat for luncheon? How was your mathematics examination? Did you meet
with Professor Schiller?* And all she could muster was "Are you all right?"

Lev hollered something from the dining room, probably complaining about the soup. She squeezed Franz's arm. "You're winded."

"I'll just wash up first, Mother." Then he said something about
rush hour and stenographers on the tram and disappeared into the
bathroom, closing the door behind him. She stood there, staring at the
door, the smooth wood, the blond fibers. The toilet flushed, followed
by the turn of the faucets, then running water. The momentary pause
as he regarded himself in the mirror above the sink. His beautiful face.
She wanted to speak with him privately before dinner, but he lingered
in there. Lev called again. Touching the doorknob for a moment, she
felt him tensing on the other side of the door. He didn't want to talk to
her tonight. He'd probably been with a girl.

At dinner, she watched him pick at his fish. Worried he would go to
bed hungry, she resolved to leave out bread and jam where he could eas-

ily find it so he wouldn't rummage through the larder in the middle of the night. Lev clapped at something Vicki said, but all Josephine heard was the proud defiance in her voice and his approving laughter. Then they started waltzing around the table, debating whether or not it was boring to waltz. Always debating. Those two could never sit calmly and discuss a topic in a civilized manner. Franz found it distasteful as well. He sat across from her, staring down at his plate.

She went over to him. "Are you feeling ill? You barely ate."

He patted her hand. "I'm fine."

She knew she shouldn't ask, but she couldn't help herself. "Are you upset over a girl? Is that why you were late this evening?"

His jaw tightened.

Lev commented on how Franz studied too hard and occupied himself with various clubs; he didn't have time for girls. After inserting a baby potato into his mouth, he stated, "It's none of our business anyway. Leave the poor man alone."

Josephine stared questioningly at Franz, but he refused to look at her, concentrating on his water glass. For a moment, the image of Franz lying on the chaise lounge, telling Dr. Dührkoop his innermost thoughts, comforted her. But he would never agree to go. She ran her fingers through his hair. He tilted his head toward her. They didn't have to speak anyway. She more or less knew how he felt just by looking at him. But tonight, he'd erected a barrier she couldn't cross. That's how it is with children, she thought, stroking his head. One minute they need you, and the next, they want nothing to do with you. Lev had been trying to impress this upon her, joking that she shouldn't have breastfed Franz when he was a baby. It had made her overly dependent on him, creating an untenable bond. Whereas with Vicki she'd hired a wet nurse.

Franz suddenly excused himself, and she felt a pang of worry. Of course Lev remained wholly unconcerned. She was always the one who worried, and he never did. Infuriating. Watching Franz walk away, she admired his broad shoulders and slim waist. He'd inherited her father's build.

· · ·

After dinner, she debated whether or not to knock on Franz's door, knowing Lev waited for her in the bedroom. Oftentimes, he fell asleep before she retired, a relief from his pawing insistence that they make love. He knew it was often painful for her, but he still insisted, quoting from that Velde book how *the key to an enduring marriage lay in mutual ongoing sexual pleasure* and how a *hell of torment* could, with work, *become a state of unending bliss.* But if she never relented, how could she blame him for his dalliances? Even Dr. Dührkoop had stressed the importance of sexual pleasure, a topic she tried to avoid with him, but since the revelation about Herr K, he insisted they explore the vagaries of her sexuality. Dührkoop supported the notion of mutual orgasm and suggested that if a woman failed to reach orgasm, auto-therapeutic measures were better than none at all.

Josephine lightly rapped on Franz's door. She heard him spring up from the bed. Opening the door, he said, "I knew you'd come."

She touched his forehead with the back of her hand. "No fever."

He motioned to the open window. "Herr Levenski is trimming the hedge again. I know you despise him."

"He's very territorial about his roses." Sitting on the foot of the bed, where Mitzi had been, judging from the black dog hairs, she noticed how Franz had put fresh ferns in a vase next to the snapshot of Wolf. She tilted her head toward the photograph. "How is he?"

"Next weekend, we're going on a nature retreat."

Josephine nodded, brushing the black dog hairs away.

Franz sat on the windowsill, the window open behind him, which made her nervous. But he doesn't need me to warn him, she thought.

He twisted around, staring into the darkness. "Of course when I'm sitting right here, he stops clipping."

"Franz, careful!"

He smiled at her. "I won't fall out."

She sighed heavily. "Is everything else all right?"

He crossed his arms over his chest.

She held out her hand to him, but he remained seated on the windowsill. "Come. Tell me."

"The Wandervogel, the particular club Wolf belongs to, doesn't accept Jewish members." He stared at her with large unblinking eyes. Her heart contracted.

"We're Aryan, Franz."

He hung his head. They had been through this countless times, faithfully following the same script. To ease him out of his discouraged state, she went over to him, massaged his shoulders, and assured him that he came from celebrated Bavarian stock through the matrilineal line, which clearly had, judging from his physical appearance, withstood all genetic influence from Lev's side of the family. She stroked his cheek, feeling the coolness of the air on his skin. "You're an exact replica of Grandfather. It's a comfort to see how he lives on in you."

Expecting to find Lev waiting for her in bed, she drew a sigh of relief at the empty room. She sat down in front of her vanity mirror, slowly untwining her coiled braid, letting her mind drift. Possibly, Lev would stay downstairs, with his cigars and whiskey. Or he might venture out, scurrying off to one of his private clubs, a distasteful habit, she thought, as he always returned home late, smelling of liquor and complaining that he was famished. He would rouse the whole household, scouring the larder for cheese and jam to make a midnight sandwich. She couldn't stop herself from springing out of bed at the sound of banging plates and knives echoing from the cavernous kitchen. Standing in her silk robe, arms crossed, she would watch him from the kitchen doorway as he hastily piled slices of cheese onto brown bread, after which he would shove it into his mouth. Upon seeing her, he would cheerfully wave, unaware of the late hour and that he had awoken her. After these nocturnal outings, he was always particularly insistent about lovemaking, which made Josephine wonder if, in fact, he did not keep a mistress but had remained faithful to her despite the many temptations he must encounter in the city at night. Listlessly brushing out her hair, the strands catching static in the warm room, she recalled Frau Blutcher's tone today when she rang for Lev. She'd sounded confused and tentative, and when Josephine pressed her, she muttered something about a haircut, followed by, "I don't really know." When Josephine said, "Well, what *do* you know, Frau Blutcher?" her voice grew tight over the line, as if she might have a nervous attack. Out of annoyance, Josephine hung up without wishing her good afternoon, something she rarely did. It was an embarrassment, to let a secretary get the better of her, when Josephine generally abided by the rule of not allowing employees to become privy to such emotions. Now, she could be sure, Frau Blutcher would triumphantly gossip that Frau Perlmutter suspected Herr Perlmutter of having an affair, and then she would weigh in, like an expert, when she didn't know the first thing about the inner workings of this family.

Lev's voice floated up from the dining room, his admonishing tone recognizable as he bantered with Vicki. Josephine put down her brush and examined her neck. Did she still look young? Turning her head to the side, she peeked at her profile. She leaned in closer, noticing a tiny row of broken blood vessels curling along the edges of her nostrils. But how could she possibly blame him, if he kept a mistress? They hadn't made love in months, not since the dinner party at the Hoffenstaldts. A mistress might relieve her of such "wifely duties" or, at the very least, shoulder some of the burden. The thought made her smile, and yet she felt guilty finding such irony in her own circumstances. Lev had arrived home tonight freshly shaven, his hair slicked back and trimmed, proof he'd visited the barber, but where had he gone afterward?

The clink of a teaspoon against a china cup interrupted her thoughts, and she pictured Lev stirring milk into his coffee, the whiteness bleeding into the black. No, she said to herself, swiveling around on the stool to face the bed, it wasn't that she didn't like sex, but rather it was the frequency of his demands, his insatiability, that overwhelmed her. She preferred the prelude to sex, when she was still cozily encased in her robe, her head on his chest, his hand stroking the length of her thigh, before the impudent meshing of bodies. She worried that she had lost all elasticity, but after birthing two children, she knew this couldn't possibly be true. Other times, it was more tolerable, even enjoyable, which led her to believe the pain was psychological. And so the extent of Herr K's sexual advances had become gradually embellished to provide her some respite from the demands of the marriage bed. Whether or not Herr K actually did violate her remained an open question, but his menacing presence was real, and she chose to interpret the past in a way that best served her in the present.

She started to take off her coral necklace when Lev strode into the room. Startled, she hadn't heard him come up the stairs, and she stared at his reflection in the mirror, her hands frozen behind her neck.

He undid his bowtie. "Can I help you with that?"

She shook her head, unhooking the clasp. The coral beads slid off her neck.

20

At night in the city, Elsa was finally taking Vicki to Romanisches Café. As they sat in the back of a taxicab, the glimmering advertisements filtered through the trees, lending Elsa's face an intimate glow that Vicki hoped illuminated her own face in the same way. As the cab turned onto Kurfürstendamm, the candelabras fastened to the tree branches swayed in the summer wind. They passed the tall glass windows of department stores and enclosed café terraces, the lit-up marquees of movie theaters and cabarets and restaurants interspersed with elongated apartment buildings. People strolled the wide boulevard, gazing up at the windows, their dark silhouettes dwarfed by the barrage of neon advertisements looming from above, as if the billboards were suspended in the night sky by invisible hooks.

The taxi driver grunted at the traffic. He had been rude from the start. Vicki almost said something until she noticed the gouge in his cheek and realized he was probably one of the war-wounded. He leaned on his horn, but this did nothing to move the long line of automobiles forward. Admiring Elsa's lavender hat with its wide up-curling brim, Vicki wondered if she looked as smartly dressed. While Elsa's hat was quite feminine, she wore tuxedo pants paired with a slim-fitting dinner jacket, and inside the slanted front pocket, she'd arranged a lavender pocket square, drawing the eye back up to her lavender hat. It was all quite a performance, Vicki thought, deciding that her black silk shift with the gold spangles was in no way daring enough. She'd gone to pains this afternoon, crimping her hair into rigid waves, which looked dated compared to Elsa's slicked-back hair. Absently touching her earrings, the new ones from Wertheim's, Vicki felt a small sense of relief that at least she had worn these. The driver sped down Tauentzienstrasse, almost passing Romanisches Café before Elsa barked, "Stop!"

Little round tables peppered the main floor under a great vaulted ceiling whose soaring arches were affixed with hanging lanterns. The heady scent of expensive perfume, luxury-brand cigarettes, and sweat hung in the air, and a roaring cacophony of chatter competed with the jazz band playing in the far corner. Every now and then a trumpet or sax riff would cut through the talk, and the clear sound of music enticed people to pause a moment and listen. An imposing red-carpeted staircase led to an upstairs gallery where men played chess while women sat on their laps and smoked. Vicki had heard of this place from her father. He used to come here on Sunday afternoons with her mother, when everyone wanted to be seen eating cake and taking a stroll through the various rooms of the café. Lev sometimes referred to it as Café Grössenwahn, or Café Megalomania, or even Rachmonisches—from the Hebrew *rachmones,* which meant "mercy"—because so many Jews frequented this place. They congregated here as if it were their personal office, lingering at the same table, nursing the same cup of coffee for hours on end. Elsa explained that upstairs the café was divided into two distinct rooms: one for celebrities and one for aspirants, rooms known respectively as "the swimming pool" and "the kiddy pool." "And I've sat in the swimming pool, believe it or not, with Egon Kisch's circle."

Sensing Vicki's hesitation, Elsa said, "You know, the famous journalist. He founded the Association of Proletarian-Revolutionary Authors."

"I know," Vicki said, when in truth she'd never heard of Egon Kisch.

The garnet-colored lanterns, suffusing a dim reddish glow, muffled rather than created light, causing Vicki to squint across the room at a man in a white dinner jacket shaking hands with two well-dressed women. After a moment, she recognized it was Wolf von Trotta, Franz's best friend.

She nudged Elsa. "There's Wolf." He had always flirted with her in an arrogant, merciless kind of way. And his ice-blue eyes seemed as if they belonged to a murderer.

"He's such a cad," Vicki added.

Elsa shrugged. "He looks ridiculous in that white dinner jacket."

Wolf noticed Vicki from across the room and his lips curled into a smirk. Nervousness flooded her, but she shook it off. Strange, how he eternally made her feel like the little sister trailing behind, the younger one who didn't know enough. She wondered if he was impressed to see her here, in such a sophisticated club, but he never appeared impressed by anything, or at least he had trained himself to maintain a cool, detached demeanor.

"Let's get a drink," Vicki said, thinking this would relax her, and Elsa flagged down a bar girl. All the girls working here looked the same, with the same slender, narrow hips, a sylph woman-child serving seductively colored cocktails, which made Vicki think of semiprecious gemstones—emeralds, sapphires, and amethysts distilled into liquid form, poured into glass bowls one had to cup with both hands. "I'll try that," Vicki said, gesturing to a waitress ferrying a fiery pink drink, the color of the sunset. Out of the corner of her eye, she saw Wolf flirting with one of these bar girls, twirling an unlit cigarette between his fingers.

Elsa suggested they go upstairs to see Egon. Lightly, she fixed Vicki's hair, smoothing it over to the side of her face. "That's better." Then she signaled to the bar girl, tilting her chin upward, a signal, Vicki gathered, indicating they were moving upstairs. Tonight, Elsa was in a sisterly mood, having forgotten the embrace in the Wannsee, when for a few seconds their limbs intertwined underwater, and for this Vicki felt relieved. Plus, she didn't really believe Elsa was a lesbian, or a *garçonne,* as she called herself, even though she boasted about her attendance at the Ladies Club Erato, a lesbian social club, which met Monday afternoons at Zauberflöte. And even though a shiver went through her when Elsa applied a dab of perfume to the nape of Vicki's neck, her cool fingertips resting there for a suspended moment, Vicki failed to extract Geza from her mind, even here, in a place he didn't know existed, a place where she would never see him. What would he think if he saw her dressed in this black silk shift with Elsa's arm around her waist as they ascended the stairs, laughing? Would he see her as frivolous, unworthy of his attentions? She guessed he was a Communist but not one like Elsa, who happily drank champagne, cherished her silk stockings, and flirted with artists.

Chess tables lined the upper gallery, allowing the players to gaze over the balustrade and consider the people below as they contemplated their next move. The "swimming pool" room was also on the upper level, and from what Vicki could see, red damask padded the walls, and a cloud of smoke floated through the open archway leading into the exclusive section. Elsa strained her neck to check if Egon was in there, but from their vantage point, they only saw the hunched-over backs of men studying a sketch someone had just completed. A few bored women loitered in the archway, smoking. Elsa pointed out one of the women, known as Little Moth, infamous for ruining a renowned musician who was no longer seen at the café. Vicki wondered what it took to ruin a man. The musician must have been desperately in love with Little Moth, who from here looked like nothing special: slight features, an upturned nose, ash-blond hair, too much makeup. Elsa added, "These girls take trips to Biarritz and Cairo, popping up here in between their travels and their men." As she said this, Vicki detected a hint of envy.

"It all sounds very decadent."

"Hmmm," Elsa replied, gazing at the smoke-filled room, searching for Egon. From one of the chess tables, a ginger-haired woman called out Elsa's name. Dressed in tuxedo trousers and a button-down white shirt, she had gone to great pains to fit her plump body into gentleman's attire. She stood behind a man with a full beard and round silver eyeglasses who hunched over the chessboard, staring at the empty squares.

Walking over to their table, Elsa whispered, "That's Emanuel Lasker and his longtime girlfriend Lise Schuler. He's a mathematician and the best chess player there is." She paused. "I know Lise from the Erato."

Vicki nodded, staring at Lise, who spoke frenetically about how Emanuel was preparing to play Thomas Grant from Chicago. "He always assumes this hooded dark stare when he plays, as if he's preparing to eject himself over the chessboard and club his opponent. Absolutely chilling."

He held up his hands, still concentrating on the chessboard. "Silence. I can't think when you're near. All this meaningless chatter."

"You might as well get married the way you two carry on," Elsa teased.

With that, Emanuel scooted back his chair and lit his pipe. "Why didn't I marry her after all these years? That's what everyone keeps asking, as if I'm letting this jewel of a woman slip through my fingers."

Lise threw back her head and laughed with her mouth open. Red lipstick freckled her front teeth. "Tell them, darling, tell them what you always say."

Emanuel shook his head, his long, gray face sagging. "I've known her for too long." Then he turned to Vicki, his cool gaze sweeping over her. "She's no longer on her good behavior."

Again, Lise laughed hysterically. Emanuel puffed on his pipe. Elsa asked if they'd seen Egon, but Lise ignored her question, inquiring where they were going next, after Romanisches. She rattled off a list of places, bemoaning the fact that Herr Wanselow ran a club in his flat called Aleifa, and despite the club's extremely liberal environment, especially in all matters sexual, he didn't allow Jews. "But I prefer the Adlon bar myself," she said, taking a sip of champagne and checking her makeup in a small octagonal compact. She powdered her nose, but this did not conceal the shadowy depressions under her eyes or how her mouth appeared predatory. Vicki felt repulsed, watching Lise apply powder, and when Lise noticed her staring, Vicki glanced away. Her head hurt from the pink drink made with gin, syrup, and chilled champagne. The conversation turned to Josephine Baker. Elsa gushed about her sex appeal, and then she smiled at Vicki, both of them recalling how they'd listened to her throaty voice on the rooftop only a few days ago, the day she cut off all her hair, which already seemed so far in the past. Because I've met him since then, Vicki thought, her life beforehand appearing in miniature, as if the roof of a dollhouse had been lifted off, revealing all the tiny chairs and beds and tables and grandfather clocks.

Lise asked, "Haven't you heard about the incident at Vollmoeller's flat?"

Vicki tried to focus on the conversation, but she didn't care about what had happened at Vollmoeller's flat.

Elsa scanned the upper gallery. "Vollmoeller's mistress only wears men's clothing."

"She's slim and beautiful," Emanuel said, examining a chess piece.

"And Vollmoeller just conducted Wagner's *Tristan and Isolde* at the Vienna State Opera."

Emanuel sighed. "Yes, I know."

"I wasn't talking to you," Lise snapped, her cheeks flushed from champagne. "Anyway, at his flat the other night, Josephine Baker was sitting on the couch half-naked, in a pink muslin apron and nothing else, talking about American jazz. Then Vollmoeller's mistress sauntered over and made herself comfortable on Baker's lap, and they fed each other chocolates."

Emanuel brought the wooden bishop to his lips. "The pink muslin looked divine on her."

Lise touched Elsa's slicked-back hair. "Smooth."

She grinned. "Bakerfix."

Lise continued to touch her hair, and then she let her hand fall casually onto Elsa's shoulder until she had her arm around Elsa. Then she gave Vicki a long desirous gaze, at which point Vicki said she had to leave. Elsa nestled her cheek against Lise's limp arm, as if it were the most natural of things, and told Vicki she shouldn't leave, because this is what people did all night; they talked and drank and danced and talked some more until dawn. She lurched forward, cupping Vicki's face with her warm hands. "You can't go, V. The evening's barely begun."

Vicki gathered up her beaded purse and her hat, trying not to make a fuss of leaving. Emanuel eyed her stoically, and Lise yawned into her drink and then whispered something to Elsa, her sloppy red mouth close to Elsa's perfect white ear. Despite Elsa's protestations that she stay for another drink, Vicki said with a smile that she really must go and slipped through the crowded smoke-filled room.

Vicki signaled for a cab, the wind rushing into her dress, the short hemline floating upward for a brief moment before settling down. Against her skin, the night air felt warm and full of summer. The electric street-lights illuminated her silk stockings and caught the golden appliqué pattern on her T-strap evening shoes. Running a hand through her hair, she still felt surprised by its shortness, how quickly her fingers sifted through the strands. Wondering if she should go home or stop by the Resi, where some of her university friends would be drinking, the image of the gloomy state library rose up before her, and she felt the urge to return there, as if loitering on the steps at night would mysteriously summon Geza.

A few cabs lingered on the corner across the street. People continued to spill out of Romanisches, replaced by a constant stream of others eager to replace them. The doorman stared impassively at the crowd, his cold gray eyes judging the eligibility of each potential patron. Waiting for the streetlight to change, Vicki sensed a familiar figure in a cream-colored dinner jacket standing nearby. Wolf. He was bragging to an older woman and her daughter about how his father was on familiar terms with von Hindenburg. Both women looked saturated in money, in long beaded crepe dresses with golden sashes. "You mean the president of Germany?" the older woman asked in a heavy French accent. Wolf glowered at her. "Of course. Who else would I mean?" The woman's daughter, who was younger than Vicki and delicately pretty, emitted an artificial laugh.

Vicki urged one of the cabs to come her way, so she could avoid Wolf, but he ambled toward her. "What are you doing out so late, little sister?"

He smelled of strong spirits.

"It's not so late."

Wolf pinched her cheek. "If you were my sister, I wouldn't let you hang around a place like this."

That old nervousness flooded her again, and it infuriated her, how he could make her feel so small and helpless without warning.

A cab honked, startling her. The driver shouted over the hood of the car, "Address, please?"

Wolf opened the cab door and told the driver to take her directly home to Charlottenburg.

Vicki slid into the backseat and banged the door closed.

Wolf stared at her through the open window. "I'll be seeing you." Then he turned away and went back to the women. They all erupted into laughter at something he said in French, which Vicki couldn't quite grasp. As the cab sped off, her thoughts ran together: she'd probably fail her French exam on Monday—she could barely catch the meaning of a simple conversation on the street—and Wolf was only an overgrown child fiddling with people's emotions, wearing that satisfied smirk, as if all women should adore him when she knew he used to kill squirrels just for the hell of it

She told the driver to head toward Charlottenburg Palace, still leaving herself the option of stopping off at the Resi. If Wolf called on her, Vicki imagined the pleasure of saying no. Elsa's recent tirade echoed through her head—a tirade Elsa had most likely read in *Der Querschnitt* or some other avant-garde magazine from which she plucked ideas that suited her: *Whenever I say no to a man, he always lectures me, for a half hour at least, on my sexual inhibitions—something all women suffer from apparently. When I still don't yield to his desires, he concludes, so sure of his lopsided logic, that I must either be a cold fish or a stupid cow. The two animals women are equated with if we don't yield to a man, when in reality it's the man himself we don't prefer. He never even considers that perhaps the odd shape of his bulbous nose offends, or that he's a boorish pigheaded conversationalist.* Vicki smiled. Yes, a cold fish or a stupid cow—that's what all this sexual freedom amounted to. Light and shadow fell across her lap from the passing streetlamps. She leaned her head against the window. In the rearview mirror, the driver peered at her from under his cap. Fearing he might be the chatty type, she glanced away, focusing on the little Opel two-seater passing by with an open top. A young woman nestled her head in the crook of the man's arm. He stroked her hair and murmured something into her neck, and she laughed, playfully tugging on his cravat. Then they sped off, leaving Vicki to wonder if they were married, if he loved her, if they were happy.

21

The last weeks of July carried a wilted, spent quality. The triumph of passing her French exam, the excitement of having free time to swim and read and go to the cinema faded in comparison to the sharp disappointment Vicki felt when she returned to the state library the following Monday now with nothing to study, and after sitting in the same seat for two hours, she left without meeting Geza. She returned a few days later, and a few days after that, only to sit alone in the ghostly room. Vicki restrained herself from going every day, although she feared that Geza might be visiting the library and looking for her on the days she failed to go. At the same time, she was irritated by how much she yearned to see him again. She spent some glorious summer afternoons cooped up in the library leafing through fashion magazines and paging through Tucholsky's *Jazz and Shimmy: Guide to the Latest Dances,* waiting for him to appear. Afterward, she went to ballet class at the Laban School of Dance, where the barre exercises felt painfully boring given how the new pianist, a young Polish girl in bifocals, banged away on the piano keys without any finesse or lightness. Leon the Russian, her favorite pianist, was holidaying on the Black Sea. His absence, and the thought of how he would suddenly break into his favorite section of *Don Quixote* during a monotonous *tendu* sequence, only reminded her of another person's absence, the person she most wanted to see, and for some inexplicable reason Leon and Geza became intertwined.

In August, her family went to Rindbach, their annual holiday spot, a small village in the southern end of the Traunsee in the Austrian Salzkammergut, where her mother had summered as a girl. Tortured by the thought of Geza going to the library to find her, she whittled away the days in this mountain town, days that stretched on endlessly without even the distraction of Franz, who had gone off again with Wolf to some vague summer retreat. Lev joked that Rindbach was delightfully boring, and Josephine retorted that this important music colony was home to Franz von Mendelssohn, who hosted the pianist Artur Schnabel, and Carl Flesch, the professor of violin at the Berlin Academy of Music, as well as various singers, such as Schnabel's wife and Jeanette Grumbacher de Jong. Over the summers, Josephine had cultivated a friendship with Mendelssohn and was an occasional guest at his villa. He had a large music room, and on rainy days, small impromptu concerts were held here. On these days, Josephine wistfully commented that listening to music at Mendelssohn's villa made her feel as if she'd been transported back to the days prior to the war, when one would sit peacefully listening to live musicians, before the radio and the telephone and the newfangled phonographs vied for everyone's attention and created an alarming dissonance.

It was after lunch, when a general laziness settled over the house. Lev and Vicki sat at the kitchen table playing rummy. Josephine ran water over a colander filled with cherries before spilling them into a bowl. She placed the bowl in the center of the table and sighed. "Remember when Franz presented flowers to the emperor, in the small square in front of the church?" Vicki nodded, thinking how Rindbach seemed to dip her mother back into the past, an effect she did not think healthy.

Josephine sat down, plucking a cherry from the bowl. "The emperor would stop there in the early morning to change from his large carriage into a one-horse carriage, which would ferry him up into the mountains to hunt chamois. The pastor chose Franz to present the flowers solely because he appeared cleaner than the peasant children. I can't recall if the old emperor even said thank you."

"Probably not," Lev snorted, dealing a new hand.

Josephine shook her head. "Eternally the cynic."

Through the open windows, Vicki stared at the chain of mountains lining the sky, above which rose the snow-covered peak of the Dachstein, standing out in blinding whiteness.

"Your turn," Lev reminded her.

Vicki drew a card. She wondered if Geza even liked her that afternoon or if it had all been in her imagination—the glances they'd exchanged, the way he had walked close to her down the street, their shoulders brushing every so often, the certainty she'd felt of meeting him again. Pretty soon it would be fall. Classes would resume, and who knew if she would ever see him? Her mind drifted over which courses she would take. Probably paleography, given by Karl Hampe, a well-known medievalist visiting from the University of Heidelberg, and most definitely Weber's course "The Crisis of the Modern Idea of the State in Europe." Maybe in the fall, I'll run into him again, she mused, since I'll be visiting the library quite often.

Lev studied his cards and glanced at her. "Pfennig for your thoughts?"

She smiled. "You'll need loads of pfennigs."

Josephine stood up abruptly, walking over to the open windows. "Isn't it strange here, without Franz?"

Lev snorted again. "He's busy fashioning himself into a real peasant."

"I feel as if he could walk in here any minute."

"You miss him," Lev said.

As she turned away from the window, her eyes pooled with tears.

Her mother: so delicate, so breakable. Even though they'd been fighting lately, Vicki realized she must be more careful with her mother. Last night when her mother had dropped a dish and broke it, she erupted into sobs. And this morning, on their walk into town, Vicki had gone ahead, purposefully losing sight of her mother, which seemed to leave an indelible mark on her fragile psyche. Back at the cottage, her mother had cried, "Is my company so distasteful that you must walk ten meters ahead at all times?" Vicki found Rindbach more tedious than ever, but for this, her mother was not to blame. She yearned for Berlin, for the brisk air and coffee at the Jockey, where the tables were so close together you could easily mingle between different groups, changing seats whenever the conversation dulled. And the way her mother wore a Tyrolean dress here, as if she were one of the villagers, and her father played along in his felt green hat with the feather fixed to the side, was utterly absurd.

Through the kitchen window, she watched her father comforting her mother in the garden. They were arguing about Franz. Her mother tearfully said that if he wanted to train in the Black Reichswehr, she supported him, at which point Lev raised his voice: "You do realize training young men for military service is forbidden by the Treaty of Versailles?"

Vicki put her head down. Her cheek rested against the cool wood of the table. Their voices floated into the kitchen; they didn't seem to care anymore if she heard their arguing. The conversation had turned from Franz to the doctor her mother was seeing. Lev said he was useless. Her mother cried, "How else can I cope with your night ramblings?"

"Cope?"

"Coming home at two a.m.!"

Vicki slowly got up from the table, and, taking a handful of cherries, she went up to her room. Sprawled across her bed, she leafed through the novel she was reading about a modern woman driven to despair by her pursuit of happiness. Not caring that her cherry-stained fingers left faint crimson marks on the pages, Vicki tossed the book aside and cursed the fact that there was no radio, no cinema, no telephone here— only a chorus of crickets. She pointed and flexed her feet and watched the shadows grow long across the wall. Picking up her book again, she read a few sentences, but the words didn't register. She'd been so foolish to assume they'd shared some sort of tacit understanding. When I return to Berlin, she thought, I will put him clear out of my mind.

Evening approached, flooding the room with a pink iridescent glow.

22

Exams had ended. Franz had done well on medieval German history, less well on French language and literature, and even less well on the forever looping problems of advanced calculus. His father had not been pleased about his barely passing score, but then he admitted to having disliked calculus when he was a student, and for a moment, the two of them shared a mutual dislike of something. But when Franz announced that he and Wolf were going to Hans Surén's nature colony on Saturday instead of his joining the family at Rindbach, Lev threw up his hands and shouted, "This *nacktkultur*! As if bathing nude and soldierly conditioning solves everything!" And then he tore off his glasses and stormed out of the room.

Wolf had failed calculus and had spent the last ten minutes cursing Professor Bilko, that damn Romanian Jew. Early Saturday morning, he and Franz sat side by side on the train, heading for the Krumme Lanke stop. At the end of this line, they would take another train one stop past Onkel Toms Hütte. Between the two small lakes, Krumme Lanke and Schlachtensee, Hans Surén held his nature retreat. Franz took an orange out of his rucksack, peeled it. Biting into a segment, a rush of citrus flooded his tongue.

He offered Wolf a piece. Wolf popped it into his mouth, continuing his rant. "From the first day, Bilko hated me. It was obvious. When he made that snide remark about Prussian militarism, he was obviously mocking my family."

"Hmmm," Franz said, half listening, disbelieving his luck. Wolf's friend Peter was also supposed to come along this morning, but at the last minute, Peter had decided to meet them at the campsite, so Franz had Wolf all to himself. The small space they shared on the train, the velvety feel of the westerly winds coming in through the window, the clean air of the North Sea intermingled with the Brandenburg countryside sweeping over the surrounding pines were enough to make him weep. The coal dust, the automobile pollution, the constant traffic and hiss of the city—he was free of it, that city his father cherished. And he was sitting with Wolf, close enough to notice how his bottom lip was dry, the skin coated over with a thin film of white, and how his breath smelled sour from last night's carousing, and how under his eyes faint shadows appeared, discoloration from lack of sleep, because he had been with Carin again. Carin, whom he'd been courting since spring.

The train halted for a moment, and they lurched forward, their shoulders brushing.

"Just forget about Bilko," Franz said.

Wolf nodded morosely.

The train started up again. It pained him to ask, but he couldn't help himself. "You were out late last night?"

"Carin wanted to see a play, but you know, I don't go in for that. We went dancing instead."

"Oh." His voice sounded hollow, weak. He hated it.

"I saw Peter after." Peter, the insipid Peter, whose face reminded Franz of a weasel.

"Really?"

Wolf shook his head. "The bastard was standing in his shorts and robe outside his apartment. Locked out. He had a girl over, but when she left, he walked her out and closed the door behind him without thinking. Utterly stupid. Luckily, there's a cafeteria next to his building, so we sat and had coffee and rolls until the sun came up. Which is why I'm shattered this morning." He stretched his arms overhead, lengthening his spine. "My neck."

Franz automatically put his hand on the back of Wolf's neck, and Wolf closed his eyes.

He bore his thumb and forefinger into the tendons, massaging Wolf there.

Wolf sighed, his eyes half-closed. "Too bad, no girls where we're headed."

"Mixed retreats are hedonistic. New Sunland with those outdoor 'fuck huts.' It's not very serious there."

Wolf opened his eyes, focusing his gaze on Franz. "You're right. It's not the same level of discipline."

"We need discipline, to revive the *volkskörper*."

He pinched Franz's cheek. "The little studious pupil, you are."

It hurt a little, where Wolf had pinched him. He wanted Wolf to do it again.

"I saw *Die Aufklärung* in your satchel."

Franz tossed the orange peels into the passing pines. "It's interesting, I guess."

Wolf raised his eyebrows. "You guess?" He looked away, laughing to himself. "Too many drawings of naked men. For my personal taste."

Franz felt his face flush. "It discusses how nudism is a form of regeneration for the Nordic race. Mostly text anyway."

"Hmmm," Wolf said, examining his nails. Perfectly filed and clipped, a pale-rose color underneath the nail. "Your sister was at Romanisches Café a few weeks ago." Wolf paused. "She was with a bunch of Communists."

Franz shrugged. Did Wolf expect him to act outraged? In truth, he didn't care so much. They moved in entirely different social circles; Vicki's bohemian friends were just as foreign to him as his fraternity brothers seemed to her.

Wolf smiled. "She's really pretty."

Franz made a face, trying to mask the jealousy he felt at this remark.

"We must make sure she doesn't fall in with that set. It would be a real shame for such a pretty girl to go the wrong way."

Franz said, "Vicki has a mind of her own. And she certainly doesn't care what I think."

Wolf glanced at the passing trees. "Just keeping an eye out."

A long silence followed. To alleviate the awkwardness, Franz punched Wolf in the shoulder.

Acting offended, Wolf said, "What was that for?"

"Get ready for the gymnastic drills, the medicine balls."

Wolf gripped Franz's shoulder. "Feels a little soft. A little weak."

He willed Wolf's hand to stay in place, or perhaps for it to move downward.

Wolf patted him on the chest. "Pace yourself." And then he gave him that brotherly smile, as if he knew best and needed to protect Franz. The train halted at their stop. They bounded into the harsh sunlight and headed for the woods.

The camp consisted of a grouping of old army barracks surrounded by a clearing where various physical drills took place. Beyond the barracks, low foothills rose into a crystalline sky. To get to Krumme Lanke, as Hans Surén explained upon their arrival, they had to walk past the barracks and take the footpath for three kilometers, until a sandy little shore appeared with lapping blue water. "The bracing cold of the water stimulates circulation—early morning and late afternoon are the times for swimming," he said, opening the door to one of the barracks. His straight back and erect posture pointed to his former career as an officer in the German colony of Cameroon. Padding down the center aisle of the barracks, he walked naked before them without the slightest hint of self-consciousness. The soles of his feet were thick and calloused from going barefoot. His slicked-back hair revealed an attractive leonine face, strong jaw, and steely blue eyes. The way his bronzed skin gleamed, Franz thought, must have been attained with oil. He pictured him smearing the oil onto his chest, his arms, his thighs. Even the backs of his hands glimmered slightly with that bronzed sheen. "Choose a bed," Surén said, gesturing to the immaculate row of bunk beds, each with its own footlocker, woolen blanket, white pillow. "But you won't be spending much time indoors." He then launched into the schedule. A five a.m. swim in the lake followed by breakfast of goat's milk and muesli, after which a series of physical drills, otherwise known as "curative gymnastics," based on the Swedish Movement Cure, would be carried out. "We don't use machines here," Surén stressed, "only one's own weight aided by medicine balls and kettle bells to attain the purest line, without the manipulation of exterior instruments." After completing the drills, one could choose between relaxing in a lime bath, sauna, or steam bath, complete with medical massage or colonic cleansing. Another swim in the late afternoon followed by a vegetarian dinner and then a lecture around the campfire. "Clear?" Surén asked, standing squarely before them. They nodded.

"Undress and leave your things in the lockers at the base of the bed."

When they hesitated, he asked them why it was so essential to go nude. "Why do you think?" He cocked his head to the side.

Wolf stared at him dumbly. Franz raised his hand. Surén gestured for him to speak.

"The sun carries curative powers so the most direct exposure to the greatest surface area of our skin creates the best results."

Surén narrowed his eyes. "A sound explanation, but a bit scientific. What I'm getting at is"—he paused to stroke his genitals with a contemplative air—"this place isn't for mere nature lovers and sun worshippers." His hand now rested on his thigh. "No. It's more than that. Much more. In the primeval forests of Germany, the Nordic solar rays once strengthened and healed our warrior nation. It was a time when the Teutons and the Cimbri spent the majority of summer daylight hours running naked and free, in top physical form as they hunted and killed and persevered in the wild, until Christian missionaries from the south clothed our ancestors' bodies in shame."

Wolf started to undress. Franz did the same. Surén watched them with nascent approval. He leaned against a bedpost, sighing. "And from there, it was only a matter of time until the devolution of man, into what we see now: the sickly, anemic, pale office worker hunched over his papers, who cannot run to save his life, round-shouldered and long-bearded, malevolent eyes peering out of sunken sockets."

"Terrible," Wolf murmured, fully naked. Franz tried not to stare at the gradations in his skin tone—tanned above his waistline and then a milky white where he usually wore clothing. Witnessing Wolf's private whiteness caused the blood to rush to his groin, more so than the bloom of golden hair between his legs, his cock, the graceful dip in his lower back, his muscled ass. Franz shivered, pulling his eyes away. Noticing, Surén said, "Come. Let's get into the sun."

Walking behind Surén and Wolf, he felt himself harden, and he tried to cover it with his hand. Surén directed Wolf to join the group practicing squats holding medicine balls above their heads. The men squinted into the sun, their arms straight and uplifted as they dipped their bodies lower and lower. "Your testicles should skim the dirt," the group leader barked when someone didn't bend his knees enough. "And you, over there," Surén said, resting a hand on Franz's back. He pointed to the pole-vaulting at the edge of the field. Franz nodded, cupping his groin.

Surén jerked Franz's hand away. "Stand proudly before your virility."

"Yes, sir." Franz began walking toward his designated group when Surén yelled joyously, "Shame is your enemy."

Franz nodded, praying his erection would die down by the time he reached the handful of men running with poles and flipping their bare, toned bodies through the air for a considerable distance. They landed on both legs, like triumphant cats. He felt as if his erect penis was the bow of a misguided boat, careening through a storm in which he'd surely drown. He tried to think of anything else besides Wolf, his mind racing for alternatives. The ugly woman on the train this morning, who kept trying to catch his eye, smiling knowingly whenever he happened to glance in her direction. Her low-cut blouse revealed a pale chest peppered with brown age spots, and her dyed reddish hair made her drawn face even more ghastly. She was the same type as the prostitute he'd visited a few weeks ago. Something sordid and poor about these women.

He looked down, relieved. Some of the men stretching and talking were quite erect, and yet they conversed with one another as if it were the most natural thing, as commonplace as sneezing or scratching your chin. The group leader, an older man wearing thick black glasses, handed him a bamboo pole. A few other men stretched their hamstrings, lying on their backs on the patchy grass, jerking their knees into their chests. The group leader, whose name was Paul Lciden, reminded Franz of his father, the way he held himself with tentativeness, his softspoken manner, the whisper of a mustache lining his upper lip. He showed Franz a few basics before he got started: this was where he must put his top hand, called the grip, on the pole, and the grip would move farther down the pole incrementally as his skill improved. His other hand should be placed shoulder-width down from his top hand. Strong afternoon sun seeped into his face, and Franz inhaled deeply, allowing the clear air to fill his lungs. For an instant, he closed his eyes, listening to the birds flitting by, the rustle of the trees, the faint wind on his chest, the sound of men sweating and grunting. He could smell their bodies—linseed oil, dirt, salt. The heady scent coursed through him.

Paul's firm hand encircled his shoulder. "Are you all right?"

Franz forced a smile. "Yes, thank you."

Paul peered into his face. "The sun is quite strong here. Take care not to get dehydrated."

He kept his hand on Franz's shoulder.

"I will take care."

"Good," he said, his warm hand sliding off Franz's shoulder. "And don't worry, it gets easier. The first day can be a shock."

"I'm not worried," Franz said, taking the pole and running with it.

At the night lecture, Hans Surén stood before the bonfire, occasionally throwing wood chips into the flames, explaining how the German nation depended on the health of their bodies, because the next war was already upon their doorstep. He spoke of his experiences in the Great War as an officer in Cameroon, how weak and disillusioned his soldiers were because the world had not only robbed Germany of her deserved victory, but her pride and strength had also been crushed. Franz sat next to Wolf, their knees touching. They wore clothes at night given how the air grew sharp, but if Surén had insisted, they would all be squatting here naked around the fire, shivering away. Surén wore loose linen pants and a linen shirt. All in white, he looked as if he were a Greek god presiding over his disciples. Wolf whispered something into Peter's ear, and Peter nodded in agreement.

Franz looked down at his sandals—they were required to wear these leather sandals provided by Surén for the weekend. His toes were long, ugly. He needed to trim his toenails. Perhaps Wolf had noticed this. Swallowing hard, he looked at Wolf again, hoping Wolf would drop him a reassuring wink, a nod, a faint smile. But Wolf listened intently to Surén's clear steady voice. "I urge you all to train during the week, after work, after study. Do not let your bodies languish, growing inactive and inert, which leads to impotence—not just physical impotence, but political and social impotence."

The men nodded, the fire throwing light and shadow across their faces. Franz thought faces looked more dramatic in the firelight, more angular and appealing. He admired the structure of Wolf's face: the straight ridge of his nose, his high cheekbones and arched eyebrows. He wanted to trace the pulsing tendons running down Wolf's neck. His hand tingled with anticipation, just thinking it. Across the fire, he noticed Paul staring at him. Franz smiled, acknowledging him, but Paul continued to stare in a more searching way.

Franz turned his attention back to Surén, who now paused a moment, his face grave. He clenched and unclenched his fist. "You see, people will tell you what we do here is merely recreational, merely for pleasure seekers, but as you have witnessed today, this is not the case."

Franz checked to see if Paul was still looking at him from across the fire and he was. His penetrating gaze made Franz nervous, slightly nauseated. The fire was dying down, the embers smoldering.

Surén shook his fist. "Sunlight! Nudity! Physical training! These are the paths to wholeness and health, as a people, as a *volk*. The Greeks and Romans, our forebears, understood this."

Wolf scooted back and bumped into Franz's knee. He turned around, irritated. When Franz started to apologize, Wolf hissed, "Quiet."

A few men sitting nearby glanced in their direction. Peter chuckled to himself, his rounded shoulders rising up and down in the most maddening fashion.

Sensing that some men had begun to drift off, their eyes wandering away from his imposing figure, Surén grew more ardent in his speech. In the distance, an owl hooted. If he listened closely, Franz could hear the lake lapping against the sandy shore. Even Surén's booming voice failed to distract him, consumed as he was by a gnawing sense of despondency. He'd hoped this weekend with Wolf would somehow revitalize their friendship and make Wolf favor him again, when it had already only worsened things. Franz was a splinter in Wolf's foot, an annoyance he wished to extract, a cur Wolf kicked from time to time.

"I will end on this note," Surén said, staring up at the star-studded sky, his voice softening, assuming a more mystical tone. "A Greco-German bloodline exists, and our return to the past will revive the *volks-körper* and strengthen the health of our race." He paused a moment and then lowered his head, clasping his hands in front of him. "Thank you. And good night." Applause erupted. Surén licked his lips, his light eyes glinting in the darkness.

The crowd dispersed into the woods, headed for the barracks. Peter and Wolf walked ahead, laughing. Franz trailed behind, feeling sorry for himself and at the same time chastising himself for such self-pity, pity that made the gorge rise in his throat. He stumbled on a loose rock, and thinking it wouldn't be so bad if he fell, he almost relished the rough ground as punishment for his weakness, but a familiar hand steadied him.

"I've got you," Paul said.

"I wasn't looking."

Paul gripped his forearm. "It's dark; you have to be careful."

Franz squinted into the darkness, but he couldn't see Wolf anymore. They'd vanished. Of course, Franz thought, by the time I get back to the barracks, Wolf and Peter will be hunched over some girlie mag.

"What did you think of the lecture?"

"What?"

Paul ruffled Franz's hair. "The lecture. Weren't you listening?"

"Of course I was."

The trees grew thicker in this part of the woods, and Franz felt as if they were walking under a heavy blanket, the stars hidden. He only heard the sound of their footsteps crunching through leaves.

"'Of course I was,'" Paul mimicked, tugging on Franz's shirtsleeve.

"You have to admit he went on a tad too long."

"Hmmm," Paul said, stopping.

Franz glanced back at him.

"Come here."

Franz hesitated.

"Just come over here a moment, will you?" Paul leaned against a tree. "Don't feel bad. I wasn't listening either."

"But I was," Franz protested.

He laughed softly, in that fatherly way. From under a gathering of fir trees, Franz could barely see him. "Where are you?"

"Here," Paul said softly.

The low hanging branches made Franz feel as if he were walking into a redolent green cave, the clean scent tingling his nostrils.

Paul took hold of his hand. It felt warm and moist. "I was thinking of you the whole time."

Franz laughed nervously, wondering if anyone could see them. He listened carefully for footsteps, for passing voices, but the stillness of the night covered them. Paul held Franz's hand firmly, guiding it down to his cock. Franz breathed in, surprised, and yet it was clear what Paul wanted. He couldn't play the ingenue forever, hiding behind feigned naïveté and poring over those pictures in his magazines, cloistered in the safety of his bedroom, as if that would satisfy him. He wanted to touch a male body, have his body touched . . . He wanted to know what it was like.

Under Franz's hand, Paul's cock rose upward, as if pulled by a puppet string. His shirt breathed open, and he guided Franz's other hand onto his chest. Franz gripped his woolly white hair there, tearing at it. Paul's breath quickened. He kissed Franz's neck, his collarbone, and then he knelt down, balancing on his knees. He unbuckled Franz's belt buckle. "We don't have much time." He used the same voice he'd used during pole-vaulting instruction, firm but encouraging.

Blood rushed into Franz's ears. The sight of this old man on his knees, looking up at him beseechingly, his eyes full of want, suddenly turned his stomach. It all seemed tawdry, vulgar, worse than sleeping with that prostitute. What would Wolf say if he saw how this old man with flabby arms begged to suck his cock? He propelled his foot back and swung it into Paul's face.

His glasses fell off. He let out a yelp. Doubling over, Paul started looking for his glasses, wildly feeling the ground.

Franz kicked him in the side. There. Better.

Paul rolled over, trying to catch his breath. "I didn't realize."

"What didn't you realize?" Franz demanded.

"I'm a bus driver on holiday. This is just a holiday for me. That's all." His mouth was bleeding and he was crying. He covered his face with his arm.

Franz ran back to the barracks, tearing through tree limbs, startled by the snapping sound of the branches, the sting of the broken-off tips scratching his arms, his face. When he got there, he stopped before the door. His hands trembled and he breathed deeply, trying to calm himself. Slowly, he opened the door and was relieved to find the lights out, bodies lying still in each bunk. He could easily slip into bed and forget about the whole mess—Paul's bloody pleading mouth, that sickening needling desire, which Franz had nearly succumbed to . . . A few errant snores vibrated through the cool quiet hall. He found his cot and started to undress.

"Where were you?" Wolf whispered harshly, his eyes glittering in the darkness. He sat on the top bunk, cross-legged, staring down at Franz.

Franz pulled off his shirt. "Nowhere."

"That's curious. I saw you with that older man. The two of you disappeared into the woods after the lecture."

Franz stood bare-chested in the moonlight. "I tripped on a rock—he helped me." His voice sounded high-pitched, panicked.

Wolf put a finger to his lips. "We don't want to wake everyone."

"Why are you awake?" Franz asked. He started to button up the front of his pajama shirt, but his fingers felt numb and thick.

Wolf smiled. "I was waiting up for you. Because I thought maybe . . . something untoward had happened. Between you and that man. And here you are, late, unsettled, looking as if you've had a dalliance in the woods."

"There was no dalliance!" Franz nearly shouted.

Wolf slid down from the top bunk and stood close to Franz now, only a few inches separating them. Franz admired the downy hair on his upper lip, the way his eyelashes curled upward, his faint thin eyebrows.

Wolf took him by the arm, and Franz felt the heat of Wolf's palm seeping into his skin through the thin nightshirt.

"Tell me. I can see it on your face." Wolf's breath smelled peppery.

Franz looked down at the floor. "It was nothing, really. He tried some funny business on me—but I whacked him across the face. That shut him up."

Wolf nodded for Franz to continue.

"He was bleeding and crying like a little girl."

Wolf scanned the darkened room. "Where's he now?"

Franz shrugged. "I don't know."

"Let's find him—finish him off."

"But, I—" He gulped down air, trying to stall. "I think he's learned his lesson."

Wolf clenched Franz's shoulder. "Don't you want to?"

Franz's heart started beating violently again, his skin prickling with anticipation. Wolf's warm hand now rested on the back of Franz's neck, and his sharp eyes blazed with excitement.

"Yes," Franz said. "I want to."

Franz and Wolf tore through the woods. They ran in their sandals, their shirts flying open in the wind.

"Turn here," Franz called out in the darkness.

"I think I heard something," Wolf said, coming up behind him.

"He's blind without his glasses. He's probably still writhing where I left him."

Wolf let out an explosive sneeze, shaking his head. "Which way?"

"Here," Franz yelled, zigzagging through the trees. His body felt light and agile, and his muscles tightened like springs. In front of Wolf, he would not let pity get the best of him, even if the old bastard cried for mercy. But as he ran and circled and cut back, he realized the old man had escaped.

Franz walked back, wondering if at least his glasses were still there, tangled in the underbrush.

Wolf came up behind him. "Looks like he got away."

Franz put his hands behind his head. "Damn."

"Hey," Wolf said, patting his back. "Next time."

He felt his eyes water with relief. Paul had gotten away. He stared at the white birches gleaming in the darkness.

Wolf swung an arm around Franz. "This place is for the dogs anyway," he said, kicking at leaves. "For perverts. And all that talk about sun exposure and nudity, Surén's not actually *doing* anything except prancing around naked all day, dipping in and out of cold water."

Franz laughed, grateful that at least Wolf seemed to favor him after what had felt like a long absence. Now it was summer, and they were together again in the woods joking about Surén and his theories, laughing about pole-vaulting in the nude. Dark low-hanging branches skimmed their heads, but every few paces, Franz would glance up at the flickering points of light dotting the sky, and he felt lucky.

23

On the way back from Rindbach, they always stopped in Nurem-burg for lunch. The Maybach acted up on the hot dusty roads; the car proved unreliable in warm weather. Lev found it annoyingly opulent for motoring in the country, but Josephine preferred it to the sweltering train, full of workaday weekenders, as she called them. At the moment, she stared at the passing countryside with a mournful look on her face while Vicki, who sat in the backseat, complained of the heat. Lev resisted leaving Berlin, often sending Josephine ahead to set up house. In the past, he'd even managed to spend just four short days in the deafening quiet of the country. But this year, with Franz away, Jose-phine refused to leave without Lev, arguing that she couldn't manage Vicki on her own given Vicki's recent moodiness and general disregard for all things familial. He thought he would appease her by staying the whole week, but everything had vexed her, from the china dish she'd mistakenly shattered, to Vicki's recalcitrance, to the lackluster concerts at Mendelssohn's villa; and Franz's absence endlessly possessed her. "What do you suppose he's doing now?" she would demand in the mid-dle of dinner, interrupting a perfectly good conversation. Or she would worry that he was overexerting himself, not eating well, and training too much. When Lev tried to reassure her that Franz could look after himself, she grew tearful, arguing that Lev didn't understand Franz, at which point Lev threw up his hands and remarked, "You're quite right there." She complained of fatigue, but when he suggested she rest upstairs, she snapped that she only wanted to be left alone. When he left her alone, reading his newspapers in the garden, she criticized him for burying his face in the papers, occupying himself with stories of distant people and places while ignoring his own family. Perhaps she was right,

Lev thought, as his eyes scanned the headlines, searching for any news of those far-off Baltic provinces . . . for news of Mitau, or even Riga. It had become a kind of habit over the years, to scrutinize the international section of the paper, in hopes of finding some trace, some small thread that might tie him back to Leah. But there was nothing today: *Yugoslavia severs diplomatic relations with Albania; Chamberlin takes off from Roosevelt Field to Germany in* Miss Columbia. Lev sat up, his interest renewed by the next item: *A total eclipse of the sun casts dark shadow over Sweden, Finland, and the northernmost regions of Russia.*

Josephine glanced at him from under her wide-brimmed hat. She squatted a few meters away, pruning her white roses.

"Did you know there's been a total eclipse of the sun in Russia?"

She snipped and snipped. "No."

"Imagine, the whole country dark." Leah must have seen it, from wherever she stood, a great huge shadow cast over the earth. Was she surprised? Frightened? What was she doing just before it occurred?

Josephine snipped more vigorously.

"You're mutilating the poor rose bush," he said.

"What do I care if the sun disappears for a few minutes in Russia?" She sighed, pulling up her long gardening gloves. "It's a dark country anyway."

"Hmmm," Lev said, knowing when to retreat. It was no use engaging her in any kind of political discussion. In her mind, Russia was bad and Germany was good and that was that.

"And why," she said, brandishing her sharp scissors through the air, "do you insist on reading about Russia, of all places. Every time I peek over your shoulder you're reading about that godforsaken place."

The high afternoon sun beat down on them. Lev wondered where Vicki was. She could dilute this brewing argument. His head itched under the ridiculous Tyrolean hat Josephine liked. He pulled it off. "Where's Vicki?"

"Upstairs, reading. She's been rather dreamy lately." She gathered up the dead black twigs, arranging them into a neat pile. "Your scalp will burn."

Lev threw the hat onto the grass. "It's not as wretched as you say. I spent four years in the east."

She faced him squarely. "Sometimes, it seems as if you never came back."

"What do you mean?" Lev demanded. What more did she want? He came back to her. He provided generously for the children. He'd played along all these years, acting the happy husband, attending her soirees and hosting dinner parties and accompanying her to the ghastly opera, box seat and all.

Her voice quivered. "I sense sometimes that . . ."

"Mutti!" Vicki called through the kitchen window. "Mutti—where's the needle and thread? I'm sewing new ribbons onto my pointe shoes and I placed it here just yesterday, and now it's vanished!" Nearly half her trunk had been filled with gleaming satin pointe shoes, a faint rose color, each pair perfectly packaged within its own rectangular paper box. When Lev had joked that there were no ballet studios in Rindbach and asked if she was planning on pirouetting across the town square, Vicki, in a characteristic outburst, exclaimed how most likely she'd die of boredom here, so she might as well sew.

"It was here, on this windowsill!" she called out again.

Thank God, Lev thought. Thank God for Vicki's missing needle and thread.

Josephine got up from the dirt and roses and strode into the kitchen.

"I only used it to mend a button," Josephine said.

"But now it's gone!" Vicki cried.

Lev closed his eyes, feeling the sun burn his scalp. His arm dangling from the chaise lounge, he stroked the grass. For a moment, a puff of clouds cast a shadow across his face. What does she know? he wondered. Does she know how often I think of Leah? How often I dream of her? Does she know I read the personal ads, wondering if anyone from Mitau is searching for relatives in Berlin? Does she know I once even placed a small personal ad in a few of the Yiddish dailies a year after I returned from the war? *Leah from Mitau—if you are in Berlin, meet me at Monbijoupark, next to the Spree River, at 10 a.m., September 14. I'm waiting for you.* He went there for a month, standing by the fountain, listening to its pitiful gurgling.

And last night's dream, still so vivid it burned in Lev's mind: they were going on holiday—not to Rindbach but some other Alpine retreat. Leah had never been to the mountains and she was giddy. He took her riding in the Maybach with the top down. Her black hair flew around her face. The road stretched endlessly before them. They had two precious days. She held his hand and wedged it between her warm thighs. He drove with his other hand. He wanted to pull over, but she told him to keep driving. "We only have two days," she kept saying, in a voice that transmitted both joy and sorrow. Zalman, Josephine, the children, his work—their lives were suspended, two days magically granted to them without obstacles. The only promise they had to fulfill was the taking of their mutual pleasure.

Lev turned his head to the side. The sun had emerged from behind the clouds, burning with heat. He breathed slowly, replaying the dream, savoring each image, each sensation. Distantly, he heard Vicki and Josephine arguing in the kitchen.

On the drive back to Berlin, Lev couldn't muster the energy to speak. His eyes burned as if sand had been rubbed into them, and his throat felt sore from having had circular arguments about which he could remember nothing. One fight in particular he did remember, as it had caused them to return to Berlin today, earlier than intended. The argument had been instigated by a fancy dress ball given by the D'Abernons, where a sprinkling of low-level diplomats and fading aristocracy dressed up in peasant costumes from Austria's rural past. Lev had gone reluctantly, finding the whole affair retrograde and embarrassing. After eating too much duck terrine and drinking too much *sturm,* a kind of fermented grape juice, he'd found Josephine deep in conversation with a ridiculous man wearing a red tailcoat and white breeches. Noticing how Lev stared at his costume and mistaking this stare for flattery, the man informed them that he had always worn this to the imperial hunt banquets in Grunewald forest before the war. Josephine had clapped her hands and said quite loudly, "Your ensemble is such a wonderful combination of elegance and simplicity." The man beamed with delight.

But Lev could no longer restrain himself. "I suppose you're an enthusiastic supporter of Hindenburg as well?" To which the man replied, "Anything to undermine the republic!"

Josephine then flashed Lev a threatening look, but he ignored her and went on to say that with Hindenburg in power, they could finally return to gorging Germany on heroic dead ideals, on philistinism, just when he thought the darkest chapter in their history had already unfolded.

The man sputtered that at least he wasn't a Bolshevik, and Lev raised his glass in mock celebration, shouting how they must continue to live as cozily as stuffed geese.

The man looked from Lev to Josephine as if he were a small child watching his parents fight. He swayed on his heels, his half-closed eyelids shimmering with moisture. It's like arguing with a fish, Lev had thought. Josephine fanned herself and said something about the heat, to which the man heartily agreed, overjoyed to veer off the subject of politics. Although the French doors had been thrown open, the room was exceedingly warm. Lev tore off his dinner jacket. Just then music started, a live performance of the tarantella. The women, in their faded flowered dresses and matching caps, swirled to and fro with their partners in the middle of the ballroom. They beat tambourines against their thighs and laughed with the feigned abandon of farmers' daughters.

Then the D'Abernons' grandson marched past in a soldier's green uniform with a steel helmet and tin drum. With his little eyes flashing under the helmet, he received many admiring smiles, which spurred him on to beat the drum even more forcibly. Josephine bent down and straightened his lapels, asking him where he got such a beautiful uniform. Lev struggled to suppress the bile rising in his throat. The music surged. The dancing women shrieked with pleasure as the men whirled them around faster and faster. "It's from my granddaddy," the little boy yelled, puffing out his chest. "You're quite the little soldier," Josephine exclaimed.

Lev had to escape this feverish room. Not watching where he was going, he bumped into an elderly woman bedecked in jewels. She dithered before him, confused, her red-painted mouth frowning. Her dyed black hair made her skin appear sickly white, and yet she was well fed, barely fitting into the corseted dress meant to imitate the country style. Multiple rings with various flashing stones graced her fingers, although one in particular caught Lev's eye: a simple band engraved with Hebrew lettering. There it was, buried in the opulence. She regarded Lev with woeful eyes. "Everyone's dying. I just heard from the director at the institute that Herr Engel has passed and yesterday my cousin as well. And then it seemed this morning my poor dog might go too, but he has thankfully revived."

"I'm sorry," Lev said, his mouth dry, his head pounding. A waft of fresh air floated into the room from the open French doors. "If you'll excuse me." He gestured to the balconies. She explained what her dog ate for breakfast. Lev nodded, stepping around her. He had to get away. Out of the corner of his eye, he saw another ridiculous man, dressed in equestrian clothing, invite Josephine to dance. Moving through the crowd toward the open air, he remembered the urgency with which he had wanted to marry her. They'd shared this urgency, this rush to be locked into a mutual bind, which now, from the outside looking in, felt like a cage he occasionally rattled in an attempt to get free.

And Leah? Would he have eventually felt the same with her, if they had married? He had left when their desire felt boundless. If he had stayed, would her body have become as familiar as an old shoe, instead of the exhilarating newness of her hair, her breasts, her skin? He didn't know. Perhaps it was unfair to only remember Leah in a blaze of passion. Perhaps he would have grown tired of her touch. And yet part of him thought: maybe not.

Breathing in the night air, relieved to be outside overlooking the vast grounds of the estate, he took out a cigarette, pausing before lighting it. He relished the feeling of an unlit cigarette in his hand, knowing he would smoke it, and yet he prolonged the moment before the smoke filled his lungs, his throat, his mouth. The anticipation is always better, sweeter, he thought.

"Where were you?"

Lev looked up from the balustrade, startled to find Josephine standing before him.

She pursed her lips, anger thinning and elongating her face.

He lit the cigarette. "I had to get some air."

"And just abandon me?"

"You were enjoying yourself with those idiots."

"Just because some people still care for the way things are done, you call them idiots."

"The way things *were* done." Lev glanced around at the neighboring balconies. Two men in top hats smoked cigars.

She started to say something, but her voice grew tight as she held back her tears. She hugged herself, looking pitiful, light and shadow playing on her face from the torches affixed to either side of the balcony. He was about to console her when she lashed out: "And what is so repellent about that little boy in his soldier's uniform?"

Lev shrugged. "It seems a bit militant, to dress him up like that."

"And when you came back, where was your uniform? Your gun? Your papers? How did those things just disappear? You think I'm too stupid to know what that means."

He felt his chest weaken, his mouth go dry. "To know *what*?"

She glanced away, into the wooded darkness. "I prefer not to humiliate you."

Of course she couldn't bring herself to say it: he had deserted, escaped, to preserve his own life over the lives of others. And she hated him for it.

He pushed his cigarette into a stone planter brimming with gladiolus. "I hate this place."

"Not even a scratch," she muttered.

He walked away from her and back into the crowded hot room.

Lev rubbed his eyes, glancing over at Josephine, who still gazed out the car window, focusing on the passing wheat fields. Though she'd acted overjoyed to see him in the fall of 1918, over the years, his early and safe return home had aroused the suspicion of her family, suspicion that eventually seeped into her view of him. And now, when she wanted to hurt him, in her most cruel moments, she pulled out this trump card, to which Lev now responded with silence. The first few years after the war, whenever she raised a question about his early return home or about his lack of medals, he defended himself. He described the bitter winters in Mitau, the marauding tribes of Cossacks, the wounds he'd treated and disinfected, the roads he'd cleared, the territory they'd gained for Germany. But he never sounded confident enough, wounded enough, for her to believe him. She would nod, but her eyes clouded over, opaque blue orbs of doubt. And for other reasons too, he stumbled when trying to convince her: between the pauses and sighs and sentences he left unfinished, there was also a love story.

Since last night at the D'Abernons', they hadn't spoken except for clipped terse exchanges. At least Vicki's presence ameliorated the icy air, but she too was lost in her own thoughts, twirling the ends of her hair, giving Lev a half-hearted smile when their eyes met in the rear-view mirror.

"Shall we stop for lunch in Nuremburg?" Lev asked.

Josephine sighed. "It's early."

"I'm getting hungry," Vicki offered.

Lev stretched his fingers out against the steering wheel. "Otherwise, it's another five hours."

"Fine," Josephine said, still avoiding eye contact. How impossible she is, Lev thought.

As they drove into town, men in brown shirts paraded down the road holding banners high above their heads. They were singing and laughing and marching along, their young faces beaming with ebullience. The cerulean blue of the sky was piercing to look at; the color made Lev's eyes water. Alongside the road, the lush vegetation of summer promised shade and respite. Lev inhaled the clean, pure scent of the country coming in through the open windows, and for a moment, he appreciated the surrounding nature, chastising himself for resisting its charms. The boys marched alongside the car, waving and smiling. Vicki waved back.

The medieval town rose up before them, the spires strong and imposing, the stone buildings quaint and squat. As they pulled up in front of the hotel, the streets were alive with anticipation. People walked briskly. The shutters of all the houses were thrown open. Women stood on balconies stringing garlands of asters. Getting out of the car, Lev wondered aloud if there was some sort of parade today.

They decided to walk into the center of town for lunch. Along the way, men tipped their hats at Josephine and Vicki. When Lev accidentally bumped into an older man, the man apologized profusely, clasping Lev's hand in both of his. Lev joked that Berliners should come here and take a course in manners. For the first time since their fight, Josephine revealed a small smile.

From three blocks away, they heard a laughing roar swelling toward them. A street band played, caustic brass instruments that made Lev wince. The noise grew in pitch as the crowd approached, moving down the street at a measured pace. Rippling in the warm wind, swastika banners hung from the facades of buildings. Moments later, the marchers came into full view, SA soldiers brandishing the black, white, and red flags of the Hohenzollern empire.

Lev clutched Vicki's hand. She flashed him an uncertain look.

After the first row of men passed, two troopers strode behind, clutching a diminutive figure, head hanging down, flopping from left to right. Dressed in drab loose clothing, muted and rumpled, she could have been mistaken for a man except for the honey-colored hair that hung over her face. As the procession moved closer, Lev felt the crowd bristling with sharp excitement: warm bodies pressing into his back, people straining to see the spectacle standing on tiptoe, their hot baited breath sweeping over his neck. Lev saw her more clearly now—a young woman, her glassy light eyes flitting from face to face, jaw locked, her mouth screwed into a grimace. A semicircle of eager bodies had instantaneously formed around the girl, and the troopers did all they could to keep the people back from pouncing, from tearing at her clothing, her skin, her hair. The crowd clapped and shouted, hurling insults at the girl, urging the troopers on. One of the troopers, after a few excruciating minutes filled with heat and laughter in which the girl started trembling, produced a pair of rusted barber shears from his rucksack. All around, people roared with appreciation.

Vicki stared at Lev, her eyes widening. "What's happening?"

He held Vicki close, one arm around her shoulders, the other one tense by his side.

The girl jerked back in refusal, her eyes squeezed shut. The trooper—a boy barely older than she was—grabbed a fistful of honey hair. Then he methodically, almost tenderly, started clipping off chunks, following the curve of her skull, careful not to nick her. Head tilted to the side, she kept her eyes closed. The closed eyes, the tilted head oddly reminded Lev of an early-thirteenth-century painting of the Madonna and Child, peaceful, flat dimensionless hand over heart, a halo of gold shimmering around her head as she sorrowfully holds her child in her arms, riddled with the foreknowledge of his crucifixion. Perhaps it was this young girl's passive resignation that triggered such a strange comparison. He didn't know. He only knew he had to leave—witnessing such a disgrace brought bile into his throat, made him want to retch on his shoes. But he couldn't move, packed on all sides with these lusty people who pressed into him, demanding blood. And he must protect Vicki. He didn't want to draw any attention, and trying to push through the crowd at this pivotal point might steer the crowd's focus away from the girl and toward them. And then, who could tell what might happen once this collective hungry gaze shifted to Vicki? He stood paralyzed with these thoughts, clenching Vicki's shoulders, hoping she didn't fully realize the severity of the situation, how awful it was. Strands of the girl's hair fell on the hot cobblestones. After the first fistful had been sliced off, people erupted into frantic applause, shouting for more. The trooper paused, held up a hand, and nodded to the crowd—he wasn't finished yet, not nearly. He would cut it all off—neuter her. A middle-aged woman next to them, her cheeks florid from the heat, sweat stains on her silk blouse, shouted, "A lesson indeed!" She was utterly enthralled, her predatory eyes watering with excitement when the trooper clipped off another chunk.

Vicki tightened her grip around Lev. "Papa, what has she done?" she whispered.

The woman overheard and pronounced with an authoritative air, "That girl has been associating with a Jewish man."

Lev glanced over at Josephine, standing on the other side of Vicki. She held her head high, staring impassively ahead, as if surmising the sunset or some other benign natural phenomenon. How did she not feel shattered by this? She, who had also committed the sin of loving a Jewish man, now gazed stonily at the poor girl. Perhaps she's afraid too, Lev thought, and she's trying to put on a strong front for Vicki, as I am. Or perhaps she's oblivious to the implications of this, thinking it unfortunate but impersonal, as if witnessing a half-dead bird twitching on the side of the road before speeding by, already on to the next thought.

When they'd finished, a few patches of uneven hair clung to the girl's scalp, her light eyes opaque and hooded, her body limp as the troopers dragged her down the street. Gone was that furious refusal, that teeth-grinding fear, as if a filmy membrane encased her, growing over her, a necessary shield against the terror of her circumstances. As the storm troopers went past with the woman, the crowd surged from the sidewalks onto the street behind her. The band struck up the "Deutschlandlied," and in all directions everyone came to attention, right arms extended in the Hitler salute, singing, *Germany, Germany above all.* Lev caught Josephine's eye—he thought she might actually sing along with her arm extended, but she only reached into her purse to retrieve her fan. She fixated on unfolding it, and then used it assiduously, as if the fan and the need for air, for relief from the heat, were the only reasons why she wasn't singing with the rest of them.

When the song ended, the procession moved on down the street. Vicki still clung to him, her eyes trained on the cobblestones, but he felt a deep sigh pass through her. Asters fell from overhanging balconies onto their shoulders. Lev touched the soft white petals, clenching a flower in his fist. When he glanced up, two women blew him kisses with both hands, their eyes laughing.

Afterward, they sat in the bar of a hotel but no one wanted lunch. Josephine pressed a glass of ice water to her forehead. Vicki kept rubbing her face. Tears leaked out of the corners of her eyes. Lev went up to the bar and ordered a vodka. He asked the bartender what had just occurred. The bartender leaned over the counter and lowered his voice. "Especially in Nuremberg, you see, it's risky for a young gentile woman to openly take up with a Jew."

"I don't understand," Lev said, heat flooding his face.

"The mayor of Nuremberg?" When Lev shook his head, the bartender continued, "Hermann Luppe—he authorized the parade. Especially after what was printed in *Der Stürmer*." *Der Stürmer* sounded vaguely familiar to Lev. Perhaps he'd seen it on a few newsstands, but it was a tabloid, the kind of paper read by laypeople who didn't know any better. But what did the paper have to do with the poor young woman, whose name, the bartender informed him, was Britta Kroll? He noticed the confusion on Lev's face and added, "Recently, it was printed that two Jewish men from Nuremburg killed a little Christian girl and drained the blood from her body for their religious rituals."

"Blood libel. We've been accused of such crimes for centuries." Lev sipped his drink, the alcohol burning his chest. He drank more. It was strange, how easily he had said "we," pointing out his affiliation to the most hated race on earth, something he would not have done in the past. And yet *we* had fallen from his lips so naturally, after witnessing such a disgrace.

The bartender scanned the room. "It was a kind of retaliation, I suppose, for the little Christian girl."

"The little Christian girl who never existed."

"Yes, I suppose that's right," the bartender said.

He finished his drink, his head lighter. "And the poor girl, the real live one I saw being tossed about like a ragdoll, she's ruined."

The bartender turned around, using a cloth to wipe the inside of a glass clean.

. . .

Josephine said, when they walked to the car, not to take it too hard; it was merely an isolated incident, nothing that reflected the whole of Germany. Lev shook his head, opening the car door for her. "They're as blond and stupid as young bulls, carrying heavy cudgels."

"Precisely my point. There's no reason to overreact."

Vicki slid into the backseat, pretending not to listen, her eyes averted under her straw hat.

Lev started the car, raising his voice over the engine. "Barbarism is contagious. Did you see the euphoria on their faces? The joy?"

Josephine laid a hand on his arm. "They're young. You just said so yourself."

Through the bay window of the lobby, Lev could see the bartender arranging bottles in neat orderly lines.

He made a sharp right, pulling out of the gravel square. "Like Franz."

"Franz has nothing to do with this."

"Which is why he's joined up with the Freikorps."

"Der Stahlhclm, actually."

"I thought he was on a nature retreat," Vicki said.

"It's all the same," Lev snapped.

When they exited the main gate of the city, a column of brown-shirted young men marched past the car and gave them the Heil Hitler salute.

Josephine smiled brightly.

Lev pressed down on the gas. "Don't encourage them."

Vicki twisted around, watching the receding figures.

Josephine rolled down her window, her hand dangling in the humid air. "I'm not encouraging anyone or anything. Do you really think someone who hasn't even finished high school can do much?"

Vicki turned back around, waiting for her father's answer.

He ran a hand though his hair. "Anything is possiblc."

With all the windows down, the sound of the engine drowned out any opportunity for further conversation, making the silence less noticeable. Vicki stared out the window, the color gone from her cheeks. Lev pretended to concentrate on the road, but his mind raced: what would happen to the poor girl? The people had stared at her with bloody lust, as if they wanted to rip off her skin, crush her bones. She looked about Vicki's age—nineteen, maybe twenty. His stomach turned. He quickly checked on Vicki in the rearview mirror. She sat passively in the backseat, watching the trees.

24

C"at."
 "Fur."
"Water."
"Ice."
"Bath."
"Baby."
"Milk."
"Warmth."
"Sun."
"Shadow."
"Husband."
"Male."
"Sex."

Josephine hesitated to answer. She was lying down in her usual position in Dr. Dührkoop's office. The coffered ceiling, she thought, must be impossible to clean, with all of its cavities. She heard his timer ticking and realized she'd been stalling. "I'm sorry. I lost my train of thought."

"All right."

She turned to face him, her cheek pressing against the scratchy wool pillow. "Shall we start again?"

He sighed, picking off a bit of lint from his trouser leg. "It's curious how you came to a full stop with the mention of sex."

"There were so many associations."

"Yes, but what was the first thing to enter your mind?" He took off his glasses. His face looked so much younger and more relaxed without them. And she could see his eyes more clearly, the dark-green color, almost amber when the light hit his face.

"Clean," she lied. But what could she say? She couldn't say the truth: sex=doctor=Dr. Dührkoop. Countless times, she had envisioned how in a fit of uncontrolled passion, he would shove the coffee table out of the way and throw her down onto the rug, admitting that yes, he was disrupting the process of transference and countertransference, but sexual repression was also extremely harmful to the doctor-patient relationship.

He raised his shapely eyebrows. "Clean?"

She shifted positions, leaning her head into the crook of her arm. "Well, yes, you see, when I was lying faceup, I noticed your coffered ceiling, and I suddenly thought how difficult it must be, to keep such a ceiling clean." She paused, gauging his reaction. "With all the crevices and such."

He glanced up for a moment and then refocused his gaze on her. "Didn't you say your mother was obsessed with cleaning the silver and the china?"

"It was the only thing she cared about."

"And it was quite obsessive, this cleaning?"

Josephine nodded, trying to anticipate where he was heading.

"She must have been especially concerned about cleaning when company came over."

She sat up even though he gestured for her to remain in a supine position. The blood rushed to her head and she inhaled deeply.

"Are you all right?" He leaned forward, touching her knee with the tips of his fingers, as if steadying himself.

She nodded.

He kept his hand there. She could think of nothing else and thought how he must feel the heat gathering under his fingers and hear her heart beating through her blouse in loud rhythmic bursts.

"Well," he said, moving his hand away to adjust his glasses. "I was only considering the possibility that the memory of your mother cleaning the silver could be linked to the appearance of Herr K, in the sense that for such social calls, your mother went to great lengths to clean the cutlery, even though, as you said, she had various maids who could have done it."

"Yes, but she never trusted they'd clean thoroughly enough."

"And when you saw your mother take out the polish, you then dreaded the subsequent appearance of Herr K, knowing that cleaning the silver also meant company was expected, and if Herr K was present, he would try to molest you, hence your subconscious association of the word *sex* with cleaning." He leaned back into his chair, pleased with himself.

She heard the next patient enter the waiting room. His eyes darted to the clock on the opposite wall. Ten more minutes. And then she would have to wait an entire week to see him again.

"I forgot to ask—how was Rindbach? Did you have a restful time?" He smiled warmly, and she felt as if they were now friends chatting over coffees. It was strange how he could unearth a deeply private childhood memory and then discuss holiday spots and music concerts in the same breath.

"Oh, Rindbach was . . ." She couldn't possibly tell him how terrible it had been—the incessant arguments with Vicki, the ever-widening rift between Lev and herself, made infinitely worse by that horrid parade in Nuremburg. She shook her head, looking down at her long skirt, feeling her naked knees just beneath the light wool fabric. He touched her hand again. "It's all right. The next patient can wait a minute."

"Really?"

He stroked her hand. A surge of gratitude rushed through her. Swallowing hard, she said, somewhat breathlessly, "There was this terrible parade in Nuremberg—we stopped there on the way back. Something to do with a girl having relations with a Jewish man. Lev was visibly upset, as was Vicki. I could tell they all thought I was acting quite cool about it when in truth—"

He interjected, "You were struggling with your own horrid history—the parade on flag day with Herr K on the balcony." Again, that satisfied look of triumph.

"Precisely," Josephine said, although she wasn't entirely sure this was the case, but she wanted him to feel good about his diagnosis. And she wanted to be his best patient, his most prized patient, the patient he would write case studies about someday, after he had cured her.

"It must have been very difficult," he lamented, noting the clock.

They'd gone five minutes over the hour. Josephine collected her purse and her parasol. Even though fall had arrived, it was unseasonably warm and she burned easily.

Walking her to the door, he added, "I did read about it in the paper."

"The parade?" A faint trace of pipe smoke emanated from his clothing.

"Lev must have been beside himself even though it was innocuous. An isolated event."

"He absolutely refuses to see how harmless the whole thing was."

"But you must know," he said, turning the brass doorknob, "Jewish brains are formed differently. After so many centuries of persecution, of witnessing war and bloodshed, nowadays with even the slightest disturbance to their environment, their pituitary gland sends fight or flight signals to the brain, thus activating the sympathetic nervous system." She waited for him to place his hand on her back, as he always did at this point.

He continued, "Which is why I have so many hypochondriac Jewish patients."

They both laughed.

Before opening the door, his hand caressed her back, and she noticed how after every session, he allowed his hand to linger there a little longer.

25

Classes resumed for the fall semester, and Vicki found "History of the Medieval German Town" far more boring than expected. The last class entailed poring over an old map of Heidelberg, examining the grid of its streets, a perfect model, the professor exclaimed, for the foundation and construction of the medieval city. The professor had also assigned them to look at a particular medieval scroll only available at the reading room of the state library, a place she was desperate to avoid. Yesterday, she'd scurried in to find her usual table, ashamed of how often she'd imagined seeing him here again, when it had all come to naught. She felt as if everyone—the head librarian in his musty sweater and the surly clerks behind the reserve desk and the students sitting nearby—could sense her furtiveness. For the next three hours, she hunched over the scroll, prohibited from taking the manuscript out of the library's premises, still half hoping she might see Geza while also dreading it. Her heart pounded whenever someone new walked into the room. At one point, she thought she saw him, only to realize the young man in the dark sweater who vaguely resembled Geza was, upon closer inspection, of an entirely different sort.

At least the pianist Leon had returned. As they balanced in passé, he added a few trembling notes, which sounded exactly as the pose felt; precarious, tentative, wavering. Balancing at the barre, Vicki focused on an advert for Chlorodent toothpaste plastered onto the side of a building across the street. She lengthened the back of her neck, tightened her stomach, rose higher onto the ball of her foot. The barre was next to a large glass window elevated above the street. Every so often, a passerby would stop and watch.

"Hold it, hold it," intoned Frau Stauffer, the ballet mistress, all in

black save for a gleaming peacock broach. Vicki tried, but already her
fingertips lightly touched the barre, a defeat. In front of her, Sabine,
with her perfectly coiled bun, balanced easily.

In the next room, cymbals clashed followed by the beating of
drums. Frau Stauffer winced, disdainful of the "expressionistic dance"
occurring "over there," as she called it, when it was only the next door
down. In response to the drums, Leon played with more gusto. Ser-
gey stretched on the floor in front of the mirrors, cradling his injured
foot. He watched Vicki impassively, and she imagined all the things
he faulted: her lack of turnout, her fallen arches, her not-quite-long-
enough legs.

The music stopped. Frau Stauffer dictated the next combination,
counting out the timing by tapping the floor with her lacquered cane.
She wanted them to close on three with a strong finish in fifth position.
Vicki half listened and leaned against the barre. She glanced out the
window and stared into Geza's face.

Startled, he backed away.

A stream of explanations reverberated through her: *It was bad luck.
I must have gone there on the wrong days, and then I went away to Rindbach without saying so, and he probably thought he'd never see me again.*

He gestured for her to come outside. The class fell silent. Leon
cracked his knuckles.

Frau Stauffer strode over to the window. "Do you know that man?"
Vicki nodded.

"I can't hear you!"

"Yes, Frau Stauffer, I know him."

Frau Stauffer pounded her cane into the floor. "I do not tolerate
interruptions! Leon, please resume."

Leon looked from Frau Stauffer to Vicki. Underneath his thick
mustache, Vicki detected a small smile. His hands hovered above the
piano keys.

"I'm sorry, Frau Stauffer," Vicki blurted. She ran outside.

Self-conscious in her leather ballet slippers and tights, chiffon skirt
and leotard, she crossed her arms over her chest, walking over to him.

Geza was more smartly turned out than she remembered. The

shabby dark overcoat was gone. Instead, he wore a Marengo cloth jacket paired with striped trousers.

He removed his hat. "I didn't mean to disturb you—I was only passing by and suddenly I saw you dancing in the window. It is very surprising."

"I'm so glad you were passing by," Vicki said, pushing back her wide hair band. "I thought I would see you at the library." Her voice carried a hint of suggestiveness, a voice reserved for flirting. "But then so many days passed."

He nodded, distracted by one of the dancers smiling in the window. "I think your fellow colleague is watching. I'm not causing a disturbance?"

Through the window, buoyant staccato notes surged to the sound of Frau Stauffer's cane thumping against the floor. "It's really no disturbance."

He put on his hat. "It was nice seeing you again, Vicki."

"Wait."

He paused in the middle of the street.

Did he not fancy her? Over the past weeks, she had allowed herself to believe the mere activity of thinking of him had brought them closer, when in reality, he was a stranger, as strange to her as any other man passing by just now. And here she was, having imagined scenarios in which they had kissed and courted and fallen in love. Her face burned from the thought of it, how misguided she'd been, how foolish.

He waited, shifting from one foot to the other, unwilling to convey even a trace of affection for her, as if any remnant of the afternoon they'd spent wandering through the city's streets had been erased from his memory and she was a distant acquaintance, someone he'd fleetingly recall in a few months' time, and after that, he would not think of her again.

She stood there, trying to think of something to say.

He nodded and walked away.

26

Inside his pockets, Geza clenched his fists, trying to appear calm, as if he didn't care, as if walking away from her meant nothing, but it meant everything. He had fought the urge to hold her delicate hands, to kiss her, embrace her—instead, he had left Vicki standing in the middle of the street, her black chiffon skirt floating up with the wind. Vicki's questioning stare, the disappointment clouding her face when he so casually said good-bye, burned through him. Walking swiftly, almost breaking into a run, Geza barely noticed the commotion on the streets— buses and motor cabs and trams jangled past. A drunken bowling team boarded an omnibus, shouting out their political views to anyone who would listen. Someone yelled back, "Damn Bolshies!" Half a block up, the sound of screeching brakes and metal against metal signaled a car crash. Who cares? Geza thought. He slowed down, trying to calm his racing pulse. But his heart accelerated when her image rose up before him again, her long white neck, the shape of her breasts visible through the pale green leotard, the way she'd tied her hair back with that thick headband, a slash of red against the dark strands. He shook his head. I have to forget her, he thought. Impossible!

It was his day off, but he yearned for the methodical work of laying bricks alongside the other men, losing himself in their banter about the subway strike, a demanding fiancée, where to buy the best Polish vodka, how the wet weather was coming. Geza saw the boardinghouse in the distance, the institutional redbrick building with its dark hall- ways, families packed into rooms, women bickering over a stolen pot, a misbehaving child. Already bracing himself for the smoky cacophony of all those poor disgruntled refugees, Geza hoped for a shred of quiet, a corner to think, to sort out his predicament.

He thought he could slip into his room unnoticed—it was nearly dinnertime, and the bedroom was vacant. The Mizurskies, the family he shared the room with, were preparing their evening meal in the hallway at the gas burner and little range. Semolina with beets and sour cream. Or potato leek soup with a few chunks of meat swimming in it. Oftentimes, they would save him some, though they barely had enough to feed themselves. Geza always declined, saying he had eaten, even if his stomach felt raw with hunger, because they had children, two boys with light hair who appeared underfed and a little dirty—the wax that accumulated inside their ears reminded Geza of crystalized honey.

As he was about to slip into his room, the lieutenant lumbered down the hallway, signaling to Geza. Lieutenant Barinov, an émigré from the Russian Revolution, an old czarist officer who in the predawn hours, after a night of heavy drinking, would wander the halls mumbling under his breath, *What has become of the czar, the Little Father? The House of Romanov? I once kissed the hand of Alexandra Feodorovna—such a milky white hand, as soft and fragrant as a flower. A hand that could only belong to an empress!* Half-asleep, Geza would overhear him whispering to another world, now lost. Having fought in the Russo-Japanese War and the Great War, the lieutenant confused battles, dates, names, and places, but it didn't matter. After dinner, Geza listened to his stories and sat with him in the slipshod library, where Lieutenant Barinov read his Russian newspapers and drank late into the night. Although his German was nearly perfect, the lieutenant preferred speaking Russian to Geza. It brought him back to the old country, before the revolution shattered everything he knew. When he drank too much, which was often, he'd rail at the Bolsheviks, how they couldn't possibly last much longer, that such a revolution was insanity, tearing the epaulettes from officers' uniforms and shooting decent men like animals in the mud. It sickened him to remember. During these rants, the lieutenant would grow more and more agitated, sweating, cursing, pacing the library as if he could slay one thousand Reds with the pointedness of his speech. Still wearing his tattered officer's uniform, he would stroke the front of it, his hands caressing the tarnished brass buttons. Geza listened with sympathy, interjecting how he also did not trust the new regime; the promises sounded too grand, the powerful always had something else in mind. They couldn't possibly want the peasants to succeed. "The rich win in the end, and that is the way of history," Geza would conclude.

But tonight, Geza didn't want to talk politics. The lieutenant waved his newspaper in the air as if conducting the Imperial Music Choir at the Saint Petersburg Philharmonic. "Geza!" he shouted. "Where have you been, my son?" Geza welcomed the term of endearment—he knew the lieutenant had lost his sons to the revolution.

He walked up to Geza, gripped his shoulder. From what Geza could tell, the lieutenant had been drinking, his light eyes glassy and rimmed with red. "You look as if you've seen a ghost," he joked.

Geza shook his head and mumbled that he'd been out in the city. Cooking smells—sizzling oil, chopped onions, smoke—filled the hall, turning his stomach.

The lieutenant gripped Geza's shoulder harder. "No, no. Something's eating at you. Come. Let's talk in the library."

They sat in front of the unlit fireplace, but there was no need to light it—the room felt overly warm, stuffy even. Someone had left a half-empty bowl of peanuts on the coffee table. They were the only ones here except for a few children who had somehow managed to escape dinnertime. The children played in the corner building an imaginary fort, instinctively keeping their voices low.

The lieutenant shelled a few peanuts. "I know. From the look on your face, it can only mean one thing."

Geza smiled weakly.

"A woman. You're thinking about a woman," the lieutenant said, gesturing for Geza to eat the peanuts.

"All right," Geza said, popping one into his mouth.

"And the problem is," the lieutenant continued, his hand diving back into the peanut bowl, "you love her, but you don't know if she loves you, or she loves you, but you don't have enough money." He paused, crunching down on a peanut. "It's the same the world over."

Geza shrugged reluctantly.

"Oh, come now," the lieutenant said. "Have some schnapps with me."

The combination of the strong apricot liquor, the heated room, the children quietly playing relaxed Geza and he slowly began to explain his situation. He loved Vicki Perlmutter—he knew this from the moment he saw her last March, but he had known her father during the war. Her father had had an affair with his aunt Leah, and this affair produced a son still living in Mitau. "Before I left Mitau, Leah gave me a letter for Lev. About their son, I assume. She made me promise to find Lev, give him the letter, but if I give Lev the letter, I bring back the past, with all its complications. And then Vicki would hate me, for ruining her family, for opening up this secret. Lev seemed happy when I saw him—he was walking with Vicki, and they were laughing over something. He already has a family. He doesn't need another one."

The lieutenant listened, his eyes bright and alert. Uncharacteristically, he didn't interrupt Geza but only stopped him now and then to clarify a few details.

Geza leapt up out of his chair, pacing in front of the fireplace. "But you see, I'm on the horns of a dilemma. If I forget Vicki, then I've lost the most important thing there is—but if I pursue her, court her, and hopefully win her, then I'll meet her father again, and this whole business with Leah will come tumbling out, which will hurt Vicki. I'm sure of it."

"You might lose her then too."

"Yes," Geza said, with an exasperated sigh.

The lieutenant leaned back into his chair, the old wood creaking. "The only thing you know for certain is if you do nothing, you will lose her. As for the rest, you don't know a thing. None of us do." He clasped his veiny hands together, his eyes darkening.

Geza collapsed back into the chair. "I suppose you're right."

"Of course I'm right," he snapped. "Can't you see how much I've lost from doing nothing? From letting the world, with all its ugly machinations, decide my fate?"

Silence filled the room. The children stopped building their fort, startled by the lieutenant's face—his usual flushed affable expression had evaporated and underneath was a hardened shell, cracked and wizened.

Geza nodded and stared down at the threadbare carpet. His ears burned. His head pounded. He knew what he had to do. "Thank you," he murmured. "Thank you."

27

His studies were suffering. Under the strain of various meetings as well as nighttime training activities, Franz often cut class and went home to sleep. He would slip through the backdoor of the kitchen, and if Marthe saw him, he pressed his hands together, as if in prayer, indicating that he was only going up to sleep, and please, if she would not disturb him. Between them grew a complicit understanding that she would not tell Josephine and Lev about how often he crept into his room and fell into bed. But this understanding followed the natural progression of how Marthe had always indulged him, allowing Franz to build forts in the garden with sheets from the linen closet, after which she would wash the dirty linens before Josephine could discover anything, or how he would shoot squirrels from a lookout point in the kitchen, even though she begged him to spare the poor creatures. Or how recently, she'd been cleaning his room and between the mattress and the box spring, she came upon his magazines. After stacking them into a neat pile, she put the mattress back in place. If his mother knew about the magazines—he shuddered thinking about it. Or anyone for that matter—but somehow the thought of Marthe knowing did not embarrass him because she carried on as before, even though he could tell from the neat little stack that she'd seen his stash. She was discreet, silent, and helpful—in short, everything a trusted housemaid should be.

He fell into bed, not bothering to change out of his trousers and dress shirt. His head pounded and his throat was parched, but he did not have the energy to ring for a carafe of water. The weak afternoon sun filtered into his room, and he curled onto his side, attempting to block out the light with his forearm.

He'd come home late last night after attending a dinner party in honor of Franz Pfeffer von Salomon, the *Oberste SA-Führung*, head of the SA, who was visiting from Munich. Recently, he and Wolf had joined the Berlin unit, known as the *Sturmbanne*. The SA itself was a large sprawling organization that Franz did not fully comprehend—it consisted of several formations known as *Gruppen*, within which were subordinate brigades that were divided into regiment-sized *Standarten*. *SA Standarten* were based in every major German city and were grouped into smaller units, known as *Stürme*, and Franz, from what he could deduce, had joined one. Twenty other young men comprised their unit. They wore brown shirts with the swastika band on the left forearm, a kepi cap, and matching brown pantaloons tucked into boots. Franz thought black looked smarter and more foreboding, which was what Benito Mussolini's men wore. Directly upon admittance into their unit, Wolf was promoted to *Rottenführer*, lance corporal, three ranks above Franz, for having done nothing except hail from a military family; Franz was only a private. Lutz, the senior officer who commanded their unit, was already on familiar terms with Wolf, selecting him as his favorite, but Franz didn't think much of Lutz—he'd been a bouncer at a nightclub, and before that had fought in the war but had been lightly wounded and never saw real combat. At least this is what the other men said.

But during night raids on villages harboring itinerant Poles, Lutz never showed hesitation. He drove the Poles from their homes and their farms, beating them with his cudgel while lecturing his men on the primacy of the soil and its connection to German blood, how the German peasant, a lost heroic figure, had been impoverished by industrialist Jews and itinerant Slavs who had settled in the countryside, displacing the true German *volk*.

They raided these neighboring villages systematically. Franz was astounded by the speed and alacrity that overtook every fiber of his being once the raid began: at sundown, the trucks pulled up into a quiet village, and at the sound of the leader's whistle, the men jumped out and attacked the Polish farmhands with rubber truncheons. Before the police could be summoned, they were off again, barreling down dusty

roads, the men beside him singing and shouting over the engine. Wolf
was always the loudest, roaring on about how he had smashed in that
Pole's face or broken an arm or pretended a man's back was a trampo-
line. With Wolf's arm draped over his shoulder, Franz basked in the
energy and heat that radiated from his body in the dark, cramped truck,
their bodies jostling together along the bumpy roads, with Wolf peri-
odically steadying himself by gripping Franz's thigh or knee. Each time
this happened, Franz drew in a short, quick breath, and he stared out at
the passing darkness, feigning nonchalance. When Wolf withdrew his
hand, the cold moon reminded him that the universe, dark and unending, was filled up with nothingness.

Afternoons were dedicated to paramilitary training known as "terrain exercises," as well as breaking up Social Democratic meetings
and standing on street corners in the busier sections of town distrib-
uting pamphlets outlining the evils of Communism, as well as how to
pick a Jew from the crowd. Some Jews, like his father, had become so
integrated into society that they appeared German, but defining traits
remained: exaggerated hand gestures, a high nasal voice, rising and falling speech patterns, short stature, weak musculature, and a deferential
countenance, verging on obsequious, which one could easily mistake
for politeness. "But remain alert to this," Lutz had explained yesterday
during lecture. His shoulders crept up, and he shortened his neck and
curved his back and hobbled toward them. "The Jew is always slightly
bent, eyes flashing this way and that for any possible threat to his person, whereas the German walks upright, limbs relaxed, face calm; he
might even bump into you and appear rude because he is not ever vigilant, ever fearful of his surroundings."

Franz heard the front door slam. He pulled a pillow over his head,
breathing in the musty smell. His eyes burned and he tried to sleep but
he kept replaying bits and pieces from last night. He'd only been invited
because of Wolf's father, who was well acquainted with Pfeffer. It was a
long drawn-out affair, beginning in the late afternoon with falcon hunting at an old estate north of Berlin. Ernst Udet, a flying ace from the
Great War, was there, and Göring, and Rudolf Diels, chief of police.

A handful of Reichswehr officers had been invited as well. They were slim, aristocratic, and overly polite and it was no wonder they longed for the return of the monarchy. Wolf had pointed out that they had chosen well in joining the SA as opposed to the Reichswehr, who were just dandies dressed up as policeman, protecting a dying government soon to be trampled.

After the hunt, they'd gathered in a vast meeting hall with wood-beam ceilings and a tremendous stone fireplace. Along the walls, the eyes of fallen deer stared down at him. The whiskey was strong, and Franz drank too quickly in an attempt to ease his discomfort, which only made him more anxious. In the corner of the room, he became transfixed by a Dürer print, *Knight, Death, and the Devil.* Staring at the engraving, he used the momentary reprieve to regain his composure, cursing himself for coming up short when Pfeffer jokingly asked how many Communists they'd uncovered in the past week. Franz had stood there dumbly, staring into his drink, racking his brain for the right number, only to be rescued by Wolf, who replied, "Thousands! And all of them are dead." Pfeffer had laughed, and then Wolf offered him a cigar. Pfeffer said, "Now, in all seriousness," and he took Wolf by the shoulder and led him over to the fireplace, where they remained, deep in conversation, for more than an hour.

Franz sulked in front of this frightful engraving, wondering why he never managed to say the right thing in the right moment. He stared at the minute ligaments in the horse's neck, which was tense and upright, as the animal maneuvered a dark Nordic gorge. Atop the horse, the knight passed by Death holding an hourglass, and following closely behind pranced a pig-snouted Devil.

He felt someone come up behind him.

"In order that you may not be deterred from the path of virtue because it seems rough and dreary . . . and because you must constantly fight three unfair enemies—the flesh, the devil, and the world—this third rule shall be proposed to you: all of those spooks and phantoms which come upon you as if you were in the very gorges of Hades must be deemed for naught after the example of Virgil's Aeneas . . . Look not behind thee." It was Rudolf Diels, the chief of Berlin police.

Franz tried not to stare at the massive scar in the shape of a V on his cheek or at the other scars below his lips, carving his chin into odd asymmetric shapes. Instead, his prominent dark eyebrows, the same jet-black color of his hair, offered a safe focal point.

"That was very eloquent," Franz said, holding out his hand.

They shook hands, and Diels smiled politely. "It's an address from Erasmus's *A Manual for a Christian Soldier,* published in 1501. One of my most preferred passages."

Franz nodded, turning back to the engraving. He couldn't bear Diels's face—his dark eyes bored into him despite his gentlemanly demeanor. Underneath the scars, Diels was quite handsome. Such a shame his face had been ruined in the war.

Diels gestured to the engraving. "The rider is undeterred, staying true to his mission. He is the ultimate embodiment of moral virtue."

"Yes," Franz said, his voice catching in his throat. "I can see that."

Diels laughed sardonically. "Well, what do I know? I'm just a farmer's son."

Franz nodded again, lost for words. Was he really a farmer's son? Diels had studied law at the University of Marburg. And he appeared polished in his cutaway suit.

The lights in the candelabras dimmed. Footmen circulated with aperitifs in filigreed glasses, signaling the start of cocktail hour. Diels toasted him, and their dainty glasses clinked together. Franz felt an overwhelming desire to escape Diels, but they stood isolated from the rest of the group, as if the engraving held a firm grip over them.

"And what drew you to the SA? Is your father a military man?"

Out of the corner of his eye, Franz noticed Wolf's fiancée, Carin, stride into the room with her friend Greta in tow. The women had been invited for cocktails, followed by dinner. Carin, in a shimmery white dress, draped a languorous arm over Wolf's shoulder. Distracted, Franz pulled his eyes away from her—from her large breasts Wolf so admired, and her bloodred mouth, and her slanted eyes exaggerated by eyeliner. She was half-Swedish but looked closer to Estonian or Lithuanian.

Franz ran a hand through his hair. "I'm sorry—I didn't catch the last thing you said."

"Your father, is he a military man?"

"My father . . ."

Diels smiled, the same polite insidious smile. "She's beautiful. I would want to fuck her too."

Carin threw back her small shapely head, laughing. Wolf and Pfeffer laughed along with her. They were standing on a sprawling bear rug, and Carin pretended to be afraid of the bear. She wiggled her little stocking foot into its open jaws, emitting a squeal of delight.

Franz felt his face flush with color. "That's Wolf's fiancée."

"Wolf von Trotta—yes, I know him. You registered together. Which leads us back to you, I'm afraid."

"I'm perfectly happy to answer any of your questions," Franz said, his tongue heavy in his mouth, his head pounding. He hated when this happened, when he split into two people—the one observing himself fumble and the one fumbling.

Diels took a pocketknife out of his jacket and balanced it between his thumb and forefinger. "What did you say about your father again?"

"My father, Karl von Stressing, was chief of the Prussian general staff." He had registered under his mother's name, von Stressing, and for all intents and purposes, his mother's brother, Karl, who had died in the Great War, was his father. He couldn't possibly imagine uttering *Lev Perlmutter* as his father's name—it sounded like a broken typewriter, muttering and sputtering without any clear delineation or active task at hand. It was a passive, inferior, easily overlooked name, which held no currency here—he refused it. The room grew louder and more boisterous. Greta, Carin's friend, waved to him.

Diels produced a cigar and cut a neat V-shaped notch into the tip. "You don't want to cut too deep or you'll ruin the whole cigar." He paused. "What was it about the SA that attracted you?"

Franz muttered something about blood and soil, and the connection between the people and the land, and how that connection must be preserved and not muddied by all the industry and speculation going on in the cities. He said the Poles and the Slavs were driving the German *volk* from their land, and as of late, they had restored some of it to the original farm owners. That should satisfy him, Franz thought, willing for dinner to be called.

Diels puffed on his cigar. "I was the Prussian minister of the interior, so of course, your commitment to the land and its peoples is important."

He paused, examining the solid block of ash that had accumulated at the end of his cigar. "But you see, the real value of the SA and the SS is how we make people feel terror. Every day."

Had Franz done this? When their trucks came into view, cresting over the hill, the red sun seeping behind the low plains, the Poles sprinted from the fields, leaving behind their scythes and sickles in the luxuriant wheat, as if they'd seen death and were trying to outrun it.

Diels cupped his hand under his cigar, scanning the room. "Do you think you could?"

On a side table next to the leather couch, there was a silver ashtray, overly ornamental, with two birds rising up in near flight on either side of the shallow dish. Franz momentarily debated whether or not this actually was an ashtray—but he already held it in his hand. Diels stared at him, his eyes dark and unblinking.

"Here," Franz said.

Diels gently rested his cigar against the side of the ashtray, rotating it until the long column of ash broke off in one even piece.

Franz's heart beat violently in his chest, and he wondered if this was what the Poles felt when they ran from the fields, when all he could see were the backs of their white shirts billowing in the wind. But why did his body tense and his heart contract, pumping blood to his muscles in preparation for instantaneous flight, when all he'd done was fetch what may or may not be an ashtray for the head of the Berlin police?

Diels slapped him on the back. It nearly took the wind out of him. "It's going to get a lot more difficult than standing around with a drink in your hand, waiting for dinner." And then Diels sauntered off, nodding to Pfeffer and a few Reischswehr officers.

Greta came toward him, smiling shyly. Oh, thank God, Franz thought. Someone to make me appear less pitiful. In her fluttering yellow chiffon dress, she still reminded him of the small girl in glasses, with two long plaits, trailing after Vicki in the snow when they'd gone to the cemetery that time to commemorate all the fallen soldiers, at the end of the war. She'd always favored him, sliding in and out of his life depending on circumstances that either brought them together or pulled them apart. They'd been pushed back together again because Greta happened to be Carin's friend, and Carin always insisted Greta join them because double dates were more social, and Carin enjoyed having people around who would laugh and drink and admire her beauty.

She lightly touched his arm. "You look quite smart in brown."

Franz frowned. "I think black would look much smarter."

They both noticed Carin and Wolf disappear into the library.

"Shall we join them?" she asked.

"I don't think Wolf would prefer our company just now."

She took a sip of champagne. "He's quite the lady-killer."

"It's true."

"And Carin fancies him."

Franz nodded, surveying the room, wondering where Diels had gone, and if the impression he'd made was as bad as all that.

"Anyway, I thought maybe we could all take a drive sometime."

"Yes," Franz said absently, "we could."

Greta beamed and said something about riding with the top down in autumn feeling so fresh and brisk that it was just the thing to enliven the senses.

Someone started banging away on the piano, playing an old military marching tune from the Great War. Everyone turned to listen, and the solemn earnest faces reminded Franz of church.

Greta's warm breath filtered into his ear. "That's Ernst Hanfstaengl—but everyone calls him Putzi."

He leaned closer to her. "Who is he?"

"Head of the Foreign Press Bureau in Berlin—his mother's American and he studied at Harvard."

The smell of her gardenia perfume was not offensive to him, as most women's perfumes were, and the high color of her cheeks, how she always tried to stand near him, aroused a certain degree of sympathy.

She touched the long strand of pearls around her neck, fingering the knot made at the end. "And Putzi's wife, Helene, dissuaded Hitler from committing suicide when the police came to arrest him after the putsch." She paused, breathless and flushed. "Isn't that amazing?"

He let his hand slide around her waist. "Yes, amazing." It didn't feel entirely repulsive, to do this.

She gazed up at him, her wide-set eyes brimming with emotion.

The room erupted into applause.

Putzi stood up and bowed with an exaggerated flourish. Greta still stared up at Franz, as if they were locked in a passionate embrace. Out of the corner of his eye, Franz caught Pfeffer looking over at him with approval. He pulled her closer, the soft chiffon of her dress sliding under his palm.

28

A few weeks later, they went motoring with the top down through the Tiergarten on a crisp Sunday afternoon in Wolf's new cherry-and-cream Opel Regent. Wolf and Carin sat in the front, Franz and Greta in the back. From this vantage point, Franz could witness, with alarming closeness, how every few minutes Carin would slide her slender fingers through Wolf's hair, the large sparkling yellow diamond on her fourth finger roving through his fine blond strands. A close-fitting velvet cloche covered her small shapely head, and the orange sequined flower pattern on the side of her hat caught the late afternoon light. Greta wore a similar cloche, but not quite as flashy, with beige felt appliquéd flowers. The brim of the hat nearly covered her eyes, but he could sense her peeking out at him, trying to read his thoughts, which even to him were vague and confused. Carin yelled over the engine about a sweet little operetta she'd seen the other night, a true relic of the fin de siècle, and how nice it was not to think too hard when going to the theater. Wolf wondered if she ever thought very hard, at which point she punched him in the arm, causing the Opel to swerve for a moment, nearly hitting one of the trees lining the road. Greta let out a stifled scream and clutched Franz's arm. When he stiffened, she pretended not to notice, and with an insistence Franz thought unsuitable to her, she continued to coil her arm around his.

What he couldn't wrap his head around was how Wolf seemed perfectly happy with Carin today, and yet yesterday he was ogling the Czech girl who worked in the university cafeteria dishing out potatoes and schnitzel. Over lunch, he couldn't stop talking about how he wanted to see her naked, how he would relish her scent of grease and sweat—*the smell of work,* he'd exclaimed. When he took up with a new woman, he told Franz all the details, almost as if he knew how much it both aroused and tortured him. Franz braced himself for when Wolf would inevitably describe the Czech's full-bodied figure, her scrubbed rural face, how she'd complied with his every fetish. It sickened him that Wolf debased himself like this, when he had Carin and Franz. Carin, who fluttered on the margins of their conversations like a carefree butterfly, happy to retreat into the background when Wolf wanted to be alone with Franz. She was too concerned with redecorating their future apartment or buying gloves at Wertheim's or throwing monthly soirees to interfere with the deeper, more serious bond between Franz and Wolf. And now with Greta, they'd reached a healthy equilibrium—he was no longer the pitied third wheel, and Wolf, it seemed, liked him all the more for it.

They pulled over for a rest in the park. Spreading a blanket down on a sunny patch of grass, they lounged in their coats and hats, turning their faces to the sun. Greta pulled out a thermos of hot coffee, and Carin placed tea sandwiches made with mustard and pickles and ham onto individual embroidered napkins. Wolf sat back on his elbows and motioned for Carin to put her head in his lap. She held up a little mug of coffee and asked, "Don't you want some?" but he only smiled back at her, an intimate knowing smile. Franz tried not to watch them relaxing on the blanket so casually, as lovers are prone to do, and instead stuffed his face with sandwiches. At least Wolf no longer asked about Vicki, which he had found particularly distasteful. Wolf lost interest after Vicki repeatedly ignored his calls. Then he started bringing Carin around, and now proclaimed he was utterly in love.

Greta watched Franz eat, cupping her hands around a mug of coffee and making passing comments about the weather predicted for the cycling races upcoming and what a shame it would be if it rained.

Franz continued to eat, nearly choking on a piece of ham. "Yes, it's a real shame," he said, stealing a glance at Wolf, who tickled Carin's nose with a fallen leaf. As if she could feel his gaze, Carin glanced over at Franz. Their eyes met. She nestled closer into the gabardine folds of Wolf's trench coat. "No need to turn all gloomy on us, Franz. The sun is shining as we speak."

Wolf grinned. "I actually see a black cloud hovering over his head."

Franz nodded, feeling the weight of the food, his throat tightening. Carin lightly kissed Wolf on the lips, and he buried his face into her neck. She laughed loudly, and then Wolf looked up, speaking to no one in particular. "Isn't she just the bee's knees?"

Despite feeling bloated and repellent—his fingers were greasy and crumbs had fallen on his trousers—he reached for a slice of marzipan tart. Greta sat as still as a statue, passing Franz long doleful looks. She wanted him to charm her, to make jokes and flirt, but instead, he stolidly ate and drank and didn't bother to wipe his hands. He was being a perfect barbarian, but what did it matter anyway? Wolf and Carin's limbs were entangled at this point—her long, slender leg encased in silk twined with his tweed trousers—and Franz felt as if he were witnessing the creation of some mythical Chimera. They cooed and whispered and tickled each other while Franz imagined vomiting over the tartan blanket. That would certainly ruin this little love nest. At night in the bathroom, Franz occasionally stuck a finger down his throat, disgusted by the sheer amount of matter he'd ingested. Afterward, he felt light and pure, his throat tingling and burning from the acidic backwash, a not entirely disagreeable sensation. Perhaps I could do it now behind the bushes, he thought.

A few blackbirds squawked overhead. Carin crinkled up her nose and said she hated blackbirds because they were ugly and made too much noise.

"Then we shall have them all killed," Wolf replied.

The light was starting to fade, and a chill permeated the air. Greta began rolling up the blanket. Carin packed the mugs back into the wicker basket. As they were leaving, a family arrived. Eastern European Jews, judging from their heavy black clothing and guttural speech. The woman wore a headscarf, and the children stared down at the ground. They spread their blanket nearby and took out a thermos. The husband started to eat without offering his wife and children any food, and they watched him eat. Franz tried not to look at them, so the family amounted to a black blurry grouping on the periphery of his vision. He could tell the others were doing the same, turning their heads away and moving quickly in an attempt to block out the distasteful scenery.

Wolf sped through the park. Greta and Carin clutched the brims of their hats. When they reached the Siegesallee, lined with white marble statues, Wolf slowed. They passed by Albert the Bear, his arm frozen in salutation.

Carin yawned into the wind and said they'd left in the nick of time. "It's disagreeable really, to encounter such types."

Greta nodded. "They should be barred from public places. It saps the enjoyment of others."

Franz saw Frederick the Great, sword at his side, followed by a string of lesser Fredericks. Even though most people mocked the over-done statues, Franz secretly loved them.

Carin checked her lipstick in a rhinestone-encrusted compact. He remembered when Wolf had bought it for her a few months ago. "And there are always so many of them clumped together like that."

Wolf sighed. "They multiply faster than fruit flies."

"It's a real problem," Franz said, his stomach knotting.

They exited the park and pulled onto the main boulevard, clogged with slow-moving traffic. Wolf said that after winning the war, gaining control over Russia, England, and Palestine, and then trying to seize Germany as well and meeting their first real defeat, the Jews had gone completely mad and were suffusing the world—especially easy America—with anti-German propaganda. He lit a cigarette, passing it over to Carin who smoked and pouted.

"All I know is the first apartment we saw—the one I fell in love with on Bellevuestrasse, right next to the Esplanade—is owned by a Jew—Bella Fromm—and she wouldn't sell it to us because we aren't Jews. Imagine, Wolf almost said his first name was Samuel or Daniel or something like that to get us an interview, but the moment she took one look at me, she hated me."

Carin passed the cigarette to Greta, who took a puff and passed it back. "You wouldn't have wanted to live there anyway," Greta said.

Carin sighed, covering her eyes from the lowering sun. "But the windows, the way they curved around the corner of the building—it was spectacular."

"If you like living in a fishbowl," Wolf said, pressing on his horn. The sound startled Franz, and he jumped in his seat.

Wolf's eyes flickered in the rearview mirror. "The thing about Jews is they're so damn jumpy. Their nerves are shot. They dart and dash from here to there as if the streets are about to open up and swallow them whole."

"It's how you can pick them out of a crowd," Franz offered, his heart racing.

Wolf held Franz's gaze in the rearview mirror. "Unless you're a quick study."

Greta described a friend of hers, Sabina, who was so elegant and refined, you would never guess her father was a Jewish tailor, and Carin added that of course there were exceptions to any race, but overall Jews were physically less attractive than Aryans. She flicked the butt of her cigarette into oncoming traffic.

Franz reached into his satchel and waved around the pamphlets that Lutz had instructed them to distribute. The moment he started speaking, the words fell flat. "If you read these pamphlets, you'll never be fooled again!"

No one said anything. After a few minutes, Greta asked what the pamphlets said, but Franz ignored her, annoyed by her insipid attempt to soften the silence. Carin looked bored and tired, not bothering to cover her mouth when she yawned.

Franz sat there, his stomach bloated and hard, full of marzipan raspberry tart and coffee and mustard sandwiches. He felt he should say something more, but he couldn't think of what. Instead, he stared at the passing cars.

They were dropping off Greta, then Carin. Wolf and Franz planned to drink and play cards at the Josty afterward. He imagined how he would let Wolf win at cards and how after a few beers, Wolf would inevitably soften toward him, and by the end of the night, all this unpleasantness would be forgotten.

But it wasn't. When Wolf pulled over to drop off Carin, the motor running in front of her family's town house, complete with turrets and diamond-shaped stained-glass windows, she leaned her head on his shoulder. "Won't you come in and say hello to Mother?"

Wolf whispered into her ear.

Franz stared down the long empty street.

"She always asks after you." Carin then motioned to Franz. "But I suppose you have to play cards with him."

Wolf twisted around, grinning in the moonlight. "You don't mind finding your own way home, do you?"

"That's all right," Franz managed, his heart sinking.

Carin gathered up her things. "Mother will be so pleased."

"Take these pamphlets as well?" Wolf slung a satchel of pamphlets into Franz's chest. "I don't have time to distribute mine, and I can't just dump them."

Carin watched for his reaction, her eyes glittering like a cat in the night.

"Yes, of course," Franz muttered.

They all got out of the car.

Franz stood on the sidewalk, watching Wolf's arm link through Carin's. They climbed the steep stone steps, Wolf's head inclined toward hers. The front door opened, flooding them in warm light.

29

On his way out to Alfred Flechtheim's soiree, Lev bumped into his son in the foyer. Franz was just coming home, after having missed dinner for the fifth consecutive night, and Lev was surprised and somewhat startled to see him. He held his hat to his chest. "We were thinking of giving up your seat at the dinner table—you don't mind, do you?" The joking tone did not make much of an impression.

Franz stared at Lev and hoisted his duffel bag over his shoulder.

"What have you got there?" No, I shouldn't have said that, Lev thought. He hates it when I ask too many questions.

"Nothing."

"I see."

Franz pushed past his father, the duffel bag banging into the glass vase perched on the entry table. White roses and water spilled onto the parquet floor.

Lev called for Marthe.

Franz made his way up the stairs.

Lev raised a hand. "Well, good night then."

"Good night," Franz called, disappearing at the top of the stairs.

He'd gone quiet over these past months, especially since the summer, as if he were conducting clandestine experiments in his room and could not be bothered to even eat dinner with the family. Lev knew he'd probably joined the Reichswehr, but the young men, from what he could gather, were generally polite in their slim-fitting blue uniforms and mainly concerned with keeping the peace, even if it meant breaking up the occasional Communist rally or whatnot. Lev didn't approve of such militarism, and he failed to see why Franz scurried to and fro as if

ferrying a grenade under his overcoat. But then again, they'd all been
lost in their own thoughts, coming and going through the house as if
it were the Friedrichstrasse train station, doors opening, doors closing,
people in and people out. When he was young, he couldn't just come
and go as he pleased—but his children preferred to live their own lives,
rejecting any semblance of a schedule, and Lev supposed in this way
Vicki and Franz exemplified the new generation.

Vicki had started leaving the house directly after dinner, always
with an excuse—a lecture, a birthday party, a new jazz club, drinks at
Die Tavern, but her fluttery erratic movements, the way she wore a hint
of pink lipstick and carefully fixed her hair, suggested she was meeting someone in particular instead of the vague list of acquaintances she
rattled off whenever Lev asked precisely whom it was she so rushed to
see. The other night, when Vicki checked herself in the foyer mirror one
last time, Lev joked, "Is he so important that you must forgo a bit of
chocolate pudding and coffee?" She had not heard him cross the living
room, immersed as she was with the curl of her hair under her earlobe.
Having been caught off guard, she did not have a ready reply.

"Aha!" Lev said. "The answer is written all over your face."

Her cheeks reddened even more, her eyes bright and glowing. It was
the look of infatuation, maybe even of love. Lev knew it well. It was not
so different from the way Josephine had been staring up at the chandelier in the living room as if expecting the angels themselves to descend,
springing out of the crystal. She always assumed this look after dinner
when, biscuit in hand, she stared upward, rapture and mystery shroud-
ing her face. And then she would turn to him, her eyes misted over, and
ask, very politely, if he wouldn't mind leaving the room.

Despite having been here a handful of times, Lev never failed to find
Alfred Flechtheim's apartment disorienting—it was all hard edges,
steel and glass and chrome, straight-backed chairs and bright white
walls and shiny fixtures everywhere, so that Lev constantly caught his
reflection in the silver border of a picture frame, in the mirror made
out of glass shards hanging precariously over a doorway, in the domed

lampshade made out of chrome. He guessed the white walls were so intensely white to better display the art Alfred and his wife collected and sold—art people mocked because they said it was ugly. But Lev poured over the Braques and Picassos and Modiglianis, taking in one picture after another as if wandering through a maze, some disturbing, some exhilarating, some incomprehensible. The spacious apartment was composed of various interconnected rooms, and Lev often found himself in an empty corridor, alone with one of Picasso's weeping women, her eyelid snagged into a sharp triangle of color, her nostrils flared like a disgruntled horse. Before the war, he might have felt the needling ache of regret encountering such paintings as he recalled his former artistic aspirations. But now, years later, a tepid admiration washed over him at the sight of others who possessed more talent, more drive, more desire. And so, as expected, the art of others grew into a pastime—he visited galleries and knew the dealers. He befriended Alfred Flechtheim, the photographer Hugo Erfurth, the painter Max Beckmann and his second wife, Quappi, as well as Beckmann's devoted patron, Käthe von Porada, a Viennese woman with slender, perfectly shaped hands. Everyone knew she was in love with Beckmann, who accepted her devotion with a gruff, superior air.

Lev wandered through the party, a glass of champagne in hand, weaving in and out of small clusters of people talking and smoking and drinking. The actress Hertha Schroeter played the saxophone in the corner, immersed in her own performance. Baby Goldschmidt-Rothschild was talking to Hermine Feist, the daughter of a coal and steel magnate who'd married into a German champagne dynasty. She had the largest collection of china in Europe, particularly Meissen, and after Baby Rothschild pulled Lev aside, introducing him as "the textile man," they resumed their conversation about stonechats. Baby Rothschild said her son had found a nest in their garden the other day. "Impossibly beautiful eggs—russet flecked, as if dusted with cinnamon." Then Hermine explained how stonechats received such a name because their high-pitched calls sounded as if two stones were clicking together. She put a hand on Lev's arm. "The way their wings constantly flutter—I'd give away half my china for their metabolism."

"Where's your lovely wife, by the way?" Baby Rothschild asked, scanning the room.

"Migraine," Lev said dryly, half listening to another conversation, one that Diaghilev, the Russian choreographer, was carrying on with Paul Mendelssohn Bartholdy. "I thought he was the next Nijinsky," Diaghilev cried mournfully, "but this Cobos, the Spaniard, he went mad and disappeared, just like that, not showing up for performances or showing up at the very last minute, unprepared, but then he would dance the most unbelievable dance, and the crowd would roar with applause—everyone made special allowances for Cobos."

Paul nodded sympathetically. "And now he's loose in Berlin?"

Diaghilev sighed. "He's the depressive type."

Lev's little cluster dispersed. Rothschild went to refill her drink, and Hermine spotted a banker she knew who'd recently had his ten-room apartment in Charlottenburg done over by Ernst Freud, son of Sigmund, whose views on clutter were as severe as those of Mies. "I must say hello," she whispered to Lev, before shimmying over to the banker. Lev thought about congratulating Flechtheim on his recent purchase— an El Greco—but Flechtheim was in deep conversation with a willowy woman who looked vaguely familiar. She nodded and jotted down notes on a notepad. A journalist of some sort, Lev thought, his stomach rumbling. Of course there was no food to speak of—only champagne and caviar dotted on endive leaves. He suddenly felt overcome by a wave of exhaustion. He wanted to sit, to recline if possible. Remembering the library with the deep leather couches, he waded through the living room, catching snippets of chatter—two women bickered over Beethoven's late quartets, a man in formal wear exclaimed how handsome Picasso was, and a young girl carried a Persian cat on her shoulder.

When Lev squeezed past Flechtheim and the journalist, he overheard her saying how a person never just feels one emotion at a time— one always experiences a layered response to the world, and art captures this best, especially portraits. She raised her voice, sensing Flechtheim's boredom. "At least the new art does this, what you collect, as opposed to the simple happiness of the Impressionists." Flechtheim laughed sardonically at the phrase "simple happiness." Lev was always struck by his full lips, which had an unnatural purple hue to them and made him seem preternaturally decadent.

Finally, the library, with its half-open door, appeared before him. A dim glow emanated from the room, and before entering, Lev heard a booming, familiar voice.

"Ugliness, the grotesque, this is part of reality—no, what I mean to say is, that *is* reality. We must capture reality, stop it in its tracks, study it, analyze it, and confront the truth, a truth that encompasses all of life—its cruelty, ugliness, and its dark beauty too."

Lev pushed open the door to find a man, his broad back facing him, and two young women in semitransparent shifts who leaned into each other on the leather sofa. The man sat on a fringed ottoman, his feet planted on either side of it, his massive knees jutting outward. Everything about him appeared oversized, bombastic, charged with energy.

"Have you read Henry Miller?" the man demanded.

The girls smiled and fanned themselves.

"I greatly admire his books." He paused and took a long gulp of his drink.

"He's only written a few books," Lev offered, speaking to the back of the man's head.

The man shrugged. "Miller doesn't shy away from extremity. What I do with images, he does with words."

One of the girls kicked off her high heels and wiggled her toes. "The way you paint, the New Objectivity?"

The man studied his nails. "Hmmm."

She yawned into her drink. "Is it German?"

The man shook his head. "What does it matter if it's German or not? It's human." He turned his head. His strong jaw and heavy-lidded eyes, his short neck and sharp profile sent a tremor of recognition through Lev.

"Excuse me?" Lev said, his voice buried in his chest. He coughed a few times. "Otto? Otto Schad?"

The man faced him. "Of course I'm Otto Schad."

Lev shook his head and laughed.

Otto jumped up and bellowed, "Lev Perlmutter! What in the hell are you doing here of all places?"

"What do you mean 'of all places'?"

Otto ran a hand through his hair. "I knew I would see you again, but I always pictured running into you at Berlin central station or the lobby of a hotel or some little bar. Flechtheim's my dealer. We met in Düsseldorf a few years back."

"You seem to be doing quite well for yourself."

"Well?" Otto roared. Then he embraced Lev and pounded a fist into his back. "I'm doing well, yes, you could say that."

One of the girls drowsed on the couch. The other one stretched her arms overhead, managing to show off her perfectly pointed breasts, which poked through the chiffon fabric. "Are you going to paint me tonight or not?"

"Lev Perlmutter. Lev Perlmutter." Otto looked at him with astonishment. "Incredible."

They spoke for a while in the library, unaware of time, of the night growing later, of the girls leaving and the party dispersing. It was as if, just by looking at Otto, Lev simultaneously inhabited two different existences: in the barracks of Mitau, smoking on their beds and listening for gunfire, walking along the icy streets, talking about women—Lev's incessant yearning for Leah, and Otto's Lithuanian, who fed him milk and cherries to heal his gout. These images collided with the present, or what had been mutually agreed upon as the present: Otto in a smoking jacket with a Brazilian cigar between his lips, explaining how he lived in the fashionable part of town and that his paintings had been selling extremely well. He looked comfortable, flush with money, the color high in his cheeks, his gold cufflinks glinting in the dim light of the library. The rough-and-tumble character Lev had known in the army was all but hidden until Otto opened his mouth. Then every obscenity flowed from it, accompanied by the same wild unhinged gestures, which so attracted women and gained the admiration of men. But how did he appear to Otto? Was he much changed? Had he grown complacent with the level of success he'd achieved as a "textile man"? No—it was simpler than all that. He was the same but older. Which was how people appeared in middle age, carrying on the same quirks, the same irritating habits, the same unattractive physical qualities, magnified by age, as if you were examining someone under a microscope, the microscope being time passing, and saw that it revealed what had been there all along: that same inherent, damning lack.

The party was in its final throes; a few people remained, passed out on the chaise lounges while housemaids cleared glasses and plates, moving through the rooms as if their limbs were encased in velvet. Alfred and his wife had retired. Max Beckmann sat alone in a corner, surly and depressed. His benefactor, Käthe, smiled at Lev and shrugged her birdlike shoulders, as if to say, *He's difficult, but I love him all the more for it.*

On their way out the door, Lev muttered to Otto, "God, she suffers for him," and Otto said, "Suffering is an art unto itself and one I'm not very interested in."

They ended up wandering the streets of St. Pauli, drinking from Otto's flask, recalling various details about Mitau, details they'd chosen to forget until now.

"Remember when it snowed and you took me to that cabal with the wonder-rabbi?"

Lev shook his head. "It wasn't a cabal. Just a group of old men and a rabbi."

"Well, it worked! My gout healed."

Three women passed, and under the harsh light of the streetlamps, their heavily painted faces betrayed their true sex. They catcalled to Lev and Otto once the cover of night enveloped them again.

Lev and Otto kept walking.

"Your gout healed because you stopped drinking."

"And then it came back," Otto admitted, "when I started drinking."

"Did you ever hear from Antonina again?" Lev asked, wanting to steer the conversation back to the women they'd left behind so that he could talk about Leah. Seeing Otto made him feel as if Leah was nearby, watching him. If he could only talk about her out loud, to someone who also knew her, she would feel more real to him, as if invoking her name would magically summon her.

Otto paused, examining the street signs. "I haven't thought of her in years. Jesus—Antonina. Who knows?"

The streetlamps shone down on them, a spectral glow.

"I never heard from Leah," Lev said.

Otto glanced around the empty streets. "I could have sworn the club was here." Then he smiled at Lev, his face loose with drink. "It's better not to harp on the past."

"Yes," Lev said softly.

"Look at me! I take each moment as it comes. The future, the past— blah—who cares?" Then Otto stuck out his tongue.

Lev tried to act amused, but he thought Otto had barbarically severed himself from the past, as if it were a dead thing. Lev tried again. "What did you do after the war? Did you end up going to your brother's in the south?"

Otto yawned. "For a bit. Then I got bored. You know, I wanted to become a famous artist. So I moved back to Berlin. And here I am!" He walked a few paces ahead and threw his hands in the air. "I must be really drunk. Can't find this damn place."

Just then a Chinese man appeared, and spotting Otto, he scurried over and whispered into his ear.

Otto nodded, and they followed him for a few blocks until they arrived at a nondescript building with a red awning.

"Wait here," the man said, and then he disappeared behind a black lacquered door.

Otto turned to Lev. "They're suspicious of Europeans. Generally, only Chinese and Malays come here."

Before Lev could ask more about this place, they were ushered into a dimly lit antechamber. Otto paid the admission, and the Chinese man gestured for them to check their coats and umbrellas. Otto then pulled out a revolver from the inside of his jacket and checked that too. Lev glanced at him, and Otto just shrugged.

The Chinese man performed a little bow, and then led them to a cellar with red carpets and vaulted ceilings. In the dim amber light, Lev noticed a few elegantly dressed Chinese men dreaming, tossing to and fro, their slim bodies splayed out on the low velvet couches. The air, sweet and moist, hung heavily. The host, a portly Chinese man, made an extravagant bow and showed them the opium pipe, dropping a small pebble of opium in its porcelain bowl, and gestured to a nearby couch. Once they were seated, he slipped away.

The calming sound of water flowing from a fountain combined with the occasional Chinese man speaking in his foreign tongue gave Lev an artificial sense of ease, while he vaguely wondered what time it was, and where they were, and why Otto carried a gun.

Otto took a tentative puff of the pipe and then paused, waiting for the effect. He passed it to Lev, who did the same. They continued to smoke. Behind them, Chinese men chatted. Lev saw a European man clutching a pillow with tassels, moaning, "Please, please don't—I don't want it."

Otto tilted his head back, gazing up at the ceiling from which drapery hung in great silk folds. "The best inspiration comes from the pipe; when I wake, the most amazing revelations come to me." A string of drool hung from Otto's lower lip. Lev felt his eyelids grow heavy. He blinked. Holding the bamboo pipe suddenly felt like a strain. He twisted the little knob in the middle of the pipe because it looked similar to a doorknob, and he imagined that another door would open, and it did.

He walked into a forest of birches. The long white trees shielded him from the hot eastern sun, and the smell of wheat and dirt instantly confirmed what he already knew: he was in Mitau again. He clutched at his belt, but he didn't have his gun. The forest was suspiciously quiet. He could only hear the crunch of his shoes treading through dry mounds of leaves. He wore civilian clothes—a three-piece suit, leather lace-ups coated in mud. I should take off my shoes, he thought, bending down to remove them. The sun beat on his neck. He glanced up at the trees, a dizzying maze of whiteness. A feral cat crossed his path, paused, and kept moving. Then he was holding his shoes, and the earth felt cool beneath his feet. He made his way to a clearing and saw a little straw hut with a thatched roof. Shelter, he thought.

Leah poked her head out of the hut. "Lev!" she shouted. "What took so long?" She looked exactly as he had left her—the same blue-black hair dazzling in the sun, the same open face, high cheekbones, delicate mouth. He wanted to run to her, touch her mouth, her hair, her skin.

She waved to him again. "Come. We've been waiting."

The hut was just there, twenty meters ahead, but with each step he took, the hut receded into the forest. He reached out his hand. "I'm coming."

She held an embroidered handkerchief into the wind. It fluttered and dipped with grace.

He paused, catching his breath.

"Why are you wearing that suit? It's broiling out. I have a clean set of clothes for you. The shirt from yesterday? I already washed it." She smiled triumphantly.

"That's good," Lev managed, afraid to take a step lest the hut, and Leah, drift farther from him.

She folded the handkerchief into a triangle and tied it under her thick mane. Then she marched toward him. "I have to come fetch you myself."

Lev nodded gratefully, feeling her cool hands on his face, inhaling the familiar scent of her: bark, mint leaves, wheat.

"There," she said, pressing her thumb into his forehead. "Better?"

"Yes," he whispered, his head lighter, his face cooler.

She took his arm. "Come."

Fruit dangled from the ceiling of the hut. He grabbed a curved yellow squash. His mother sat on a dusty cushion drinking mint tea. She shot him an accusatory look. "We thought you'd never come, but here you are."

Leah looked at the squash he held in his hand. "We're waiting until sundown to eat. But sit. Here's tea."

She served him strong black tea, and his mother told Leah not to fuss over him too much because he didn't appreciate it anyway.

Leah ruffled his hair and sighed.

Then his mother stated that Josephine was suffering from heatstroke. "Such a delicate thing," she added.

Leah sat down next to Lev and wrapped her cool white arms around him.

"Where's Josephine?" he asked.

Leah yawned. "She's convalescing with her mother."

The light outside faded. It was nearly sundown.

"Her mother's dead."

Leah patted Lev's hand. "Such a shame."

Lev's mother shook her head. "That woman would never have withstood the revolution. In the end, it's for the better."

Leah turned to Lev. "Will you get us some wood? We need some wood to make a fire."

Lev agreed. His mother and Leah smiled secretly to each other, thinking he did not notice this exchange. He left the hut, convinced he was married to Leah now, and somehow, Josephine understood this arrangement.

He wandered into the forest. Pink streaks ran across the Prussian blue sky. The sun, an angry ball of red, descended behind the foothills. He searched for firewood. Leah had described its whereabouts, but her description bore no resemblance to his surroundings.

Halfway behind the foothills, the sun dropped out of view, and then it was night. Lev stumbled on the low-lying bushes and uneven ground. He steadied himself against a tree, struggling to adjust his eyes to the sudden darkness. The moon rose up, full and luminescent. Lev tried to ascertain how far he had gone and from which direction. The goal of getting the firewood faded, and now he only wanted to return to Leah and the hut.

He heard a low guttural moan, and peeking around the tree, he saw his son howling at the moon. His son's head was a lion's head and his arms were wings. The bottom half of his son's body was human; he still wore his military slacks and black boots.

Franz swiftly turned toward Lev, his leonine eyes glowing in the darkness.

"Franz?"

Franz blinked back at him.

Lev tried to speak. No words came.

Franz threw back his head and howled, this time louder, as if in pain.

Lev spoke Yiddish, the only language he could summon. *Franz, are you hurt? Can I help you?*

Franz shook his head back and forth. He didn't understand Yiddish. He flapped his wings in frustration and emitted a series of high plaintive yelps. Lev remembered holding Franz to his chest when he was newly born—his eyes barely open, his mouth down-turned, he cried incessantly, red-faced and angry at his arrival in the world. If he could only tell us what's wrong, Lev had said to Josephine, feeling a sinking helplessness as he held the screaming creature, who tapped his balled-up fists into Lev's chest.

Franz let out another low moan that sounded akin to *Father*.

"I'm coming for you," Lev said, but when he moved, his legs felt heavy and sluggish.

Despondently, Franz wandered off into the woods, shaking his head, flaring his wings.

Soft velvet rubbed against Lev's cheek. He pulled away, inhaling the sweet thick air. Opening his eyes, he was startled to find the moon-shaped face of the portly Chinese host hovering over him. Lev checked his watch: five a.m.

The host bowed and offered Lev a cup of hot bitter tea.

After taking a sip, Lev slowly sat up with a pounding headache. Otto was rubbing his eyes. The other men were standing up, their legs shaky, except for two Chinese men who had taken even more opium and were still asleep.

Lev glanced around with distaste, for the other customers and for his unsettling, opium-induced dreams. His eyes burned and sweat had dampened his shirt.

Otto grinned. "Well?"

"Is it common to have hallucinations?"

"I was just fucking twenty women, including Marlene Dietrich."

Lev nodded soberly. "Sounds nice."

They stumbled into the antechamber. The host drew the heavy curtain, closing off the main room, and then went to retrieve their coats.

When Otto shoved open the door to the street, the gray morning light stung Lev's eyes.

The host, handing Lev his coat, smiled graciously. "Come again soon," he whispered. "It was a pleasure, watching you dream."

30

Since they had returned from Rindbach, Lev had begun leaving the house at night on a regular basis. After dinner, he casually folded up his napkin and told Josephine he would return later. In an attempt to soften the blow of his nocturnal outings, before leaving he would caress her cheek, and say, "I won't be as late as last time," as if this offered some sort of consolation. He never said where he was going, and she didn't dare ask, in part because she feared what he might say, and in part because she knew he would resent such interrogations. And few things were more distasteful to her than pushing a man into a corner, forcing him to behave properly or say something he didn't mean. Her friend Sophie, who had lost her husband in the war, used to scream after him when he left the house, as if he were a hunted animal. Afterward, she knocked on Josephine's door in a panic, her eyes wet and searching, muttering how he had gone off somewhere but didn't say where, and Josephine had tried to explain that this demand to know his whereabouts only drove him farther afield.

Josephine sat alone in the living room, staring out at the spacious garden, its few dark corners filled with rhododendrons, the patchy ground sprinkled with lilies of the valley. The rest was a properly ordered garden, intricate paths lined with blooming roses and fuchsias, so from where she sat, the view, which extended over the wide lawn, made her feel a perfect sense of equilibrium. But her eyes kept traveling back to the dark undergrowth, and although it amounted to such a small portion of the garden, those unruly spots seemed to undermine its overall beauty and shape.

If Lev didn't want to tell her where he'd gone off to, then she would certainly not stoop so low as to inquire. She sighed, leaning back into the chair, uninterested in the magazine article she was skimming about how bias-cut dresses were all the rage. She glanced around, aware of every sound. The rustle of her skirt against the chair seemed overly loud, but then again, the rooms were so still and silent, she imagined sheets draped over the furniture, as if they'd left for summer holidays. Vicki was not at home either, now that young women went out freely at night without chaperones, something Josephine still found hard to accept. Every now and then, she heard Franz rumbling around in his room, but the other night when she had knocked on his door, he opened it with such an affronted look on his face, she slunk away, mumbling an apology.

Fingering the biscuits on the silver tray, the same shortbread biscuits her mother used to eat, she turned her gaze back to the garden and was reminded of how her grandfather on her mother's side used to sit on the terrace in a brown velvet jacket with a rug over his rheumatic knees, even in summer. And the two surly greyhounds lying next to him, his loyal companions; he loved those dogs so much—oh, what were their names again? She racked her brain but couldn't think of them. When the weather was fair, he'd take a ride after the midday meal. The carriage waited at the entrance of the estate with the manservant poised to open the front door the moment her grandfather emerged from the dining room, his cheeks flushed with satiation. Her mother would dress her in a stiff navy frock and place her in the carriage next to her grandfather, and they would ride around and admire the summer residences of the Hohenzollern kings.

As she bit into the biscuit, the lightbulbs in the chandelier flickered on and off with a strange spark. She carefully put the half-eaten biscuit down on the tray. The lights flickered back on. Yes, it was certain: Mother must be sending her a signal through the lights. Whenever Josephine thought about her with a strong intent, aided by the biscuits, the lights flickered in this odd way, a sure sign her mother was still here, but just in another form. Josephine took another bite of the biscuit. What did she want to say? Why was she not at peace?

Mitzi wandered into the living room, beckoned by the scent of the biscuits. The dog glanced around dolefully and then took her time settling down, circling three times before curling up next to Josephine's feet. Well, she thought, if I went to Balthazar's church, Lev would strongly disapprove, even though Dr. Dührkoop had recommended him. Lev relied on science, insinuating that faith was medieval, a device to uplift and control the peasants when, after a day in the fields, they stood in awe before soaring buttresses and rose windows saturated with color. She could hear his voice now: *Of course under those circumstances anyone would believe in God!* A callous, cavalier argument, she thought, finishing off the last of the biscuits.

Sleepily, Mitzi raised her head, hoping some shortbread crumbs might have fallen from above.

The trip to Balthazar's church, located in southwestern Berlin, required her to take two trams followed by a rushed fifteen-minute walk, after which she finally reached the middle-class neighborhood where the minister had converted his small apartment into a makeshift church and meeting place for like-minded spiritualists. The afternoon traffic had made her dreadfully late, and climbing up the steep carpeted staircase, she feared they wouldn't admit her. It would be much more convenient, she thought, if he conducted his sessions at a more reasonable hour, but as the pamphlet explained, the spirits were most voluble during the "in-between hours," when the sun was either rising or setting.

An older woman at the door, wearing a simple navy dress with a high white collar, introduced herself as Sister Grete Muller. She pressed another pamphlet into Josephine's hand and then ushered her into a dim living room filled with an overwhelming number of books, hanging portraits, and an odd assortment of miniature cat figurines, their eyes inlaid with colored glass. In the middle of the room, ten chairs were arranged around a wooden table. Behind the table hung a large cloudy mirror, and Josephine caught a glimpse of herself in it. Sitting next to two elderly women, she looked slightly out of place in her molded felt hat, given the modest surroundings. She touched the rhinestone pin fastened to the side of the hat, which caught the late-afternoon light, and debated whether or not to remove it. Besides the two women, who were whispering rather loudly, a girl, probably about eighteen, sat at the edge of the circle, nervously fingering the buttons on her blouse. Her uneven complexion and the way she fixated on the empty chair behind the table, presumably where Balthazar sat, made her appear disturbed. But isn't everyone here somewhat anxious and disturbed? Josephine thought, pulling off her ivory kid gloves. The loud whispering of the two women interrupted her thoughts. Hearing Balthazar's name, she strained to listen.

"He's from Altenburg and his father was a bricklayer," one of the women said, adjusting her crocheted shawl. The other woman whispered harshly, "He lost both parents and a sister to cholera. That's when he began seeing the dead. As a young child, he'd been prone to visions, but the visions grew so powerful after the death of his parents, he went to a healer in Zwickau, who informed him that such visions were not a sign of illness but evidence of his strong powers as a medium."

The woman in the shawl shook her head. "Thank the Lord for that healer in Zwickau." She sighed. "It's been a real comfort, seeing Hans again."

Who was Hans? Josephine wondered. Her son? Husband? Whoever he was, most likely she'd lost him in the war, and for a brief moment, Josephine quietly thanked God that Franz had been too young for the war. She lowered her head. *Please God,* she prayed, *please protect him until the end of his days, or at the very least, let him die after me.*

A middle-aged couple entered the room followed by two elderly Russian men who shuffled their feet. The men carried on a conversation they'd been having on the street, the street being no different to them than this dimly lit, sanctimonious gathering.

Sister Muller closed the door and walked into the middle of the circle, standing in front of the table. "Now that we're all assembled here this evening, I would like to express my deepest gratitude for your contributions, which have greatly helped us remain afloat, even during the most trying of times," and as she rambled on about various meetings and lectures scheduled for the upcoming fall season, she passed around a little alms box, and each person discreetly slipped a few marks into it. Sister Muller's voice, soothing and lilting, together with the lack of fresh air in the room made Josephine drowsy. She read over the pamphlet in an attempt to appear engaged and alert.

The Technique

Derived from the Greco-Roman tradition, with some later Christian adjustments, our technique dictates that four people, or six, or eight sit around a table made of solid oak. Do not allow five people to participate, for Christ was murdered with five wounds, and odd numbers generally (but not always) invite baleful forces. In the center of the table, place a glass bowl filled with olive oil. The oil's warm golden color is soothing to gaze at, for living and dead alike. A single drop of fresh blood drawn from the finger of a volunteer (remember, a young virgin is best!) will be blended into the oil. During the séance, concentrate on the bowl of oil and blood.

Outside the circle, a bell, a steel knife, and some rock salt will be placed at strategic points to defend against any malevolent spirits who may choose to make themselves known.

The Process

During the séance, please do not speak or raise your voice. Only Father Balthazar will speak. Refrain from coughing, sneezing, or any other adjustments made to your person, including but not limited to: touching the face, smoothing the hair, rubbing the eyes, fiddling with clothing or jewelry, etc. These movements, no matter how deft and discreet, only remind the spirits of the painful truth that they no longer inhabit a corporeal form.

Maintain a serious and reverential attitude toward your surroundings. Do not laugh. The dead can no longer laugh with true abandon, and therefore such displays of cheer offend them.

Sister Muller held her hand to her heart, beaming at everyone around the circle. "And now, let us welcome our holy prophet and esteemed conduit, Father Balthazar."

A smattering of applause followed, after which an adjoining door opened and out stepped Father Balthazar, smiling broadly in his royal-blue suit, the same blue Sister Muller wore. Fat and energetic with a curly white beard, his cheeks red and puffing, he was most definitely of this world, and the image Josephine had carried in her head, of the cool remote prophet, evaporated. He held a leather-bound Bible to his chest and lowered his gaze for a moment, closing his eyes. Everyone else, including Sister Muller, followed suit, so Josephine also closed her eyes. Balthazar then read from 1 Samuel 28 as an introductory prayer, after which he placed the Bible on the table with a piece of quartz resting on the open book. He surveyed the group, nodding to the middle-aged couple.

Balthazar started to speak in a deep resonant voice, "Welcome, friends. We are gathered here tonight to make contact with the Other Side. The conditions are strong—the energy is vibrant and free of pathogenic currents, which often block contact. If you experience asthma, sleep loss, or severe headaches, you may be restored to health by evading these disease-causing currents streaming through the world around us by simply following a particular regimen . . ." He paused a moment, lost in thought. "Please see me afterward if you experience such symptoms. But now to the matter at hand."

The two elderly women leaned forward. The couple stared at Balthazar with searching, predatory eyes, as if he alone held the key to their happiness. The young girl looked down at the pamphlet in her lap, biting her lower lip. Josephine folded her gloves into her purse, trying to make the least amount of noise. Sister Muller set a glass bowl filled with olive oil on the table and then positioned herself to the right of the table. Balthazar sat behind it and spread his large sun-spotted hands over its surface. He assumed an odd, blank expression. The robust bloom drained from his cheeks. He closed his eyes and he suddenly appeared shrunken and wracked with fatigue.

Sister Muller asked, with a hint of severity, "May we have a volunteer?" The young girl raised her hand, and Sister Muller motioned her to come forward. The girl sat down in front of Balthazar. Sister Muller carefully pricked her finger with a sterilized needle and then squeezed little beads of bright red blood out of the girl's index finger, the drops falling into the olive oil, a performance that transfixed and repelled Josephine. Sister Muller nodded, signaling for the girl to return to her seat.

Then she solemnly faced the group. "Concentrate on the bowl of oil and blood and send a message out to the departed and invite him or her to make themselves known to us so that we may open the lines of communication." Josephine stared at the blood and oil. The sight of it nauseated her—the viscous thick liquid, the swirling red drops.

Balthazar cleared his throat and shook his head back and forth like a horse. He mumbled something and coughed. He shook his head back and forth again, the sagging skin under his chin swaying along with him. His eyes squeezed more tightly shut. "My knees, my knees—they feel cold, damp, aching. Does anyone here know someone with aching knees?"

No one spoke. Josephine fidgeted with the metal clasp on her purse, feeling slightly sorry for Balthazar. Many of these mediums came up short, and she imagined how disappointing it must be for those who truly believed in it, such as the couple across from her, who looked on the verge of tears.

Balthazar put his forehead down on the table and mumbled something, his lips moving against the wood. Then he picked up his head, his eyes awake and blazing. "There's a heavy rug over my knees and I am cold, even in summer. Even in the height of summer, at our villa in Charlottenburg with the flies buzzing around the fruit, the fruit under the muslin cloth, and our two greyhounds, Gaspar and Prima, at my feet as I sit all day on the terrace, the rug over my knees—oh my knees, my rheumatic knees!" He gasped, doubling over, and in the same moment, Josephine let out a sharp cry.

Sister Muller rushed over to Balthazar, and he nodded reassuringly. A general disturbance erupted, and people started whispering among themselves.

Sister Muller shouted, "Silence!"

Josephine felt her heart race, a chilled sweat drenching her chest. She didn't know if she should speak or not—she frantically tried to recall the pamphlet's instructions. Sitting very still, she raised a hand. Sister Muller gestured for her to speak.

Her throat felt tight and parched. "It's my grandfather Frederick."

Balthazar grimaced, his light eyes now glassy and opaque. "Yes, my child."

She glanced at Sister Muller, who nodded for her to continue.

"I was trying to contact Mother before—I didn't know it was you."

"What's happened to you? What's happened?"

"Everything's all right, Grandfather." She wanted to go to him, to touch him, but Sister Muller had warned against touching the medium during a trance.

Balthazar shook his head. "The bloom is off the rose."

Josephine's eyes stung with tears. Sister Muller knelt down beside her. The other participants looked bored and annoyed, especially the middle-aged couple, who glared at her.

Balthazar kept shaking his head sadly. "That boy of yours. That boy."

She lurched forward, only to be restrained by Sister Muller. "Franz?"

"Hmmm," he said, his milky eyes surveying the room.

"What about Franz?" Josephine cried.

He yawned. "Such a shame, that fine boy of yours."

Josephine tried to remain calm and receptive to the spirit, to not threaten its presence, but she burst out, "Please—I don't understand. Could you be more clear?"

Balthazar started groaning about his knees again.

Sister Muller enveloped Josephine, holding her close. The strong scent of cardamom and cloves emanated from her clothing.

Balthazar raised a limp hand and waved.

The participants looked crestfallen when Sister Muller announced the session was over and to please leave quietly.

Josephine gripped the sides of her chair, frozen in a state of suspended shock. The two Russian men stood up in a huff, grumbling that today wasn't their day. The others left reluctantly, half hoping Balthazar would revive himself and summon another spirit. But he did no such thing. Sister Muller had moved him into the adjoining room, where he lay prostate on a tattered velvet chaise lounge, one hand covering his eyes, the other hanging down, his fingertips grazing the rug. Josephine remained seated—she couldn't possibly leave now. Sister Muller ferried a glass of ice water into the other room, and then Josephine heard Balthazar moan, "My head's pounding." Sister Muller answered soothingly, "Of course it is, darling—especially after what you've gone through; such a strong willful visitation. It will take a few days to recover."

Through the half-open door, she only saw Balthazar's feet, in soft-soled leather slippers, hanging off the edge of the chaise.

He wondered aloud, "Have they all gone?"

Josephine clutched her purse to her chest. "I'm still here."

"Come in," he called.

Sister Muller had propped him up on the chaise, with multiple pillows supporting his back, a heavy wool shawl over his shoulders. He looked warm and feverish, and with his peaked cap removed, his bald head was as opalescent as a pearl. He held out his hand, and Josephine instinctively knelt down beside him, taking his hand in hers. Sister Muller stared at them with an exaggerated grimace of sympathy, which perversely reminded Josephine of an Edvard Munch painting—the agonized face, the sunken cheeks, the startled dark eyes peering out at the world.

"We didn't mean to frighten you, but when the spirit presents itself, we must welcome it and provide a hospitable, receptive atmosphere." He sipped his ice water. "But it can be quite a shock—this is your first time?"

Josephine nodded.

Sister Muller readjusted the pillows behind his back. He coughed, his chin doubling into his chest. Then he observed Josephine with wide, clear eyes. "I know you're afraid, but please try to understand that this is normal—especially the first time the spirit presents itself, the visitation tends to be quite strong, quite insistent—he had attempted contact for quite a while."

Josephine touched her chest reflexively. "The lights always flickered whenever I thought of my mother, who died last fall; I mistakenly thought she was trying to contact me."

Balthazar nodded. "Entirely understandable."

"But what I don't understand is this business about Franz, my son. Could you tell me anything more? Any feeling you might have about him?"

He touched his forehead and sighed deeply. After a pause, he murmured something into his beard.

Sister Muller put her hands on his shoulders.

"Why are they never satisfied?" he cried.

Sister Muller massaged his shoulders.

His cheeks reddened. "Always more, more, more, until I drop dead myself one day from overexertion!"

Sister Muller lowered her face next to his, their cheeks touching, and shushed him. Then she motioned toward the door, indicating Josephine should leave.

Josephine rushed out of the room, but then Balthazar called weakly, "I apologize, my dear. It's all been very taxing, you see."

Before leaving, Josephine paused on the landing above the stairs and heard Balthazar demand dried dates and a cup of tea with a stick of cinnamon. Sister Muller cried out that she wasn't a dumbwaiter, and Balthazar moaned about his pounding head.

She closed the apartment door and pressed her back against it, unable to go down the stairs and out into the world again, but at the same time, unable to return to Balthazar and Sister Muller, who were now yelling over the price of dried dates.

31

It had started growing darker earlier, so this evening when Vicki left the ballet studio, the sky was no longer an inviting violet but a stark sapphire, the first stars brightening. In less than half an hour, she was meeting Elsa at the university to hear Rabindranath Tagore, a scholar and literary genius, who also happened to be incredibly handsome, according to Elsa, although Vicki secretly wished they could go see *The Girl from Tauentzien Avenue* at the UFA Palast. Only in the cinema's warm darkness, when the live orchestra played Offenbach before the newsreel, and then the heavy green curtains parted to reveal the screen illuminated by a preternatural light, soon animated with images that softened the day's aggravations and anxieties, did she experience a relaxed happiness. But no—Tagore it was. Pulling her felt hat nearly over her eyes, as she had seen Elisabeth Bergner wear it in a magazine, Vicki anticipated the hard wooden seats of the lecture hall, the inevitable hobnobbing afterward when students clamored to get a signed copy, the way Elsa would gush over his mystical and enlightened demeanor. She buttoned up her coat with one hand, the other rummaging through her purse in search of change for the U-Bahn. If she didn't have change, then she'd have to stop at the cigarette kiosk across the street, which would only delay her further. Removing herself from the oncoming stream of pedestrians, she reconsidered the time. At best, she would arrive fifteen minutes late, and they might not allow her into the lecture hall. All the tickets would be sold, unless Elsa had saved her a seat, which was unlikely, because Elsa herself was always late.

She walked back toward the ballet studio, in the direction of home, but home was distasteful. She wasn't speaking to her mother at the moment. A few nights ago, she'd taken her father's side about how grotesque, how inhumane that rally in Nuremburg had been. Even though it had occurred in August and it was now October, whenever she pictured that girl dragged along by those troopers, their big ugly hands on her, and then how they shaved off her shining hair, and that middle-aged woman who watched in rapt attention as if she was at the cinema, the images stung. How the subject of Nuremburg had even come up escaped her, but Franz and her mother had chimed in, saying there must have been more to the story, that a young girl doesn't just end up in such a situation without a reason for it, however misguided the reason is. And then Franz had described the good work of the National Socialists, how many of them had fought in the Baltic after the war and regained land, how they'd set up soup kitchens for the unemployed and the wounded, how they only wanted to restore Germany's honor. Her father replied they were merely a fringe group, unworthy of dinner conversation, and then he smiled casually at Vicki, a smile she didn't entirely believe.

She stopped short in front of the ballet studio, noticing the outline of a familiar figure. He stood in front of the window, staring into the empty studio, and then he looked down, boring his hands into his coat pockets, and the gesture made her heart leap—yes, it was him. But he had made it perfectly clear that day. She could still slip into the arcade on her left, and he would never see her. Avoiding such a meeting was the discreet, rational thing to do. Of course this was not at all what she wanted, what her whole body wanted when she felt herself moving toward him, her mouth trembling, her steps light and wobbly.

"Geza," she said, a little too softly.

He kept staring into the empty studio.

She swallowed hard. "Geza."

He glanced over at her, breaking into a soft smile.

"What are you doing here?"

He shrugged. "Waiting."

She touched her hat, pulling on the brim. "For what?"

He grinned and made a vague movement with his hand. "For you, and here you are. It is magic."

"Oh," she faltered, embarrassed. "Ballet class ended an hour ago.

You would have missed me if I hadn't turned back. I was actually supposed to hear Rabindranath Tagore at the university." She hesitated. "But I'd much rather see a film, to be honest." *Stop explaining so much. He doesn't care what you were going to do, or didn't do.* She shifted on her feet, restraining herself from adding even more meaningless details.

His eyes lit up. "I love the cinema. *The Golem* was good."

She stared at him, remembering how cold he had been to her, how he had practically run off, and yet now he acted as if that had never happened.

"I should be on my way," she said.

"But weren't you supposed to hear the lecture?"

"It's too late now."

"So you have a few hours?"

Vicki blushed with pleasure. This was exactly what she wanted him to say.

They ended up at a French café along the arcade. The tables were placed closely together along the wall, and Geza motioned for her to take the seat facing outward. He signaled for the waiter with a brusque movement of his hand and ordered two glasses of red wine, and for a moment, he seemed worldly, as if he had studied the city and its inhabitants and picked up on their idiosyncratic customs, disguising himself as one of them.

Then that silly song, "Mein Papagei frisst keine harten Eier" (My parrot doesn't eat hard-boiled eggs) came on. Geza stared at her expectantly, and in a moment of panic, Vicki blurted out, "Actually, there was a Berlin lady who took her chambermaid to court because the maid had given the woman's ancient pet parrot hard-boiled eggs to eat, even though the song plainly states parrots don't eat them. The parrot died. The judge dismissed the case out of hand."

"That's silly."

She shifted in her chair.

A long pause followed. She wanted to ask him many questions, but unlike most people she knew, he didn't seem like the type who relished the chance to talk about himself. Instead, he sat across from her with a half-amused expression on his face, as if he was surveying the crowded café, and her, from a cool distance.

The waiter placed down two glasses of red wine.

She took a hurried sip. "Did you hear about the Berlin cat burglar?" Not waiting for his reply, she continued, "He robbed Hugo Stinnes, who was staying at the Adlon with his wife, and then a Swedish businessman spotted the burglar but didn't want to catch him because he was at the hotel with his mistress. But it didn't matter anyway because the burglar fell from the first-floor balcony and broke his leg."

"What happened to the cat?"

She smiled apologetically. "Oh, I don't know."

Normally, a young man would laugh, or at least pretend to, and make some funny quip in return, at which point they would exchange various inane comments for the rest of the evening. But he just sat here, uninterested in this form of repartee without which she felt afloat. What did he want with her anyway? She sighed and glanced down at the scalloped edge of the place mat. He took a long sip of wine and then reached across the table for her hand. "Vicki—I owe you an apology about the other day."

She drew in a breath, wondering if she should take his hand.

"I knew your father in Mitau, and when I found out you were his daughter, I tried to stay away from you. I didn't want to complicate matters. I still don't."

"You knew him during the war?"

He nodded and drank more wine. Then he ordered some schnapps. The crowd had thinned, and a sonata played, casting a melancholy air over the place.

She took his hand. It felt calloused and sweaty. She clenched it in hers. "What was he like then?"

Geza stared down at the table. "He was one of the good German soldiers. He helped us, gave us food in winter. He took me shooting for birds."

"He helped you and your family?"

"Yes," Geza said. "And we remain grateful."

"He doesn't talk about the war," Vicki said, playing with her brace-let, a thin gold chain that reflected the light.

Geza shrugged. "Most men don't."

"How old were you then?"

"Fourteen."

She calculated his age now: twenty-three. An attractive age, six years her senior. But did he find her too young and inexperienced? She drank more wine and felt her cheeks flush. "You should meet my father again—he'd be happy to see you after so much time."

Geza made an offhanded gesture. "As it is, I'm not staying in Berlin. I'm going to Palestine."

"Palestine?"

"There are quotas, and you need money, which is why I'm working in Berlin first."

"What kind of work?" she asked, thinking he didn't care to meet her father or care for such formal introductions, which were expected when a boy called on a girl regularly. Was she a casual passing fancy? She forced herself to listen as he told her how he'd started off working as a nightclub errand boy in the western districts. "I could have gotten into some trouble there, if it wasn't for Felka."

Vicki tried to ignore the sudden stab of jealousy when he mentioned this woman's name. "Felka?"

"A Polish whore." When he saw her startled look, he rejoined, "Oh, it was nothing like that. She saw me standing on the corner of Frö-belstrasse, a greenhorn in the big city selling these little brown paper packets. I thought it was only headache powder—that's what my boss said—but of course it wasn't. As I was about to get picked up by a cop, she intervened on my behalf. I think she knew the cop. Seeing how frightened I was, she let me stay with her for a few days. Central heat-ing and a sofa were appealing. Under all that paint on her face, she was delicate, almost pretty, and when she asked me, after she had undressed, why I didn't want to sleep with her, do you know what I said?"

Vicki shook her head.

He leaned forward, lowering his voice. "I once saw this beautiful girl, all in white, walking with her father on Charlottenstrasse. I've never been able to forget her."

Instantly, she felt her face grow hot. Staring down at the silverware, she asked, "Where are you staying now?"

"At a boardinghouse on Grenadierstrasse." Then he explained how it was a way station for Jewish refugees from the east. Many had arrived from the Russian POW camps after the war. They came from Ukraine, Romania, Lithuania. "Of course," he added, "they all plan to move to Holland or America or Palestine. But you know, it's not so bad. Sure, it smells of cooking oil and old bedsheets and hordes of people living on top of one another. Old Jews smoke pipes all day, playing chess. Screeching children run down the halls. In the sleeping rooms, families squeeze together, packed as tight as sardines." He laughed, shaking his head. "Never enough space."

She nodded and tried not to seem overly concerned—he might think she was too sheltered, too rich. Maybe she was.

He sighed, running a hand through his unkempt hair. "It's better than dying for the czar or the Kaiser or being massacred by a horde of Cossacks."

The music had stopped, and the waiters were stacking up the chairs.

He smiled sadly. "It doesn't mean I don't miss home sometimes."

"What is it like there? My father only told me a few things."

"How can I describe the feeling of home to you? I'm not a poet." He frowned, his thick eyebrows knitting together. "There are so many things I could say."

She took his hand and pressed it to her cheek.

He sighed. "When I'm especially missing home, there's this song."

"Sing it to me."

"I can't," he whispered.

"Please," she said.

His voice, soft and lilting, began, *"The wind and I, we're two of a kind; no house or yard or body to shed a tear over us."* He stopped.

She leaned over the table. "Keep going."

He shook his head.

"Please," she said.

He pulled her toward him, her waist folding over the edge of the table.

His mouth tasted of apples, of the orchards that must grow there, of the warm earth and the strong sun and the sweat that peppered his chest. He gripped the back of her neck so even if she wanted to stop kissing him she couldn't, but she didn't want to stop.

32

It was almost Christmas. When the sun rose, it was soon eclipsed by the onset of early evening, lending the city a damp and dark feeling and yet this aching coldness contrasted all the more greatly with the heat radiating from her body whenever she thought of him. Daylight was sparse, but the city made up for it with the mingling of lights shining from illuminated store windows onto the wet sidewalks, the warm glow of streetcars passing by. Fir trees lit with electric lights decorated squares and parks and gardens. Hand in hand with Geza on the city streets, Vicki felt Berlin was opening up to her, revealing all her riches, riches that had been obscured for many years but only needed the life and breath of new love to unveil them.

The Tiergarten, a park Vicki believed she knew so well, became a mysterious expanse, a winter-white maze of paths and hillocks where they wandered for hours in the cold, warmly encased in their heavy coats, making the occasional stop for hot chocolate and cinnamon rolls.

And Geza showed Vicki the Temple of Solomon, or, rather, an exact replica in every respect of the one described in the Bible, using papier-mâché and balsa, gold paint instead of real gold and cedar wood. Herr Frohmann from Drohobycz proudly traced his long finger over every single detail: from each curtain to crenellation, the temple was constructed to scale, he explained. Vicki and Geza stood before this miniature revelation, displayed in the back room of a bar, which smelled of fish. "Marvel at its beauty. Admire its precision. The temple will be gone in two days," he said, lording over his creation. An old Jewish man in a skullcap swayed before the temple, humming a hymn under his breath: *Kim, kim, Jisruleki l aheim, in dein teures Land arain . . .* (Come, come, Jerusalemer, come home to your beloved homeland.)

Geza explained how Frohmann carted his temple from ghetto to ghetto showing it off, praising it, and old Jews stood before it, forlorn, praying and weeping, as if they were at the Wailing Wall in Jerusalem, as if they had come home.

"But you see," Geza said, "we will build roads, not temples, in Palestine."

Walking back outside into the cold, Vicki said, "You should meet my grandmother—you sound just like her."

"Now we are meeting grandmothers?" Geza asked, unable to mask his pleasure.

Vicki shrugged. "You still won't come see my father."

He kissed her nose, then her forehead. "I told you. I don't think he wants to be reminded of the war, of the people he knew then."

Vicki peered up at him. "Why not? What was so terrible?"

He pulled down her knit cap. "There. Now your ears won't freeze." He cupped his large hands around her head—it made her feel safe, warm.

"Why change the subject always?" she persisted.

A light flurry swirled around them.

Geza shook his head. "You know, Vicki, for such a worldly girl, I thought you'd understand my hesitation." He paused, his eyes twinkling.

"You're teasing me."

"I'm not."

She gave him an imploring look.

He stroked her cheek. "Okay, maybe I tease a little. But can't you see? I'm poor, from Eastern Europe, and a Jew—do you really think that's who your father had in mind for you?"

Vicki pouted. "I don't care what he has in mind."

Geza murmured into her hair, "Of course you do."

She stamped her boots on the icy sidewalk and shook her head. He kissed her wetly on the mouth. She inhaled his breath, the milky scent of him.

"Now show me where your grandmother lives. It can't be far from here," he said.

. . .

Vicki first met her grandmother when she was nine years old, just after her father returned from the war. Before that, she only had one grandmother, Marie, whom they visited on Sundays. Vicki used to feed chocolate-dusted macaroons to the corgis, and Marie sat, all in black, on the sofa with Josephine. There were dried rose petals in bowls, menthol drops, dainty teacups, and an assortment of sweets. The visits were long and tedious, and because they were both bored, Franz and Vicki often fought, but Marie would smile kindly even if they spilled tea or crushed a cookie into the rug or accidentally ripped the velvet curtain off its hanging rod. Agatha, Marie's sister, was less forgiving. Vicki thought it a sign of life's blind cruelty that Agatha, who was in good health, despite her insistence that she wasn't, continued to live, while Marie, the kinder of the two sisters, had suffered a long agonizing death from cancer of the pancreas.

When she met Mara, Lev's mother, Vicki felt shy and nervous around this woman who was more beautiful and much younger than her other grandmother. And she didn't look like a grandmother, in her high heels and modern dress. She smoked and talked and pre-pared food, all the while conversing with her cats. After they ate salty foods Vicki had never tasted before, Mara pressed Vicki to her chest. Vicki heard Mara's heart thumping through her thin silk blouse as if it might explode. Stroking her hair, Mara had murmured, "Your mother has hid you away from me for so long. And now I finally get to hold you in my arms, my little bird. My little *bubeleh*." Her father stood by sheepishly. But when Mara carried on about her misfortune, ask-ing how was it possible she did not know her only granddaughter until now, Lev said something in a different language, and Mara fell silent. Vicki later learned that the language was Yiddish and Mara was Jewish, which made Lev Jewish and also maybe meant Vicki was Jewish. But what did it mean to be Jewish? No one could give her a clear answer. She thought of her old schoolmate Sybilla, who was Jewish, and she wondered what they had in common. They both had dark hair, dark eyes, and pale skin, but Sybilla wore thick glasses and feared horses whereas Vicki loved horses and had perfect vision. And Vicki still wore a St. Christopher around her neck, and her mother said she was a Christian. They still went to church on Sundays and they still recited their prayers before bed, and Vicki still believed in Jesus. When she had asked her father to explain, he told her fantastical stories about the Israelites—which was apparently another name for people who were Jewish. He told her about Queen Esther, who married Ahasuerus and saved the Jewish people, and about Yael, who saved the Jewish people by killing a man with a tent peg, and about Judith, who triumphed over the Assyrians by also killing a man, Holofernes. Sometimes Vicki wondered if Mara, by the way she cursed and smoked and furiously chopped onions to mix into sour cream, was a direct descendent of those sword-wielding heroines. And now, although Vicki would never call herself Jewish if someone asked, and she certainly had no intention of taking up the religion as her father had impressed upon her the importance of assimilation, of being German first and foremost and not falling into antiquated habits, living, as they did, in an age when nationality, not faith, determined one's path, she couldn't help but feel a strange wonderment whenever she visited the Scheunenviertel and looked into the windows of restaurants at the Jews sitting there with their tall fur hats and dark clothing, hunched over newspapers and small plates of food. And how did they see her? Was she an intruder, a curious Berliner, a shiksa (as Mara called Vicki's mother), or, possibly, as Jewish as they were?

The last time she saw Mara, Vicki had helped her distribute flyers for a KPD rally. It was just before she'd met Geza, before so much had changed. She thought they were taking an innocent stroll through the old neighborhood, perhaps stopping for a coffee, until she noticed Mara's bulging purse. The purse was filled with flyers, which had to be stuffed into envelopes and mailed to a list of people. Such subversive activity, Mara joked, was conducted in the basement of the yeshiva. Vicki couldn't leave her grandmother stranded at one of the folding tables in the basement, a stifling room absent of any fans, especially when people her own age greeted Mara, hugged her, and asked after her health, before returning to their tasks, diligently folding flyers and slipping them into already-addressed envelopes. Not only would they think she was a bad granddaughter but a bourgeois one to boot. And so she ended up sitting next to Mara, folding flyers into perfect rectangles, pressing her fingers along the creases, and Mara then stuffed them absentmindedly into envelopes, all the while using this opportunity to point out the eligible bachelors in the room. "That's Arthur Oertelt—with the glasses, next to the radiator. He's training to be an engineer. He's quite tall—he's sitting down so you wouldn't know—and look at his broad shoulders. Not a trace of baldness on his fine head of hair. Never marry a bald man. They're forever insecure and will cling to you. Next to him is Julius Levin, but everyone calls him Julo. A very talented artist, I've heard. Woodcuts. Comes from Stettin, up north, from a good family. They'd hoped he'd go into business, but it seems painting has consumed all his energy. He was engaged until very recently. His fiancée had this dog, a little white Pomeranian, very sweet, but she insisted it sleep in the bed, even though poor Julo has allergies. He said it's either me or the dog, and who do you think she chose?"

Vicki suppressed a laugh.

"A pity, really. Now he's single." Mara grinned. "And over there, by the window, Stefan Lazar, the Romanian; he's a little older, but—"

Vicki patted Mara's hand. "It's okay, Nana. You don't have to worry about me."

"Worried? Who said anything about worry?"

"I don't lack invitations."

Mara fanned herself with an envelope. "I'm sure you have plenty of company—but it's the *kind* of company you keep that's important in life."

Vicki glanced around at the young men and women working quietly alongside one another, and she thought of her friends who danced on tables, wasted hours at the cafés, wore turbans and monocles and stenciled their eyebrows into an expression of eternal surprise. They competed for the best table at Romanisches, and when they failed, they sulked for days, as if the world had crumbled.

Vicki sighed, handing Mara a stack of folded flyers. "University boys from good families take me out dancing. To be honest, I like the dancing more than I like them."

"Yes, but these boys, I'm sure none of them are Jewish."

Vicki shrugged. "I suppose not."

Mara held an envelope in the air, as if trying to determine which way the wind blew. "You suppose?"

Vicki conceded that none of them were Jewish.

Mara clucked her tongue. "So casual about these things."

A young, vigorous man walked into the basement carrying an electric box fan over his head. Everyone stood up, clapping. He plugged in the fan and took a bow.

Mara and Vicki remained seated, squarely facing each other.

"You're always saying it shouldn't matter—where you come from, your religion, and now you say this?"

"It does matter who you marry, my little *zumer-feygele*." With the back of her hand, she stroked Vicki's pale, soft cheek. The electric fan whizzed, its brass blades slicing the thick air.

Mara leaned in closer, her cloying perfume tingling Vicki's nostrils. "You are one of us."

Vicki frowned, doubtful of this.

She clutched Vicki's wrist with her steely grip. "There will always be *us* and *them*."

Vicki resisted the urge to argue, and instead she said it was too hot down here and proposed to buy Mara a glass of cold cider, her favorite drink.

Undeterred, Mara kept talking on the way out about how blood never lied, and Vicki shared this blood, no matter how blond her mother was or how German Lev claimed to be. Walking up the concrete steps to street level, Mara described the Cossack hordes that careened through her village when she was a child, in their black boots atop black horses, "as if a black wind perennially swept through the streets, taking some of us with them, leaving others of us for dead. And all I could do was watch through a broken window."

Vicki tried to reason with her, but the busy street, with its honking cars and lumbering buses, only seemed to bewilder Mara more. "That sort of thing happened in the countryside among the uneducated where modernity hadn't yet reached," Vicki explained in a soothing tone. She led her grandmother across the street, toward a café. "It's like still being afraid of the dark in a city where streetlights blaze every night." A policeman blew his whistle, stopping a car so that Mara and Vicki could cross the street.

Stepping onto the curb, Mara regained some of her composure. "Look what happened to Rathenau."

"That was ages ago, Nana."

"Only five years." Mara shook her head in dismay. "A German Jew who made his distaste for Jews widely known, and still they shot him."

"The foreign minister, or any public figure for that matter, is always someone's target. Don't forget, the killers committed suicide afterward."

Mara nodded, muttering, "I suppose it was an isolated event." As they entered the café, she brightened. "There's Sammy!"

Sammy, the same young man who'd procured the fan earlier, ferried a crate of soda bottles out of the café. She whispered into Vicki's ear, "A real prize, in my opinion. And a *chalutz,* no less. Training how to be a peasant when for generations we were so proud to work with our minds. They say he's moving to Palestine."

Sammy nodded to Mara and Vicki. Walking over to him, Mara appeared sprightly, coy. Vicki admired his bright blue eyes and how he held the crate with ease, his forearms strong and tanned from the sun.

"You got us that fan, and now soda too?"

"I'm bringing the comrades some soda, yes."

Mara clapped her hands together. "A leader among men."

Now, with Geza on her arm, walking into the damp wind, Vicki wondered if Mara would say the same about him. He was Jewish, a worker from Russia, her home country, and he wanted to immigrate to Palestine. Would she praise him the way she had praised Sammy?

They paused before the deserted courtyard leading into Mara's house.

Ducking under the archway, Vicki said, "It looks dark inside."

One of the cats had pressed himself into the windowpane, his orange-and-white fur smudged up against the glass. She tapped on the glass. The cat purred and purred. Then she rang the bell, feeling a rush of nervousness. What if Mara was home? What if she didn't like Geza and then reported back to her father? Her parents still didn't know about him.

They waited a few minutes. Vicki shrugged. "She's probably at a KPD rally."

"I love her already," Geza joked.

Turning to leave, Vicki said, "Let's go to that place Elsa likes. I'm hungry."

The café was inside a cozy boathouse on pilings over a lake. A handful of tables scattered around the small dance floor. They ordered simple food: onion soup, beer, cucumber salad. Geza ate *pirozhki* and herring. After lunch, they danced, although Geza danced haltingly, giving every step a long thoughtful pause. He preferred to just hold her close, his long fingers spreading over her back, caressing her thick wool sweater as if it were her skin, occasionally running a thumb down the length of her spine, which sent shivers through her. Vicki imagined his naked body pressed up against her nakedness, his bony hipbones skimming her pelvis, how she would cup his shoulders and urge him into her with confidence, as if she had done this many times, when in truth, she was still a virgin. At night, alone in her girlhood bedroom, she pushed a lumpy pillow between her legs and squeezed her eyes shut, pretending Geza lay with her under the creamy sheets, their bodies entangled in the darkness, his laughing eyes encouraging her, wooing her, loving her. When he held her close, she teased him, whispering into his ear, "Can you take me someplace?" He would gently stroke her hair and whisper back, "Not much longer." "What if I can't wait?" she pressed, only half teasing now. "I don't want to take you like this," he would say, sweeping his hand out as if she expected them to make love in public, on a café tabletop. "I want to make you my wife. Properly," he would add with a touch of indignation. His resistance both charmed and frustrated her, but she accepted it, burrowing her face into his chest, embarrassed, flattered, and full of want.

After dancing, they walked out on the wooden deck that stretched over the water. They stood together at the rail and watched a chain of black swans gliding past.

Geza gripped the railing, his knuckles white. He gazed at Vicki.

She knew from his pained expression what he was about to say. They had been over this before, countless times.

"Come to Palestine with me. I leave in the spring."

Vicki sighed and turned away from the lake, leaning her back against the railing.

"Don't look like that," he said.

The thought of not going with him made her whole body ache, but she also couldn't imagine telling her family good-bye, Berlin good-bye, her friends and studies and all of Germany good-bye. Besides, her family didn't even know he existed, let alone that she was in love with him. First, he would have to agree to meet her father.

A shot fired off in the distance.

She sighed. "You think it's better for us to live there."

He kissed her neck. "I like how you said *us.*"

Vicki snuggled her face into his chest, inhaling the smoke that always lingered on his clothing from the boardinghouse.

He stroked her hair. "And yes, better for us, because we are *Jews.*"

"My mother isn't even—"

He pressed his lips to hers. She closed her eyes, willing the present moment to suffice, but it never did. He always had to talk about the future.

He ran a finger along her chin. "Your grandmother is both Jewish and a Communist. Two strikes against you!"

She laughed and pretended to punch him in the arm.

Someone had turned on the jukebox and a garish polka floated over the deck.

He set his forearms against the railing and stared out at the black lake. "In all seriousness, Vicki. What I'm about to say, you're not going to like, but the fact is, you don't understand the way things really are from your vantage point."

" 'In all seriousness, Vicki,' " she repeated.

His jaw tensed. "I wish you wouldn't mock me."

She turned around and assumed his same position, knocking her elbow into his.

"The fact is, a new language is developing. *Ubermensch* means 'superman.' If you're Aryan. And *untermensch* is 'subhuman,' for Jews. And then there's *strafexpedition.*"

"Punitive expedition."

Geza nodded. "That's right. I've seen the storm troopers on their *expeditions* into the Jewish and Communist neighborhoods. I've seen the men left behind, bloodied, barely breathing, badly beaten. It's a pogrom." He drew a breath. "Which is why we have to leave."

A heavy mist gathered over the lake. Vicki shivered in her coat and thought back to the rally in Nuremberg, to the girl tossed high in the air, to the way her father pensively stared out the car window afterward, and how her grandmother had said she would move to Palestine, if only she were younger.

"We have a right to Palestine. Not because it was once our homeland but because no other country will have us." He concentrated on the wooded forest across the lake, as if Palestine were just there, within reach.

She took his hand and kissed the top of it. From inside the café, a raucous laughter erupted.

"Is that a yes?" His voice vibrated with hope.

She bit her lower lip. The gunmetal sky tipped into evening. "There's still time."

He looked away, disappointed.

She caressed his shoulder. "Come to the house and meet with my father."

After a long pause, he said, "All right."

"Next Sunday?"

"Next Sunday," Geza repeated.

33

Geza arrived freshly shaven, little nicks visible along the underside of his chin. He smelled faintly of lime cologne and wore his best suit. His polished oxfords with the square toes were new and stiff and creaked when he walked. Vicki spotted him though the living room window, striding nervously up to the front door, a bouquet of white roses accented with holly in hand. It was the Sunday after New Year's, and the family was recovering from various celebrations and parties.

Lev sat in the living room reading the paper. He said, in a droll tone, "So you say I know this young man?"

Vicki caught her reflection in the gilded mirror hanging on the opposite wall. She looked older, more sophisticated, a bit leaner. Love had fashioned her into a woman.

The doorbell rang before she could reply.

Marthe opened the door, ushering Geza inside and taking his coat. He paused in the foyer.

Lev raised his eyebrows expectantly, a slight smile playing on his lips.

Vicki sat upright in her chair. "Where's Mutti?"

Lev motioned upstairs. "Changing."

Geza hesitated in the archway separating the foyer from the sitting room. He held the flowers awkwardly away from his body. Marthe, sensing his unease, took the flowers and said she'd put them in water straightaway.

Vicki smiled at Geza and motioned for him to come into the room.

Lev didn't bother to look up from his paper. Perhaps, Vicki thought, he was trying to act unimpressed, but it was rude.

Geza took two loping strides into the room, his shoes creaking along with him. "Hello, Herr Perlmutter?" He extended a hand.

Lev glanced up from his paper. For a moment, neither one of them said a word. Vicki glanced at her father. The color had completely drained from his face. He gripped his chest. "Geza—what are you doing here?"

Vicki went over to Geza, taking his arm. "This is the young man I've been telling you about."

Lev ran a hand through his hair. "I'm shocked to see you. I had no idea you were in Berlin." He remained frozen in the armchair.

Geza shifted from one foot to the other. "If anything, I tried to stay away, but . . ." He glanced guiltily at Vicki.

The sound of Josephine running down the main staircase and calling out to no one in particular, "Are we finally going to meet Vicki's beau?" interrupted him. Color rose up into Geza's face, and he stared down at the floor. Vicki had gone to great lengths to describe her mother to him, but she always ended up criticizing her for her rigidity, her allegiance to a disappeared world, her inability to understand the new way of things. "She's impossible—just impossible!" Vicki would say, pouting after yet another disagreement they'd had. And now he was about to see Josephine for himself.

Josephine burst into the room, flustered, her hair twisted into a chignon. She wore a long burgundy crepe skirt with a wide belt cinched at the waist. Peering around the room, she touched her earlobe, checking to confirm the back of her earring was securely fastened. "Marthe didn't bring tea? And please—turn on the lights! It's dreadfully gloomy!" She shook her head. "I'm sorry—no one ever seems to do anything around here unless I tell them to."

Geza extended a hand. "It's a pleasure to finally meet you, Frau Perlmutter."

She smiled politely, but Vicki recognized the tightening of her facial muscles due to his strange Russian accent, poorly cut clothes, new stiff shoes, and the fact that he was, at the moment, trying too hard. She gingerly took his hand.

"Geza Rabinovitch," he added.

More tightening of the facial muscles. "Geza Rabinovitch," she repeated airily.

"I knew your husband in Mitau. He's a good man."

Lev lit a cigarette and then immediately put it out. "Yes, we tried to help the local population when we could."

"What a coincidence," Josephine said.

Attempting a smile, Lev grimaced.

Vicki switched on the lights. Above them, the chandelier buzzed before emitting an amber glow.

Marthe brought in tea and ginger biscuits, placing the tray on the low glass coffee table. For a moment, no one spoke as Marthe arranged the teacups. Vicki tried to read her father's face, but he assumed a non-committal expression of neutrality, as if listening to a radio program on winter gardening methods. When Marthe left the room, a tense silence hung there. The bleak white sky cast a dull pallor over everyone's faces.

Josephine busied herself with squirting a wedge of lemon into her tea before asking Geza where he lived and what his line of work was. He explained that he had been trained as a bricklayer, but now he taught various agricultural methods to those wishing to immigrate to Palestine at the Berlin Zionist Bund.

Lev frowned. "Are you planning to move there?"

Geza hesitated. Vicki gave him an encouraging nod. "Yes," he said.

Josephine winced. "The tea's extremely hot." She blew over her teacup. "A shame, after only just meeting, to be separated by such a great distance." Then she looked up and smiled brightly.

Vicki scooted to the edge of her chair. "Well, yes, that's the thing, you see . . ."

Lev's hands curled over his knees, his fingers tensing. "And when do you plan on moving to Palestine?"

"May," Geza said.

The two men stared at each other.

Josephine clapped her hands together. "Actually, I heard cigarette cases are manufactured in Palestine, by Jews slaving away in workshops."

"We're beginning to build up some industry, that's true," Geza said, holding Lev's stare.

"The other day on Friedrichstrasse I saw the most charming little cigarette case in the window of an antique shop—it was inlaid with mother-of-pearl—and I thought to myself: did a Jew make that in Palestine?"

Lev glared at Josephine, who continued, "But then of course, it was overpriced. The man wanted to bargain with me, but I think that sort of thing is vulgar." She delicately selected a biscuit from the tray and offered it to Geza.

When he declined, she said, "Oh, please take one—you look hungry."

Vicki stared at her mother, mortified.

Lev stood up. "I need to speak with Geza in my study."

Vicki shot him a defiant look, and Lev added, "Alone."

34

I'm going to marry your daughter," Geza said once the door closed. "This is how you ask permission?"

"I'm not asking for permission." Geza touched the edge of the imposing walnut desk behind which Lev sat, arms crossed, his lips pressed into a grim line.

"I'm asking for your blessing."

"Speak German," Lev said sharply, but then he felt guilty. He should soften his tone. He had known Geza and liked him as a boy. And Geza could tell him about Leah. His pulse raced at the thought of this, and yet he feared to ask: Did Zalman and Leah live happily as man and wife? Had Leah forgotten him entirely? Was he alone holding the vigil, nursing the past back to life when there was nothing left of it? He felt his ears burn. Contesting thoughts ran though his head, blending into a chorus of confusion: Did Geza tell Vicki about his affair with Leah? Or had he the tact to withhold such details? Did Leah still love him? What was her life like now?

Lev rubbed his eyes, his head pounding. "I find it peculiar how the two of you"—he paused—"came together."

Haltingly at first, Geza explained how he met Vicki at the state library. "She forgot her pocketbook on the desk, and so I brought it out to her." Growing more animated, he dipped back into Yiddish, relating how he never wanted to meddle with Lev's life, but after seeing Vicki not only at the library but then again on the street, near her ballet studio, he couldn't ignore such a string of coincidences. "I had no idea she was your daughter," he lied, thinking back to that spring day, Vicki on Lev's arm in her white dress, the melodic enticement of her voice ringing through the trees.

Geza continued, "And so, when Vicki finally agreed to have a coffee with me, I was overjoyed. Because for months—I promise you—I avoided her when I discovered you were her father, but I thought of her constantly."

Looking at Geza, who now rested both hands on the edge of his desk as if he would dismantle it, Lev remembered his own boldness, how unthinkable it was to ask for Josephine's hand in marriage. Her father had hated him, but maybe it wasn't so much hate as pain. Pain that now seeped into Lev's bones at the thought of losing his daughter to this man—to any man—who might take her away. Even worse, Geza planned to take her to a strange land where Jews carved matchboxes in the blistering sun. Didn't he see it was safer here than in that hotly contested stretch of earth parceled out between Arabs and Jews?

In addition to this, Geza was not who he imagined for Vicki. He worked with his hands. He spoke Yiddish and wanted to grow fruit in Palestine. Vicki had been raised for an entirely different life—one filled with ballet recitals, art exhibitions, silk dresses, and soft lighting. Eventually, she would live nearby, in her own large house with housemaids and cooks and wet nurses for her children. Her husband, refined and reflective, would have a profession that required skilled training—a doctor, a lawyer, a musician. Lev thought he had secured this, exposing Vicki to various cultural pursuits, steeping her in luxury. She studied French at the university, and only a few months ago, she had described how much she loved translating Flaubert into German. Now she had chosen the exact opposite: dirt, heat, labor.

Lev cleared his throat. "Geza, you must take into account how Vicki"—he paused, trying to deliver this next part as delicately as possible—"might not want to give up everything she is accustomed to." He gestured around his richly decorated office. "Even if right now, in the throes of infatuation, it seems as if she might."

Geza paced the length of the room. Lev could tell Geza rejected what he'd just said by the way his face calcified into stony disappointment, thinking Lev knew nothing of real love. Well, that's youth, Lev thought. Always forging ahead with strident opinions, never once wondering if they could be wrong. Oh no—it was always the older generation, the generation that had lived longer and amassed more experience that was wrong.

Geza paused in front of Lev's desk. From this angle, he appeared even taller than his two meters. "There's something else."

Lev felt as if someone clenched his heart, draining all the blood from it.

Geza handed him an envelope, yellow and worn. In faded pencil, written on top: *Lev Perlmutter*. "She wanted me to give you this."

Lev held the envelope with two hands, as if handling a delicate object. "Thank you," he said, choking over his words.

Geza nodded and started to leave the room.

Lev sprung up from his chair. "Wait."

Geza stopped in front of the door.

"Does she have a hard life?"

Geza glanced around the study, at the leather-bound books lining the shelves, at the charcoal etchings encased in gilded frames, and the luxuriant Oriental rug beneath his feet. He swept his hand out before him. "It's all relative, isn't it?"

"Yes," Lev said softly, feeling the worn envelope in his hand, as if Leah were just there, beneath the thin paper.

Realizing Geza was about to reenter the living room, reenter the world of Vicki and Josephine, the world he had sacrificed so much for, Lev said hoarsely, "Don't tell Vicki."

Geza's hand cupped the porcelain doorknob. "I won't. I don't like involving myself with other people's affairs. But—"

"There's a stipulation," Lev said. "There's always one."

Geza gazed at him. "All we want is your blessing. That's why I'm here today—what happened then is not my concern."

Lev sunk back into his desk chair. "All right, all right. You have my blessing. Mazel tov." Then he slid the unopened letter beneath a paper-weight, the one with the monarch butterfly frozen under the rounded glass, its emerald wings spread.

35

Mitzi sauntered into the living room. Josephine called to her, but she went straight to the door of the study, sniffing the dark oak. She sank down, her nose pressed under the door, and waited.

Josephine sighed, pouring more tea into their cups. "They've been in there for ages."

Vicki nodded, staring into her tea.

"Do you know where Franz is? He said he would be home by now."

"I don't know."

Josephine shook her head. "So strange, how he disappears."

"He's joined up with the brown shirts."

Josephine got up, carrying her tea over to the window. She gazed out at the skeletal trees, the barren branches shaking in the wind. "I don't see why they have to keep them away from their families, up all hours of the night."

From behind the door, Lev raised his voice.

Mitzi let out a low growl.

"Oh, stop that," Josephine said.

Vicki joined her mother at the window. She set her teacup down on the windowsill. "They're training for another war. That's what Geza says."

"Another war," Josephine echoed. Her eyes, usually blue and sharp, appeared opaque and misted over. "And Franz will fight."

Vicki impatiently paced the room, picking up an ashtray and setting it down, fiddling with the tassels hanging from the velvet drapes, twisting the candles deeper into the silver candlesticks. She flopped down on the velvet sofa, propping her feet up on the ottoman.

Josephine remained by the window. "At least he'll be a hero, fighting for Germany, as Grandfather did."

The thought of Franz fighting usually sent her mother into hysterics. *If any harm comes to him, I'll perish,* she often said, her eyes welling up. But a calm air had settled over her. She stood frozen by the window.

Vicki lit a cigarette, the ashtray cradled in her lap, anticipating that her mother would reprimand her for smoking. But Josephine didn't notice. She only traced her finger along the frosted windowpane. "It's already been predetermined anyway. We can't change the future."

Vicki held the smoke down in her throat for a prolonged moment before speaking. "What are you going on about?"

Josephine turned away from the window, the color high in her cheeks. "I know it must seem strange, but sometimes . . ."

Mitzi let out a series of sharp piercing barks.

Josephine winced, putting a hand to her head.

"Mitzi, stop," Vicki demanded.

The dog settled down again, nose to rug.

A few blackbirds squawked, settling on the branches of the linden tree.

Josephine stared at the birds. "Most people think they're bad omens, but actually, they're not—they travel between our world and the next."

Boring her cigarette into the chrome ashtray, Vicki said, "I hate blackbirds. They scare me."

From the kitchen, they heard the beginnings of dinner: a pot clattering, Marthe instructing the new kitchen maid on how not to burn the roast, the chopping of onions as the blade hit the cutting board.

Vicki looked at her mother. Something was different about her, as if the contours that normally outlined her face had smudged, turned blurry. "What did you mean before, about something seeming strange?"

Josephine smiled and straightened her skirt. "Silly. I already forgot."

Vicki gestured to the closed door. "It's nearly dinnertime."

"Well, what did you expect?"

"What do you mean?"

"There's quite a lot to discuss when you bring someone home, like that."

"Such as?" Vicki demanded.

Josephine settled into the couch, adjusting her long pleated skirt. "Oh, Vicki. Please."

"What?" she cried, already knowing what her mother meant.

Her mother plucked a piece of lint from her skirt. "Don't force me to say it."

"Oh, Vicki, please!" Vicki shouted in response, causing her mother to flinch.

Vicki stood up, restraining herself from kicking over the crystal bowl filled with glass-spun candies. She used to think they were so pretty— the red, green, and purple candies. And she used to laugh when guests would plunge a hand into the bowl, tricked into thinking the candies were real. But now the idea of such glass candies as mere ornamentation mocked the very fact that women waited in line for bread only to be turned away, and police beat workers for striking when all they wanted were fair wages. And her mother sat before her, shrouded in the past, filled with predetermined ideas, as if all she had to do was watch the world go by through the window of her comfortable living room—well, it was sickening.

Lev stepped out. "Everything all right?"

"Yes, of course," Josephine said.

Lev rubbed his eyes and made an effort to smile.

Geza stood behind Lev and winked at Vicki. She mouthed, *I love you.*

Once outside, she begged Geza to tell her what her father had said.

Geza squeezed her hand. "He gives us his blessing."

She gazed into his dark eyes. "Really? He wasn't upset? He looked so unsettled."

He grinned. "Of course he doesn't want to lose his only daughter to a poor immigrant, but other than that, it went swimmingly."

"Geza, please don't joke. Really, what did he say?"

They didn't notice Franz striding up the narrow pathway.

"What's happening here?" Franz wore his high black boots and brown cap, his gray coat with brass buttons.

Geza mocked a military salute.

Franz pulled off his black leather gloves. "What are you selling?"

Geza and Vicki looked at each other, holding back their laughter.

"You're not authorized to sell commercial goods on private property."

Geza grinned. "Excuse me, Herr Perlmutter, but I'm not selling anything. I'm visiting your sister."

Vicki coiled her arm through Geza's. "It's true. He just met Mutti and Papa. Don't look so shocked." Trying not to explode with laughter, she bit her lip.

Franz clenched his jaw and shoved his gloves into his coat pocket. "Vicki, is it some sort of joke, pretending to know this Jewish peddler?"

Geza suppressed a smile. "Excuse me, Herr Perlmutter, although I happen to be of the Jewish persuasion, I am not a peddler."

"Stop calling me Herr Perlmutter!"

"That's your name, is it not?"

Franz shook his head in disgust and shoved past them, slamming the front door.

Geza and Vicki burst out laughing, holding each other up by the elbows while nearly collapsing on the icy steps. Their eyes filled with tears, their voices were hoarse, and each time it seemed their hilarity had finally died down, Geza performed a military salute, clicking his heels together, and their laughter renewed with greater force.

36

On his way to Rabbi Landauer's, the frigid January wind cut through Lev's overcoat. The contents of Leah's letter reverberated through him, blotting out all other concerns. He could not think or eat or sleep since he had read it two days ago. Even smoking provided little relief. He snapped at Josephine and stared absently at Vicki when she chattered on about the Zionists' good work in Palestine, building a new Jewish nation. Even when Franz had stormed into his study, ranting about the impossibility of such an unholy union between Vicki and Geza—*That Eastern European ingrate,* he had shouted—Lev sighed and mumbled some half-hearted explanation, causing Franz to stare at him in disbelief. The letter, the letter, written in her hand, was all that mattered. He couldn't wait for Franz to leave him in peace. Then he locked his office door, despite Josephine's entreaties that he join them for dinner, despite the fact that he could hear Franz yelling at Vicki and Vicki mocking him, her taunting voice floating under the door: "But look at you, in your ridiculous boots and brown trousers!" Inside the smoke-filled chambers of his office, he spread the letter out before him, his hands shaking, his throat parched. He removed his reading glasses and put them on again. He straightened his tie. He rubbed his eyes, as if to confirm the veracity of the object before him—a letter from Leah, a letter he had been waiting to receive forever.

June 9, 1925

22 Aspazijas Boulevard, Riga 1050
Soviet People's Republic

Dear Lev,

I have wanted to write you for so long, but many things prevented me from doing so. Before I begin, I pray you keep in good health and that you are happy. I have been praying for you since the day you left, seven years ago. Seven years! Such a long time, and yet, it feels as if you were just by my side, dancing with me at Altke's wedding and walking through the apple orchards. As you can see, I learned how to read and write. Geza taught me. He has grown into such a strong and willful man . . . hopefully this letter will reach you through his hands. I wonder what you think as you read this . . . I pray you are not angry with me for contacting you, for interfering in any way. I fear this, but I am writing to tell you what happened after you left.

I waited for Zalman to return, as we all did. Every day, after the war ended, we waited. The Red Army swept into Mitau and said we were liberated from the Germans. They said we were free citizens of the Soviet Republic and that the czar and all the old ways were dead. People danced in the streets but I felt only sorrow. Some of the men returned to Mitau, some of them didn't. Zalman never came back. He died in the Carpathian Mountains, just as I thought. The pharmacist's cousin was wrong. Every day I curse her for feeding such lies, but what is the good? You are gone and I am here.

A year later, the Spanish plague visited our town. Many died, mostly young able-bodied men and women, mothers and fathers, not what you would expect. The old people and the children survived. Geza left at this time to escape the sickness spreading, and we went with him, to live with relatives in Riga where the infection levels were lower. If he had not convinced us to leave, I would probably be dead too.

You have never left my thoughts, my heart, my blood; as I write this, there is someone who will always remind me of you, someone for whom I would sacrifice the whole world—he is the reason why I left Mitau; he is the reason why I stay alive, why I breathe in and out each day. Lev, he is our son, the fruit from that night at the end of September, the last time we joined our bodies together in the Sukkot hut under the stars, during the festivities of my sister's wedding. His name is Aleksander, but we call him Sasha. Today is his birthday. He is six.

I can't tell him who his father is because any woman who had relations with a German soldier is a whore, a traitor to Russia, and any child from such a union a disgrace to the state, a reminder of German occupation. So I tell him his father died heroically in the war, a soldier who defected from the White Army. But other people—relatives, relations from Mitau—they know the truth, and soon it will become impossible to keep up this fantasy for Sasha.

He is fragile—sensitive, with bad nightmares and fevers that seize him for twenty-four hours and then disappear. I worry about his future here—the revolution turns more fervent every day. Officials come to check papers, to check background, age, health, religion, financial status, parentage, and they ask neighbors about us and ask us about the neighbors. They write many notes in little notebooks and they never say anything. Just ask questions and more questions. Then they leave but always reappear after one month, like a clock, as the expression goes.

So I have decided, after much contemplation, to leave Russia. We are going to America. We set sail for New York in three months. I already have our berths reserved. Zlotnik's brother, Misha—remember Misha? He lives in New York and works as a cobbler. He has been there for two years, and now he has a wife and three children. We will stay with him for some time, until I can secure a job as a seamstress, or even as a domestic. I hear New York is a golden city with tall glass buildings and also a squalid place with rats and dirt and garbage and no space to breathe . . . I don't know what we will find, but at least Sasha will be free.

Please do not misunderstand me. I am not writing because we are in need of money. Sasha and I live comfortably, in a house with our relatives. There is always food, and we sleep in warm beds. Sasha studies hard at school. He wants to be an artist and he likes music. He draws many things—flowers, butterflies, squirrels, even portraits! You would feel proud if you saw his drawings. Some of them are quite good.

My only thought is perhaps you could see us before we leave for America.

Just once. To properly say good-bye.

Love,
Leah

Lev paused on the U–Bahn platform, forgetting the route he usually took to the Scheunenviertel even though it was where he grew up, where his mother still lived, where he was going now. After reading her letter, he kept hearing Leah's voice, a mixture of sadness and triumph, of love and resignation. And now? Where was she? Had she really gone to America? He couldn't imagine Leah, in her scarf and heavy clothing, her provincial ways, taking a giant steamer to that city made of concrete and steel. But she had learned to read and write. She sounded older in the letter, more world-weary, more aware of the pitfalls such a letter could cause, which was why she had waited so long to send it. His hands trembled when he reached into his pocket for change, his head pounding with the thought that it was too late, too late to find her, and yet a sharp urgency tugged at him, because he still might have a chance, somehow, to find her.

People rushed down the steps to the underground, bumping his shoulder, stepping on the heel of his shoe. He didn't even feel it. Normally, he would have acted offended, perhaps said something in passing, but why? Maybe that woman in the herringbone coat was rushing to see her lover and, forgetful of herself, brushed past him. Who was he to remind her of manners? Or the elderly man who had flicked his cigarette butt in Lev's direction, what did he care if some ash sprinkled Lev's trouser leg?

Lev stumbled down the concrete steps, passed through the turnstile, absently bought a ticket, while the echoing noise of trains arriving and departing buffeted him from all sides, as if he floated in the midst of a wild sea. He waited on the platform, staring into the dark tunnel, bracing himself for the roar that never ceased to startle him upon the train's arrival. A boy stood next to him, the tips of his shoes too close to the red line, until his father pulled him back. "I've seen fellows fall to their deaths on the tracks," the father said, gripping the boy's hand. Lev felt the urge to say, *I have a son your age. Aleksander.* His son, conceived the last time he made love to Leah in the apple orchard under the white branches, the moon glimmering through, the hurried apologies afterward as he explained to her that he was leaving, because the Russians were coming and the war was ending. And because Zalman was returning—a piece of hearsay, a miscalculation, which had led him back to this life, a life that now clung to him as heavily as a wet cloth through which he could barely breathe.

He almost forgot his stop but was reminded to disembark by the flood of Jews in black kaftans standing up. Lev followed them off the train, thinking of how Rabbi Landauer's elongated face and hands always reminded him of an El Greco saint; troubled, sad, malnourished. The last time he had seen him—when was it? June, at the start of summer—Vicki had cut off all her hair, and Josephine complained about the sputtering ceiling fan. Yes, such trifling concerns had masqueraded as real ones. After visiting his mother, Lev had found Rabbi Landauer wandering the streets, confused, a glazed look in his eye, rambling on about vegetarianism and his spiritual upheavals. Lev had comforted him, took the rabbi by the arm, tried to talk some sense into him—Lev smiled. Yes, he had felt so very stable and secure with himself in comparison to the wandering rabbi, devoid of his skullcap, devoid of his faith. And now? He was worse off than the rabbi. Worse because the woman he loved had probably vanished forever into the roving masses of New York, worse because he had a son he would never know, worse because two and a half years ago, when Leah wrote him, he might have had the chance to be with her again, to start another kind of life. And worse because Geza, who planned to spirit his daughter away to Palestine, was the only person who could help him find Leah. He cursed Geza for waiting so long, for withholding such precious information. And now it was too late. *Too late. Too late.* Lev squeezed his eyes shut before pressing his thumb on the doorbell. Perhaps the rabbi would have some advice. There was no one else he could turn to.

Clothing hung from Rabbi Landauer's body despite how his wife, an enterprising woman who owned two hairdressing salons near Potsdamer Platz, pushed food onto his plate, complaining how he didn't eat anything anymore. "No more meat, no more fish, no more game or fowl and yesterday he condemned beets!" she said, bustling around the kitchen while Lev and the rabbi sipped black tea.

The rabbi shrugged. "I don't like the bloodred color of that particular kind of root."

Lev had just explained his state of affairs, or as he preferred to say, "the unhinging of all order" to the rabbi: Geza Rabinovitch from Mitau had arrived on his doorstep two days ago and announced his plans to marry Vicki and take her away forever. And Lev had recently discovered Franz's SA membership card, but the name on the card was Franz von Stressing. He didn't know what was more upsetting: that Franz had joined up with the brown shirts or that he had used his mother's name to do it. He sighed and thought about saying more, but he couldn't bring himself to admit what truly troubled him: *I love another woman. We have a son whom I've never seen. They might have moved to America.* The other things—Geza and Vicki's engagement, Franz's SA membership—were potentially solvable, open to discussion, whereas Leah inhabited a secret chamber in his dreams. He held back, knowing that once the confession escaped, the secret chamber would be torn open, and keeping the two worlds separate was not only a comfort but a necessity.

The rabbi pursed his lips and frowned. "And what of Josephine? What does she think of Franz joining the SA?"

The rabbi's wife paused a moment in the kitchen, straining to listen. Yes, Lev thought, this will make good gossip to retell on the balcony of the synagogue, surrounded by your womenfolk. He could already see her holding court, fanning herself while doling out various details plucked from this conversation. Lev rubbed his eyes. He didn't care. Let her hear how much he regretted marrying a gentile. He sighed. "She's the least of it."

The rabbi nodded. "But you were experiencing marital difficulties in the past, were you not?"

"Our problems have intensified."

The rabbi's wife brought in a refreshed pot of tea and poured more into Lev's glass. "If the marriage is sound, you can weather any storm," she said, smiling down at him, her blond curls tucked beneath a headscarf. Before returning to the kitchen, she glanced at the plate of food the rabbi had left untouched.

The rabbi leaned back into his chair. "My wife's right."

Lev rubbed his eyes again. "What does Geza want there? To start a banana plantation on the Sea of Galilee so that Vicki can battle water snakes all day? We're Europeans; for us it's entirely out of the question." He paused. "Even America would be more civilized." *Even New York*, he thought. *Where Leah is.*

"Hmmm," the rabbi said, piercing a pea with one of his fork prongs. "I've heard New York in particular is quite barbaric." He brought the pea to his lips but then, upon further consideration, placed his fork down again. "Perhaps France would be better."

Lev glanced at the mound of peas on the rabbi's plate. "Have you boycotted peas as well?"

The rabbi took a small sip of tea, barely opening his mouth to let the liquid enter. "In France, the Jewish problem has almost ceased to exist after the Dreyfus affair, which resulted in quite a favorable outcome for us, no?"

Lev slung one leg over the other. "And here?"

Rabbi Landauer stared at him. Lev hadn't noticed until now how the rabbi's eyes were too close together, throwing off the entire symmetry of his face. The spacing of the eyes—it was something one could never alter. The rabbi scratched his patchy beard, steel gray at the tapered tip, a burnt auburn around his mouth and nostrils. The rabbi's beard reminded Lev of the frayed and threadbare blanket Franz had toted around as a child. He'd refused to relinquish it for washing or mending, taking immense pleasure in its worn-down quality, just as the rabbi now stroked his beard, taking comfort, Lev imagined, in its raggedness.

The rabbi leaned forward, inspecting the grain of the wood running along the table. "We have assimilated with ease, this much is true. But . . ." He looked over at his wife, who had installed herself in the corner of the room, shuffling through the afternoon edition. She glanced over the top of the paper. He cleared his throat. "We pay a price. We must constantly prove, at any given moment, that we are German before we are Jewish. And in these modern times, what does being Jewish mean beyond this constant arguing, each group convinced they are right and the others wrong—the Zionists, the assimilationists, the

Jews from the east clinging to their ghetto ways while trudging down our cosmopolitan boulevards, wearing those faded dark clothes and tall fur hats, gathering frowns from the rest of us?"

"Many people are anxious," his wife barked from the corner.

Lev turned toward her. She continued reading as if she had never spoken.

The rabbi shook his head. "You exaggerate."

She shrugged and turned the page.

The rabbi continued, "A few of our friends talk continuously about the National Socialist movement, which really is anti-Semitic, but people are overreacting, growing hysterical, when the important thing is to remain calm. We must be the first ones to act in moderation, to model this behavior for our depressed nation so that reason will return here . . . We must wait for the economy to reestablish its equilibrium, for the republic to regain its footing, for the losses of the Great War to dissipate, for the pain of the reparations, of so many dead, to lessen." The rabbi slumped back into his chair, as if the stringing together of so many words had greatly tired him.

His wife snorted and straightened her paper. Muffled laughter could be heard from one of the bedrooms off the hallway. A gray cat scampered into the living room, looked around, and darted back into the hall, the little bell on its collar tinkling. Lev wondered if the rabbi's laughing daughters would leave their father someday too, for Palestine or some other place.

"But in the meantime, we must practice discretion." The rabbi then folded his hands over his chest, as if preparing for eternal rest.

His wife mumbled, "What he means is discretion to the point of disappearance."

The rabbi raised his hands in supplication. "Must you always interject?"

Lev jerked his chair back from the table. "Geza spoke of the 'housetrained animality of the German Jew,' of our feigned civility, our adopted customs, our so-called gentility, how cleanly shaven we skip off to temple—God forbid we call it synagogue—sporting our bow-ties and monocles, wrapping our prayer books in the editorial page of a newspaper so it will attract less notice." Lev paused, drawing a breath. "Are we only German on the condition that we not appear too Jewish?"

The rabbi fingered his beard, trying to suppress a small sarcastic smile. "I didn't realize you attended synagogue, let alone carried a prayer book."

Lev paced the room. He couldn't think clearly. And looking at the gray-faced rabbi didn't help matters. One of the rabbi's daughters dashed across the hall, trying to hide. She giggled behind the door. Lev could see her dark eyes glinting through the doorjamb.

"I argued with Geza for over an hour, during which he tried to convince me that there's no other way for the Jews short of moving to Palestine. I called him a fool. I forbade him to take Vicki away to that wasteland. I explained how there are so many possibilities here. *Berlin is not Russia*, I kept saying. *Berlin is not Russia*."

"Forgive me . . . who is this Geza?" the rabbi asked.

"I helped his family during the war," Lev mumbled, leaning against the wall next to the bay window. He had slept poorly last night due to an argument Josephine started the minute the lights went out. She spoke into the darkness about how it wouldn't be so bad if Vicki went to Palestine, as opposed to gallivanting around town with Geza, which had already caused a stir. Of course, Lev yelled, she didn't care if Vicki made matchboxes in the beating sun—as long as their social position remained intact. Josephine fell into a crying fit, behavior Lev had anticipated, and instead of comforting her, he turned onto his side and pretended to sleep until three a.m., when real sleep overtook him. But then he had another dream about Leah—this time, he met her at Grand Central Station in Manhattan. He knew from pictures how it looked, like a golden paradise of travel. She was dressed in a dove-gray fitted suit, stockings, and heels, a real modern woman without a trace of the shtetl on her. She held their son by the hand, and he stared up at Lev. His eyes were green and luminous, brimming with a mixture of accusation and hope. Lev was about to embrace his son when a mechanical voice over the loudspeaker announced the last train to Mitau. In a gust of wind and smoke, Leah and his son were swept away with the rushing crowd. He had awoken feeling as exhausted as he was the night before, the early morning light seeping through the velvet curtains. His ears hurt, filled with the sound of trains.

The cat rubbed up against Lev's leg, purring, then jumped onto the windowsill. The rabbi's three daughters had planted themselves in the middle of the living room sorting through a bag of marbles. They swapped marbles for dolls and dolls for marbles in an endless negotiation. The rabbi had disappeared, leaving behind his skullcap on the white embroidered tablecloth.

His wife gently touched Lev's shoulder. He could smell the lacquer she used in her hair.

"He went to wash." She handed him his coat and hat. Her daughters did not look up from the game, their heads bent together, creating a natural barrier between their world and the dull worrisome one of adults. The soft clinking of the marbles against the hardwood floor had a soothing effect on Lev. "I'm sorry for your troubles," she said, walking him to the door.

Lev tipped his hat. "Don't let the rabbi starve."

She smiled, her bottom teeth crowded. "We all do what we can do."

37

"He might leave for a month, and I barely care!" Josephine sat up to emphasize her point, even though she knew Dr. Dührkoop preferred her to remain lying down. She had worn her most fetching outfit: a Vionnet dress in crepe de chine, cut on the bias, which caused the fabric to subtly cling to her body. The way her knees showed when she sat down had at first embarrassed her, but she now thought it was quite daring and seductive, and every time she looked down to see her knees peeking out from the pleated hemline, it brought color to her face, color she hoped made her appear more youthful and appealing. It was an unseasonably warm day for March, after weeks of rain and grayness, and he had opened the window next to the chaise. The humid breeze brought little goose bumps to her arms and collarbone. She rubbed her bare arms. He watched.

"Lev plans to visit New York on business, you said?"

She leaned into the pillows, one arm draped over her hip, the other dangling over the back of the chaise. "I don't know if he's leaving for certain . . ." Her voice trailed off. "He said something about brokering an exclusive import/export deal with Rhodes Hart, an American textile firm. The enviable type of linen they produce in New York is apparently not available in Germany. Lev thinks it will sell here."

The doctor shuffled through his notebook. An unlit cigarette dangled from his lips. His shirt not perfectly ironed, his eyes bloodshot—she wondered what kinds of troubles he harbored but resisted the urge to ask. He would only deflect her concern, reminding her that she was following the predictable pattern of transference, and if he engaged in it, he would be subjecting the analytic relationship to the dangers of countertransference. He had once explained this many months ago, when she had asked after his mother's health and he had stiffened, as if the very thought of revealing even the smallest trace of his private life proved utterly repugnant.

"And I keep thinking back to the last time he left, at the start of the war, and how terribly upsetting it was. Now, I scarcely care where he's going. Or when he'll return." She stared down at her satin pumps and felt a stab of guilt. How could she say this so offhandedly, as if discussing someone else's husband? And yet in this room with the damask wallpaper, coffered ceiling, and onyx figurines, it felt true.

Dr. Dührkoop rubbed his eyes. "I see." He lit his cigarette and stared out the window.

Did he see? He was distracted; that was for sure. She felt cast out, jealous of the thoughts clouding his mind. She almost raised the problem with Franz again, but that was a tiresome subject. After the first séance with Father Balthazar, she had rushed here in a panic, racked with anxiety over his incantation about the bloom coming off the rose and Franz getting into some trouble he refused to discuss further because he had a headache. Dr. Dührkoop had patiently explained how some individuals, such as mediums, have a particularly strong connection to the collective unconscious allowing them to channel feelings and intuit certain events, but he impressed upon her that it was not always accurate; it was merely a helpful tool in the process of her own unearthing of past traumas, dreams, and memories. Worse still, after that, Father Balthazar stopped contacting her grandfather. She still returned every week for the séance in hopes that her grandfather would reappear. She now understood the urgency, the desperation, of the other participants whom she had initially mocked. For the past weeks, she had described all of this to Dr. Dührkoop in great detail—but she could tell it bored him. Suddenly, he stood up and shut the window with a sharp bang.

She jumped a little.

He leaned against the window and stared at her.

"Oh—that reminds me of my mother. A buried memory. It just came to me in a flash."

He nodded for her to continue.

"She was always closing all the windows because she said one would catch cold that way. Even on stifling hot trains in the middle of summer, she would slam down the windows, as if the air carried an infectious disease. I remember sweating in the train compartment, wanting to take off my stockings, the sweat dripping between my thighs."

Dr. Dürhkoop's eyes gleamed with renewed interest. "That's very interesting." He paced the room, stopping every few steps as if a revolutionary thought had just occurred to him. "And how did you feel on that train?"

Josephine shifted on the couch. Sweat gathered under her arms and between her legs. She felt the urge to rub herself against the bunched-up couch cushion. She moved slightly back and forth. "Trapped," she said, her voice hoarse. Her pearl-gray stockings stuck to her thighs—she wanted to peel them off. All at once, she was fifteen, trapped on the train with her mother, full of unnatural urges, as well as being a woman of thirty-eight.

He now stood behind his desk. He had rolled up his shirtsleeves, the blond hairs soft and fine along his forearms.

"Trapped?"

"I couldn't do what I wanted."

Planting both hands down on his desk, he leaned forward.

She couldn't stand up—a wetness had amassed in her underwear, and she was certain it would show through her crepe de chine dress. She didn't even have a light coat to wear over it, for the way home.

"What, then, did you want on that train?"

His face was kind—she could tell him. And if she couldn't tell him, then there was no point to analysis. No point to any of it. He always said she must be honest with him. Entirely honest. "I wanted to—" She paused. She could still say something else, anything else: *I wanted to open the window, feel the wind on my face, slap my mother, run away.*

He sat down on the couch and took her hand. His proximity made her head light. She gripped his hand. "I wanted to masturbate."

"Josephine." He rarely said her name but it sounded much more beautiful coming from his mouth. She buried her face into his shoulder, inhaling his scent of cigarettes and tea and lavender. *He must put dried lavender in his dresser,* she thought. *Or perhaps his mother places it there. As* if such movements had already been choreographed, she hoisted herself onto his lap, straddling him. She pressed her face into his neck and rubbed against him. He slipped his hand into her underwear, inhaling sharply at the wetness he discovered. With the other hand, he caressed her back, fingering the brassiere under the thin fabric. "God knows the damage of those early repressive years. But we are returning to a primal state of freedom, before judgment, before shame, before mothers and fathers," he said.

She nodded and bit his neck, tight pleasure spreading and flowing from the epicenter of clitoral nerves he so nimbly manipulated.

Afterward, she sat upright on the chaise. He sat opposite, in his usual chair. The session had run over; it was nearly two o'clock. The next patient had arrived, but after repeated knocks on the door, he left. Quietly exhilarated, Josephine buttoned up her blouse. After a pause, he tapped the long column of ash from his cigarette into a nearby ashtray and leaned farther back into his chair. It squeaked. "Well," he said, raising his eyebrows, "what just occurred would have been unthinkable two months ago. But the floodgates have opened." He smiled sympathetically.

She smoothed down her skirt. "It's still quite unthinkable."

He had since reopened the window and a tepid breeze blew into the room. "In the confines of this office, what we have is a safe environment to reenact past trauma *consciously* so that it may be integrated into the psyche with a greater degree of understanding."

Josephine nodded, trying to conceal her pleasure at the thought of repeating such an exercise.

"Good," he said, snapping his notebook closed. "Until next week."

"Until next week," she repeated, standing up.

He led her to the door and pointed out how they'd run over time. "I won't charge you for it," he joked.

She paused, touching the brass doorknob. "How's your mother?"

He hesitated. "It's been—" He stopped short. He touched her face, his thumb gliding down to her sleek collarbone. "I shouldn't burden you with my troubles."

She took his hand. He squeezed it and opened the door. Before them, thick bars of sunlight flooding the empty hallway shimmered with visible dust. She started to leave, but he took hold of her elbow and explained, haltingly at first, how his uncle had recently died, leaving a vast estate behind for his mother to manage in Grunewald forest but it was all too much for her at this age, so the problem naturally fell on his shoulders. They were trying to sell it, but the estate had already devalued greatly since the war. It proved too expensive to keep. "Yesterday, I let half the staff go. Some of them have worked there since the last century." He took off his glasses and cleaned them with the edge of his shirt.

"I'm so sorry."

He nodded with resignation.

Without thinking, she took him into her arms, holding him tightly against her. His chest crushed into her chest, his chin bore into her shoulder blade, and tunneling into her ear, his breath, at first uneven and labored, grew as quiet and calm as a Bavarian lake at night.

38

S he's been gone for ages."

"Carin's in Paris?"

"With her mother," Wolf said, ordering two more beers. "Shopping for her bridal trousseau. Apparently the best lace is in Paris." Four empty glasses stood between them. Wolf's eyelids shimmered with sweat and his long lashes made him look particularly feminine, especially in the dim lighting of the bar. They sat on barstools sharing sausage cut into coin-sized pieces. Wolf's knee brushed up against Franz's, and it gave him a momentary thrill, despite knowing the futility of such sensations. Today, they had trained near the Staaken military airfield. Physical drills with no breaks. Barking out the occasional order, Lutz watched with a satisfied smirk, pacing the damp field. In one exercise, all the boys stood in a line, one behind another. The last in line had to hold a medicine ball and crawl through the legs of the other boys all the way to the front; then the next would go. Looking up through the tunnel of gaping gym shorts was paradise: the muted color of the jockstraps, the shadow of pubic hair, some dark, some light, muscular legs planted in a V, inner thighs taut. Franz had fumbled the ball twice, the grass grazing his face, and emerged from the tunnel of legs with dirt on his lip, his brow shining with sweat, to the sound of Lutz cursing. He was clumsy and stupid. He lacked basic agility. He needed to repeat the exercise. Franz acted disappointed, but inside he was singing.

After training, Wolf proposed they stop off for a beer in a local bar—the heavy wood paneling and rustic feel of the place appealed to them. When they walked in wearing their brown uniforms, Franz noticed how the other men glanced in their direction, some of them nodding with respect. The bartender gave them the first two beers on the house.

Franz shifted in his chair, thinking about all the Parisian lace Carin was buying for her trousseau, and if she only knew that Wolf had fucked that Ukrainian girl who worked in the university cafeteria last week. Ukrainian or Czech? What did it matter? He was getting married. "It's June seventeenth?"

Wolf ran a hand through his hair. "You remember the date of my own wedding better than I can."

"Don't you want to marry her?" Franz cringed at the hopefulness flooding his voice. He would have to practice producing more definitive statements in short bombastic sentences. He would have to start sounding like everyone else.

"Of course I want to marry her," Wolf retorted, mimicking the slight elevation in Franz's voice—that hope.

In the corner a group of men started singing a drinking song. Arms over shoulders, they swayed on the long wooden bench, their shirts unbuttoned, chests blooming with hair.

"What about the Czech you fucked?"

Wolf slapped him on the back of his head. "What's it to you?"

Franz shrugged, looking down.

"I know. You want to hear all my dirty details. Peter says you want to fuck me."

He kept looking down, so Wolf wouldn't see the redness spreading all over his face. He had to say something quickly, something definitive and cutting. Something to make them both laugh, to disperse the panic rising in his chest. "Peter's the one who wants to fuck you."

Wolf smiled.

There. A short, nonemotive reply. The hot embarrassment lessened. He touched his face—it felt cool and white again. He looked up from the floor and stared at the murky mirror behind the bar. The room took on a tilted quality as the lights grew dimmer, more golden. The workmen, swaying fluidly, laughed. They clinked glasses, white foam flowing over the rims. *"Zum Wohl!"* they shouted. Franz thought about the customary words, what they meant: *To your completeness, to your fulfillment.*

The bartender poured Wolf and Franz complimentary shots. He

gave Franz a sidelong smile, and for a second, the idea of sex glittered between them.

Wolf stuffed a few extra marks into the tip jar, and the bartender bowed. Even though he was young, he was Old World—the bowtie, the genuflecting, the complimentary drinks, the way he seemed to know his place, the miniature portrait of the emperor behind the wine cases.

Wolf restlessly glanced around the room. He would want to leave in a few minutes, and it always stung a bit, when he so instantly tired of Franz's company. It was warm here—Franz felt the comfort of Wolf's closeness, the way his elbow inched toward his own, and the latent excitement of the bartender's glances, the robust male singing interlacing their conversation.

He blurted out, "I need your advice." And then he told Wolf about how Vicki was seeing a Jew—a real Jew from Galicia who wanted to take her to Palestine. She had been brainwashed by this Jew, thinking Palestine and Zionism and Communism were the true paths. Worst of all, his father welcomed this Jew into their home with open arms. His father knew the Jew from the war, from the poor little Russian town where he'd been stationed. But he's an upstart, an arrogant little Jew who thinks he owns the world, thinks he can just take away his sister and disgrace the family. "The pride of the chosen people," Franz added sarcastically.

After a pause, Wolf said, "Does this Jew have a name?"

"Geza Rabinovitch."

The tips of Wolf's fingers met. "The only solution: we kill him."

"Kill him," Franz repeated. Plainly spoken, laid out bare before him, it felt clean and pure. Franz envisioned bones on the beach, bleached by the sun, the ocean washing over them, making the surfaces smoother and smoother. Blindingly white bones. That was all Geza would amount to.

Wolf pushed back his barstool, one knee jammed up against the counter. "It's a job for us, the SA. There are precedents. This won't be the first time a Jew oversteps his boundaries. We've got to rein them in lest they grow too certain of themselves."

"And Vicki, even if she can't realize it now, has gone too far. She says she loves him, but how can she? She'll be terribly unhappy if she marries him, if he takes her away to Palestine," Franz said, his voice gaining conviction.

Wolf nodded and slammed his fist down on the counter. "You're right, Franz. Such a beautiful girl as Vicki shouldn't be sacrificed because we stood by and did nothing. She's always felt like my little sister too." Wolf's face was sweating, his neck blotchy. Perhaps he'd had too much beer, Franz thought. Or perhaps he still fancies Vicki. Either way, they would stop Geza together. The thrill of talking so confidentially with Wolf pulsed through him.

The bartender, using a damp cloth to clean the nearby tabletops, stopped for a minute, as if transfixed by the hatching of their plan.

Wolf then took Franz's arm and explained in a low urgent voice how Franz should not tolerate Jewish scum polluting his family line, because even though his father was a Jew, he was the better kind of Jew, having refined himself into a respectable member of society and marrying a gentile, which made Franz and Vicki children of mixed blood: *mischling*. But if Vicki married Geza and procreated, this made her a full Jew again and their children would be full Jews and there you have it: *genetic regression*.

"Genetic regression," Franz echoed, catching the bartender's eye. He was young—maybe eighteen judging from his smooth tan skin, the way he wore his hair parted on the side, the clean white part healthy and neat.

Wolf waved a finger in front of Franz's face, his speech slurring. "We can't let it happen."

The bartender shoved the rag into his back pocket. All the tabletops were shining. The group of workmen had left, leaving behind the heady scent of sweat and hard labor. The sound of dishes clattering from the kitchen carried into the main room. Wolf ranted on about Jewish tentacles spreading over the surface of the earth, unchecked. "They are like octopus—octopi! Fists in every pot of gold!"

The bartender produced the bill, and Franz paid up. He was a good bartender—discreet, expedient. Wolf staggered to the door, and Franz said, "Call him a cab." The bartender nodded.

Wolf hung in the doorway, his head lolling. For the first time, Franz noticed a physical defect—Wolf's head was extraordinary large, almost baboonlike.

"I can drive myselth home," he sputtered. Then he slumped into a nearby chair, his eyes half-closed slits.

After the cab left with Wolf asleep in the backseat, Franz lingered in the bar. He was the only one left besides two waiters quietly eating their dinner in the corner. The bartender came over and offered Franz a cigarette.

"I don't smoke."

He took a long drag. "A purist." Then he squeezed Franz's arm, and Franz tensed at his touch. "You probably have one hundred percent oxygen in your blood. Maybe you'll get a medal for it." The boy's amber eyes lit up with mockery.

Franz leaned back into the chair, tracing a circular stain on the wood. "You think we're ridiculous?"

He shook his head, sitting down next to Franz. "I admire the new movement—the energy, the unity, the infusion of hope for all of us. It's really something."

Franz took the cigarette from the boy's mouth and put it out. "You'll ruin your lung capacity."

He put Franz's hand on his chest and breathed in and out. "How am I doing, Doctor?"

"Strong."

The boy guided Franz's hand downward. "I'm Manfred. But you don't really care, do you?"

"Not really."

His amber eyes lit up again with that teasing mocking glee.

Franz's heart accelerated at the sight of the boy's sloping jaw, his long swanlike neck and perfectly proportioned head, as if molded by a Roman sculptor.

They ended up in the back room—a threadbare couch, an old radio, peeling wallpaper, the smell of kitchen grease hanging in the air. Despite the coarse atmosphere, Manfred was considerably gentle. He preferred a lot of kissing and caressing. His breath smelled of vermouth. He barely had to shave because his hairs were so fine and light. Franz touched his face, his mouth, his long neck. Then he wrestled him to the ground, calling him a weakling. The carpet smelled of cigarette smoke.

"Are you really going to kill that boy?" he asked.

Franz ruffled his hair. "Wolf always talks that way when he's drunk." Then he bit Manfred's shoulder and pressed into him. Sweat sprung up on the boy's skin, and Franz licked his smooth chest, circling his tongue around Manfred's berry-colored nipple.

"Bite it," Manfred said, cupping his palm behind Franz's neck.

Franz took a little nibble.

"Harder."

He looked up, resting his chin on Manfred's smooth chest.

Manfred ran his fingers through Franz's hair and then hoisted Franz up to eye level. His metal belt buckle bore into Franz's stomach. "Does that hurt?" he asked.

"No," Franz said in a high whisper.

"Well, it's uncomfortable regardless, keeping these on," Manfred said, taking off his trousers, but he stopped when he noticed Franz staring at him, silent and still.

"Is this your first time?"

"No," Franz lied.

Manfred smiled and playfully flicked the hair out of Franz's eyes. "It's okay. I can tell it is." Manfred cupped Franz's chin; his hand felt warm and dry. "Let me show you."

Someone hollered good night and shut off the lights in the hallway. A door slammed.

"You don't have to—" Franz stammered. He should leave, forget all this—already he had failed, but then he inhaled Manfred's scent. It reminded him of warm milk and almonds mixed with the sharp sting of his own nervous sweat. He stared at Manfred's bare chest, as smooth as wood, a rich walnut. Manfred's warm hands slid down Franz's forearms. "It's all right, really."

"Really?" Franz asked, feeling foolish.

Manfred kissed him on the mouth. The kiss was tidy, just the right amount of saliva. Franz felt his muscles loosen, his stomach soar with excitement.

Manfred buried his mouth into Franz's shoulder blade and bit him hard. Then he sucked the place where he had bit him. Franz sighed—a long sigh filled with all the times he had wanted to do this with Wolf but couldn't. He pulled Manfred into him, their belt buckles clashing. They both laughed. Then Manfred slid off his pants and Franz did too. They stood before each other, naked in the darkness except for the white moonlight filtering through the small dirty window.

Manfred carefully turned Franz around, his hands massaging his abdomen, his thighs, his chest. "See?" He breathed into Franz's neck.

Franz gulped, feeling Manfred's hardness pressing up against him.

"Don't worry," Manfred said, planting little kisses on Franz's neck. "We're alone and free now."

39

Coming in from the fields, she needed time to let her eyes adjust to the darkened room of the meetinghouse. She pulled off her straw hat, fanning her face. It was hot for April. Before her, she squinted at the outline of Zev and Maya Dubinsky, huddled over a newspaper article. They were discussing something intensely, as usual. They proved incapable as long as Vicki had known them, which had only been the last two weeks, of tepid table talk: *Pass the salt. How was your day? Will it rain tomorrow?* No, no. For them, speech was solely reserved for heavy drawn-out discussions regarding the immigration process, the illusion of assimilation, how Europe was a bourgeois fantasy waiting to crumble, how they must sever all ties to their Diaspora existence and begin anew in the Middle East. Which began, of course, with the assigning of a Hebrew name that was either the equivalent of one's European name or bore some relation to it.

"Aviva!" Maya called, motioning for Vicki to come over. She still had to get used to her new name, which meant "spring" in Hebrew. Because of the presence of the *v*, it was the name that sounded closest to her real name. As it turned out, there was no Hebrew equivalent for Vicki.

Vicki wiped her brow with her sleeve. "What are you reading?"

Maya beamed. "Zev just published an editorial in the *Jewish Daily Forward* about the necessity of Labor Zionism."

"It's only a little article." Zev shrugged, chewing on tobacco, which Vicki found unnecessarily vulgar. How did Maya stand it? She had grown up in Paris, the daughter of White Russians who had fled Saint Petersburg on the eve of the revolution, whereas Zev hailed from some backwater town near Odessa. Maya had swept her long dark tendrils into a French twist and then covered her head with a shimmering green scarf. Even in the heat, Maya didn't break a sweat, despite the tight floral dress she wore just for digging potatoes.

Maya waved the newspaper in front of Zev's face. "The whole bottom half of the second page—I would hardly call that little!"

He took it from her and rolled it up into a baton. "What I should have said, but I'm too much of a coward to say, is this: what the Jews are seeking in Palestine is not *progress* but a *state*. When you build a state, you make a revolution. And in a revolution there can only ever be winners and losers. This time around, we Jews are going to be the winners." He grinned, tapping the rolled-up newspaper against his thigh.

"Congratulations anyway, on the editorial," Vicki said, feeling uncomfortable all over again. Last night at dinner, she had offhandedly complained about tending to the baby animals because it was boring, smelly work—the calves just stared at her all day with their doleful blank eyes, and when she stopped moving for one second, they took the opportunity to shit on her shoes. A few people laughed in recognition, including Geza, but Zev ate his rice without looking up from the plate, his jaw tensing, before launching into a tirade about the importance of Jewish work: young Jews from the Diaspora would be rescued from their effete, assimilated lives and transported to remote collective settlements in rural Palestine where they would create a living Jewish peasantry, which inevitably, though unfortunately, excluded the Arabs. Under the table, Geza had squeezed Vicki's hand. He understood, at least, how difficult it was to suddenly shun her European upbringing and trade it in for this. Even if *this*—a line of dirt ever present under her fingernails, the rarity of a shower, singing songs she didn't know the words to—was what they wanted. Or said they wanted. And every night, cupping her face with his rough hands, Geza promised, "It will be different once we get there. It will be different."

Vicki did hope the kibbutz, Beit Alfa, would be different. And she knew, as Geza reminded her, that she should be thankful to Zev. He had arranged a place for them here, at the *hachshara* training center in Skaby, southeast of Berlin. *Hachshara,* Vicki learned, the Hebrew word for "training," was the name for Zionist preparatory and training centers where young people received instruction at no charge prior to immigrating to Palestine. More and more Jews were applying to make aliyah, and the Jewish Agency for Palestine guaranteed a certain immigration quota, which the British mandate authorized. But Geza pointed out the most important thing: if they immigrated through one of these centers, they could make the quota and not pay a thing. Otherwise, it was very expensive.

At least this training center was located on a sprawling old farming estate. The Hechalutz had dormitories for the Young Pioneers built on the property. Agricultural chores were carried out in the morning. In the afternoons, they attended classes on Jewish subjects including religion and Hebrew. Then the evenings, called "social evenings," were dedicated to Jewish spiritual life—traditions, customs, rituals, all of which Vicki knew nothing about to the point of embarrassment. Not knowing a word of Hebrew, she didn't understand the songs and poems, but she noticed most of the others acted the same way, mumbling their way through the words, mashing them together, and then ending with gusto on a certain syllable to convince themselves and others of their dedication. In Skaby alone, eighty *chaverim* waited to immigrate. You were supposed to serve two years before immigrating, but somehow Zev had gotten Geza and Vicki on the passenger list for the *Pacific*. They were to set sail in June. Even though Vicki knew she should feel lucky, her heart pounded with the same question pounding through everyone's heart here: *If it works, and we really get a place on the ship, what awaits us?*

In the white moonlight, she lay in her cot, next to Maya, who slept peacefully, asking herself this question—what would it really be like? She pictured sandbars, the lapping of turquoise waters, cerulean skies, stone walls bleached the color of bone, and muscular Jews striding, their tanned arms swinging, singing their Hebrew songs. Or at least this was what she was supposed to imagine. What they wanted her to imagine, the Mayas and Zevs of the movement. And what, in her worst moments, in the small hours of morning, her mind racing, her chest coated in sweat, did she actually imagine? No shade, save for a lone and withered palm. Scorching sun burning her scalp as she picked tomatoes with bloodied fingertips. Communal bathrooms and shared meals. Her skin perpetually coated with a fine layer of dust kicked up by the wind.

Punching her pillow into a shape that would induce sleep, she drew in a sharp breath at the thought of leaving her father. It wasn't as easy as they said, leaving family behind to start a new family, a different, better kind of family. Her father—their after-dinner debates, the way he gave her flowers on her birthday and took her to the ballet, his wry smile, always ready to engage her in witty repartee. Even for her mother and Franz, she felt a pang of regret, leaving behind the familial disputes and irritations for new disputes and irritations in an unfamiliar terrain, with those who did not share her blood. And good-bye to Berlin, good-bye to all that? Maya called it a mechanical city, a frigid inferno with its snub-nosed cab drivers and rivers of automobiles honking at nothing, but she didn't see, or want to see, the wide shaded boulevards of Charlottenburg, window shopping at Wertheim's, the ladies in their ermine collars and pillbox hats, the placid waters of the Wannsee in the height of summer, the jazz bars and the dancing girls and the sidewalk cafés crammed with people who were endlessly arguing, debating, and contesting the ideas of the age.

No, she didn't see it. Vicki watched Maya sleep, her thin arm flung over her face. She snored lightly, joining the chorus of snorers. A milky purple light filtered in through the dusty windows. It was almost six. Soon there'd be a knock on the door, followed by a general rousing: stretching and yawning and disheveled hair. Bleary-eyed and barefoot, they would stumble over to the sinks, splash cold water on their faces, and prepare for another day of physical labor. Vicki savored these last moments before the sound of that knock—it felt luxurious to just lie here in bed, the pillow balled up under the crook of her arm. Thankfully, she only had one more week tending to those calves. And then they would return to Berlin, and she would prepare to leave. Forever.

Last night after dinner, after Zev's whole speech about Labor Zionism, she and Geza had stood out on the porch, watching the hazy sunset disappear. He smoked a pipe, a new affectation he'd taken up. Vicki suspected he thought it made him appear more manly, older and world-weary, when in fact, it looked a bit silly sticking out of his mouth as if he were a sea captain.

She sighed, leaning against the post. "How does animal husbandry pave the way to my Zionist future?" She was half joking, but at the same time her voice cracked and she felt tears well up in her eyes.

"Oh, Viv," he said, coming up behind her. He called her Viv now, short for Aviva. It sounded more palatable to both of them. He wrapped his arms around her waist and perched his chin on her shoulder.

"Do you miss your tutus and rose petals?" he teased, alluding to a ballet recital where she'd performed, in white tulle, a variation from *La Sylphide*.

Her throat tightened. From inside the main house, she heard them singing in Hebrew. Under her blouse, Geza's hands spread across her stomach. "The thing is, ballet is a—"

She sighed. "Bourgeois fantasy. I know."

"Viv, I sympathize."

She turned around to face him.

The singers stopped, and then someone began to recite a poem.

"Do you really?"

He tucked a loose strand of hair back into her floral scarf. "Yes, really."

She wanted to shake him. He always relied on this light teasing tone, on his lopsided grin, even when things felt serious. Especially when things felt serious. Feeling the heat rise in her chest, she was about to tell him that maybe she couldn't do it—she barely had any skills and learning Hebrew was impossible. A backward language, writing from right to left. It made no sense. None of it did.

The strange intonation of words drifted through the screened-in windows. They listened for a moment. Then Geza admitted that of course it would be very hard for her, at first, to leave behind such a comfortable Europeanized existence. She noticed how he avoided saying *bourgeois existence,* as that phrase had been so overused it ceased to mean anything.

She leaned her head against Geza's chest, feeling herself forfeit to him even though the fight she wanted to start still simmered within her. The voices picked up again, and this time singing was accompanied by the slapping of a tambourine. Geza started rocking her back and forth, humming under his breath. She resisted, but he twirled her out and then rolled her back into him. He plucked off her scarf and started waving it in the air as he crossed one foot over the other, dancing a circle around her.

"Geza, stop!"

He danced more wildly, his arms curving over an imaginary ball, and then, flexing his palms, he shot his arms upward. Having donned her scarf, he stomped his feet, his hips sashaying from side to side as he repeated this wavelike arm movement.

Vicki leaned against the post.

"C'mon."

Suppressing a smile, she shrugged.

"You should try."

She made a disparaging gesture. "This?"

"Folk dancing, yes." He pulled off the scarf.

Everything was wrong with it—the pronouncement of the heel crashing down first, the lack of turnout, the clapping and the stomping. Peasant dancing. With scarves and tambourines. The dancers actually sunk closer to the ground whereas the whole point of ballet—what she loved—was the elevation, the ethereal, otherworldly quality of floating through space, the boxed tips of her pointe shoes skimming the floor as she *bourréed* across the stage.

The sun dipped behind the blue hills. She no longer had to squint at him. Shadows filled the porch with what felt like a mire of gloom. Geza walked over to the far corner of the porch, gazing out at the wooded forest.

She went toward him but then stopped. "I'm sorry—it's just—that type of dancing seems coarse."

"A lot of things are going to seem coarse to you."

She fiddled with the clasp of her watch—the gold watch her father had given her when she'd turned seventeen. It had an alligator band, bright green, the color of emerald.

He breathed in deeply, his back expanding under his thin white shirt. "But the taste of freedom is, at first, the same as the taste of bitterness."

"Did Zev say that?"

A line of lemons balanced along the porch railing. He took one and inspected it. "I thought of it. Just now." He flipped open a pocketknife and cut the lemon in half.

Vicki stared at the glistening white fibers, the seeds embedded in the flesh. The sharp sour scent spiked her tongue with saliva.

Without much thought, he threw the halved lemon over the porch railing.

"That's a waste."

Geza shrugged.

She came up behind him. "Think of the labor that went into growing that lemon."

He swung around, smiling. "My good little pioneer."

"Maybe I am," Vicki said, nestling back into his embrace, listening to the pulse of his heart, to the swish of his blood traveling through his veins.

He smoothed down her hair, his hand lingering on her earlobe. "You don't wear earrings anymore."

Vicki laughed. "What good would earrings do me here?" Her voice carried an unexpected sharpness.

"I like the lapis ones, the way they swing around your face."

"Papa gave them to me, after I cut my hair."

Geza continued smoothing down her hair. Mosquitoes buzzed around them, one landing on Geza's white shirt, searching for flesh. She flicked it off with her forefinger and sighed. "Do you think he's devastated, about my leaving Berlin?"

"Well . . ." He paused.

She pressed her ear into his chest, to hear his beating heart again. If only he really understood how much she was giving up. Of course she believed in the cause and standing on the "right side of history," but the reason she had agreed to give up her studies, her papa, her city of light and shade, had nothing to do with Labor Zionism or the Promised Land. He was her promise—I want to be where you are, she thought. So simple. She pulled him closer. "Why are you quiet?"

Geza fingered the line of her bra though her shirt. "I had a coffee with your father. A few weeks ago. He's coming around to the idea of us leaving. You shouldn't worry so much."

She glanced up at him, her eyes filling with tears. "But he seems so sad lately, so troubled. After I leave, who will he joke with? Who will he talk to? God knows how he gets along with Mutti. And Franz barely speaks to him. And why didn't you mention the coffee until now?"

Geza scratched his patchy beard and avoided Vicki's questioning stare. "Let's go inside," he said. "We'll get eaten alive out here."

"Wait." She pressed her body into his. "I don't want to go back in there yet."

In her embrace, his body felt restless and tense. She could tell he was thinking something, something he wouldn't tell her.

They stared at each other in the darkness.

"What is it?" she finally asked.

"When your father first heard the news, he was upset about our departure. But he's searching for something too, something he cares about deeply. His life is not only as it appears to you, or to me. What can we really know of another man's life?"

"He's my father," she said, her voice breaking.

He cupped her face in his hands. "Even I have secrets," he said, his tone light and playful again.

"What secrets?" she asked, wondering why Geza had waited until now to mention the coffee with her father, and what the two of them had spoken about for so long the first time she brought Geza home to meet her family. But he avoided the subject of these discussions with Lev as elegantly as a skilled acrobat, gliding in and out of her questions by posing other questions, until she forgot her initial question or gave up.

He curled an arm around her waist, guiding her back to the house.

"Oh, you know. Once we passed a man who spat out chewing tobacco on the sidewalk, and you said it was a vile habit, so I vowed never to let you know I chewed tobacco. I know you prefer white shirts on men, and so I went out and bought five white shirts. And I don't even like white shirts! They get soiled so easily. I started listening to jazz, because you love Josephine Baker and Sam Wooding. I borrow the records from Herr Zakrevsky at the boardinghouse and play them in the afternoon, trying to feel what you must feel when you hear the music." Geza shook his head, laughing to himself. "I can hardly stand it. Gives me a headache."

Vicki giggled. "Sam Wooding? Did I really say I liked him?" She poked him in the side. "And I never said I prefer men in white shirts—how ridiculous!"

Geza buried his face in her hair. "You did. You did," he murmured, guiding her back into the house filled with singing and light.

40

These days, whenever Lev thought of his marriage he saw the ruins of a beautiful Greek temple. Doric columns erected against a sharp blue sky. The pediments still intact with friezes of the Trojan War: fallen heroes, serene goddesses, bucking horses, the overall structure in place despite countless attacks from barbarian tribes. People still visited and placed their hands on the cool stone, channeling what was lost. They said to themselves, taking a snapshot, What a pity. In those days, it must have been spectacular.

Yes, spectacular, Lev sighed, thinking back to the Ice Palace, where he had first spied her twirling slender figure, and the chance afterward to share a coffee with such a remarkable creature didn't seem possible back then, especially with sand in his pockets and those stiff new shoes. But it became possible. The opportunity to know her unfolded before him like a runner of the finest silk rippling down a flight of stairs. Boldly, before her governess lumbered over, he had turned down the edge of her glove and kissed the inside of her wrist. Right there in the café. An unthinkable thing to do then. In return, she gave him a breathless glance, conspiratorial in nature, as if they were in it together. He had not seen that look for so long. Not since the war. Not since he returned from it and she pretended to be happy he'd come home, and he pretended to be happy because she acted happy, but she wasn't and neither was he. Because he returned not more German but less. Without medals, honors, or distinction, without even a wound to show for his bravery. Less German, more Jew. Lev knew what she thought of him behind her silent eyes: shirker.

After the war, he had started visiting his mother again. He walked the dog when Josephine went to Mass on Sundays. He no longer felt the charm of her Christian ways, no longer admired that little golden cross she wore around her neck. And what did Josephine detect behind his eyes? Leah: the gleaming white birch trees, their bodies moving beneath them. He had left his lifeblood in that small dark corner of the world, scanning the papers for news of Mitau, for any trace, any clue, of Leah.

With only his memories and dreams, he muddled through the years, convincing himself he was lucky—they hadn't lost everything in '23; their healthy children had gone to the best schools. Lev kept getting promoted until he became director of Bremer Woll-Kammerei textiles. Josephine threw dinner parties, entertaining guests with her effortless sparkle, but afterward, alone in their bedroom, she was worn out. The rosy flush of her cheeks evaporated as quickly as all that champagne they drank. People complimented him on his wife's charms, perhaps imagining how after the party, she was sexually ravenous, fulfilling the promise of her coy smiles and touches on the elbow. If only they knew about the invention of Herr K, how she turned her back to Lev in bed, how the next morning she acted as if everything was fine, pouring coffee from a gleaming chrome pot.

And Dr. Dürhkoop—what good was he? It had been nearly a year of treatment. Lev had seen him strolling through the Tiergarten. He wore his hat tipped at a jaunty angle. When Lev told Josephine how he'd seen the doctor in the park, she'd turned positively red. Maybe, Lev sighed again, he should be the one seeing the doctor. What would the good doctor say about his vivid dreams of Leah, how he'd been going back to that opium den without Otto, because she existed only there, in the ether and the smoke.

Until now. He could board a steamer next week and find her in New York. Find his son. He had even fabricated an impressive lie to Josephine about visiting a textile firm in lower Manhattan to procure a certain type of linen. Keeping the dates vague, he had created a flexible window of time during which he could leave. Josephine had seemed surprised, making a sarcastic comment about how special the linen must be to travel all that way, but then she didn't ask about it again. His comings and goings no longer concerned her. But Lev still didn't know if Leah was in New York for certain, and if she was, he needed an address. He knew the city was geographically small, a long thin stretch of land, but filled with tens of thousands. She might have moved to another city by now. She might never have left Riga at all.

When Lev met Geza for coffee a few weeks ago, Geza had acted subdued and dismissive. He said he didn't know where Leah was. She might be living in New York, or she might not. He had seen her two years ago, when she gave him the letter in Riga, and she had not said anything about America. When Lev begged him to find out, at the very least, if she had left for America, Geza nodded reluctantly.

"And if you can, her address in New York?"

"Don't abandon your family," Geza said, stirring cream into his coffee. "What good would it do now? Think of your wife, your children."

Trying to suppress his mounting anger, Lev cried, "You're taking away my child! My Vicki! What does it matter if I stay here now? I've already given up so many years of my life."

"Think of the upheaval," Geza kept repeating, as if immigrating to Palestine did not qualify as upheaval.

Lev's heart contracted at the thought of Palestine, the place where he and Leah had once dreamed of moving, the place where his only daughter would live. Clutching his chest, he looked around at the other passengers on the tram to see if anyone noticed, but no one did. The woman across from him chewed gum, her lips smacking together in a rhythmic motion. How closely people resembled farm animals. Lev shook his head. He had dressed too warmly for the weather, and inside the train car, it was hot and stuffy—people never wanted to open the windows, even in the heat. An antiquated superstition about catching cold. He was sure if he tried, an old woman would start protesting, only to be joined by other old women until he would be faced with a chorus of them, all clutching their throats and pointing to the open window. No, it wasn't worth it.

Instead, he felt sweat trickle down his sides and thought about how Easter was this weekend, and surely Josephine and Franz would go to church, and how Passover fell the night before. Would Vicki still go to church? She had become quite the Zionist, and he was sure Judaism was part of her cultural training. They only wanted good earnest Jews in Palestine, not the aesthete assimilated ones who shirked the Sabbath and shopped on Yom Kippur, who felt embarrassed to walk next to their Yiddish-speaking caftan-wearing brethren from the east.

The train jerked forward and back. A few more stops until he reached the Scheunenviertel, where his mother, he could be sure, would be waiting with recriminations.

Every time he saw her, she looked a little older.

"You're late," she barked, shaking out a sheet in the front yard before hanging it on the laundry line.

Lev took off his hat. "The train was crowded."

She motioned for him to follow her inside.

"Where are the cats?" he asked, his eyes adjusting to the darkened sitting room.

"Out back in the sun. They stay by me less and less. Traitorous creatures."

In the kitchen, she stirred a large pot on the stove. The aromatic blend of parsley, carrots, and freshly made matzo balls made Lev's mouth water.

"Here. Taste." She held out a large spoon pooling with hot yellow broth, cupping one hand under it.

Lev gingerly bent toward it.

"I'm not going to poison you!"

He took the spoon from her. "It's hot." He blew over it.

She leaned against the stove, her arms crossed. Lev noticed she'd recently had her hair done, dyed a jet black to match her eyebrows. She tapped her foot impatiently. He swallowed down the warm liquid. It was too salty.

He said it tasted wonderful.

"I'm serving it Saturday night. For Passover."

One of the cats sauntered into the kitchen.

Lev raised his eyebrows.

She fidgeted with a dishcloth. "I know. I know. But it's nice, having the Nardovitches here for Seder. And then afterward, we play charades and drink the pear-flavored schnapps from the old country."

"Sounds enjoyable."

She pulled a cigarette out of her apron pocket. "Don't mock me."

"I'm not mocking you."

"Yes, you are."

He asked for more soup. "I just remember how you used to rail against religion, saying it would destroy the revolution, how it was a beautiful distraction. That's all."

Mara turned her back to him, pouring a generous amount of soup into a bowl. "I was younger then, the way Vicki is with her Zionism."

She sat down next to him at the table. "I don't mind beautiful distractions so much now."

"You think it's Zionism she loves? If Geza wanted to move to Johannesburg, she would move there too," Lev said, feeling compelled to finish the soup with his mother sitting there watching him. Thoughts flitted around his head, and he entertained telling her about each one before discarding it: the discovery that he had a son, his affair with Leah, whether he should try to find them in New York under the pretense of procuring a certain type of linen. The problem was, if he told his mother one thing, the rest would tumble out. He could never just dip his toe into the water with her—it had to be a full immersion.

He finished the soup, balancing the spoon against the lip of the bowl.

"When is Vicki leaving?"

"June," Lev said, his voice catching. "I've even agreed to help them with the passage fare. Otherwise, she'll still leave, but they'll have to travel belowdecks. Think of the stench, the filth."

Mara motioned for Trotsky to jump into her lap, but he stood watch next to Lev's chair, hoping for scraps. "Vicki will be happier in Palestine," she said firmly and then added, "You're celebrating Easter, I assume?"

"Naturally."

"Hmmm," Mara said, taking his bowl away and placing it in the sink.

Over the sound of the running water, she reminded him that Christians still believed the Jews killed Jesus. "It's the myth they cling to, so they can hate us a little longer. For all eternity," she added, shaking the pot dry and placing it upside down on a dishtowel. Then she recounted some recent attacks, honing in on the more disturbing details, almost with relish.

She sat down again, her eyes tired. "But it's the season, isn't it? We're making matzos out of their children's blood. Yes, yes, it's only the season. This too will pass. We've said this to ourselves for centuries."

She went into the living room and fell into the deep leather armchair where Lev's father used to sit and smoke.

Lev watched her from the kitchen doorway, feeling the usual mixture of guilt and irritation. She was old. And manipulative. She was alone. And she reminded him of this whenever he came to visit. Her husband had died many years ago, and she mourned him, but she was happier without him.

Mara closed her eyes and murmured that she felt tired, motioning for Lev to go. "Oh," she said, rubbing her forehead. "Did you hear? About Rabbi Landauer?"

Lev shook his head.

"He's gone. Poof! Just like that."

"What is this insane story?"

"That's all I know," she said, her hand over her eyes. "Someone saw him boarding a ship in Kiel," she added.

"I don't believe it," Lev said.

She shrugged. "What's not to believe?"

He left her sitting there, a diminutive figure blending into the oversized chair. She barely stirred when the door shut.

Lev stopped by the rabbi's apartment to disprove what she'd said, although as he climbed the steep stairs to the fourth floor, his chest pounded as if some mysterious organ in his body knew it was true. When he got there, the rabbi's daughters were huddled together on the rug, clutching their cat, their faces red and blotchy from crying.

Smoking up the kitchen, the rabbi's wife yelled over the hiss of frying potatoes what a horror it'd been. She shook the pan and speared one of the blackened baby potatoes with a fork.

"He left! Just like that. No note. No explanation. For three days, I thought he was dead, crumpled up on the street from starvation, dehydration. But no. Someone saw him boarding a ship to America. Then they had the gall to ask, 'He's going to send for you, yes?' when I was already in tears. What did they think? Would I be in tears if he'd sent for us? They only want to see me suffer!" She waved the fork in the air, the potato steaming. "I thank Him for the hair salons. At least business is booming. But . . ."

"You're alone."

She sighed, putting down the fork. "Solitude is worse than poverty."

From the other room, they heard the girls fighting over the cat. Then someone dropped the cat, and the animal scrambled up from the ground and raced down the hall, its little bell ringing.

She looked at Lev, her eyes swollen and bloodshot, and managed a bitter smile.

"Is there anything I can do?" he asked.

She took the frying pan off the stove. "Would you like some?"

Lev stared at the blackened balls of starch, and with the tenderness he knew a woman in her position longed for, he said he would very much enjoy some of those potatoes.

The food heavy in his stomach, Lev wandered through the old neighborhood musing at the men who still insisted on wearing their *peyes* tapering down the sides of their long white faces. Others wore caftans and fur hats, even in this spring air. Packs of children ran by, some of them bumping his shoulder. He used to call out and reprimand them, but today, he didn't have the energy. Let them run, Lev thought. Soon they will stop running, and they will lumber through the streets because they will feel the burden of living, how tiring it can be, how a multitude of thoughts will pulse through their heads, all competing to be heard, and their children will mercilessly abandon them, their wives will turn cold in bed, their own youthful skin will gradually start to sag and crinkle until they are no longer recognizable, not even to themselves.

He passed the old synagogue on Heidereuterstrasse and pictured the rabbi leaving from the port of Kiel, with its massive steamers hovering on the murky horizon. Did he think of his sensible wife, his three young daughters, his gray cat with the bell around its neck, when he boarded the ship? *Life is so terrible it would have been better not to be born. Who is so lucky? Not one in a hundred thousand.* The rabbi had often repeated this Yiddish proverb in jest, but maybe, all this time, he had dreamed of escape. Could Lev really do the same? Leap over to New York and find his beloved Leah? And then what? Would he stay there with her and attempt to construct some salvageable existence in that barbaric city? Was he capable of abandoning Josephine the way the rabbi had abandoned his wife?

Vicki was prepared to leave her familiar world behind, but she was young and energetic. And of course, the glow of new love motivated such grand gestures. The greater the obstacle, the more intensely lovers swore their allegiance to each other—the real test would come once Vicki and Geza moved to Palestine. Only then would they have to contend with the ordinariness of daily life, which was much more detrimental to a love affair than their current reenactment of a Shakespearean tragedy.

Yes, it was much more detrimental, Lev thought, crossing the street for the U-Bahn station. When he had struggled the most—those long arguments with Josephine's parents, how they forbade her to see him, the clandestine meetings in the Tiergarten—he was more in love with her then, before she became his wife, before he really had her. He remembered the surprise, a few years later, after Franz was born, at the blandness of her bare ankles, how thin and birdlike they looked. Once, she had dangled her foot so sensuously before him, and his blood surged through his veins, a sensation gradually replaced by the irrevocable thud of marriage. But then the war came! The war, the war! Another obstacle of grand proportions to nudge them back into love. And it had worked for a while. He remembered coming home after work on a Friday afternoon and telling her that he was joining up and how tender, how expressive, she suddenly became, her eyes flooded with hot tears. They sat in the courtyard. She touched his face, his hair, his neck, murmuring that she couldn't survive without him, that he might die over there, and then she would be the young widow forever in black—a role, Lev realized when he had returned home in one piece, she actually yearned to play. He smiled sarcastically to himself and, not paying much attention, accepted a flyer someone handed him.

Only later on the train, did he unfold it from his coat pocket to see it was a National Socialist advert. *Citizens! Do not believe that the Germany of misfortune and misery, the nation of corruption and usury, the land of Jewish corruption, can be saved by parties that claim to stand on a foundation of "facts." Do not relent!* The image of a storm trooper, his chiseled profile overlooking an expanse of green hills and farmland, dominated the page. Lev balled up the flyer and let it drop between his knees. He wondered if Franz handed out these flyers, his heavy messenger bag filled with this trash. Kicking the balled-up paper under his seat, Lev reminded himself that it wasn't entirely Franz's fault. Over the years, Josephine had encouraged his innate militarism to blossom. She had smoothed down his lapels and complimented his SA uniform. She spoke of the Great War as if speaking of a haunted love affair: the sacrifices they'd made, the food they'd gone without, the faith they'd maintained even in the face of all that death. How she'd scoured the house for metal, how she'd refused to accept flour and butter from her mother because it was unpatriotic, how she'd tended to the wounded soldiers in that makeshift hospital set up in the train station—she spoke of all this as if it were the most magical time of her life. No wonder Franz had grown inebriated with war.

41

Franz had been going to Manfred's hole of an apartment on Dragon-erstrasse ever since that night in the bar. Manfred shared the apartment with his aunt and her family, all six of them crammed into three little rooms. Manfred's room was separated from the main room by a frosted-glass window. The place was loud and dirty, but they always found their little corner of peace behind the frosted-glass pane, even though when they lay naked in bed, bedbugs would crawl back and forth over their intertwined limbs. Manfred's aunt and uncle didn't seem to notice what went on behind the glass pane. If anything, they appeared grateful for his presence, as if he elevated the squalid atmosphere in some way. At first, Franz felt the need to protest, saying they shouldn't see each other, especially not at night, when they would be tempted to indulge in their "mutual weakness." But Manfred just kissed him on the mouth and said if they couldn't abstain, then clearly it was the right thing to do! Lulled by how easy and free Manfred acted, how natural and almost commonplace he made it all seem, despite how inherently wrong Franz knew this was, walking home one evening after a bout of lovemaking, Franz thought to himself, however illogical, that with Manfred, it was all right. As long as no one knew.

During the day, Manfred worked at a construction site in the Tier-garten district, close to Franz's house. He was usually up on the roof, carrying tiles. Franz would invent excuses to visit him, admiring Manfred wearing nothing but an undershirt, working among real Berlin proletarian types. Manfred's head almost touched the trees, the new spring leaves fluttering around his brown curls. On his break, he would walk with Franz through the park, swinging his water canteen, and Franz would recite some lines from Faust. And then Manfred would tell him about his supervisor, a little Hungarian who was always making obscene remarks. "What a horror!" Franz would add, and then they would laugh about it. After glancing around, Franz drew him close, his young muscular body, full of boyish energy, pressed up against his. He knew it was a risk, to walk with Manfred in this way. He imagined one of his mother's friends seeing him with this worker type, but he couldn't imagine his mother's reaction—the thought sometimes made him burst out laughing because he didn't know what else to do. It would be so horrible if she knew. An abomination, yes, she would say so. Part of him believed this too, which was why he sometimes forced himself to stay away from Manfred for a few days. He moped around his room, feeling his blood slow, his whole body weakening, dying. He fasted, punishing himself for wanting Manfred, while his mother brought up bowls of broth, bread, and chocolate on a serving tray. He never touched the food. Instead, he stared out the window at the bloodred roses in the garden below, feeling lightheaded, imagining himself tumbling into the air and hitting the ground. How tragic, they would say. He imagined his mother weeping over his dead body. Weeping and weeping. Vicki would cry too. His father would shake his head, confused, as he always had been about Franz. But how light and free Franz might feel, to be rid of this body, a body that wanted so much, more than he could give it.

Eventually, hunger overwhelmed him and he devoured a chocolate bar, and with the taste of chocolate still in his mouth, he would run to Manfred's apartment as soon as dusk fell. Manfred knew to wait so they could follow the established routine: he undressed Franz, scolded him lightly for staying away so long, and then admired how thin Franz looked, tracing the run of his ribs with his fingertips. Last night, Franz had predictably shown up on Manfred's doorstep famished, ashamed, in need of reconciliation. Manfred mothered him, made him toast with jam. They ate in bed. Franz stayed until first light, something he'd never done before.

This afternoon, they walked past the horse path, the smell of manure stinging their nostrils, giddy as truants. Franz had skipped out of Lutz's lecture on the importance of hygiene during wartime to see Manfred again today. He knew it was indulgent—he felt as if he might get caught somehow, but he didn't care. Under the shade of trees, Manfred wondered why Franz needed to learn how to brush his teeth without a toothbrush. An orange-chested bullfinch flitted from one branch to another.

"Well, when you're in the trenches, see . . ."

Manfred laughed. His full lips, his upturned mouth; he always appeared to be smiling at something. "I just don't understand. Seems arbitrary, like Lutz has invented these lectures to give himself something to do."

Franz playfully slapped his baton against Manfred's thigh. "There's going to be another war on, you know."

"Then I better learn how to brush my teeth in a trench."

Franz murmured, "You stay at home. I'll defend the Fatherland."

"Shall I knit you legwarmers and send chocolate bars?"

"Yes, please," Franz said, fluttering his eyelashes.

Manfred giggled and gripped Franz's body, which sent a sharp spasm of fear and excitement through him. Franz backed away.

"If you won't let me touch you, let's at least go look at the polar bears and the walruses."

"My sister and I went to the Zoological Garden, when we were little." He nipped Manfred's earlobe.

Manfred pulled off his cap, fanning Franz's face. "You're teasing me now. Careful." Then he backed Franz into a nearby tree and kissed him. For a moment, it was only their faces touching in the shaded darkness, the fullness of Manfred's lips against his own, the restless desire to undress him. But they would have to wait until this evening, behind the frosted glass.

He quickly let go of Manfred when they heard a horse approaching. Wolf trotted toward them, riding an enormous steel-gray gelding. Its tail flicked. "Where were you?"

Franz ran a hand through his hair. "I was . . ."

Wolf gestured toward Manfred as if shaking an insect off his hand. He rocked back and forth in his saddle, grinning. "Fucking like animals fuck."

Manfred stood to the side, his body tense.

"We're only taking a stroll." Franz's voice reverberated through his head—it sounded weak, feminine. The sun beat down.

"We were only taking a stroll," Wolf mimicked. He clapped his hands together. "What do you think Lutz will say about this?"

"Lutz is an ass."

Wolf slid off his horse and shrugged.

He slung an arm around Franz's shoulders and grinned at Manfred. "Would you mind leaving us?"

They watched Manfred walk away through the tall grass and the trees.

Wolf stroked the side of his horse, the back of his hand caressing the large canvas of gray-white hair. "Secluded here." The horse bent its neck to retrieve some grass. "He's good-looking," Wolf added.

Franz stared down at the fallen acorns and the crushed chestnuts and the dirt, kicked up in clumps where Wolf's horse had halted abruptly.

"And all that time, pushing Greta on you."

Franz felt his cheeks burn, his ears turning crimson. The sun shifted behind a cloud. "It doesn't mean—" he started, but he didn't know how to finish the sentence. He leaned against the tree, his arms crossed over his chest. It was better to say nothing.

"Let's keep this between us." Wolf touched his arm and relief flooded through Franz. Then Wolf squeezed his shoulder, a little harder than necessary. "Anyway, I came to find you for another reason. I was thinking about the Jew."

The sun drifted out from behind the cloud, shining down on them again. Wolf turned his face up to it and closed his eyes. Franz noticed that his eyelids were sweaty. "You know—that dirty little Jew your sister's running around with." He sighed deeply, enjoying the momentary warmth on his face.

"Geza?"

Wolf opened his eyes and focused on Franz. "When are you going to kill him, as we discussed?"

"I haven't planned it out yet, exactly." Again, he sounded vague, indecisive. I must stop that, he thought. I must announce a date, a time.

Wolf laughed, leading his horse back to the path.

Franz followed him and Wolf said over his shoulder, "A half-Jew yourself, you should feel scandalized by such pride, his thinking he can whisk away your sister and ruin all the social progress a family such as yours has made."

He got back up on his horse and motioned in the direction Manfred had gone. "I didn't mean to frighten him."

Franz nodded, panic budding under his skin, little pinpricks. Would he have to kill Geza tomorrow? Or the next day? He had never killed anyone. Only beaten up a few Poles.

"Big white teeth. Good skin. He must have grown up in the country," he added, adjusting his saddle. "Greta's been invited to Vicki's good-bye party at some apartment near Moritzplatz. That's where you will do it." He spoke crisply and cleanly, as if dictating a timetable of when trains were due to arrive and depart. "I'll be there to make sure it goes off smoothly."

"When is it?" His voice caught.

"Next Monday. Nineteen hundred hours."

Then he cantered off, waving as he went, his body moving with the horse's body to the point where Franz could no longer distinguish between horse and rider.

42

The house was calm and filled with white sunlight. Vicki pulled the curtain aside and shoved open the bedroom window, feeling the warm spring air against her bare arms. Languishing in a state of undress, she wore a long V-neck tunic patterned with an oriental motif, and a silk sash around her head. Tossing a few dresses aside, she looked in the oblong mirror and held one up to her body. Glittery and beaded, with alternating panels of satin, she would have no use for such a garment in the Holy Land. She imagined plucking tomatoes in this beaded affair. Ha! That wouldn't do. And Elsa was more than happy to inherit it, having already expressed a keen interest in Vicki's clothing, which was, she said, "unfit for the kibbutz." And her favorite peach satin evening pumps with the buttoned straps and Cuban heels? Would those have to go too? She put them on, clicking her heels together in front of the mirror, about to break into the Charleston when she heard the front door open. Their voices echoed in the foyer as they discussed how the rector looked gaunt. "But he's always been a slight little man," Josephine said in her high theatrical voice. Franz mumbled something back. Yes, it was the voice her mother reserved for church on Sundays, for socializing with a certain set of women who always needed impressing. It was definitely not the voice she would use when she would have to explain how her only daughter was moving to Palestine with an Eastern European Jew to work on a kibbutz. Vicki flopped down on the bed and stared up at the ceiling, pulling the silk sash off her head. She wound it around her hand, wondering what her mother had said this time, about her daughter's absence from church. Was she feeling ill, perhaps? Had she suffered an allergy attack from all the pollen in the air? Had a terrible toothache swelled up the side of her face?

Last night, Vicki had been at Elsa's flat for Passover seder with Geza, Maya, Zev, and Elsa's new boyfriend, who was a radical journalist. They had dipped bitter herbs in salt water. They had reclined on pillows and drunk red wine. They had recited prayers, their hands hovering over the flickering candlelight, the Hebrew less foreign on her tongue now.

"Hello, hello," her father called, coming inside with Mitzi, whose long nails tapped over the parquet floor. He preferred walking the dog to sitting in church, an arrangement Josephine had accepted for many years. He couldn't be bothered with God anymore. At least that's what he said. Vicki had expected her mother to barge into her bedroom this morning and demand she attend church, given it was Easter Sunday, but she left the house quietly with Franz, careful not to wake Vicki, as if such scenes were irrelevant because Vicki had already erased herself from the family. But when the door had slammed shut, the sky a milky purple, Vicki pulled the comforter over her ears and tried to squelch the bereft feeling that enveloped her, the feeling that she had been purposefully left behind, even though she didn't want to go.

Downstairs, they were discussing when luncheon would be served. She sighed, heaving herself up. She would have to get dressed eventually. The smell of that ham baking in the oven with the mustard crust nauseated her. An insistent, somewhat insidious smell, it penetrated the rugs and pillows, it floated up the staircase and weaseled through the space under her door. She went over to the window again and jerked it up higher. Then she sat on the windowsill and lit a cigarette. Just then, a solemn knock on the door.

"*Entrez,*" she said jokingly.

Franz opened the door, hesitating on the threshold.

"You look as if someone's died," she said, swinging her bare legs from side to side.

He forced a smile and asked if he could come in.

She waved her cigarette in the air. "I said enter!"

He closed the door behind him. "In French."

She rolled her eyes. "Which is unpatriotic. I know."

"Remember when you got in trouble for that at school?"

"I always got in trouble."

He glanced around her room, and she could tell he was taken aback by the Zionist pamphlets that littered the floor, how she'd hung a portrait of Theodor Herzl on the back of her armoire, how her evening dresses were strewn together in the corner, how a pamphlet entitled *Immigration to Palestine: A Process of Cultural Re-Integration* stood open on her desk.

She tapped her cigarette ashes out the window. "Right on Herr Levenski's roses. That should make you happy at least."

"So it's tomorrow, this good-bye party?"

She jumped off the windowsill and hugged him tightly. "You'll come? Oh, I didn't think you would. I know how much you hate that crowd. But if you come, I promise not to . . ."

He pulled away from her. "Are you really going to marry him?"

She blushed a little and put on a turban with blue feathers that had been lying on the bed. "We're emigrating first."

Franz nodded, pacing the room, stepping over the pamphlets, the discarded shoes, the empty suitcases.

"But, yes, I think so," she added.

He stared down at the carpet.

"Don't you have anything to say? How about 'Congratulations'? How about 'Safe travels'? Nothing at all? Everyone else seems to have something to say about it." She frowned and pulled off the feathered turban, tossing it into the corner with the dresses.

"Vicki, you—" He leaned into her desk, accidentally knocking over a book. It landed facedown with a thud. "You've got to think about the larger implications. You've got to think of our family."

She had moved behind the bamboo screen and was shimmying into a summer shift, the yellow one with the scalloped hem and boatneck collar. She zipped up the side zip, her tan skin flashing for an instant, reminding her of how dark she turned in the sun if she didn't wear a hat and gloves. How dark she would get working in the fields. How dark and unrecognizable. Dusky, almost. She stepped out from behind the bamboo screen, smiling. "But you'll come? Meet my friends?"

From downstairs, Lev called out ceremoniously, "Luncheon is now being served." Then he rang a little bell, and Mitzi barked sharp joyous barks.

"How does my hair look?" she demanded.

"Fine."

"Fine?" She leaned closer toward the mirror, scrutinizing the slight wave rippling through her hair. "But it sort of lacks shape."

"You should cancel the good-bye party." He cracked his knuckles in quick successive cracks.

Using a circular brush, she tried to curl the ends of her hair upward. "I hate when you do that. Makes my skin crawl."

"Mother's already suffered enough with you leaving, but then to throw a party, making a spectacle."

He grabbed her arm.

"Ouch." She pulled her arm away, inspecting the red marks he'd left there. "You always take her side. Always."

"If you left peacefully, instead of this big ballyhoo you're planning . . ." He breathed quickly, cracking his knuckles again.

"Franz—what's wrong?"

Lev called from the bottom of the stairs, "The ham is getting cold!"

She shook her head. "You look as if you've taken the whole world on your shoulders when it's only Mother."

Studying the carpet, Franz dabbed his forehead with a handkerchief.

She hooked her arm through his. "Let's not be late for the all-important luncheon," she said, rolling her eyes.

Leading him down the stairs, she added, "You know, you look so much smarter in a suit and tie, as opposed to that silly brown uniform." She tightened her arm through his and dropped a kiss on his cheek.

43

They had been carrying on for months now. It was an actual love affair, despite the disappointing fact that she never saw him outside of his office. But he said it had to be that way when she'd suggested they stroll through the park one afternoon. It was hot and stuffy in his office. She wanted to get outside, with him on her arm. When he reminded her she was married, she went on about how exhilarating it would feel to walk arm in arm under the linden trees, to ride horses, to share iced tea, to amble along the hedged pathways, passing people they might know, or might not know, but either way, she would be publicly linked to him—the good, kind doctor, the handsome, empathetic man who resembled Mahler, who often misplaced his eyeglasses, and when he did find them, they were inevitably smudged with her fingerprints. "You have traces of me on you everywhere," she had said, pinching a stray blond hair off his shirt and fluttering it against the side of his face.

But how wonderful would it be, if she were truly his? Josephine asked herself this as she walked to his office on a warm Monday afternoon in the beginning of June. Two young men who looked as if they'd been dipped in bronze strolled past, their hair parted on the side and slicked back with some kind of pomade. They didn't even notice her—but why should they? She was as old as their mothers. Recently, she'd looked down at herself during an inopportune moment, only to catch sight of the loose skin gently swaying from under her thighs as the doctor thrust himself forward and back. Luckily, the doctor did not see this. He was quite concentrated on a point just above her head, where the arm of the velvet chaise curled into itself.

Halfway there and already she was sweating, despite taking the pains to apply extra borated talcum to her underarms before leaving the house. At least the blouse was loose-fitting with flared sleeves so that when the wind blew, it provided relief. She had applied a little rouge to her cheeks, even though she'd often criticized Vicki for wearing makeup during the day. Well, a little color lent her cheekbones dimension, brought out the blue of her eyes, and made her appear flushed, vibrant, girlish. She didn't want to seem old to him, especially because she was *old*—or rather she was *older* than he was, by a good seven years. She paused in front of Bruno Kuczorski's before crossing the street— the double-breasted sports jacket featured on the headless mannequin would look beautiful on him. And paired with a crimson tie and those suspenders too? *No*, she thought. *I'm always buying him little presents. He pointed out last week that I was overcompensating because I'm married and can't be with him normally, so then I shower him with trinkets instead.* She looked longingly at the sports jacket before the light turned and she crossed the street. *No, I mustn't,* she reminded herself, dabbing her forehead with a handkerchief. Sweat trickled down between her breasts, and she caught her breath, thinking how he would lick that spot and then nestle his head against her, and she would run her fingers through his fine wheat-colored hair.

His building rose in the distance, and her heart leapt at the sight of the stone edifice, so stately at the end of the street. Picking up her pace, she wondered if the passing people detected how her heart throbbed and her mind tumbled forward, envisioning the glass door overlaid with ironwork, how she would push the buzzer and he would ring her inside, and she would nearly gallop up the winding staircase to the second floor, where he would be waiting to undress her.

Clip, clip, clip--the sound of her heels against the pavement reassured her that she was still here, in this moment, despite such rabid anticipation. She stopped and rearranged her wide-brimmed hat. She knew it was out of fashion, but the close-fitting hats provided no protec-

tion from the sun, and lugging a parasol around had become an affectation reserved for the elderly. Heliotherapy, Josephine Baker's glistening
skin, Coco Chanel photographed on the French Riviera—tanned skin
was all the rage, and she smiled, remembering how she had gone to
great lengths to keep her complexion alabaster white. Once, she'd even
used a lightening powder with lead. And now all she saw were young tan
bodies, arms and faces and legs exposed and basking in the sun, soaking
up the restorative rays, white teeth flashing, and laughing at someone
like her, who still longed for a little bit of shade.

In front of his building, she lingered before the white roses spilling
from the planters. She admired their purity—white flowers were absolutely the best. A ladybug tentatively crawled down a green stem. She
ran her fingertips over the creamy petals. It was as if nature's beauty
magnified when she thought of him, of his gentle fingers running down
the length of her spine, as if her spine was a chain of rosary beads that
he so lovingly counted upon for reassurance, for evidence of God. But
not in the mystical sense Father Balthazar spoke of Him. She pressed
the buzzer, shuddering at how awful the last session had been. Father
Balthazar had felt the need to share his visions of an approaching apoca-
lypse with everyone. Most of his attendees were psychologically fragile,
but this didn't stop him. He described the snowcapped Alps of Austria drenched in blood, red rivers streaming down mountains, flooding towns and cities, oceans of blood. Whenever someone asked if he'd
made contact with a relative from the other side, he waved a dismissive hand and then launched into yet another discussion of his Blue
Book, a collection of his dreams, memories, and visions. The Blue Book
apparently reflected the world's psyche—the two were intertwined, he
insisted. Therefore, he could more or less see the future, and it was
covered in blood. When anyone from the group pressed him, he grew
petulant and said he could not possibly elaborate. But he assumed the
same ghostly pallor, the same mystical air as when he had spoken about
Franz many months ago, and it left Josephine with a foreboding chill.
    When she got to Dr. Dührkoop's office, she was overheated, and
having forgotten to eat lunch, she felt dizzy. She asked him to open the

other window behind his desk for cross ventilation, but the window was stuck from the recent rains. He made an offhanded gesture. "The only thing left to do is take off your blouse."

She blushed and unbuttoned her blouse. To fill the silence—he always required her to begin the conversation, even now, at this stage in their relationship—she told him how she couldn't help herself from mentioning his name to Lev. "I talk about you so often, he must be growing suspicious. But everything reminds me of you—the brand of tea we had yesterday was the same brand you drink, and I had to point out how the orchid in a shop window looked similar to the type you cultivate, and when we ran into some friends of ours, I complimented the man on his bowtie, thinking to myself that I would buy you one just like it. It was crimson, with little white polka dots."

He smiled good-naturedly and told her to continue.

"And I just," she said, sliding out of her silk blouse, "I just feel, when I say your name, I'm suddenly lifted out of that continuous wheel of domestic drudgery: supervising Marthe and ringing the plumbers because the tiles in the shower have come undone due to poor grouting, and now there's a leak under the staircase, and reminding Lev to speak to Herr Levenski because he cut down our hedges, once again, for the sake of his beloved roses, which are bloodred and, frankly, quite overdone."

She draped her blouse over the arm of the couch. Glancing down at her chest, she smiled appreciatively at her hardened nipples, which were making themselves known under the tight satin brassiere. "Lev barely protested when I said I couldn't attend Vicki's good-bye party this evening. As if he's almost giving me permission to be with you."

Dr. Dührkoop nodded. "As if his subconscious already knows."

"That's right," she said.

"We all know much more than we think we know." He went over to her and unclasped her brassiere, sliding it off her body. She drew her shoulder blades together and arched her back, a trick that made her breasts appear more pert. He balled up her bra and stuck it into his back pocket. Then he took a step away and said that he wanted to admire her from there, as if she were a Grecian goddess ascending from the bath. "Having washed yourself, surrounded by fauns and lush veg-etation, your fresh naked body only visible to me as you reach for your robes." He spoke excitedly, pushing the coffee table up against the wall to make more space in front of the chaise, where she lounged, enjoying the gentle breeze blowing over her bare torso. Feeling languorous and desired, she said how refreshing it was that he didn't always insist on mounting her, the way Lev did.

"Yes, well," the doctor said, giving the coffee table one last push, "I suppose that has to do with the innate lustiness of the Semitic peoples. You can't blame him, really."

After they made love, which was somewhat swift and brutal—for the first time, the doctor insisted upon entering from behind while Josephine balanced on hands and knees in the middle of the rug, he announced he had a surprise for her.

"Surprise?" she asked, nestling her face into the crook of his arm. They now lay on the chaise again, and Josephine was trying to forget about the last ten minutes. She supposed in some ways all men were the same—they found such erotic pleasure in not having to look into a woman's eyes during penetration, preferring a view of the buttocks, the back, the neck, as much more enticing than the open question on her face in that crucial moment. She sighed. "You've already surprised me quite a lot today."

He patted her naked thigh. She followed the shadows playing on the far wall and mentioned again that she felt guilty for missing Vicki's party this evening. "I suppose it's about to start, judging from the light."

"Hmmm," he said, his eyes closed.

"But if I went, it would seem as if I were giving her my blessing."

He murmured that she sounded exactly like her own mother when she ran off and married Lev.

"You're right," she said, twisting his nipple. "Maddeningly so."

"Ouch," he said, pulling her hand away.

Then she felt herself growing serious, and not knowing if she should say this next part, she said it anyway. "The truth is, I couldn't wait until Friday to see you. I couldn't wait the week out. It was too painful."

His fingers roved through her hair, which was down and loose around her shoulders. He pulled on it and tilted her head back a little. She continued, "When I'm not with you, I feel as if I'm lost, stranded on a barren island with these towering waves threatening to crash over me."

He sprung up from the couch. "Don't move." He went over to his desk and riffled through the drawers. He was naked, sitting behind his desk, and she was naked, lying on the chaise. Watching him, Josephine wondered if he'd even heard what she just said, or if he was willfully ignoring her, finding such an admission of need distasteful, overbearing? Glancing down at her white legs against the velvet cushions, she suddenly felt overly exposed, as if her translucent skin betrayed her, revealing the bluish-purple spider veins in delicate tangles on the outer edges of her thighs, and that ugly yellow bruise, the size of a coin, on her shin from forcing open a drawer—it had slammed into her leg after having been closed for so long.

"Ah, found it!" he exclaimed, startling her. He held up the retrieved item—a record. Then he trotted over to the gramophone, glancing down at the record sleeve. Giddy, buoyant, she enjoyed watching him like this, as if he had momentarily returned to boyhood. She rolled onto her stomach and balanced her chin on the arm of the chaise. He adjusted the needle to the correct track and motioned for her to come. She walked over, the late afternoon sun flashing against her bare white skin, and she pressed her back against his chest. He molded his hands over her ribcage. "Close your eyes," he whispered.

The rich, vibrating voices of Tristan and Isolde floated above them, singing their ghostly love duet: *O sink hernieder, Nacht der Liebe, gib Vergessen, dass ich lebe.* (Descend, oh Night of Love, grant oblivion that I may live.)

He whispered into her ear, "They're in the forest at night, together at last."

Her eyes flooded with tears, thinking how Tristan says the realm of daylight is false and unreal; the lovers will only be united in the long night of death.

The tenor's and soprano's voices swelled and bloomed, slipping and sliding over each other, rising and falling with each new declaration of love, just as the doctor's chest rose and fell against her back. She looked down at his young hands on her pale skin. He cupped her breasts and mumbled something into her neck. She knew he would want her for a little while, for as long as the night would last, allowing them to roam in the forest of their pleasure, but he would eventually cast her out and start a real life. It was why he had chosen to play her act 2, scene 2—an unconscious choice, of course, but even the doctor could not be entirely aware of the implications of his actions. None of us can, she thought.

44

Franz had awoken at first light, his chest pounding. He bolted upright, gripping his knees, his undershirt damp. It's the way of war, he thought, his hands now shaking as he affixed his removable white collar, starched and pressed, in front of the mirror. He would leave in one hour. All day he had prepared. The switchblade was inside his left pocket underneath his vest. He patted his chest, the faint outline of the knife comforting. If he happened to miss with his pistol, he would use the blade while everyone was still disoriented by the gunshots. This is what Wolf advised. They had met last night, and Wolf had said, "I'll be there, watching. The paramount thing is not to panic like the little woman you are." He had gripped Franz's shoulder, kneading it like dough, which left faint purple bruises. Franz noticed them this morning in the bath, and normally, he would've celebrated any evidence of Wolf on his body, but the bruises only indicated his weakness, the fragility of his skin. He picked up the handgun, which lay on his dresser, a Mauser C-96 9mm, used by Wolf's father, who had killed many French with it. A better story than his father's—he had returned with no gun, no uniform, no medals, dressed in tattered civilian clothes. He and his mother wondered what Lev had really done in that Russian town besides some translation and light desk work. "Fussy work" was what Franz called it. "An unwillingness to sacrifice oneself for the greater good" was what his mother had once said.

He sat down for a moment on the side of his bed. He stared at his knees—smooth, hairless. He could still back out. He started sweating at the thought of reversal, retreat. Wolf had already told their unit. Now, everyone knew about it, so it had to happen. Lutz even came up to him a few days ago and solemnly shook his hand, complimenting Franz on his good work, and then added, "We are well aware of the sacrifices you've made." Franz had said, "For Germany." And Lutz said, "For Germany." After this, it seemed there was a general air of reverence whenever Franz walked into a room. Men of higher rank nodded to him, and one of them invited him for lunch at his private club.

Franz picked up the gun, a recoil-operated, locked-breech, semi-automatic pistol. The safety was located at the left side of the hammer and locked the hammer when engaged. Its most recognizable feature was its nonremovable, fixed-box magazine, located ahead of the trigger guard, which could hold up to ten rounds. The other thing he liked about it was the beautifully shaped handle, lightweight and practical, and the wooden shoulder holster. He straightened his vest and slipped the Mauser into his inner chest pocket. Yes, it was slightly bulky, which was why he would wear a linen jacket over the vest. He parted his hair to the side and combed it down with some tonic. Leaning in closer to the mirror, he noticed a few hairs sprouting upward, refusing to stay down. He dipped the comb in more tonic and heard a knock on the door.

"Darling?"

"Yes, Mother."

She tried the door handle. He froze before the mirror.

"I'm going out now."

"Yes, Mother."

"I feel terrible about missing Vicki's party."

"Yes, Mother."

"But the meeting . . ." She paused.

He sat on the edge of the bed and smoothed down his pants.

"It's for the Association of Christian Mothers, and I . . ."

"You must go now, Mother. Don't be late."

"All right," she murmured.

Through his bedroom window, he watched her walking to the tram. She looked quite fetching lately, taking more care with herself. He admired her from a distance—her long white form, her wide-brimmed hat. He smiled, thinking how unfashionable it was to wear such an antique hat, but it was admirable, how she clung to that bygone era. Today, women were strident and ugly, flashing their bare flesh, shimmying their shoulders and thighs underneath the thinnest of sheaths. Walking down the street, they offered the same grotesque thrill as a peep show. He paced the room, breathing deeply. In part, he was doing this for her. She didn't deserve to flush with shame after services, when one of the church ladies asked about Vicki and she airily made up some lie about allergies or a toothache. How could she admit her only daughter was marrying an *Ostjude*? A disgrace. A sickening disgrace. He leaned out the open window, staring down at the red roses blooming with vigor. He projected a potent ball of spittle into the roses before slamming the window shut.

Walking to the tram, his pulse accelerated. He straightened his tie; this always calmed him. As long as he looked presentable, he felt capable, competent. The jacket worked well, hiding most of the bulk. He smoothed it down. Waiting for the streetlight to change, a man observed him, an old man in a worn-out suit. He tried to catch Franz's eye. Then he barked, "I like your jacket!"

Franz winced, feeling his nerves sharpen.

"White! Gets dirty easy!" the man added.

"Yes, it does," Franz replied, willing the light to change.

"But you can always launder it!"

"You can, yes."

The light changed. Franz walked briskly away from the man, who lumbered after him, clutching his walking stick. The man smiled benignly at another passing pedestrian. Some people just like to chat; he didn't notice anything in particular, Franz thought. I just have to get on the train to Moritzplatz without incident. It's a simple plan, he told himself.

On the train, he sat next to two women who smelled of strong perfume. It nauseated him. They talked about a purse. A beaded purse without a handle. A clutch, they called it. They both wanted one, but the purse was too expensive.

"A week's salary!" the girl exclaimed.

The other woman nodded sadly. "But if I work overtime," she said, bumping his shoulder. Franz jerked away. "Excuse me!" he said hotly.

Both of the girls smiled with condescension. The train rattled and swayed, pushing her into him again.

"Is a woman's touch so repellent?" she joked. She had no eyebrows and reminded him of a ferret.

Franz stared at the man across from them, leafing through the paper, bored.

"Well," the other girl said, "you can't win over everyone." Then they erupted into inane laughter.

Franz clenched his jaw, thinking he had already drawn unwanted attention. Possibly, they could sense how much he wished to be left alone, which only spurred them on. After a few moments, their laughter subsided and they resumed their discussion about the clutch.

Franz felt his head empty and grow light. It was really happening.

45

Monday, June 11, 1928

Maya flipped through a film magazine on the bed, a glass of iced tea on the side table next to her. She leaned over and took a long sip from the straw. Vicki smiled at her through the smudged mirror propped up against the wall. She was getting ready for the party. The small bedroom in Maya's apartment trapped the late afternoon heat. The sun beat against the green shutters, which had been opened at a slant, allowing a small amount of air into the room, but not enough.

Vicki gestured at Maya's languid pose. "Enjoy this while it lasts."

Maya looked up from an article, the page spilling open to reveal a large black-and-white photograph of the film star Lil Dagover wearing a snowy-white mink.

Maya shrugged, one strap of her slip sliding off her shoulder. "At least there'll be straws in Palestine. I hate drinking without one. Ice makes my teeth ache."

Vicki stepped into her dress. "There won't be straws."

Maya tossed the magazine aside. "Of course there will be!"

"Can you zip me up?"

Maya sighed and got up from the bed. Standing behind Vicki, she said, "You paint such a black picture."

"It's only . . ." She paused, waiting for Maya to finish gliding up the zipper. "They keep telling us how hard life will be, how much work needs to be done. When will we have any time to enjoy ourselves? Isn't that important too?"

Maya turned Vicki around to face her. "They say this because they

433

want people to immigrate who are truly committed. No dilettantes need apply."

"I'm not a dilettante!"

Maya tried to hold back her laughter. "I never said that."

Vicki looked down at her dress, a soft cream shift with two deep front pockets. "Is this too plain?"

"It's perfect."

Vicki forced a smile, but warring thoughts flitted through her head. She pressed her thumbs into her temples. Should she wear the lapis earrings her father gave her, or was that too sentimental? In the next room, someone flipped the radio dial through the stations, pausing on a jazz quartet. That would be all right, if they played jazz. Had they purchased enough alcohol for the party? Her father would hate this place, hovering on the edge of conversations in his three-piece suit. She could already envision him tasting the cheap wine with displeasure. And her mother had developed another one of her famous migraines.

It was Monday and they were leaving Thursday. Three days. Half of Vicki's things were packed in boxes standing in the middle of her room, the other half strewn around this apartment. In the past weeks, she'd been sleeping here most nights, sharing a bed with Maya, preparing coffee for Zev and Geza in the morning, going over lists and supplies they would need, their collective life already taking shape. Sometimes, it jarred her when Maya, wearing one of Vicki's dresses, a dress she favored, accidentally splashed black tea onto it. Conveniently, Maya only stained Vicki's dresses while somehow making sure her own dresses remained pristine. But then Vicki would push this thought away, because they shared everything now, and she reminded herself that the idea of personal belongings was petty and overly individualistic. On the collective farms, women even shared the burden of breast-feeding, the children belonging to everyone. And so owning a dress, saying it was yours, carried no weight in the Holy Land.

Maya was now rummaging through a box of clothes. "Everything's already packed. I can't find anything to wear. Did you hear the Katz twins might stop by?"

Vicki shook her head, deciding she would wear the earrings. She remembered when her father gave them to her as a present last year, before she'd even met Geza. How odd it was: only a year ago she was dreading French exams and fighting with her mother about cutting off her hair, and then she went to the library and her life changed. Forever.

Maya sighed with exasperation, a lavender dress draped over her shoulder. Actually, it was once Vicki's lavender dress, the one with the low-slung sash.

"And the sculptress Renée Sintenis."

"She's coming?" Vicki moved her head from side to side, pleased with how the hanging lapis earrings swayed along with her.

A string of beads hung from Maya's forefinger. The lapis beads that were meant to match Vicki's earrings. "You don't mind, do you, if I wear this tonight?"

"I . . ." Vicki began. A lump gathered in her throat.

The bedroom door swung open, and Zev stood there in his suspenders and white undershirt. "Hello ladies! You're looking lovely."

Maya charged him with a pillow. "We're only half dressed!"

He grabbed her waist and pulled her into him. She half struggled to get free.

"This black slip is more than enough clothing," he murmured.

Vicki glanced away, embarrassed. Breaking the silence, she asked, "Where's Geza?"

Maya had freed herself and was now sliding the lavender dress over her head.

"He went to get tea lights," Zev said.

"It's not a funeral," Maya protested, turning around so that Zev could button up the back.

"Candles are festive," he added.

"Candlelight makes everyone beautiful," Vicki said, stepping into her high heels.

The party had started an hour ago, and already the room was buzzing. A woman in a headscarf was talking to Vicki about the need for nurses.

And elementary school teachers. Her hand skimmed Vicki's bare shoulder. "Making the desert bloom is not just an agricultural endeavor."

"I see," Vicki said, scanning the room for her father, wondering if he'd arrived yet. The woman's black eyes, the way she held her gaze so intensely, made Vicki nervous.

"But you see," the woman resumed, undeterred, "the children are raised in communal children's homes. Mothers work in Palestine!"

Vicki nodded, noticing that Greta, her old school friend, was talking to Maya. It gave her a funny feeling to see them together, as if two disparate parts of her life had collided for a moment, before floating away again. She was surprised Greta even came; they hadn't seen each other in months, and when they spoke for a few minutes, trading polite questions over the thumping jazz, Greta appeared ill at ease. She had overdressed for the party and tugged nervously at her gloves. Well, Vicki thought, watching the woman's chapped lips form words and sentences about communal child care, Greta was in love with her brother, something she wouldn't wish on any woman, seeing how he avoided her, stationed on the other side of the room in deep conversation with Wolf. Every so often Greta's gaze floated over to the fireplace, where Wolf and Franz stood, using the mantel as a base, as if it was their own little fiefdom.

"Scheduled breast feedings provide relief for active mothers," the woman intoned. "For example, while you work in the olive groves, I breast-feed your child, and vice versa. They are all our children."

"Hmmm," Vicki said, trying to catch Franz's eye, hoping he'd come over to her, but he stared at the floor while Wolf whispered something into his ear.

A little girl tugged on Vicki's hem. She made a squawking sound and stared up at her mother with round anxious eyes.

"Oh, Netta." The woman hoisted the little girl up onto her hip. "What are you doing?"

The girl scrutinized Vicki's earrings, her little fists clutching her mother's blouse.

Vicki smiled. "Do you like them?"

She buried her face into her mother's shoulder while still peeking at Vicki, her eyes trained on the dangling lapis stones.

The woman smiled apologetically. "All the new people here make her shy. She's normally very independent."

Vicki excused herself and went outside to find Geza, who had disappeared from the party. She flattened her body, pushing through the crowd, but was stopped various times along the way by well-wishers, congratulating her on making aliyah, their drinks raised upward, as if the Holy Land hovered just above their heads.

The night had cooled. She paused a moment on the landing, listening to that language her mother shunned and her father hid away, a language that carried an elusive taboo, a language she now used with ease, the syllables having grown familiar on her tongue, despite how Geza kept telling her Hebrew, not Yiddish, was their new language, and she must keep practicing. She saw Geza and her father sitting side by side on the top step, their backs hunched over in the same way, their kneecaps nearly touching. But then Geza said something that made her father's back stiffen, and she called out, "Having secret conversations without me?"

They turned around and produced the same jovial grin.

She motioned to her father. "You're here."

He stared at her, his face mournful and tired, and she felt a stab of guilt. He got up and announced, "Tonight is a celebration. Where's the champagne?"

The three of them walked arm in arm back into the hot living room. Out of the corner of her eye, Vicki saw Maya talking to the woman in the headscarf. The little girl wandered nearby, clutching a stranger's leg that she mistook for her mother's. Maya waved Vicki over, but Geza pulled her in close, and she turned away from Maya to kiss him, inhaling his scent. For a moment, the hum and flow of the party froze, and she felt as if it were just Geza and herself encased in a cocoon, and the rest—the music, the people, her friends—stood outside of it. Was this love, to feel so closely tied to one person that the world, with all the people in it, existed apart from the intimate knowledge that passed between them?

She traced her finger along his lower lip, and he squeezed her shoulder, tilting his head toward the crowd. "I'm going to make sure no one's glass is empty."

Their intertwined hands broke apart.

Lev took Vicki's arm. "Keep me company for a while—I don't know anyone here," he whispered.

Vicki giggled. "But you've always been so good at mingling, Papa."

Lev shook his head. "No, that's your mother."

Despite all the music and chatter, and the heat of other bodies jostling past them, she gave him a long look. His dark eyes were glassy, radiating a faint melancholic light. "Is there something—" She paused.

Lev threw up his hands. "Whatever happened to that champagne I brought?"

She started again. "Papa—is there something you're keeping from me?"

Someone turned up the music. A few couples started dancing the Charleston in the middle of the room, their feet pounding on the wooden floor.

"Because we've always told each other everything," she added, trying to suppress the sensation she might cry right there in the middle of the party, with everyone looking.

He stroked her cheek. "You've always been so very astute." Breaking into his sunniest smile, he added, raising his voice, "Go dance—don't worry about your old papa. Everything's as it should be." He stepped back, taking a little bow.

The music thumped through her, vibrating up her legs, into her chest. "But Papa," she said, reaching for his arm. She wouldn't give up this easily. Even if Geza evaded her, her father would not.

Lev grinned again. "Where's Geza? You two should be dancing!"

Vicki glanced over her shoulder and saw Geza pouring beer into a long glass, making a show of it, while a man wearing a panama hat laughed. Then she saw Zev spin around, his face tight with anger. He punched Franz in the arm, but Franz kept moving toward Geza as if he had something urgent to say. Her father's face clouded over, and for a moment their eyes met, and she felt her throat tighten and go dry. She tried to scream but she was breathless. Lev grabbed her arm and pulled her down to the floor before leaping up and hurling himself into Geza. A gunshot ricocheted through the room.

46

Tonight, he would get the information from Geza about Leah's whereabouts. Geza had promised him this much, and he knew that in the meantime, Geza had made inquiries, writing to Leah's relatives in Riga and Mitau. But what if Geza hadn't received any news yet? What if letters were lost in the mail? If Leah wasn't in New York, Lev would abandon the lie he had already told Josephine about Rhodes Hart textiles and pretend the linen deal had fallen through. Or, if she was there, he must book his ticket, confirm first class, and prepare. Prepare to meet his son. Prepare to see Leah again and reopen the wound of having left her in the first place. But the uncertainty was driving him mad, as if he could only ever balance on one foot, and was eternally hopping from one to the other like a dancing monkey. During dinner last night, he tried to contain his anxiety, pouring himself a generous glass of red wine. He listened to Josephine go on about a certain kind of orchid. She wanted some for the rooms upstairs. He nodded in agreement. She added that Dr. Dührkoop kept the same orchids in his office and they were absolutely stunning as well as resilient. Then he made some quip about how everything Dührkoop had must be fabulous. Josephine scowled and left the table.

Either way, he would find something out tonight. Walking in this unfamiliar part of town, he mused over his situation and smiled sardonically. How many men, he wondered, glancing down the street, carried the burden of an icy wife, a long-lost son, an old lover in a foreign land, children who were choosing to leave him behind, each in their own particularly painful way?

He sighed, readjusting the bundle of lilies he carried, careful not to crush them. In his other hand, he held a bottle of champagne, relishing its coolness through the paper wrapping. Where was Zev Dubinsky's apartment anyway? He hadn't been around here in years, having become insulated by the streets connecting his house to his office and to the park. He frequented the same cafés and bars along Unter den Linden and on occasion made a foray into the city center when he was feeling restless. But Treptow: Red, working-class, the streets darker and dirtier than the verdant light-filled parks of Charlottenburg. It made him depressed. He trudged along, checking the street addresses. Judging from the sidewalk littered with pamphlets and a torn KPD banner, there must have been a recent rally. He stepped over the banner, strewn with leaves. Was he in the right place? He was about to ask the news vendor outside a tobacco shop when a young couple walked up to a building, smiling shyly at him before climbing the steps. She carried a bundle of tulips wrapped in newspaper and his hand floated over the small of her back. A woman opened the door and welcomed them in Hebrew. This must be the place, Lev thought, straining to see through the linen curtains into the front room where people milled about. He suddenly felt apprehensive and stood there watching the hostess, who smiled at him in a fitted lavender dress, a dress he faintly recalled Vicki wearing. She beckoned him inside, and with her shiny hair and dark lipstick, she looked too cosmopolitan for this group of earnest pioneers.

"Welcome, welcome," she said to him, taking his coat and his hat. "You must be Vicki's father," she added, flashing another smile.

"Yes," Lev said, wondering if he really looked so old. Or was it a certain paternalistic air he gave off, both anxious and judgmental, as he surveyed the room?

"Who else would bring such a nice bottle of champagne, and these stunning lilies?"

Lev smiled politely and the young woman, now cradling the flowers against her breast, introduced herself as Maya—Maya Dubinsky. The name echoed in Lev's head—she was one of Vicki's new friends, also immigrating to Palestine. On the same ship, he believed. She took his arm and offered him some kvass. Noticing his hesitation, she asked,

"Or wine?" He nodded and she melted into the crowded living room, heading toward the kitchen. He admired Maya's Levantine eyes, her long back, the way that dress clung to her body.

Lev hovered on the threshold, wondering where Vicki was and wishing he had a drink to hold in his hand. The place, packed with young people, was decorated in the Bauhaus style, but on the cheap, so instead of appearing linear and Spartan it looked as if they could only afford one glass table, one iron lamp, one plush cube-shaped chair, and against the wall, one long metal bookcase crammed with used books. Jazz blasted from the radio balanced on top of the radiator. Hors d'oeuvres had been hastily assembled and put out on the coffee table without much thought to their presentation. A mixture of Yiddish, Hebrew, Russian, German, and Polish whizzed around the room. An aggressive-looking type hooked his arm around Maya's waist and gave her a kiss. That must be her husband—Zvi, or Zev? He looked like a Polish Jew with that fiery mustache and stocky build. And he seemed quite proud of his prize: Maya's French accent and slanted eyes, a sexy pioneer for sure. Lev grinned. But at least this Zev didn't carry around the same look of blank fear the other young men here did—it was strange, such strong youthful men with prominent jaws and broad chests and muscled forearms, they wandered around the room in a trance, as if they didn't know how they'd arrived at this point, about to cross the great ocean, the future a murky promise. Maybe the strong *halutzim* weren't so strong, Lev thought. But the women were right at home. They chatted comfortably with one another, alight with laughter, their eyes flitting around the room. They refilled drinks and rearranged the platters of pickled vegetables. Without women, Lev mused, taking in the blank white walls and the oblong glass vases devoid of flowers, there would be nothing. Against the far back wall, he was surprised to see his mother chatting with the rabbi's wife, who wore an expensive-looking hat, peacock feathers plastered to the side of it. His mother caught his eye and waved him over impatiently. She probably wanted him to talk with the rabbi's wife, to fall in love with her, and leave Josephine. He overheard a young man discussing the kinds of trees that grew in the Holy Land. "Olive and fig and orange," the man said. "Maybe lemon too."

"Citrus? I doubt that," a woman rejoined. "But definitely almond trees, the ones with the white blossoms. So lovely."

"Lev!" Geza yelled, weaving through the crowd with two glasses of beer. He hugged him with one arm, and Lev felt relieved that at least Geza was not wearing *peyes* and a yarmulke, as some of the young men here did, but had cropped his hair short and was clean-shaven. His dark eyes sparkled when he gestured to Vicki, explaining how Maya had taken Vicki under her wing, helped her along in the process, which was important and would be even more so once they arrived there. Then, as an afterthought, he asked about Josephine, and Lev explained she was home in bed with a migraine. Really, though, he wasn't sure where she was.

Lev squinted through the crowd at Wolf, who leaned against the mantel, smoking. He was overdressed in a three-piece suit and shiny spats, and although he tried to appear casual, the way he smoked his cigarette and declined the offer of a drink all seemed oddly choreographed.

Geza waved to some men, both rugged and of towering height. They ate herring smeared on black bread and waved back, their mouths full and chewing. They have no manners, Lev thought, trying not to linger on the idea that in Palestine, Vicki would be surrounded by these types, that she might come to think, within a few years, that it was acceptable to eat while standing, to greet a guest while munching on a hunk of bread, and forgo the use of a napkin because it was a bourgeois pleasantry. *Barbarians!*

Geza took Lev's arm. "Can we speak?"

They sat outside on the steps. Geza began in Yiddish, "First, I want to thank you. For helping us with the passage fare."

Lev answered in German, "This way, at least, you won't have to travel between decks in steerage. It will be more comfortable."

"Yes, more comfortable." Geza paused. "I have the information you asked for." He reached into his breast pocket and pulled out a scrap of paper.

Lev took it. The paper, the words, burned through his palm: *11 Rivington Street, Apartment 3B, New York, New York.* He stared at the address. "Well," his voice softened, "she's in New York," he added in Yiddish.

"What are you going to do?"

Lev folded his hand over the paper. "I'm going to New York."

Geza sighed. "I understand, but . . ."

Lev took his arm. "What is it? Is there something else you're not telling me?"

"No, no. Nothing else. Her cousin in Riga sent this address after I requested it."

"Yes, but what if she's met someone? What if her circumstances have changed?"

Geza smoked with a stoic expression on his face. Lev felt a flash of irritation—how easily Geza sat here, witnessing the uneasy mixture of excitement, panic, and fear flooding through him.

Lev stubbed out his cigarette on the step and took a deep breath. "Thank you. For the address." He patted Geza's knee, giving his next words added weight. "And thank you for keeping this between us."

Geza jutted his chin forward. "We give and we take."

"There you are!" Vicki called from the open doorway. "Having secret conversations without me."

They both twisted around, jarred by her voice.

She stepped away from the bright warm room and walked out onto the landing, hands on her hips. Her eyes, luminous in the lamplight, chastised them. She wore the earrings Lev had given her last year, the lapis lazuli ones from Wertheim's. He wondered if she would wear them in Palestine, or if such items would be deemed culturally unnecessary, distracting baubles.

Lev stood up, touched her face.

"You came," she whispered, looking as if she might cry.

"Of course!" Lev said, slipping the piece of paper into his trouser pocket. "Now where's that excellent bottle of champagne I brought? Or have the barbarians already devoured that as well?"

They went back inside, Geza's arm linked around Vicki's waist, and Lev's arm draped over Vicki's shoulders. Glancing over at her smiling face, the way she kissed Geza on the cheek and he pulled her close, Lev knew, as much as he resisted it, this was whom she had chosen. And this choice would dictate the way she was going to live, raise her children. All this future reverberated between them as they walked hand in hand back into the party.

The number of people in the room had multiplied. Maya wanted to introduce Vicki to a woman in a headscarf, who held a small child to her chest. Geza said he wanted to make sure no one's glass stood empty.

Before she could disappear into the crowded room, Lev took Vicki's arm. Her skin still felt as warm and milky as it did when she used to throw her small arms around his neck, begging to be carried.

"Keep me company for a while—I don't know anyone here," Lev whispered.

Vicki giggled. "But you've always been so good at mingling, Papa."

Lev shook his head. "No, that's your mother."

Vicki gave him a long look, her large eyes watering. "Is there something—" She paused.

Lev motioned to the makeshift bar in the corner. "Let's have some champagne!"

She started again. "Papa—is there something you're keeping from me?"

He smiled immediately, trying to mask the panic spreading through him. Did Geza say something to her? Make some sort of allusion? He could tell Vicki didn't know everything, but she knew something.

Someone turned up the music. A few couples started dancing the Charleston in the middle of the room, their feet pounding on the wooden floor.

"Because we've always told each other everything," she added, glancing down. Her face turned blotchy and flushed, the way she looked when she cried.

He stroked her cheek. "So astute." Breaking into his most winning smile, he added, his voice sounding overly loud and false to him, "Go dance—don't worry about your old papa. Everything's as it should be." Then he took a step back, bending slightly at the hip. He wanted Vicki to dance with the others, to revel in the freedom of youth and new love, to revel in all the things he felt he had lost.

"But Papa," she said, reaching for him. Lev could see she wasn't willing to forfeit so easily. What had Geza told her?

He grinned again, trying to suppress the mounting anxiety that everything would soon crack open. "Where's Geza? You two should be dancing!"

Vicki shook her head, exasperated.

Out of the corner of his eye, Lev saw Franz making his way toward Geza. A stern concentration clouded his face. He went swiftly, economizing each movement. Wolf followed Franz closely, as if tracking him. A sharp unpleasantness pricked Lev's tongue. Both boys were tense, their eyes bright and jumping. Lev wondered if they were leaving because of some heated argument. He recalled how Wolf had once fancied Vicki. Perhaps Wolf had said something nasty to one of the *halutzim*. Inside his pocket, Lev clenched Leah's address.

Franz reached under his jacket into his vest, his elbow jutting out, which accidentally jabbed Zev's shoulder. Geza was pouring a drink for a man wearing a panama hat. The stream of brown liquid tunneled from the bottle into a long glass. Zev swung around and punched Franz in the neck, missing his face, but Franz kept moving, and the short jerky way Franz's arm had reached into his vest sent Lev into motion. He pulled Vicki down to the ground and then leapt up, pushing a man in wire-rim glasses aside, reaching for Geza. At the deafening sound of gunfire, Lev embraced him, the two of them hurtling to the floor. The woman in the headscarf screamed. Lev clutched Geza's chest and saw blood. A smarting pain seared through his shoulder and forearm. His whole body throbbed. Some of the women were crying. Overturned chairs blocked the doorway.

Zev cursed at the top of his voice, "Where did that bastard run to?"

Franz and Wolf were gone.

Zev, Geza, and a pack of men ran out into the night. The front door swung open. Vicki clutched Lev's good arm and yelled for help. Maya was comforting the woman with the headscarf, who was still screaming.

Her baby crawled the perimeter of the room, playing with a wooden spoon. Someone had knocked over the radio and it now lay on its side, emitting static. Whiteness started pressing down around his eyes, and Lev faintly asked someone to call an ambulance. Vicki nodded and said something he didn't understand.

"Wait," Lev whispered, gripping Vicki's wrist. "Is Geza all right?"

She nodded, tears streaming down her face. Then she faded out of his field of vision, replaced by the rabbi's wife, who bent over him and took his face in her cool hands. "It's mainly your shoulder. The ambulance will be here soon. Can you feel your right arm?"

"I think," he said, his mouth as dry as cotton.

The woman moved his head onto her lap and elevated his arm above his chest. "Hold it up?"

He nodded, staring at the chandelier, which was missing two lightbulbs.

She ripped off the arm of her blouse and tightly wrapped the silken sleeve around his wound. "What is your level of pain, on a scale of one to ten?" she demanded.

"Ridiculous questions," Lev sputtered. He noticed his mother peering over them. She looked anxious and shook her head. "No matter what the circumstances, he always has to argue."

The rabbi's wife smiled, and again Lev noticed her crowded bottom teeth—he wondered why some people had good teeth and others didn't.

Ambulance bells rang down the street, coming closer.

47

After two weeks, Lev came home from the hospital, his arm in a sling. He had suffered nerve, muscle, and tissue damage. Shredded tendons. The exit wound, larger than the entry wound, was healing more slowly than expected. After the long hours of surgery during which the bullet was excised, they dressed the wound and then immobilized the limb in a plaster of Paris splint. Lev now carried his plastered limb around in a sling over his chest. The doctor told him he would lose movement in his arm, but how much he couldn't yet say. Right now, it just felt numb, and it itched. When he returned home, Marthe was the only one who acted normally. She made up his room with flowers from the garden and fresh-smelling sheets. She fed him barley soup and prepared his favorite dish, knishes, or as Marthe called them, dumplings, filled with potato and cheese, slightly browned in the oven so that the edges were crispy.

Vicki floated through the house, her eyes glazed with tears, her feet encased in a pair of burgundy slippers she refused to take off. She always looked as if she had just been crying, her eyes swollen and bloodshot. She had decided to move home until things settled, but the settling of anything seemed quite far off to Lev.

Franz had disappeared the night of the shooting, along with Wolf. Zev, Geza, and a handful of Zionists scoured the city for them. The Berlin police were also on the search. They paid visits to Josephine, Lev, and Vicki at the house, questioning each one of them about Franz's whereabouts.

Vicki assured Lev and Josephine that Geza was not planning to kill Franz. "After all, Franz will be his brother-in-law. But he wants justice.

We all do," she said, adding that Geza still feared for his life, and that Wolf, not Franz, was most likely the true culprit.

Yesterday, when Geza came to the house to visit Vicki, he took Lev aside and told him there was a warrant out for Franz's arrest, for attempted murder. The Berlin police were searching for Wolf too, as an accomplice. Geza promised Lev they did not want more blood. "If it wasn't for you, I would be dead," he added. "And he could return anytime to kill me. With his SA brothers."

Lev shook his head, feeling the burden of standing, as if he could barely support himself. He wanted to lie down, drink something cold. His arm throbbed. He steadied himself against the marble table in the entryway. "You know, when I found out he'd joined the SA, I did nothing."

Geza pursed his lips. "Yes, but . . ."

Lev clasped Geza's arm. "And now he's scared, on the run somewhere—he never would have done it without Wolf. You must understand this."

Geza gently removed Lev's hand. "But he did it."

Lev sighed, thinking about this conversation with Geza, padding through the halls in his socks. He hadn't the strength to ask Geza if he'd said anything to Vicki about Leah—and it seemed Vicki had moved on to more pressing matters anyway. She'd spent many hours alone with Lev, sitting at his bedside, and she could have easily used such an opportunity to ask him again about the secrets she knew he kept from her, but she didn't. Instead, Vicki fussed over him, fluffing his pillow and worrying that he didn't eat enough, imploring the nurses for better food, different food. She insisted on shaving his stubble and even used his favorite lemony aftershave so he smelled more like himself, less like starched hospital sheets.

Lev stopped short, listening to Vicki and Geza whispering in the sitting room. They thought he was sleeping upstairs and had left the door half-open. They disagreed over something, and, no longer whispering, their voices grew sharp. Lev took small quiet breaths, pressing his back against the wall.

They talked about how their trip to Palestine had been delayed; she and Geza planned to take another ship in a month's time, but Vicki felt uncertain.

"I can't leave now. Papa's barely healed. And Franz's disappearance. . ."

Geza sighed heavily. "Vicki. Listen to me. That is precisely why we must leave as soon as possible. If there ever was a sign—"

"A sign, a sign. Yes, I know—more Jews are getting killed, lynched. This is only the beginning."

"If your brother had another chance, he would try to kill me again."

Lev heard Vicki emit a hoarse sob. He hung his head—of course, some would call his son a murderer. And now it was too late—Franz had slipped out of his grasp into the hands of violence. Franz, half-human, half-animal, winged with the head of a lion, groaning in the moonlight, flickered before him. Yes, he had been forewarned. He should have known.

Vicki stood up from the sofa, and Lev backed away from the door. She paced the room. "The police have been notified of Franz's disappearance. They'll find him and throw him in prison, or worse. But I know it was Wolf. Wolf was the one who put him up to it. He's always acted strangely toward me."

"Vicki, I can't wait here like a sitting duck, wondering when I'll get a bullet through my back."

"Please don't hate him!"

Lev watched through the doorjamb. Geza now walked over to the window, where Vicki stood, her arms crossed over her chest. He whispered something into her hair and embraced her. She dissolved into his arms, and he rested his chin on her head, his eyes scanning the street.

Well, Lev thought, they will leave Berlin. Geza will convince her. And he was right—it was dangerous for him to stay here. Vicki would see this when she calmed down, when things settled, as they all kept saying. Lev smiled halfheartedly. At least he still had Leah's address in New York. When they released him from the hospital, his clothes had been folded into a neat square bundle, wrapped in brown paper, tied with a white string. His shirt was gone, but his trousers and socks, watch, wallet, cufflinks, and bowtie had been preserved. Before Marthe could get to it, Lev unwrapped the package, and as if receiving a present, he found the scrap of paper still inside his front trouser pocket, her address on it. Thank God. He stowed it away in the top drawer of his bedside table. When he went to sleep, he stared at the closed drawer, knowing that when he was better, he would get to New York.

Since Franz's disappearance, Josephine had fallen into a veritable depression. She stopped changing out of her silk pajamas. She took all her meals in bed on a tray, leaving most of the food untouched. When Lev suggested she at least rouse herself to see Dr. Dührkoop, she cast him a withering stare, as if the very notion was wildly insulting.

"What good can the good doctor do me now? Franz is gone, and it's my fault he's gone," she had said.

When he tried to console her, she burst into hysterics, moaning how she knew something was wrong, could sense it, but she'd been overly involved in her own affairs, too selfish to detect his troubles budding before her. The only thing that comforted her was the idea of hiring a private investigator to find Franz and to inquire into the events of that night. Perhaps he'd been threatened prior to the party? Perhaps it was an act of self-defense? Perhaps Zev, and the rest of those Zionists, had provoked him to violence? When Lev said no, he had been at the party and had seen it happen, and nothing of the sort took place, Josephine sunk back into her soft pillows and covered her face with her hand, and whispered, "I'm tired. Leave me alone."

Lev sat on the edge of her bed, his arm in the sling. Even though he was the one who had been shot, Josephine suffered a harder blow. She rambled on about Father Balthazar, how right he had been, how she should return there. But she never left the house. Her migraines multiplied. She couldn't sleep at night, so she slept fitfully during the day. For once, she and Vicki agreed on something: it was Wolf, not Franz, who held the blame. Wolf became the house villain, the dark force tearing their family apart, the one they must steel themselves against. But Lev knew better—he blamed Franz *and* he loved him. He wanted to scream at his son and rock him in his arms. The women, though, they had to take sides.

48

One month later, Geza, Vicki, and Lev drove from Berlin to Hamburg. Nothing had been settled. Franz was still missing. If the police found him, he would be charged with attempted murder, followed by a prison sentence. How long the imprisonment would last they still didn't know. Josephine threw herself into daily hysterical fits, even when Lev told her there were ways to appeal this. Lev, when he spoke with his lawyers, took copious notes to understand each eventuality. He had only just begun to familiarize himself with the new language of legal jargon, and he kept turning over various terms in his mind, as if the repetition would provide some clarity. He had even arranged a meeting with Wolf's mother, who had received him coldly and told him she knew nothing of her son's whereabouts, although there was a rumor Wolf had fled to Vienna.

The drive had been long and silent as each one of them contemplated what lay ahead. Because of Lev's arm, still in a sling, Geza drove, and Vicki sat in the backseat, with suitcases piled up next to her. In three hours, Vicki and Geza would be boarding the RMS *Mauretania*. The steamship would travel up the Elbe into the mouth of the river, which spilled out into the open, unprotected North Sea. They would then pass through two straits: the Strait of Dover and the Strait of Gibraltar. Once they entered the Mediterranean, Palestine would be waiting for them, blazing with harsh heat. Or maybe not. Maybe they would find refuge in the shaded warmth of olive groves. Maybe they would eat oranges for lunch and swim in the sea. Maybe they would marvel at the fecundity of the summer harvest and feast at a long wooden table, sharing bread and wine and stories. This is what Lev hoped for her, despite his misgivings, despite his fear that she would live a difficult life full of rocky soil and blistering sun, of backbreaking labor and little luxury. He had not prepared Vicki for this. He had not brought her up to work with her hands, to chop onions in a kitchen filled with other women chopping onions. He tried to act happy, but he was not. And she knew it. But what could he say, after Franz had tried to kill Geza?

There was nothing left to say. Except farewell, safe journey, write often, at least once a week—I'll worry otherwise. I'll become sick with worry. No—he couldn't say this last part because he was already sick with worry, they all were, after the shooting. Instead of the jubilant car ride and the confetti-filled departure Lev knew Vicki had imagined for herself, they were somber, introspective, each peering out a separate car window.

He had to appear calm and encouraging. It was his role and they expected him to fulfill it, even on such a morning as this, with the fog clearing and the cargo ships docking in the port, dwarfing Vicki and Geza. They gazed up at the massive steamers that appeared like moving buildings with rows and rows of little windows out of which an occasional person would stare down at them.

Perched on their suitcases, Geza and Vicki fussed over their belongings, wondering where Zev and Maya were. Lev teased, "Maybe they changed their mind at the last minute, decided Berlin wasn't all bad." But then he stopped, noting the anxiety on their faces. Of course. They imagined something much worse: Wolf and his SA friends had resurfaced, taken Zev by surprise.

Vicki frowned. Geza slid their passports into his vest pocket.

At least, Lev thought, lighting a cigarette, the Mediterranean was warm and temperate, more hospitable than the Baltic or the North Sea. Taking off his jacket, he winced. The dull pain in his shoulder caught him off guard, but the wound was healing. Slowly. Despite tissue damage, there was minimal infection. His jacket hung off one arm. Vicki was too preoccupied with organizing various documents to notice. Geza chatted with another family about the trip over, what supplies he had packed, and the family nodded at him with trust and approval. They glanced over at Lev, and Geza explained that Lev wasn't coming. The father and mother, Jews from the east, gave him a sympathetic glance, their faces full of pity.

The morning turned into a humid, overcast day with the sense that the sky was pressing down on them. They stood together on the dock, eyeing the gleaming white *Mauretania*, with its woven life rafts dangling from either side of the deck. Up top, the crew arranged sun chairs for the more fortunate passengers, and Lev felt a small shred of comfort that at least, if Vicki wanted, she could lie in one of those chairs and take in the air. Other families were saying good-bye. Other girls Vicki's age hugged their mothers and fathers. Lev stared at the parents with a sense of shared loss. He almost felt the urge to ask them about their children, why they were leaving, but he stopped himself from making such a sad spectacle, from seeking commiseration with strangers.

"Oh, Papa. Let me help you." Vicki slid his jacket off his arm.

"Thank you, *liebling*."

She gave him a halfhearted smile. "You'll come visit?"

"And stay in a hut without a proper toilet?"

"You make it sound so barbaric."

"Well," Lev said dryly, "it is."

She swept the hair out of her face and tried to appear as if his comment didn't bother her.

Lev gestured to Geza, who was immersed in a discussion with the same family about how best to combat seasickness. "He's good at taking care of things."

She folded Lev's jacket over her arm. "We take care of each other."

Lev murmured, "Of course."

She touched his good arm, and he felt her motherly gaze upon him. "You'll be all right?"

"Yes," he repeated automatically, embracing her. He inhaled her clean hair, closing his eyes.

She looked up at him, touched his face. "You'll send word—if Franz turns up?"

"Of course I will, *liebling*."

.   .   .

Already, a queue had formed alongside the docked ship. The passengers eyed the vessel as if it were a living breathing entity that would either destroy or brighten their lives. The crew members lowered the gangplank. And that sound, the distinctive whistle of steam releasing through the smokestacks, flooded Lev with a sharp fear. He hugged Vicki closer. His shoulder throbbed.

Geza hovered on the outskirts of their embrace before stating rather formally, "We should collect our things."

Vicki let go of him, her lips pursed. He could tell she was trying not to cry, and he yearned to hold her a little longer.

People started boarding. Geza and Vicki stood there restlessly, wondering if they should get on too. "I don't want to be late," Vicki said, glancing around at the other families lining up.

"What difference does it make? The berths are reserved. In a few weeks, you'll be wishing you could jump off that ship."

Vicki smiled, but the way she fidgeted with her gloves and gazed with longing at the steamer betrayed her—she couldn't wait to leave him behind. It was so characteristic of youth, to rush into the future as if one's present circumstances proved anachronistic to the point of embarrassment. A luxury, really, for life to feel so suddenly intolerable you could immediately alter it, whereas Lev, in middle age, tolerated a great deal, maybe too much, for the sake of constancy and calm. And yet the question burned within him: how much longer until he could leave for New York, now that he was delayed by a slow-healing wound, a son in trouble, a maze of legal questions, a hysterical wife?

The fog cleared. Lev winced at the sharp sun breaking through the clouds, his eyes watering. The sun's glare blurred the image of Vicki adjusting her hat. He blotted his eyes with a handkerchief and took a deep breath. Voices in the distance yelled, *Vicki! Geza!*

Maya and Zev ran toward them, breathless, full of apologies: their car had broken down, and at the last minute, they caught a train; they never thought they would make it but here they were. "I left the car in the middle of the road," Zev said triumphantly. "Whoever finds it can have the lemon."

"Thank God," Geza said, embracing Zev.

Vicki hugged Maya, and after a suspended breath, Maya asked, "Tell me honestly, am I wearing too much powder?"

Vicki's eyes pooled with tears. "You look beautiful."

The line of passengers waiting to board had diminished. From the railing of the ship, people waved scarfs and hats at those who'd been left behind. A fat grandmother wailed on the dock, her massive arms shaking. An older man, her husband, comforted her, which only agitated her further. A sister cried for her departed sisters; they promised to send for her once they settled in Gedera.

Suddenly, there wasn't any more time. Vicki and Geza embraced him. Maya and Zev argued about which satchel contained the dry bread and smoked fish. Geza said the tickets were in his inner vest pocket, and Vicki added, "We'll be the last ones to board if we don't hurry!" "Let's go!" Zev roared, and in a whirl of kisses and mazel tovs, after one last embrace from his daughter, they left him standing on the dock.

They disappeared into the ship. Lev couldn't bear to stand there and wait for them to emerge onto the deck and wave. He couldn't bear to wave back and watch the ship float down the Elbe until it grew smaller and smaller.

The fat grandmother stared at him. She was crying and sweating, her face a porous mass of regret. Her husband, his back stooped over in what seemed to be his permanent position, smoked a cigar. Lev tipped his hat at her and started to walk away, over the floating pontoon that connected the dock to land. Even as he crossed the bridge, the lapping shores of the Elbe at his back, he could still hear her indignant cries from far off, the cries of an old, bitter woman who believed everything she loved was on that ship.

49

Together on the deck of the *Mauretania*, their bodies pressed up against other bodies, all of them strained to see Haifa Bay. The deck railing dug into her stomach as Vicki tried to get a better view. She leaned so far forward that if she wanted to, she could easily have pitched herself into the crystalline waters. But Geza held on to her. Maya's damp arm pressed into hers, and she could feel the rise and fall of Zev's powerful breath as he too took the measure of this place called Palestine.

They were exhausted, with dark shadows under their eyes and dirty hair that smelled faintly of fish. They had not washed their clothing in weeks. Her skin felt tight with dryness. The air here carried no moisture compared to the humid summer air of Berlin. But they had survived the trip, she reminded herself, gazing up at the sky, saturated with such an intense blue that her eyes stung. Little white egrets flew overhead, squawking with relish.

Geza squeezed her sweaty hand in his. "Look," he said, pointing to the coastline. The view of the city from the sea: cerulean sky, gold sand, white houses gleaming on the hillside perched above the port. As they approached the harbor, illustrious ships lay anchored in the roadstead between Acre and the foot of Mount Carmel. Along the curve of the shore, purple flowers swayed in the wind. Palm trees were scattered across the hills. All the way from Acre to Mount Carmel stretched a green luxuriant park, which appeared to run on forever.

There was no more complaining, as there had been for weeks on end, about the swarms of anopheles mosquitoes that carried disease, about the earthquake last July near the Dead Sea, or about how Tel Aviv was a brash and bourgeois city built on sand, no different from the capitalistic cities of Europe. When Geza and Vicki protested, explaining they were not going to Tel Aviv, the other passengers shook their heads and said eventually that's where the exiles from Europe always ended up. "It's too tough for them on the kibbutz," they added. "Too lonely even though you are always surrounded by people." And then a rabid argument would break out, between Zev, who proclaimed it was one's national duty to work the land, and a man wearing a three-piece suit, who only wanted to find office work in either Tel Aviv or possibly Jerusalem, where he had relatives.

As the ship floated into the harbor, there was no more energy left for such febrile disagreements. The whizzing sound of the anchor plummeting into the water sent a tremor through the crowd. Vicki stared at Geza, gripping his hand, and he smiled back at her. It was the smile he reserved for the most tense and worrisome moments. They saw Arab sailors pushing lighters out into the water from the shore; these barges would transfer them from the moored ship onto land.

From the ship to the lighters, the sailors handled them as if they were discarded packages they would rather dump into the ocean. But even after the long, arduous journey, floating in this barge steered by hostile hosts, there was no misery, only joy when they saw the cliffs of Mount Carmel and the purple-blue mountains of Galilee. Some of the passengers spontaneously started singing Yiddish folk songs from the old country, about returning to Jerusalem, even though this was Haifa.

Gripping the sides of the rocking lighter, she thought of her father. By the time they had reached the deck, he had vanished. She had called out his name, but the drone of the great ship departing the harbor drowned out her voice. The only person who seemed to hear her cries was the grandmother quivering on the dock. That grandmother wailed not only for her departed children and grandchildren but for everyone on that ship. And everyone on that ship had felt a communal sense of guilt for leaving behind a grandmother, whether living or dead, in the Ukraine or in Berlin. When they reached the open sea, people passed around a bottle of vodka, and it was one of those times when drinking with strangers was a blessing.

. . .

At the port in Haifa, masses of people strained behind a barbed wire fence, desperate for news from home. The British policemen used their sticks and camel-hide whips to hold back the crowd. Vicki clung to Geza. They were waiting for Maya and Zev, who were on the next lighter.

Geza told her they would go to the bathhouse, where they would be separated for a short time during the physical examination, after which they would be taken to the disinfection facilities to receive shots for typhus and smallpox.

"Don't leave me," Vicki cried.

He calmly reminded her of what they had discussed on the ship, about the entry procedures. A policeman blew a whistle. The crowd quieted for a moment.

"It's all right," he said, wiping a smudge of dirt off her chin.

To get to Beit Alfa, in the middle of the Jezreel Valley, they took a bus. Geza, Maya, and Zev were relieved and filled with euphoria that they had passed the entry procedures smoothly, even after their belongings had been searched, their skin pricked with needles, their naked bodies examined. Vicki wondered how they were immune to the worries that consumed her: How long would it take to reach Beit Alfa on this bus? When would she get to wash some clothing? Where would they sleep? Her feet itched and she desperately wanted a shower. But I mustn't say this, she thought, swallowing hard.

Passing through Haifa, she noticed all the construction. Skeletal scaffolding shrouded buildings, soft-drink stands with the sign *Gazoz* stood on every corner. A woman sitting in the next row pointed out that they were passing through Hadar Hacarmel, a neighborhood where lots of Jewish immigrants lived. Vicki took in the bustling shops, the coffee-houses where women sat outside drinking from elegant saucers, fanning themselves. There was even a cinema—her heart leapt at the sight of the marquee rimmed with unlit bulbs.

Behind them, Zev and Maya chatted with a pioneer who had arrived six years ago. He spoke about how, to Europeans, Palestine was all romance, and people who liked romance should stay home. "The instant they arrive here, such misty dreams evaporate and what's left is a rough and rocky place, a hard life, unsuitable for the fainthearted." He raised his fist and shook it. "We need soldiers, not frail refugees. Better not come at all than come only to run back home."

Geza patted Vicki's knee. She managed to smile, and he grinned as if none of this mattered, what others said. She stared at the passing acacia trees. Through the open windows, the air felt bone dry. The pioneer droned on, saying that there would always be a war against the Arabs and the English, against the cold nights and the desert heat, the immovable rocks and the innumerable grains of sand, a war that could last for thousands of years.

Geza whispered into Vicki's ear, "He certainly loves the sound of his own voice."

Vicki squeezed his hand. He squeezed hers back in three short bursts, which meant: *Don't worry; I love you; it will be all right.* The scent of eucalyptus trees and citrus groves filtered into the bus, and she inhaled these sharp clean smells, smells that were new to her.

Beit Alfa, the kibbutz where they were going to live, was still off in the distance, nestled against the Gilboa Mountains. There, while plowing the fields, the pioneers had uncovered the mosaic floor of an ancient synagogue illustrating the lunar Hebrew months—a sign, Zev said, that Beit Alfa was a good and blessed place.

They passed an Arab village with fields full of rocks. Vicki and Geza stared at the Arab children, who stood in front of ramshackle houses. The children stared back.

Sitting nearby on the bus, an older man in oriental dress wearing a tarboosh and smoking a *beedi* coughed hoarsely.

He must be an Arab, Vicki thought, and she self-consciously averted her eyes from the passing village.

The man coughed again and then asked if they had recently arrived in Palestine.

"Yes," Geza said solemnly. "This morning. Via Berlin."

The man said he had been living in Palestine for thirty-five years.

Originally, he was a Jew from L'vov, but now he had a big house in Tel Aviv and traded in cotton wool. He had just returned from a business trip to Beirut and was on his way to visit his sister in Safed. He owned a factory called Lodzia that produced cotton socks, which he informed them were quite popular, despite the heat. "People wear the socks under their sandals. They don't like their toes getting dirty. Strange, but I'm not complaining." Vicki and Geza nodded politely. As they exited the Arab village, the businessman muttered, "They live like pigs. The children are dirty, the adults more so." He then pointed to the exact spot where Abraham had cast out Hagar and Ishmael from the land of Israel, as if he himself had witnessed it.

Geza tilted his head in that particular way, which suggested debate. "But you see, the Arabs have been bought out by the Jews, who purchased the land from Elias Sursuq, an Arab and a businessman, like yourself, who didn't mind selling Arab land for the right price. Of course they're angry. Of course they're poor. Their land has been sold out from under them by one of their own. You should not mistake poverty for ignorance."

The man shrugged. "They throw stones. They start trouble."

The terrain turned rocky and Spartan.

They passed the rest of the ride in silence.

The bus turned off the main road, traveling inland, when finally the valley revealed itself. Fertile, swaying with wheat and sunflowers, it was a green and cool reprieve. From a distance, Vicki and Geza gazed upon their new home. They saw rectangular huts scattered across the settlement. They saw cattle milling about, corralled behind wire fencing. They saw chicken coops and groves of pomegranate trees. They saw tractors plowing the fields. They saw a large white building in the center of town. They saw stout young palms sprouting up haphazardly, without much design or order to their placement.

The bus stopped in front of the entrance to Beit Alfa, indicated by a rusty metal sign. Vicki gripped the seat in front of her. Young men, in caps and work boots, strode with purpose across the main square. A few women, working in the communal garden, peeked out from under their wide-brimmed hats at the bus. A line of children wearing bonnets and bloomers held bunches of wildflowers to welcome them.

Vicki steadied herself against Geza. He squeezed her hand three times. Then he moved down the aisle of the bus, falling behind the other passengers. She followed him. Other people's voices, some familiar, some not, floated behind her; they discussed the heat, their hunger, where they would put all the suitcases. She could only focus on the back of Geza's neck—if she looked at the line of hopeful, dusty children holding flowers, if she turned around and saw Maya's stained dress, if she glanced down at her own dirty feet encased in sandals, she knew something inside of her would break. And so she didn't.

Vicki stepped off the bus. The children squinted up at her, wildflowers skimming their delicate chins. She knelt down, her bare knees pressing into the dry earth. Cautiously, a little boy stepped forward from the line of children. She gave him a secret wave, as if they were the only two people in this great valley. He hesitated, his dark eyes scanning her face. She held out her hand. It trembled in the hot, dry air. He saw her trembling hand and he came closer. She sensed Geza standing behind her and the suspended breath of everyone watching.

The boy thrust the flowers toward her. Her fingers brushed his small, warm palm when she took them.

"Beautiful," Vicki said in Hebrew.

He beamed.

The women hunching over their lettuce beds, the dusty travelers from the bus, the men who carried pickaxes over their shoulders— everyone clapped and laughed affectionately. The boy smiled shyly, tucking his chin into his chest.

Vicki inhaled the sharp wild scent of the flowers; dirt, light, earth. Geza's warm hands cupped her shoulders, capturing the heat beneath them, capturing the sun and all it gave life to. She closed her eyes and let her future begin.

Epilogue

Cementerio de la Recoleta, Buenos Aires, 1953

It has become a kind of ritual, this communion with the dead. Lev roams freely here at dawn and avoids this place in the midday heat, when the tourists visit, commenting on how the graves, as palatial as miniature homes, are charming.

Once a German woman had gasped, her platinum hair catching the sun, that these little houses were just so *fascinating*. So much money dedicated to the dead, she had said, pressing together her gloved fingers. Lev had pretended he did not speak German and merely nodded. He walked away, down the broad path that cut through the cemetery, littered with leaves and shadows. He had to stop and catch his breath, leaning on the stone knee of a seated soldier gazing at lost battlefields. Lev could still hear the German's chirping voice reading the gravestones. She butchered the Spanish.

The heavy January heat is getting to him. He loosens his tie and fans his face with a Panama hat. No, he decides, the dead are not fascinating. Nor are the dead truly dead. They haunt him without warning, and suddenly, his eyes smart when he sees Josephine's long elegant back against the frosted living room window. She bends over, sewing a brass button onto Franz's coat. Or he sometimes hears the rolling sound of his daughter's voice when she used to sing in the kitchen, a popular love song—what was it, he wonders, in 1927? It must have been something imported from America, one of the jazz tunes Berlin went crazy for. He racks his brain, but only later, biting into the buttery fluff of *pan dulce*, will the melody resurface, and he'll whisper the name: "Ich bin von Kopf bis Fuss auf Liebe eingestellt," "Falling in Love Again," the English version, sung by Marlene Dietrich, whose face always reminded him of snow and loneliness.

Lev leaves the cemetery and turns the corner, passing the old man selling flowers. The sharp sweet scent of gardenias wrapped in brown paper carries Josephine to him again, when he used to kiss her behind the ear and inhale the gardenia scent she sparingly sprayed there, in the nested darkness only available to a husband. And yet the whiteness of the flower, the purity of the color, reminds him of Leah.

Lev returns to the cemetery the next morning, when the light-blue sky carries a purplish tint, the half-crescent moon still visible, a ghostly white outline of what the night had been. At this early hour, the cats rule. They luxuriate among the graves. They sulk and stalk Lev for food. Some find rectangles of morning sun hitting granite steps commemorating generals, and they lounge there, lapping up the heat. A black-and-white kitten is fond of sleeping on the marble foot of an angel. A calico sits upright at the entrance, pausing to lick her paws. Lev loves the old brown cat. This cat seeks him out, rubbing his knotted hairy back against Lev's shoe. He rolls over, his paws dangling limply in front of his chest, white and soft with intermittent patches of pink skin. Bits of dead leaves hang from his whiskers. Lev has named him Der Puma because he has survived.

After strolling down the aisles of shrines, Lev finds a bench in the sun and sits down, paper in hand, although he never reads the paper here. He places it next to his thigh, a tightly rolled-up baton of ink. What is there to know? He has already seen the worst of what humans are capable of. Anything that follows is merely a muted stream of regret. He would rather sit here, in his own square of sunlight, and think of how in January the streets of Berlin are bitterly cold and slick with ice, how the wind blows wetly through your overcoat, how the linden trees are stripped of leaves. Maybe Josephine is still there, among those linden trees. Ah, no—the trees have been blasted from their roots. Their street, Charlottenstrasse: a pile of rubble. He hopes she fled to the Bavarian countryside, where she could bake apples on Sundays and wear that glittering diadem he had once bought her. He pictures her walking among the farmhands, through the wheat fields, in one of those long sweeping black silk dresses she wore before the Great War, with the high collars and the billowing sleeves. And on her flaxen head, she wears the diadem with the shining yellow stone at its center. Pagan queen of the harvest.

A high whistle interrupts Josephine wading through the wheat. A woman with a scarf tied around her head calls to the cats. Lev knows her. She arrives every morning at eight. She pulls a tin barrel full of milk through the wide path of the cemetery until she sets it down and mixes it with water. The cats follow behind her, a roving cloak of fur, waiting for the watery milk.

The sun rises. Lev takes off his linen jacket and rolls up his shirt-sleeves, revealing his weathered skin. Bulbous blue veins run down his forearms. His arms used to be so white, as pale as birch trees, his mother would say, but after eighteen years here, they have browned, like leather left out in the sun. Good enough for skinning, he thinks soberly.

The cats lap up their breakfast, crowding around the crone's skinny ankles. Lev's stomach grumbles. It's time for *medialunes* and *café con leche*. In his first years here, he missed certain things: the flat matches he used to buy in Berlin that fitted his waistcoat pocket, his small cigars, and black tea in a glass, Russian style, with mountains of sugar poured into it. He used to ask for black tea in a glass at his customary café on Avenida de Mayo, and they laughed at him good-naturedly, but brought it out steaming hot, as requested. Still, they cajoled him into trying *café con leche*. They would serve it on the house. After so many times, he grew used to the milky coffee and now prefers it. Strange, how certain tastes change, even after so many years, even when he used to think, *Who can eat dessert for breakfast?* But here he is, eating the buttery bread, stuffing it into his bearded mouth, enjoying the rinse of milk and sugar and coffee sliding over his tongue. Little flakes of pastry fall onto his dark trousers. He dusts them off dismissively.

This is the way things are now: breakfasting at "his" café every morning after a stroll through the cemetery. Because he's always up before sunrise, he converses with the whores. Sometimes, they tell him their troubles: an errant boyfriend, a cousin who won't move out, that they're too busy or not busy enough. He brings them cigarettes. The women are beautifully tired, especially when they have taken off their shoes, their high heels dangling from their fingertips as they make their way home.

And watching blond Germans, former soldiers of the Reich, and dark Jews eating in the same café amuses him. Their proximity. And now it is the blond German who will be hunted, tracked down, interrogated. At least this is what Lev hopes for, even if it means his own son would be hunted. But Franz died before the war even began.

Three weeks after Vicki and Geza left on the *Mauretania*, the Berlin police found Franz working on a farm in Grunewald forest. When they brought him home, his face was dirty and rough, his skin weatherbeaten. His blue eyes stared at Lev with incredulity. He cried in his mother's arms and said Wolf had talked him into it, a terrible mistake. Josephine rocked him and shushed him and said of course, Wolf was to blame. Their tears intermingled. Before Lev's eyes, they fused into one, mother and son, as Franz burrowed his head into the folds of Josephine's silk robe.

They threw Franz in prison for five years. For five years, Lev battled to get him out. The complexities of the case multiplied—the murder weapon had vanished, Wolf had fled the country while Franz stood for the kind of disobedience the government insisted on squashing, although more and more, Berlin flourished with bright violence. Bloody riots. KPD demonstrations. Semitic-looking pedestrians attacked at random on train platforms.

In the midst of this, Lev wrote Leah a letter. He explained how he had received her address from Geza two years too late. He wrote about what had happened to Franz. At the end, he added: *When he's released, I'll come for you. Wait for me? Please wait for me,* he added, not wanting to sound presumptuous, to demand so much after so long. He didn't know if she still loved him or if she had found someone else. He didn't know anything about her life until she wrote back.

November 11, 1928

11 Rivington Street
New York, NY

Dear Lev,

I am overjoyed to receive your letter. I think of you every night, when the moon shines brightly down through the window, the way it once did in Mitau, lighting up the birch trees. I wonder if there's a place for us, if there ever will be. And yet I understand how you must sort out the trouble with Franz—you cannot abandon your son during such a time. You must help him. Get him out of the prison and lead him away from violence.

My days are very busy working as a seamstress in a small shop. At least it's not a factory, but it's sweltering in the summer and frigid in the winter. We still live with Misha and his family in a small apartment with two rooms—there's not much space, but we help each other. Sasha and I sleep in a Murphy bed—have you heard of this? It disappears into the wall during the day, and then at night, we pull it from the same wall. Sasha thrives in this metropolis. He plays baseball in the middle of the street with other boys and he draws at the dining table. Intricate sketches. He wants to become an artist, but I want something better for him—a lawyer or a doctor. He delivers newspapers early in the morning before school. I have included a photograph of him with this letter. Certain expressions, the way he shakes his head when he's displeased, remind me of you.

We have been lucky enough to meet some distant relatives from the old country. Benjamin and Rose Dubrowensky from Riga, but they now go by Dubrow. They are planning to open a cafeteria in Brooklyn next year, and they have already promised Sasha a job clearing tables. Rose is Misha's second cousin and she married Benjamin a few years ago. Benjamin is from Belarus and has taken an interest in helping Sasha—they can't have children, which I suppose is one of the reasons for their generosity.

I yearn for the day when you will find me. I might be old by then.
My black hair has already faded, and living here, I don't laugh as often.
But perhaps there will still be a trace of the girl you knew in Mitau.
    I am waiting.

                                        Love,
                                        Leah

Lev still carries the small black-and-white photograph that tumbled out of her letter. It's in his wallet, faded and frayed from too much handling. His son balances on a wooden plank over muddy tracks, with a large sack slung over his shoulder. He wears lace-up boots and a short wool coat, and he's about to throw a rolled-up newspaper over a clipped hedge. He looks suspicious, his hooded eyes staring into the camera from under his cap. The weather seems damp and cold, the trees bare. Lev has always wondered where this picture was taken and who took it. Somewhere beyond the skyscrapers and busy streets, perhaps a neighboring town outside the city. His son's eyes, rounded and dark, both accept his circumstances and rebel against them.

In 1933, Hitler took control of the Berlin police and released all prisoners affiliated with the SA and SS. When Franz was freed that spring, Josephine emerged from her long dark depression, and Lev began to plan for New York.

Franz slept in his old room. He enjoyed the comfort of Marthe's cooking, and he hesitated to leave the house. Josephine made Lev promise not to mention the night of the shooting. "He's fragile," she kept reminding him. But, as Lev predicted, after a few weeks, Franz started leaving the house again and disappearing for long afternoons. His place at the dinner table was once again empty. He had rejoined the SA as part of the Hilfspolizei (Auxiliary Police). He handled his parents with care, explaining how Göring had recently uncovered plans for a Communist uprising. During these conversations, color flooded his cheeks. His blue eyes flashed. Josephine listened, her face frozen in horror. She begged Lev to pull him out of the SA, away from all political activity.

"I will talk to him," Lev had said, knowing such talk would do nothing, turning over in his mind the booking of his berth to New York, the warmth of Leah's hand in his, the fluttering of her soft eyelashes across his face.

Two months later, Franz was shot in the chest three times. It happened when he emerged from a tenement building on Bernauer Strasse, a working-class part of town. Early dawn, the rosy sunrise illuminated the ugly apartment blocks. Franz paused in the doorway of the building, lingering above the chipped cement steps. His dress shirt billowed open and he started to button it. Fiery hues drenched the sky, the intensity of such colors reflecting the passionate night he'd just spent with Manfred. He had two more buttons left, a tie folded in his back pocket, when the bullets tore through him.

The night before, Lev and Josephine had sat at the dinner table, wondering if Franz would join them. Lev remembered how Josephine was nervous, pulling on her rings, asking Lev, even though she knew he didn't know, where Franz was. Franz had not been sleeping at home, and every morning, Josephine swung open the bedroom door, distressed by the sight of Franz's perfectly made bed. Lev shook his head. His thoughts were far away, focused on one central task: he was leaving tomorrow for New York. It had all been arranged. Josephine thought it was for business, for importing linen.

Early the next morning, Lev's suitcase was packed, resting open on top of his bed. He rang for a cab and waited for it to come. Marthe knocked softly on his bedroom door, and he thought he was leaving forever. Finally, after years of deliberations, of creating imaginary business deals in New York only to erase them, he had decided to leave Berlin and find Leah. But that morning Marthe didn't announce the cab. Instead, staring down at the carpet, she told him Franz had died last night. An officer was waiting downstairs in the foyer. Fat tears trickled down her neck. Josephine was still asleep; she didn't want to disturb her. "It's an awful shock," Marthe had said, her hand over her heart.

"An awful shock," Lev had repeated, sitting down on the bed.

· · ·

Perhaps the Communists wanted to make a point. Perhaps the Zionists had been waiting for their opportunity to avenge Franz's attempted murder of Geza. Perhaps, perhaps. The shooter was never found. The only discovery the police made was where Franz had slept that night, where he had most likely slept for countless nights: the apartment of Manfred Berres, a construction worker and part-time bartender, twenty-four years old. He said Franz was an old friend who needed a place to stay. He didn't know anything about his political activity. They simply drank together and played cards. Manfred had lurked on the edges of the crowd during the funeral, fists stuffed into his pockets. Staring at the fresh brown soil thrown over the coffin, he wouldn't meet anyone's gaze. He didn't stay for the whole service but walked off into the bright harsh day, his eyes trained on his paint-splashed boots, his shoulders hunched. He reminded Lev of an old man who had lost some vital part of himself as he shuffled off into the trees, zigzagging aimlessly between them.

Franz could be here, in this café, Lev thought bitterly, motioning for the waiter. The young Argentine came over, bowing slightly. He was handsome, with gleaming dark hair slicked back with gel. His eyes were smiling and he asked Lev if he wanted more coffee. Franz was about the age of this young man when he died. He would be forty-five now. Lev couldn't stop himself from calculating his son's imaginary age, comparing him to other young men he spotted in cafés, on the street. *Does he really resemble Franz?* he would wonder while buying tomatoes at the open-air market. *He has his cheekbones, but his eyes are different.* And then he would walk away, tomatoes in hand.

After Franz's death, Lev delayed his departure for New York. A few months turned into a year. Suddenly, it was 1934 and people were leaving. People were jumping out of windows. People were discussing the merits of Shanghai, the only city in the world that didn't require an entry visa. People were selling off armoires, silverware, Meissen china. People were asking far-flung relatives to write letters of recommendation so they could move to England, America, or South Africa, where they could work as domestic servants when they had only ever employed domestic servants. Lev tried to get a visa for the United States, but for that year and the following one, the quota was already filled. Lev told Josephine she should leave Berlin too because war was coming. "You've always enjoyed Paris, and you have cousins there," he suggested. But she refused to leave the city where her son's body lay. She refused to leave her last surviving aunt. She refused to leave her girlhood memories of the Kaiser and the Empress, even though the red-and-white banners, with swastikas fluttering in the wind, blotted out any semblance of another kind of past. And she refused to leave Dr. Dürhkoop, who had turned out to be a much more devoted and enduring lover than either Lev or Josephine had anticipated. He wanted to marry Josephine. And he did not care for children, so the fact that she was over forty was a great relief to him. One of Lev's most vivid memories—he could not count the number of times he replayed it—was when they came to see him, the good doctor and his wife. In making their love public, they acted as giddy as children. They asked him to consider a divorce. Their tone was both pleading and decisive. Josephine sat across from him with a strange ecstatic light in her eyes, a light he had not seen in so many years that his chest caved, and he threw up his hands and said, "Mazel tov!" All three of them burst into laughter, relieved, elated, slightly embarrassed. And then the doctor said with a tinge of formality, "It's for the best, with the new race laws."

"New race laws?" Lev repeated. He had heard about these new laws, but there were so many proclamations flooding the paper and the radio, he paid little attention to the news back then. The doctor straightened his back and shifted in his chair, and explained how the Law for the Protection of German Blood and German Honor prohibited marriages as well as intercourse between Jews and Germans, and so by releasing Josephine from their marriage, Lev was complying with the law. They were asking him out of politeness. And then Josephine added that the law also forbade the employment of German females under forty-five in Jewish households. "So Marthe's coming with us."

"Marthe's over fifty, at least!"

Josephine sniffed and said something about how Marthe most likely would prefer it.

"I see," Lev had said, although he did not see. He felt as if he was newly blind, especially after losing Marthe, which stung sharply. She had always been on his side. Next, Josephine would demand the monarch butterfly paperweight or the ivory hare with the amber eyes he so lovingly would hold in the palm of his hand.

A year later, after failing to procure a visa for the United States, Lev was lucky just to get out of the country, let alone choose where he wanted to go. Quotas to immigrate to England or America were filled, which was explained in a labyrinth of bureaucratic jargon from the American and English embassies and consulates, where queues wrapped and curled around blocks. It was risky to queue for too long. The SS randomly plucked people from the line and bundled them into police trucks; they ended up in a detention camp, a work camp, or some other unidentified place.

He could go to Palestine, but judging from Vicki's letters, it was a rough and hard country, no place for old men. The other choices were Australia or Argentina. He had heard that criminals shipped from England had founded Australia, and he pictured their troublemaking descendants hungrily roaming the outback. So he picked Argentina. Overnight, punitive taxes for leaving the country were magically invented. Lev had to declare all properties, savings, pensions, and valuables before he was granted, by the Office of the Security Service for Jewish Emigration, a stamp in his passport that read *Einmalige Ausreise nach CSR:* good for a single journey.

He arrived at the port of Mar del Plata, Buenos Aires, in December 1935. The air was warm and balmy. First thing, he took off his jacket and unbuttoned the first two buttons of his oxford shirt. Summer in December, he thought, surveying the long stretch of white, hot sand. A few people ran into the water and then sallied back out again, taunting the lapping shoreline.

.   .   .

Lev stirs his coffee with a little spoon, which emits a tingling sound as the metal hits the porcelain. Later he had learned, in a somewhat desperate letter from Josephine, that the doctor had left her. Apparently, because she had been married to a Jew the doctor felt this tainted him professionally. He had also stopped receiving dinner invitations from certain social circles because they now found him to be an unsuitable guest at their table. Lev couldn't help the small cruel smile that played on his lips when he read her tiny scrawl, the franticness of having been left pulsating through the intricate cursive. Of course she didn't dare ask outright if she could join him in Argentina, but there was a searching, hopeful quality to the letter that suggested she would come if he asked her to. He wrote back: *I'm so sorry to hear of your troubles. I wish you well in these turbulent times. Fondly, Lev.* Maybe, when the bombs started falling, Josephine had escaped to a friend's bunker in Grunewald forest. Maybe she was trapped under a pile of rubble in the middle of Berlin. Maybe the Russians rolled over her body with their tanks. Maybe she took a holiday to Switzerland or Sweden and never came back. He didn't know. He only knew Josephine's polite and somewhat apologetic letters stopped arriving by the spring of 1943. After that, there was no trace of her, as if she had never been his wife. He takes a sip. The milk has made the black coffee cloudy and beige.

The door of the café jangles and in walks a girl who reminds him of Vicki, when Vicki was young. The short, dark hair revealing delicate white earlobes. The curious, quick eyes. The easy grace with which she surveys the pastries behind the glass and gestures to the swirled Danish. She takes it and pays in one smooth sinuous movement. They live in Tel Aviv now, having only survived the kibbutz one year. After the birth of their child, a sickly boy named Theodore, they felt different about their national obligations. Lev knew this would happen, but of course he had to sit back and watch it, witnessing through her turbulent letters all the strife and worry they put themselves through when he could have simply told them kibbutz life was unsustainable, except for the most ardent. Reluctantly at first, Geza became a shop owner. Now they have five shops scattered throughout Tel Aviv that sell household goods, and they are quite profitable. Who knew dishcloths and peppermills and sieves would be so popular? Vicki teaches French at a high school. She is a good teacher; engaging, encouraging, the students love her. Lev remembers with a half smile how much she hated French. He tells anyone who will listen about Vicki, his daughter the French teacher who lives in Tel Aviv. Theodore has grown strong and healthy, and they say he looks like Lev, the same mistrustful eyes, the same olive skin and wavy chestnut hair. In the fall, he will start at Hebrew University in Jerusalem. He wants to be an archaeologist. Good, Lev murmurs, good.

Filled up with coffee and bread, he leaves a few coins on the table and ambles out into the street. The strong sun hits his face; another bright day, the same enduring blue. Rain will not come until April. Until then, the days will be bone dry, his sitting room filled with sunlight, the windowpanes dusty. He lives in Palermo Viejo, in one of those old ornate family homes, which has been subdivided into apartments. The neighborhood is full of small quiet streets opening into shaded court-yards, cobblestones strewn with the lavender petals of jacaranda trees. Irrepressible bougainvillea sprouts over whitewashed walls. When he looks up, he sees balconies lined with caryatids, private terraces hous-ing potted plants amid chaise lounges for taking a coffee in the sun. He passes front doors made of oak set behind impressive ironwork, doors to protect marble entrance halls and salons with painted ceilings, even if the paint is peeling. There is no tango on the street corners, as all the tourists expect. But there is a horse-drawn cart operated by an old man selling soda water. The cart rattles by Lev's window every morn-ing to deliver wooden crates stacked with green siphons. Up ahead, Lev spots the knife sharpener, dragging along his whetstone on an odd wheeled contraption. He blows his harmonica to announce his passing. The chemist is opening his doors, and the scent of eucalyptus wafts into the street.

Lev pauses at the corner, the eucalyptus tingling his nostrils, and debates whether to turn or keep walking. The thought of his apartment, his narrow bed, a late morning nap, followed by a cool shower is appeal-ing, but so is his favorite stationery store, which sells the most expensive and beautiful pens, heavy paper, and leather-bound notebooks that he likes to buy and leave empty. Once, for a lady friend, he purchased one of these notebooks, crimson leather with a little strap that kept it closed. She complained that if he wanted to buy her a book, why did he buy her an empty one? It is a reason, among many others, that this lady friend is no longer a friend. But women, at his age, are a hassle. It takes too much energy, and he has too many memories, to charm a woman into thinking he is the sort of man who enjoys polo and picnicking, who will buy her baubles and insist she looks beautiful in a newly acquired pair of earrings, when she does not.

He chooses to go home, taking Avenida de Mayo, where in sidewalk cafés Spanish anarchists debate politics. But it's still early and the chairs stand empty. Waiters are setting tables, opening up umbrellas, and washing the sidewalks with mops and buckets. Lev carefully steps over the soapy rivulets. A man in a white suit is already sipping a glass of sherry. *He starts early,* Lev thinks. *The moment he wakes, the memories must begin again, like a vengeful lover returning each day with more bad news.* Lev doesn't drink until dusk. If he allowed himself to start earlier, he fears it would be as early as this man, maybe earlier. The man senses Lev looking at him. Lev tips his hat and keeps walking. He probably wants company, someone to talk to over a bowl of salted marconas. There's too much to say, so it's better to say nothing. Lev's story, how he got here, where he came from, tires him. He can't stand to recite it another time, to another stranger.

Turning the corner, he catches sight of himself in the window of a leather-goods shop for wealthy gauchos. Riding boots and polo belts are on display. An expensive saddle is featured on a wooden horse. A man once tried to sell him an estancia down south, in Las Pampas. *This is the land of Jewish cowboys,* he kept saying, grinning widely, his mouth full of fillings. What would Josephine say, to find him atop a steed, arrayed in the Western style? *A Jew on a horse?* That's what she would say.

Lev shakes his head, snorting at the memory. He studies himself in the glass. His girth has widened. His nose is more bulbous, and his ears have elongated, as if someone hung weights on the bottom of his earlobes to stretch them. He doesn't remember when he started to look old, but it has happened. And Leah, what does she look like now? Has she retained her youthfulness, as some women do despite old age, or did youth fall away from her, peel off of her, as it did with Josephine, who, in the end, reminded him of an empty cornhusk. He'll never know.

Once, he had a chance to know . . . if Franz hadn't been shot, if the quotas weren't full, if another war hadn't broken out, if Rose Dubrow hadn't died of shingles, if . . .

By 1939, Benjamin Dubrow owned five cafeterias in Manhattan and Brooklyn, and he was soon opening one in Miami. Murals on the walls. Trays laden with delicacies from the old country. Sunlight streaming through tall glass windows looking out onto busy streets. One long mirrored wall where you could eat and watch who came in and out. A place to nosh, kibitz, and argue the fate of the world was how Leah had described it in her letters without the slightest hint of irony, as if she was trying to convince Lev to eat there too. *Sasha enjoys the work because famous writers and intellectuals gather here on Saturday afternoons, discussing the catastrophes happening across Europe. Thank God we are here and not there.*

Soon after this letter, another followed about Rose's death. And then a long stretch of silence in which no letters arrived from New York. But a war was on, and Lev thought perhaps the mail had been delayed or circumvented. Never, Lev thought, his stomach turning, did he imagine Leah's next letter, brimming with apology as well as an alarming frankness. Benjamin Dubrow wanted to marry her. It was 1942, and her fate, as well as the world's, was held in the balance, a swinging pendulum of uncertainty. Didn't she see fate was always uncertain, always swinging? No, not like this, not like now, she replied, which was why she had accepted Dubrow's proposal, along with his promise to pay for Sasha's education followed by the offer that Sasha could manage the Eastern Parkway location of Dubrow's after he finished his studies. *Please understand,* she wrote. *I'm only trying to make a life for Sasha. And Dubrow is a kind man. He doesn't expect much besides companionship, understanding, the things everyone wants.*

Lev wrote back that of course he understood, even though he had smashed things afterward. The monarch butterfly paperweight in shards across the room. The hare, one of its amber eyes missing from crashing into the windowpane. Lev pictured Dubrow as a well-satiated man in a fur coat, which he wore with a dash of vulgarity that was accepted, even celebrated, in America.

In the same letter, Lev wrote that it was true; he didn't know when he could get to New York, and with the war, who knew the future? Of course he wanted the best for Sasha and the best for her. Dubrow, it seemed, would provide generously. Wincing at the banality of such lines, he told her to be happy and think of him only once in a while. *Perhaps it's best if we don't write much after this—you'll soon be a married woman, and I don't wish to hamper your happiness with memories of our past, a past that is barely alive without much promise of a future.* It sounded hard, callous, written when he still simmered with anger. After he sent the letter, he only felt regret.

Frantically, he sent her other letters, gentler ones explaining how he had wrongly expected her to wait for him, as if she was encased in a glass tomb where time didn't move, and he understood how the necessities of life must have pressed down on her—Misha's cramped apartment, how such a savage city demanded she take their son's future into account, the need for reassurance where he could provide none, but he still loved her, longed for her, and promised that the moment the war ended and he could get on a ship, any ship, he would come for her, take care of her.

She never wrote back. The war ended. A yawning absence followed, vibrating with this one truth: he had lost her.

Turning away from the shop window—Lev can't look at himself anymore—he sees that across the street, on a green bench, a young couple embraces. Their bodies awkwardly intertwined, they kiss, and the kiss creates a world between them. Sitting on the same bench, a man lounges with his arms crossed over his chest. He sits so close, but they don't see him. They will never see him.

On his street, the sidewalk juts upward, breaking open, and Lev stumbles over the uneven ground. Steadying himself, he pauses. The young couple from the bench strolls behind him, taking their time. They laugh and caress each other, trading endearments. To him, Spanish still sounds like a release of butterflies, fluttering, erratic, punctuated with movement. Lev smiles when the girl raises her voice, mocking indignation.

Thoughts flit through him as he gropes for his keys, his fingers rummaging through spare change, receipts: Did they spend the night together? Where is the girl's mother? Finding his keys, he switches from being the father to the enamored son: Does the boy love this girl? Will he ask her to marry? Again, he is the father and hopes, for the girl's sake, this is what the boy feels.

When did I last feel love like that? But he doesn't have to ask. Leah. The name has become mythic, ghostly, a lost artifact in a lost world. *Where are you?* he wonders, unlocking the door to the great crumbling house. *Where are you?*

Acknowledgments

I must thank the brilliant, beautiful, and wise Lexy Bloom for urging me to write this book and for telling me to keep going, my fabulous agent, Alice Tasman, for believing in me, the wonderful and sensitive editorial guidance of Deborah Garrison at Pantheon, and the astute editorial assistance of Anne Eggers. My mentor and hero Professor Aimee Bender, for her invaluable notes and moral support throughout this process, helped make this book what it is. I am forever grateful for the foresight of Jennifer Pooley, for getting this book into the right hands. I am also so appreciative of the encouragement of Professor Tony Kemp and Professor Emily Anderson at the University of Southern California, as well as the support of the Creative Writing and English Department at USC. Thank you to Professor Wolf Gruner at USC for his historical insight and assistance with the German language. My gratitude also extends to Micheala Wolf for her help in checking all things German. I must also thank Evan James, Rachel Artenian, and Richelle Persampieri for their generous hospitality in providing me with a quiet space to write. My gratitude also, always, for the meaningful friendship and never-ending encouragement of Deborah Netburn. And thank you to John Haule, for his sage advice and expert listening.

I am hugely indebted to my father, Joel Landau, and my mother, Arlene Landau, for their unending support, and to the rest of my family: my beloved children Lucia and Levi, Susan Landau and Brad TePaske (particularly for his ornithological expertise), Lauren Cadish and Patrick Griffin, Betty and Anders Westgren and the entire Westgren clan in Sweden and beyond. For her longstanding support and friendship, thank you to Ania Vichniakova, and thank you to Paula Kaufman for her enthusiasm through the years. Thank you to my esteemed colleagues for generously reading my work: Josh Bernstein,

Emily Fridlund, Bryan Hurt, Lisa Locascio, Bonnie Nazdam, and Jessica Piazza.

And last but most certainly not the least, my talented and incredibly supportive husband, Philip Westgren, who never stops believing in me and has helped me every step of the way.

I would also like to acknowledge the following writers and sources that helped in the research, writing, and inspiration of this book:

Max Beckmann, *Self-Portrait in Words: Collected Writings and Statements, 1903–1950*

Walter Benjamin, *Berlin Childhood Around 1900*

Elena Ferrante

Stolen Voices: Young People's War Diaries, from World War I to Iraq, ed. Zlata Filipović and Melanie Challenger

Felix Gilbert, *A European Past: Memoirs, 1905–1945*

Anton Gill, *A Dance Between Flames: Berlin Between the Wars*

Mel Gordon, *Voluptuous Panic: The Erotic World of Weimar Berlin*

Eva Hoffman, *Shtetl: The Life and Death of a Small Town and the World of Polish Jews*

The Weimar Republic Sourcebook, ed. Anton Kaes, Martin Jay, and Edward Dimendberg

Count Harry Kessler, *The Diaries of a Cosmopolitan, 1918–1937*

Erik Larson, *In the Garden of Beasts: Love, Terror, and an American Family in Hitler's Berlin*

Vejas Gabriel Liulevicius, *War Land on the Eastern Front: Culture, National Identity, and German Occupation in World War I*

Irène Némirovsky, *Suite Française*

Sabine Rewald, *Glitter and Doom: German Portraits from the 1920s*

Joseph Roth, *What I Saw: Reports from Berlin, 1920–1933*, and *The Wandering Jews: The Classic Portrait of a Vanished People*

Tom Segev, *One Palestine, Complete: Jews and Arabs Under the British Mandate*

Edmund de Waal, *The Hare with Amber Eyes: A Hidden Inheritance*

Eric D. Weitz, *Weimar Germany: Promise and Tragedy*

Robert Weldon Whalen, *Bitter Wounds: German Victims of the Great War, 1914–1939*

Arnold Zweig, *The Face of East European Jewry*

Stefan Zweig, *The World of Yesterday*

About the Author

Alexis Landau studied at Vassar College and received an MFA from Emerson College and a PhD in English Literature and Creative Writing from the University of Southern California. *The Empire of the Senses* is her first novel. She lives with her husband and her two children in Los Angeles.

A Note on the Type

The text of this book was set in Ehrhardt, a typeface based on the specimens of "Dutch" types found at the Ehrhardt foundry in Leipzig. The original design of the face was the work of Nicholas Kis, a Hungarian punch cutter known to have worked in Amsterdam from 1680 to 1689. The modern version of Ehrhardt was cut by the Monotype Corporation of London in 1937.

Typeset by Scribe, Philadelphia, Pennsylvania
Printed and bound by Berryville Graphics, Berryville, Virginia
Designed by Iris Weinstein